WORM CAVE

Martin Van Pelt

This is a work of fiction. Names, characters, places, and incidents either are the product of the author's imagination or are used fictitiously. Any resemblance to actual persons, living or dead, events, government facilities, business establishments, or locales is entirely coincidental.

Also by Martin Van Pelt

THE CIRQUE

Cover artwork by Jerry Phillips

Author can be contacted at

thecirquenovel@hotmail.com

FIRST EDITION

ISBN: 1505477360
ISBN 13: 9781505477368

The corn was a deep green, high, and tasseled. What was the musical? *Oklahoma*? The corn as high as an elephant's eye? She and her classmates had done that play back in the eighth grade. Or had attempted it.

Well, this corn was maybe up to a horse's eye. Maybe not Oklahoma standard, but it was high and tasseled.

She glanced in the mirror again. A red Buick Regal with Georgia plates had passed the old Ford truck and was impatiently coming up on her bumper. It passed her in a big hurry doing at least seventy, but the pickup driver was still holding his distance.

A city girl through and through, she thought as she looked at her watch. It was a Timex Indiglo with a white face, black hands, a date, and a cheap compass on the band. Press a button on the case and the dial would glow blue at night. The Explorer model. It had been bought some years ago at Costco for $39.95.

In a former life, Hilly had once known all about expensive watches—Rolex, Omega, and Piaget—but she had never seen the attraction. Her Timex, which to her surprise now said 3:06 p.m., kept almost perfect time with the atomic clock.

Two miles ahead, the road ran straight for Batavia. She could now make out the green shade trees that marked the town's limit and a church steeple or two.

Batavia was tucked up against that large ridge in what looked like a pretty setting.

The first order of business was a place to stay, something for dinner, maybe a big, overloaded cheeseburger and fries—after all, it had been a long time since that Slim Jim. Then maybe a run before it got dark. She was keeping the weight off, but it was getting difficult.

———

Hilly guessed it had probably been about twenty-six years since the last time she had been down here in Batavia, Kentucky. Actually, she had only been here twice despite the fact that she acknowledged her roots were in this town and county. The first time had been as a little girl, maybe six years old, soon after her alcoholic father had wrapped himself and the Buick around an oak tree. The second visit had been right after graduation from Michigan State and before the army, when Hilly had driven her mother, Rose, down here in the old Dodge Dart to see relatives. Her mother's eyes were failing. Hilly figured it was probably some form of what everyone now knew as macular degeneration. Her mother couldn't drive anymore and had retired from the auto plant early. She had coaxed Hilly into the trip. The mother–daughter adventure had been fun, but it was their last trip together as it turned out. Her mother, who had a lifetime two-pack-a-day habit, had succumbed to lung cancer a few years later. Hilly had flown home from Europe for the funeral and found herself alone. Hilly had no brothers or sisters.

But her roots were here. She knew if you went back far enough she was somehow related to the namesake of this county, Hiram Walker. Hilly had done some research on him through Google. Mostly, Hiram Walker, was a big blowhard politician from the Revolution.

After her mother's death, Hilly had sworn never to smoke anything again and lead a healthy life. Unlike President Clinton, she had inhaled plenty in college.

As she drove closer to town, memories of the two visits came flooding back, and she looked to the left for the big white farmhouse just outside of town. She remembered the house was set back, with a long gravel drive with a strip of grass in the middle. Out by the road there had been a tin mailbox with a red flag. The house and red barn had sat against that high ridge under some immense trees. There had been a spring back in the bushes in the backyard that she was told to keep away from. The smell of hay had been everywhere.

Actually, it was her grandmother Lucy who had the real Kentucky roots, having been born right in one of the upper bedrooms of the farmhouse. Hilly had dim memories of her grandmother; she had died early, too. Another reason for Hilly to fear her genes. Grandma had been raised in Batavia until World War II, when she, as a young new bride with her new husband, had headed North to work in the big defense plants for good money as did many thousands from the South. Grandma had eventually helped build thousands of B-24 Liberator bombers at the big Ford factory just outside Detroit at Willow Run. Grandpa had been soon drafted and served in England as an Eighth Air Force mechanic, servicing those very same bombers.

As a kid, Hilly had heard all the old stories at Sunday dinners. Now, as a grown woman, she realized there was a certain symmetry to Grandma and Grandpa. She built them, and he serviced them.

———

The Greatest Generation for sure, she thought as she looked for the lane.

Ahead was the old mailbox with the red flag.

Hilly slowed. Yes, she thought, that was surely the mailbox and drive she remembered.

As she slowed even more to take a good look, she glanced once more in her rearview mirror. The old Ford pickup was still there, and slowing to keep its distance.

The house was still painted white and sat among the same large trees. There was a large blue box truck parked near the barn and what looked like the same red Buick Regal that had just passed her parked near the house, but she couldn't be sure. Though distant, Hilly thought she could make out the word "Furniture" in white letters on the truck. The house was still perhaps a half mile away, down that long lane.

Hilly accelerated.

The Batavia town limits was barely two miles away.

The pickup truck was still behind her with the sun visor down.

Hilly decided to stop and confront the driver somewhere in town. Soon a sign proclaimed:

BATAVIA

POP. 7,982

Hilly passed the sign and entered the town limits.

The first business was a convenience store and gas station. The Lasso and Go! Eight pumps.

Next was a True Value Hardware store and lumber yard. Larson's Lumber. Just past Larson's Lumber was a large metal building with tall garage doors. As Hilly drove by, the doors were open and there was at least one car up on a lift. Ben's Auto Repair. The business the flagman had mentioned.

Opposite Ben's was a large car dealer, Kingston Ford. There was a new pickup in the showroom, along with a smaller sedan. Outside, colorful flags flapped in the hot breeze over other new models.

A side road joined 153 after the Ford dealership. Hilly saw it was First Avenue, and 153 was now Main Street.

Traffic had picked up a little now that she was in town.

There was a school up the next side street on the left. Second Avenue. The school looked fairly new with a lighted football field beyond. A large sign above the bleachers read WILDCATS!

Hilly glanced at her rearview mirror.

The old Ford four-by-four with the primered red front fender was signaling and turning into the Lasso and Go!

Hilly hesitated, thought about making a U-turn and confronting the driver, but instead thought better of it. It had seemed a little suspicious, but it was probably just some local farmer or hunter returning to town.

Route 153 acquired curbs and sidewalks as Hilly continued toward the town square just ahead.

A few blocks later, she came to the Fireside Motel, whose sign featured a row of orange and red flames. A large red neon sign announced NO VACANCY. It didn't look good, but Hilly decided to try her luck. She pulled into the motel's asphalt parking lot. The motel was an L-shaped, two-story building that filled up half the block along Fifth Avenue. A one-story addition in front just behind the sidewalk had another red neon sign in the window: OFFICE. The motel's parking lot was filled with yellow and orange construction trucks and equipment. A maid's canvas hamper overflowing with sheets was parked outside a second-story room.

A Chevy Suburban sat in the first parking spot next to the office. A round logo on the passenger door read "USK." Then in smaller letters, "University of Southern Kentucky."

Hilly pulled in under the office's portico and put the Honda into park but left her car idling. She laid her sunglasses on the dash and opened the door. Even in the shade, the late afternoon heat poured into the car.

Entering the motel's office, she heard a doorbell chime somewhere in the interior. The motel's air-conditioning was cranked up, and the lobby felt downright frigid as the blast of cold air hit Hilly full on.

Inside the lobby a counter ran from wall to wall with a hinged partition that could be lifted to either maneuver behind the counter or gain access to the front. An open door in the rear of the office offered access to living quarters; Hilly thought she could hear a TV.

Three large windows enclosed the public portion of the lobby. Two of the windows ran along the front just behind the sidewalk and a yellow fireplug. The other window looked out under the portico and toward Hilly's Honda.

Inside the front windows were two lounge chairs that, considering their plaid upholstery, appeared to be straight out of the 1970s, as did the brown shag rug covering the lobby's floor. Between the chairs was a low coffee table piled high with magazines.

Against the far wall was a coffee machine and a stack of Styrofoam cups. Next to the coffee machine was a rack with colorful brochures advertising local attractions.

On the wall behind the counter was a key rack. Five rows of brass hooks. Six in each row and all empty.

It didn't look good thought Hilly. It confirmed the NO VACANCY sign.

Below the key rack was a sign: CHECK OUT 11 a.m.

A silver service bell sat on the counter next to a glass ashtray piled high with butts. Just as Hilly put her hand over the bell, a woman emerged from the back room.

The woman coughed and said, "Hold on, I'm a comin.'"

She took small steps and looked down at each one.

She appeared to be in her midseventies and slim. She was dressed in a nice pair of dark-blue slacks and a flowered blouse. She also wore a nice pearl necklace with matching earrings. She had on makeup and a fifties hairdo.

Hilly felt a little underdressed in her Nikes, cargo shorts, and T-shirt.

The woman came to a stop behind the counter, looked up, and gave Hilly the once over from head to toe. She took a pull on a long, filtered cigarette, probably a Virginia Slims, blew the blue smoke out of the side of her mouth, tapped an ash into the overflowing, glass ashtray, and asked, "Can I help you, honey?"

Hilly answered, "Yes, ma'am, I'm looking for a room for a few days."

The woman took another pull on the Virginia Slims and tapped it again on the ashtray.

"None of this ma'am stuff. Name's Peggy. I'm the manager. Sorry, honey, but I'm full up. What with all the construction workers these days. I had one room left until about an hour ago due to a cancellation, but them spelunkers and their teacher from the university got the last room and I didn't really want to give it to 'em. There's seven of them, two queen beds, you add it up. I'm guessin' three of them are sleepin' on the floor in their sleeping bags and the other four are doublin' up. Didn't seem to bother 'em none."

The motel manager looked around Hilly at the Honda. "Say, you wouldn't be Miss Walker would you?"

Hilly replied, "Yes, I'm Hilly Walker. How in the world would you know that?"

The woman took another drag. Same routine. The ashtray was now maxed out.

She blew the smoke sideways and said, "Those Michigan plates, honey. I guess there's some people expectin' you today or tomorrow."

Hilly was speechless.

The motel manager continued, "L. T. Rice hisself stopped by yesterday and gave me the particulars in case you stopped here first. Never liked the man. He said to tell ya he's got a room for ya at the Bluebird."

"The Bluebird?"

"The Bluebird Motel. It's the only other one in town. Just keep goin' east on Main or 153 through the town square and it's three blocks. Main and Ninth. On the right."

Hilly turned to leave, still somewhat puzzled, "Thanks, ma'am...er, Peggy."

"Anytime, honey. Wish I could've put you up here at the Fireside instead of those university people. There's two girls in that party, too. Wonder where they's sleepin', huh? It's their business these days, but I don't like it none."

Hilly pushed open the lobby door.

Peggy continued and laughed, "You tell that old bitch Ethel at the Bluebird hello."

Hilly turned and said, "I don't understand, Peggy."

"Oh, don't worry. I'm teasin'. I didn't mean nothin'. We've known each other all our lives. She's nice enough."

"OK."

"And one more thing, honey. Welcome to Batavia."

CHAPTER 10

The Square

Hilly pulled out of the Fireside Motel's parking lot and onto Main Street. Within half a block she came to the northwest end of the town square and one of the two stoplights in town. The other light was on the northeast corner of the square. Both were red at the moment, and Hilly came to a stop.

It was the end of a workday, and the square was busy with pedestrians and traffic.

Completely dominating the north end of the square and to Hilly's left sat a large gray limestone church with a tall steeple poking above the trees—one of the steeples Hilly had seen from a distance. Embedded in the steeple was a large, ornate clock.

Hilly decided to take a lap around the square. The driver of an old Ford Taurus politely beeped his horn just as Hilly wondered whether it was legal to turn right on a red in Kentucky. *I guess it is,* she thought as she made the turn.

Two- and three-story buildings lined the square.

On the corner was a Rexall drugstore. Two large, familiar signs in blue, gold, and white ran along both sides of the building above the large windows displaying goods. Another sign hung above the sidewalk over the door. Hilly hadn't seen one of these old drugstores since she was a little girl; she thought the brand had just faded away into one of those huge multinational conglomerates. Maybe they just hadn't taken down the signs yet. She wondered if there was still a soda fountain inside and would have to investigate.

Two traffic lanes and diagonal parking ringed the square.

The cement curbs were high two-step affairs with parking meters mounted above each spot.

The Taurus driver who had honked at the red light cut Hilly off as he dived into one of the diagonal parking places.

Hilly braked and muttered under her breath, "Jerk."

Along the west side of the square were various stores: shoes, tobacco, hobbies, menswear, a barber shop with a rotating pole, and what looked like a dress shop, Mary's.

Next to the dress shop and the last store on the block was a Subway sandwich shop, which somehow seemed very modern and didn't fit in with the rest of the square.

On the south end of the square stood another building constructed out of the same gray limestone as the church on the other end. It was a large, square building with fluted columns, above which large letters proclaimed, Walker County Courthouse. Just to the west of the courthouse was the firehouse with two bays. A red fire truck and an ambulance were parked on the apron.

Hilly passed the firehouse and made the turn across the south end of the square in front of the courthouse. On this Monday afternoon, people were busy making their way up and down the courthouse steps.

Next to the courthouse was a low, one-story, more modern red brick annex. Above its stainless steel–and–glass entry door, polished stainless steel letters declared it the Walker County Sheriff's Department. A brown Chevy Tahoe was parked in front. It had a light bar on its roof and a large decal of a badge on the front door.

The square itself was grass, and diagonal walks with several nicely varnished wooden benches were scattered throughout. A few people sat on the benches in the late afternoon sun talking and gesturing. Politics, family, the weather, more than likely.

The walks met in the middle of the square at a tall memorial of some kind. Hilly figured it to be a war monument judging by a soldier on each side with a gun.

She turned in front of the courthouse and continued north.

The first building on the east side of the square and the one nearest the courthouse was the post office, constructed of the same gray limestone. There was no diagonal parking in front of the post office; rather, a drive-up mail box had been mounted at the curb.

Next to the post office was a restaurant of some sort. Two tall windows flanked the front door. Above the windows and door was a large white sign with red letters, Worm Café. What a name for a restaurant, Hilly thought, perplexed. What could possibly be on the menu in there?

She also noticed above the Worm Café in a window on the second floor the name L. T. Rice in gold letters, below which, spelled in an arch with the same gold letters, was Attorney at Law.

There was a doorway between the restaurant and the next building which housed the town's movie theater, the Victory. The three-sided marquee extended over the sidewalk and ticket window, and currently playing on the Victory's two screens was the latest Star Trek movie, *Into Darkness*, and *Silver Linings Playbook*. Not first-run films but good choices. Hilly thought if she was here long enough, she might like to see both movies again.

Hilly made the green light at the north end of the square and turned right on Main Street once again.

On the northeast corner of the square was the Eastern Kentucky Bank and Trust. Although the building had a date of 1880 chiseled into a corner stone, it had been modernized with an ATM near the front door.

As promised by Peggy, two short blocks later on the right was the Bluebird Motel.

Hilly noticed on the north side of Main Street, opposite the motel, was a small supermarket, Johnnie's.

She pulled into the motel's parking lot, and Lilly's tires crunched on the gravel.

CHAPTER 11

The Bluebird

The Bluebird Motel was indeed blue.

It was a long, one-story building along Ninth Street. Like the Fireside Motel, it was L-shaped. Its wood siding was painted a pleasant dark blue with contrasting white trim and a dark gray shingled roof.

The office looked to have been modernized with larger windows facing the parking lot and sidewalk

A large sign on the office roof sported the name Bluebird Motel, with a not-quite-Audubon-quality painting of a bluebird with an orange breast carrying a piece of grass or straw. No neon at the Bluebird.

She pulled up in front of the office and left Lilly running. The office door was locked, but there was a button—either a buzzer or a doorbell.

As she waited for someone to come to the door, Hilly turned around, shaded her eyes, and looked at the Bluebird.

The motel looked to be a relic of the 1940s, and, whereas the Fireside was definitely showing some wear, the Bluebird was as neat as a pin and obviously well maintained.

Evidence of fresh paint was everywhere, and the evergreen bushes in front of each parking space were neatly trimmed.

As with the Fireside, the parking lot was full of construction vehicles and pickup trucks, but the place seemed more relaxed.

Hilly guessed fifteen rooms, each with a window air-conditioning unit humming in the front window and a brass lamp by the door.

A canopied sidewalk ran along the front of the rooms.

Hilly turned, buzzed again, and waited.

Under the office window was a planter full of multicolored pansies.

And under the planter hung a white sign with red letters. NO VACANCY.

Shit, thought Hilly, as the office door opened.

Standing in the door was a woman who appeared to be easily in her mid-eighties. She had bluish-white hair done in a perm and was wearing a pink bathrobe and slippers. She appeared somewhat stooped over.

The woman backed up and held the door open while motioning Hilly to come into the office. Hilly opened the screen door. Again, the air-conditioning felt frigid, just as it did back at the Fireside.

Hilly slipped by the woman and entered the small office. An open registration book and service bell were on the counter. There was a couch under the sidewalk window and a rack with local attraction brochures. As in the other motel, a door led back to some kind of living quarters.

Behind the counter on the wall was another almost-empty key rack. Hilly saw three rows of five hooks and one lone key under the number 15. Maybe there was hope after all.

Above the key rack was a large NO SMOKING sign.

The woman took her place behind the counter, the registration book front and center.

Before Hilly could speak, the woman said in a gravelly smoker's voice, "I'm Ethel. You must be Miss Walker?"

Hilly had begun to believe there were no secrets in this small town. She asked, "My Michigan plates again?"

"Heavens, no. I'm not that sleuthy. Peggy over at the Fireside just called a minute ago. Said you were on the way. We've been expecting you for a few days now."

Hilly replied, "That was kind of her. She said to tell you hello."

Ethel answered with a scratchy laugh, "I'll just bet she did."

"Do you have a room for a few days?"

"Sure do. That old coot L. T. Rice saw to it last week. You must be some kind of VIP." She turned slowly and lifted the last key off the rack, "Number fifteen, the last room on the end. One of my nicest, but I say that to all my guests."

Hilly took the key and asked, "How much for the room, and do you take Visa?"

"Rooms are forty-five dollars a night," Ethel answered, "and I also have a weekly deal. And, yes, I take Visa, but your room charge has been taken care of, Miss Walker. I was told to tell you that."

The old woman turned the registration book around and handed Hilly a pen on the end of a chain. "I need your name, address, model car, and license plate number."

Puzzled, Hilly took the pen and began to fill in the blanks. "Who's picking up the room charge?"

"I suspect L. T. Rice himself is paying, but" she laughed, "don't worry, knowing him, he'll charge you double somehow down the line."

Hilly finished, and Ethel turned the book around.

She exclaimed, "Hildegard Walker, just like our county, huh?"

"Please just call me Hilly."

"My full name is Ethel Ferguson, but call me Miss E. like the rest of the town does."

"Sure, Miss E."

"There's a bunch of those dam workers staying here and around town. A tough lot, but they know to keep it down around town. And this is a dry county, Miss Walker. No drinking on the premises. I won't tolerate it or any other misbehavior."

"I see. No trouble from me, Miss E."

"If anybody bothers you, let me know. My nephew is the sheriff, and he's only a few blocks away. Everyone knows not to mess with him."

Miss E. fumbled around under the counter and handed Hilly two business cards.

"By the way, Miss Walker, my nephew left his card and said he would like you to drop by his office tomorrow morning around nine o'clock if it's convenient for some kind of meet and greet. Didn't say what it was about. And old L. T. left his card, too, and said to drop by his office around ten o'clock, if possible. Both places are just a couple of blocks through the alley. Near the courthouse."

Hilly looked at the sheriff's card. Roscoe Ferguson, Walker County Sheriff's Office. Serve and Protect. The second card read, L. T. Rice, Attorney at Law. Hilly slipped both cards into her T-shirt pocket and turned to leave. Before she was out the door, Miss E. added, "Doughnuts from Johnnie's and coffee here in the office in the morning. Best doughnuts in the state."

CHAPTER 12

The Worm

Hilly stepped from the shower and dried herself. She had stayed in many hotels in her life. Too many, she thought, including some five stars in Europe, but she had to admit that the Bluebird was above average. The towel she was using was large and fluffy and smelled fresh. The room and bathroom, although small, were immaculate and well kept. The queen-size bed was firm, although probably a tad too big for the room. A flat-screen LCD TV held a good selection of channels. And a vase full of bright flowers sat on the desk.

Most importantly, the air-conditioning unit below the window was putting out ice-cold air on the high setting. It was the small things that counted.

Hilly selected a pair of well-worn Levis and another T-shirt from her overnight bag and pulled on her Nike running shoes. She tucked the T-shirt into her jeans and checked herself out in the mirror on the back of the bathroom door. Not bad, she thought.

The first order of business was something to eat. That Slim Jim was a distant memory, and her stomach was growling.

She felt tired after the long day. Her planned evening run would have to wait until morning.

She picked up her keys from the desk, along with her Swiss Army knife, wallet, cell phone, and spare change, and stuffed all of them into her pants pockets.

She picked up her sunglasses and the room key, which was attached by a small chain to an awkward block of wood with the room number. The room key itself was a relic. Most motels and hotels used electronic key cards these days. She switched off the lights and set the air-conditioning to low.

Stepping out, she felt the heat again—although now that the sun was lower, it was a bit cooler.

She twisted the outside knob to make sure it was locked.

The only restaurants in town seemed to be the Subway and that other café on the town square with the strange name. Since they were only a couple of blocks away, Hilly decided to give Lilly a rest and walk the short distance.

Ethel, or Miss E., had mentioned cutting through the alley, so Hilly walked to the street in front of the motel and turned right around the end of the motel. Sure enough, an alley ran behind her room toward the town square.

There was nothing remarkable about the gravel alley. It came out on the town square between the sheriff's annex and the post office. Utility poles ran along one side. Some garages backed up to the alley as well as a few Dumpsters. Not surprisingly, mail trucks were parked behind the post office. The sun was getting lower and was shining in her eyes.

Hilly sensed someone behind her and turned. The man was tall with dark hair over his collar. He wore old Levis, a plaid shirt, and a dirty baseball cap with some equipment manufacturer's name above the bill. The shirt was not tucked in. The cap's bill and sunglasses hid his eyes.

He appeared to have followed her around the end of the motel and into the alley, and he was keeping his distance, just as the man in the old Ford pickup had done a few hours earlier.

Hilly reached into her front pocket and made a fist around her pocket knife. Chuckling to herself, she released her grip. This was a little town in Kentucky, not the streets of metro Detroit.

She walked from between the buildings into the town square.

The county courthouse was closed, as were the rest of the businesses around the square, including the Subway. Maybe the movie theater would open later.

So the restaurant with the funny name it would be.

As Hilly rounded the corner, she glanced back and noticed that the man in the alley was gone, vanished somehow.

To her left some movement caught her eye as a large black female deputy came out of the sheriff's annex. She wore a light brown uniform shirt and dark brown uniform pants. A black stripe ran down the outside of each pant leg. Dark brown epaulets on each shoulder matched the pants. She wore no tie, and her collar was unbuttoned. A gold badge was pinned above her left breast pocket. On her feet were brown sensible work boots with a high shine.

As Hilly watched, the deputy walked to the brown Chevy Tahoe. She hitched up her gun belt and, after hefting her bulk up into the driver's seat, gave Hilly a smile and a wink. She shut the door, started the engine, and backed into the square.

As Hilly walked to the café and watched the deputy drive by the movie theater, she thought to herself that it was evident the law enforcement of Walker County knew all about her arrival in town, too.

Three parking places down, Hilly noticed a red Buick Regal. The car was angled away from her and she couldn't see the license plates.

Hilly looked through the restaurant's windows. The lights were blazing. Two ceiling fans were rotating. A Formica lunch counter with shiny rotating stools lined the café along the right wall. The seats of the stools were covered in red vinyl. Along the left wall were perhaps eight booths. And along the back wall were three more. The booths were covered with the same red vinyl.

At the back wall, a swinging door with a central window opened into kitchen.

The large wooden front door was painted dark green. The door had a large central window and a brass handle. It was in an alcove a few steps in from the sidewalk with a high narrow window on each side.

On the window to her right was stenciled "Camas L. Worm, Proprietor."

Before she opened the heavy door, Hilly looked for a posted menu but guessed the Worm Café just wasn't that kind of place.

The place was packed and noisy and hot. People were talking loud. One man was standing near a booth with four other men and arguing about something. A waitress at the next booth behind him was taking an order. She was a tall, striking blonde, had maybe an inch or two even on Hilly, with a few tattoos on her arms, but at the moment was slouched with pad in hand.

Then Hilly noticed three Korean men in suits in the first booth and at the next booth were three more men in suits.

Crowded into two of the booths along the back wall were some young people with an older man.

The stools at the counter were all taken. Three of the men were older and wore bib overalls and kept their equipment ball caps on as they ate and talked. One man was squirting a liberal amount of ketchup on his steak.

There was one empty booth at the back near the kitchen door.

As Hilly pushed the heavy door open further, a brass bell attached to the upper door frame tinkled loudly, announcing her entry. Everyone suddenly looked her way. The noise and clatter stopped completely, and the Worm Café went silent except for the ceiling fans swishing overhead.

CHAPTER 13

Cheeseburger And Fries

Hilly stood still with her back to the door. The brass bell over the door tinkled again as the door swung shut behind her.

A man standing behind the cash register asked, "How many tonight, miss?"

The man was small. Hilly had an easy three or four inches on him. He was dressed in a white shirt with the sleeves rolled up tightly above his elbows, revealing several tattoos on each wiry forearm. Over the shirt and dark pants, he wore a long, food-stained apron tied behind his back at the waist. Two ballpoint pens and a pencil protruded from his shirt pocket. He wore his grayish hair long and tied back in a ponytail, mostly covered with a hair net.

The man smiled as he jockeyed a toothpick back and forth and asked again, "Welcome to the Worm Café." A slight nod. "I'm Camas Worm, proprietor." He asked again, "How many tonight, miss?"

Hilly found her voice and turned her attention from the diners to him. "Just me."

The man picked up a menu and said as he turned, "Follow me. I believe we have a booth in the back open just for ya all."

Hilly began to walk down the middle of the café, suddenly thinking of the old joke wherein the waiter with the bad limp says, "Walk this way!"

The man walked the length of the café behind the counter as Hilly followed.

Hilly knew she was no shrinking violet; she considered herself pretty tough, but this whole situation was very weird.

The men at the counter, even the ones in the bib overalls, rotated on their stools and followed her progress. One very large man still had a fork up to this mouth.

As she walked by, Hilly could feel the eyes on her back from the Koreans as well as the men in ties at the other two booths.

In the fourth booth sat three tough-looking men. The man on the outside—silky maroon shirt, gold chain necklace, and Elvis Costello glasses—seemed to be checking her out intensely.

The tattooed waitress was watching Hilly, tapping her pink-eraser pencil on her lower teeth.

The man who had called himself Camas Worm was ahead of her and came around the end of the lunch counter.

Hilly caught her breath as she saw an old Colt .38 stuck in his waistband just inside the apron. No one could miss it. She wondered, did he carry it all the time?

Camas Worm arrived at the empty back booth, produced a rag from his pocket, and proceeded to make a show of wiping off the table and one of the red vinyl seats. He straightened the salt and pepper shakers, the chrome napkin holder, and the yellow mustard and red ketchup squeeze containers as Hilly arrived at the booth.

The waitress passed with her pad and opened the kitchen door. Before the door closed behind her, Hilly thought she saw the man from the alley cooking over the grill. He had a hair net on, but it looked like the same person.

Camas Worm bowed and motioned for her to have a seat. Hilly scooted into the booth.

The older man with the students studied her. In fact, as she glanced around, everyone was still looking her way. Nothing had changed.

Camas Worm stood at the end of the table as Hilly picked up the menu.

He said a little too loudly, "Welcome to the Worm, Ms. Walker."

Hilly nodded, still pretending to study the menu. Another person in this town who knew her name. She didn't question it this time. She was sure Miss E. had telegraphed her departure from Room 15 at the Bluebird. In fact, she was sure all the people in this restaurant knew her name somehow. It was turning into a great *Twilight Zone* episode in her mind. This booth had no doubt been kept empty for her and watched over by this strange owner and the tough-looking waitress. It looked to Hilly that some of the customers had also waited for her to make an entrance.

Camas Worm extended his hand to the menu and smiled. "Everythin's good at the Worm, Ms. Walker. I'll give you a minute or two to decide. Trisha will be back to take your order."

Hilly nodded.

Then he leaned in and said in a low voice, almost a whisper, "You don't know it yet, Ms. Walker, but you and me got a lot in common right now. Be careful is what I'm sayin'." Then he straightened and turned back toward the front of the café. He went back behind the counter, stood with his hands on his hips, and gave his customers a stern look and said loudly, "What you all lookin' at? Git back to your eatin'."

Slowly, the other diners turned their attention to their meals.

CHAPTER 14

The Long Way

After the strange meal at the Worm Café, Hilly decided to pass on the shortcut through the alley and take the sidewalk back to the Bluebird. The sky was now overcast, the square was descending into twilight, and sprinklers were swishing back and forth watering the grass, the sidewalks, and the wooden benches.

Hilly stopped under the movie theater's marquee. All was dark. According to a sign, the theater was only open for business on Friday, Saturday, and Sunday.

The food had been good, as promised, at the café. Heck, she thought, might as well just call it the Worm like everyone else. The cheeseburger had been big, at least a half pound. Cooked to perfection. The fries were special, too, with just the right amount of crispness. And to finish it all off had been a tall, creamy chocolate milkshake. All of it slowly making its way to her thighs.

Mr. Worm wouldn't let her pay no matter how much she protested. She had given the waitress a generous tip.

Hilly continued to stroll slowly north toward Main Street, casually looking in the store windows. She stopped to check out a small jewelry store. It was closed, but she noticed the display window had not been emptied for the night.

Someone stepped out of the Worm. It was the waitress, although she had changed out of the skirt and tight blouse into jeans and a Harley-Davidson T-shirt. Tips, Hilly guessed.

As Hilly turned around and continued to walk, the waitress pulled a butane lighter and a pack of cigarettes from her pocket. The lighter flared as she began to follow Hilly along the east side of the square.

Hilly ambled along and then quickly turned the corner in front of the bank. The streetlights had come on along the darkening street, and she continued quickly along the sidewalk. She was in the shadows between the two buildings and backed up against the bank's limestone wall.

It didn't take long before the waitress ran around the corner and stopped, seemingly puzzled that the sidewalk ahead of her was empty.

Hilly stepped out of the shadow and smiled, "You'd make a pretty lousy tail, Trisha."

The waitress started and licked her lips. The tough façade she had affected in the restaurant faded for a moment, then came right back.

Hilly noticed the Harley T-shirt hung loose and there was a telltale bulge on the left. She wondered whether everybody in this town was armed. Most likely.

The waitress lapsed into her tough-girl slouch, took a drag on the cigarette, and said, "I don't know what you mean, Ms. Walker. I was just headed home after my shift."

"Call me, Hilly, Trish. And here's another tip. Don't go running around a corner like that."

Trish nodded.

"Did your father send you to see me back to the Bluebird?"

"Oh, he ain't my father; he's my husband."

Hilly blinked and then asked, "What's going on in this town with me?"

"I don't know what you mean, Ms. Walker…er, Hilly."

"C'mon, Trish, I've been escorted by someone ever since I was ten miles outside of town today."

"Sorry, it ain't for me to say, Miss Hilly. Camas just wanted you seen back to the Bluebird. All I know is he's worried."

"Worried about what? I never even met him until tonight."

"All I know is that there's some deal about an inheritance."

"Who was the man helping in the kitchen?

"That's one of Camas's brothers, Leroy."

"Does he drive an old Ford four-by-four by chance?"

"Why, yes, an old white one. How'd you know?"

Hilly ignored the question. "And all those people in the café?"

"I hear most of them was waitin' to maybe talk to you. They knew you was probably coming up from the motel to eat, but Camas told all of them to talk to your lawyer, L. T. Rice, up on the second floor, if they wanted to talk to somebody. He told them all not to bother you whilst you ate, or else."

"Or else what?"

Trisha took another drag on the cigarette. "You know, or else. Camas and his brothers and cousins have a pretty fearsome reputation around these here parts. Always have. Believe me, they's no people to fool with."

Trisha dug into her tight front jean pocket and pulled out a handful of business cards. She handed them to Hilly. "Most of 'em left a business card or two for you. Camas wanted me to drop these off with Miss E. at the motel office, but seeing how we're talking right here, I guess I'll just give them to you."

Hilly took the cards, quickly shuffled though them, and whistled quietly to herself. World Mart, Fugawa Motors, Forsyth Travel Hotels, Friends of the National Parks, Sierra Club, the University of Southern Kentucky. Quite a mix. All had phone numbers, no doubt cell phones, penciled on some blank part of the cards. Three were billion-dollar-plus international businesses. Hilly slipped the cards into her T-shirt pocket. She nodded at the waitress's waist. "Do you know how to use that gun, girl?"

The waitress touched the butt of the gun under her T-shirt, "Oh, yes, ma'am, I've been around guns all my life, and I was in the regular army three years. I was even in the military police for a short while helpin' out but I'm guessin' I'm a little rusty followin' people, huh? I shot expert though. Everyone knows I'm the best shot in the family and pretty fearless." She hesitated and said with a little humor, "And that's saying something in this here family, believe you me." She added, "But I'm much better with a rifle than a pistol."

"Iraq?"

"No, ma'am. Afghanistan for a year, but that's been a while back. I'm still in the reserves now and might be sent back, they say. I'm startin' nursin' school up in Lexington in the fall."

Hilly didn't doubt any of Trish's story and resisted giving the other woman a hug as they set out to walk the two blocks to the Bluebird.

CHAPTER 15

Mirror To Mirror

The red Buick Regal was parked in the shadows beneath the trees next to the white farmhouse. Three men sat silently waiting in the dark car facing the highway a half mile away. The Buick's engine had been turned off but not before the power windows had been lowered. The night was hot. Flashes of distant lightning played through the clouds. Thunderstorms had been predicted for the morning hours.

The man in the backseat held a cigarette in his right hand. His arm dangled out the open window alongside the outside of the door. He brought his arm back inside and took a drag on the cigarette.

The passenger in the front seat nervously tapped a finger on the padded dash.

The driver, a man with thick, black-framed glasses, sat with his hands on the steering wheel in the ten-and-two position.

The passenger in the rear dangled his arm back along the door and broke the silence. "Where in the fuck is he?"

The front passenger chimed in, "Yeah, he's late, Phil. I don't like it when people are fucking late, you know."

The rear passenger leaned forward a little bit, "Hey, it's fuckin' hot back here. Start the fuckin' engine and turn the AC back on for Christ's sake."

The front passenger chimed in again, "Yeah, Phil it's hot in here."

The driver sighed and spoke up. "Shut the fuck up. Both of ya. You two are the biggest fuckin' babies I've ever had the fuckin' pleasure of working with. He'll be here. It's only been ten minutes. Somethin' probably held him up in town. Christ!"

The passengers were silent again. The rear passenger brought his arm inside again and took another drag on his cigarette.

The driver turned around. "Put that fuckin' cigarette out for Christ's sake. You're lightin' the whole car up with every puff of that cancer stick. And I'd better not find any ashes on the seat back there." He turned back around.

The rear passenger grumbled a little to himself but did what he was told and flipped the cigarette out the window onto the grass.

The driver straightened. A pair of headlights was coming along the highway from town.

As the three men in the Buick watched, the headlights slowed and turned toward them down the long lane.

The driver turned on the Buick's parking lights.

The driver in the oncoming car switched off the headlights but left the parking lights on, as he approached. The other car was a brown Ford Crown Victoria, known by every cop and taxi driver as a Crown Vic. It had a pair of red and blue lights mounted in its grill and a heavy, black push bar mounted in front of the front bumper.

The Crown Vic driver expertly pulled alongside the Buick, his driver's side mirror missing the Buick's side mirror by less than a quarter of an inch. The Crown Vic came to a stop and the driver powered down the window with a whining sound.

The Ford's driver stared down the Buick's driver for a moment, until the Buick's driver simply said, "How's it going, sir?"

The Ford's driver answered, "You really fucked it up in Detroit, boys. She wasn't supposed to make it this far. You were supposed to detain her somehow. Use your imagination. The court date is this Thursday morning. Atlanta isn't happy with you."

The driver of the Buick swallowed and pushed his glasses up on the bridge of his nose. "We just missed her by a day, sir. We couldn't find her, and then one of her neighbors said she was headed down here. We drove like hell hoping to intercept her somewhere and just caught up with her a couple of miles outside of town."

"Well, now she's in my county, and it's a little more complicated thanks to you fuck-ups."

The Buick's driver chuckled a little but regretted it.

"What's so funny?"

"Yeah, we just had dinner with her a few hours ago at the Worm."

The Ford's driver raised his voice a little. "You what?"

"Yeah, we was eatin' at the Worm, and in she walks just like that." He snapped his fingers just above the steering wheel.

The rear passenger leaned forward. "Nice bod, too."

"Yeah, nice ass." The front passenger added.

The Ford's driver tilted his head and stared at the Buick's passengers.

The rear passenger said defensively. "Well, she does. Right, guys?"

The Buick's driver turned around, "Shut up, Frank."

The Ford's driver turned his attention back to the Buick's driver. "I supposed she saw you three assholes in there, and you probably blew your cover. Idiots." He paused, then asked, "Anybody talk to her in the restaurant?"

"Naw, that mean little son of bitch that owns the place obviously knew she was coming and pretty well made it clear to everyone not to bother her or else. And it appeared there were others in there that wanted her attention."

"Or else what?"

"Well, he did have a pretty big old pistol stuck in his belt."

"Like I said, Atlanta isn't happy with you three. You should've handled all this up north. Delayed her for a few days or a week. That's all. It's not good other people are involved now. You're to back off and let me handle things for the time being. Clear on that?"

"C'mon, tell Atlanta to give us a break."

"This woman, from what I'm beginning to hear, might be more than a match for you three tough guys."

"Give us a chance. We can handle it."

"Not now. Tell me you're clear on that."

The Buick's driver raised his hands in mock defense. "Yeah, we're clear. Right, fellas?"

The other two men in the Buick nodded.

The Ford's driver asked, "Where are you staying?"

"We got rooms at that Best Western out by the interstate."

"Yeah, I know it. Keep your cell phones handy and on at all times. I don't want to hear you left your phone in your room while filling your mouth with pancakes over at the Waffle House or something."

"No problem."

The Ford's driver changed the subject and pointed out the front window. "You got this place cleaned up for the time being?"

"Yeah, finished up this afternoon. Last truck for a while I guess. Only Alvin is left up on the hill tending to things. And he isn't too happy about staying in that tent for the meanwhile either."

"Too fucking bad. Atlanta isn't happy that production is going to be down for who knows how long, because you three goofballs fucked up and didn't take care of her up north like everyone planned."

The Buick driver whined, "But they got to understand…"

The Ford's driver slipped the car into reverse. "Just shut the fuck up. And stay by the phone like I told you." He powered his window up, backed the car onto the front lawn, and disappeared down the long lane, turning his headlights on just before he eased onto the highway.

The Buick's driver started the car, turned on the air-conditioning, and powered his window up. As he put the Regal into gear, he muttered to himself, "Asshole cops."

The rear passenger powered his window up as the car began to roll forward. "What'd I say, anyhow? I was just makin' an observation."

CHAPTER 16

Meet and Greet

The sky was beginning to open up as Hilly neared the Bluebird at the end of her run. She picked up the pace. Lightning struck somewhere on the ridge to the north. Minutes later a thunderclap rolled over the town.

She made it just in the nick of time to the safety of the motel's office porch as large drops began to pound the parking lot.

She bent over with her hands on her knees for a moment. When she caught her breath, she walked the length of the motel to her room under the protection of motel's long porch roof. Her heart was beginning to slow as she unlocked her room door.

The morning run had been a good one. Perhaps four miles. East down Route 153, past the town limits, and a mile or two farther. The countryside alternated between wooded hillsides and farm fields. A few houses and barns were scattered along the road, set back in trees here and there. The sun had been shining for the first half of her run, but then dark clouds had begun to move in over the ridge, distant thunder could be heard, and she thought it was time to turn around.

Hilly had spotted the old Ford four-by-four with the red-primered fender on a hillside parked behind some brush. She was going to meet with the sheriff in a little over an hour and would ask him about this strange family and what was going on.

When she emerged from the shower, the rain was still pounding on the roof and creating big puddles in the parking lot. Hilly didn't have to make any big decisions about what to wear today to meet the sheriff and that mysterious lawyer, L. T.Rice. She had only brought one set of good clothes, a light blue silk blouse, her favorite, gray dress slacks, and a pair of black pumps with a medium heel.

She placed her favorite gold chain necklace around her neck as she turned, looking at her image in the bathroom door's full-length mirror. Not bad, she thought again. She tilted her head as she added simple gold earrings and an old art deco gold pin that had once belonged to her mother. Her hair was still damp and would soon dry. It had been cut a little shorter than she really liked it last week, but it would have to do.

Looking at her watch, she thought she would be able to stop at the motel office and snag a cup of coffee and one of those doughnuts Miss E. had raved about.

The rain had stopped by then, and she took the wet sidewalk to the town square. No alley this time. As she rounded the bank on the corner, she glanced up at the big clock in the gray church's steeple. 8:57. Hilly picked up her pace. She hated to be late.

Before she entered the sheriff's office, she tossed her coffee cup into a trash barrel near the front door. The chocolate cake doughnut and coffee were as advertised. Delicious.

Behind the counter of the Walker County Sheriff's Office was a heavyset, older woman wearing a frown and a print dress. Another younger woman was sitting at a radio console against the far wall and talking on the telephone into an industrial-grade black handset.

The frowning woman had a file open in front of her and was furiously writing something on a notepad. Without looking up, the woman at the counter said automatically, "Be right with you, honey." Then she looked up, stopped what she was doing, and said politely, "Oh, Miss Walker, excuse me. Good morning. The sheriff is expecting you." She lifted a portion of the counter and motioned Hilly forward. "Please follow me."

Hilly followed her down the hallway to a door at the rear of the building, feeling as if she had grown up in this town.

One side of the door was a full-length window. Stenciled on the window was a gold badge, and below:

ROSCOE FERGUSON

WALKER COUNTY SHERIFF

The woman entered the office and motioned Hilly to follow her.

The carpeted office was spacious and nicely air-conditioned. A large man was standing behind a big mahogany desk along the opposite wall and hurriedly hunching himself into a nicely tailored sport coat. He was wearing matching tan linen trousers, a light blue dress shirt, and a yellow-and-brown striped tie. As the man finished pulling on the sport coat, Hilly noticed a holstered Glock 19 on his right hip and a gold badge clipped to his belt on the other side. The man had himself organized and stood behind his desk with a large smile.

The woman made the introduction, "Sheriff, this is Miss Walker. Miss Walker this is Sheriff Ferguson."

The sheriff leaned across his desk and offered Hilly his right hand. Hilly walked forward two steps and took it. She felt as if she had taken the paw of a large grizzly bear. Sheriff Ferguson stood well over six feet and was closer to three hundred pounds than two hundred pounds if the roll of fat over his belt was any indication. He also appeared to be closer to seventy than sixty but with a full head of light brown hair turning to gray. The sheriff released his grip and indicated for Hilly to sit in one of the upholstered armchairs in front of his desk. The smile remained and he asked, "Do you prefer Ms. or Miss?"

Hilly smiled back, "Actually, I prefer Hilly."

"Hilly?"

"It's short for Hildegard."

The sheriff remained standing, looked down, and tapped a paper on his desk with a forefinger, then looked back up.

"Hildegard, of course. Well, my mother played a trick on me, too, and named me Roscoe, but you can just call me Ross." He hesitated. "Or just Sheriff, like everyone seems to prefer around here."

Hilly answered, "Actually, Sheriff sounds better to me. I'm used to it."

"Given your background, I guess so."

Sheriff Ferguson then sat heavily into his large, upholstered swivel chair behind the desk. The woman stood by the door awaiting further orders. The sheriff noticed her and said, "Where are my manners? I'm sorry, Hilly, but you haven't formally been introduced to Alice. Hilly, Alice. Alice, Hilly."

Hilly turned in her chair as Alice came forward to politely shake her hand. "Pleased to meet you."

"Likewise."

Alice looked impatiently at the sheriff, "Anything else, Sheriff?"

The sheriff looked at Hilly and asked, "Anything to drink? Coffee? Water? Royal Crown soda?"

"No, I'm fine." Hilly thought, Royal Crown? It had been a long time since she had heard that brand.

Alice turned and left, shutting the door behind her.

The sheriff smiled and said, "A little secret, Ms. Walker…er, Hilly. Alice is the person who really runs this office. I'd be lost without her."

Hilly knew that to be true. Everywhere she had worked there had been someone like Alice keeping it all together somehow. Hilly turned and faced the sheriff again. To her left was a wide, crank-out window with a view of what looked to be the employee parking lot. A brown Ford Crown Victoria with a push bar was parked in the first spot. To her right, in the corner, stood an American flag and what she assumed must be the Kentucky flag. It was dark blue with gold lettering. Hilly could only read the word *Commonwealth*. On the wall near the flags were framed pictures of President Obama and a man who must be the governor of Kentucky. Behind the sheriff was a long credenza and, above that, bookshelves attached to the wall. Hilly had seen the same setup in every commanding officer's or politician's office she had ever visited. It was known as the "trophy wall," and Sheriff Ferguson's ran true to the stereotype.

On his credenza and shelves were various Lucite-encased awards and framed photos. There was a somewhat-faded color photo of the sheriff with a woman and two teenagers, a boy and a girl. Hilly recognized some familiar names and logos. Lions Club, Kiwanis, VFW, American Legion. Also on the credenza was a handheld radio in a charger showing a green light.

What interested her, though, was a black-and-white eight-by-ten photo. It depicted five soldiers standing in front of an army UH-1 Huey helicopter with crossed sabers on the nose. 7th Cav. Three of the soldiers were kneeling in front, and two were holding flight helmets behind. One of those standing in the back with a flight helmet was obviously the man sitting before her—although much younger, much thinner, and with a little more hair.

Hilly spoke first, "With all due respect, Sheriff, I'm not quite sure why you wanted to see me this morning."

The sheriff answered, "Well, Hilly, it's about those unpaid parking tickets."

"Parking tickets, I don't…"

Sheriff Ferguson cut her off and laughed. "Hey, just kidding. Actually, I was just being selfish in wanting to meet you first before everyone else."

"Everyone else? I still don't understand."

"People like the mayor and others."

"I'm still puzzled."

"You haven't been told?"

"Told what?"

"Well, Hilly, you are about to become one of the biggest private landowners in Walker County, which is kind of appropriate because I hear the county was named after a relative of yours a long time ago."

She didn't know what to say except, "Yes, way back on my father's side."

The sheriff continued, "Rice tells me about nine thousand acres including the west half of Worm Ridge."

"Worm Ridge?"

"That big hill north of town."

Hilly suddenly had a small glimmer of understanding but couldn't yet put it together.

"Anyway, I've probably said too much. You're meeting with Mr. Rice this morning, I hear, and he'll tell you more."

Hilly nodded and remembered what Trisha Worm had said the night before about an inheritance. Nine thousand acres? Jesus. Rice, the lawyer, had been secretive but had been insistent her presence was needed and that the inheritance matter was urgent. She had guessed maybe the old house and barn. But why the bodyguard?

The sheriff picked up a pair of reading glasses, adjusted them low on his nose, and tapped the papers in front of him on his desk. "I know people who know people, and I wound up talking to a Detroit PD captain by the name of Patton."

"General George?"

"I thought he said his name was Donald?"

"Inside joke."

"Oh, I see. Well, he had some high praise for you."

Hilly remained quiet.

"I told him I was thinking of hiring you myself, but after speaking to him, I don't think I can afford you."

Hilly thought to herself that law enforcement is a small, tight world and Patton was an asshole for talking to Sheriff Ferguson. And Ferguson was an asshole for delving into her past and talking to Patton. It was a world she wanted to leave behind.

The sheriff tapped the paper again, "You retired recently from the Detroit PD as a first-grade detective?"

Hilly replied curtly, "Yes, in April. I put my twenty in, and that was enough working in a war zone. Time to move on."

The sheriff continued to read to himself. He gave a low whistle. "Graduated from Michigan State, ROTC. US Army for seven years, served in Germany and the NATO headquarters in Brussels, military police, eventually promoted to captain. Detroit PD for twenty years, three letters of commendation and a medal."

The sheriff continued, "Detroit PD, robbery and homicide. One of the commendations was for closing down a blood diamond smuggling operation working alongside Interpol and other European agencies."

Hilly replied, "The jewel smuggling operation was via the Saint Lawrence Seaway from European cities like Antwerp and Amsterdam. I had investigated the same type of smuggling while serving in the military police in Brussels. My former European contacts were useful, and working with some other agencies we were able to help bust a big jewel smuggling ring working on the East Coast and in the Midwest."

Hilly briefly recalled the two years back in Europe undercover. It was an exciting time worthy of a novel. Expensive cars, expensive clothes, and five-star hotels. In the end, a lot of folks eventually went to prison for those African diamonds. And she fell in love with Switzerland again.

The sheriff looked over his reading glasses, "You speak a few languages Patton said?"

"Yes, I'm pretty fluent in French and German."

"You've run marathons he said? And Captain Patton also said you can be a bad ass and to watch out. Martial arts he said?"

This was sounding more and more like an interview of some kind. Hilly let out a breath, "Yes, Sheriff, I'm a third-degree black belt, and my best marathon time is four eleven, but that was a while ago."

Hilly pointed to the eight-by-ten black-and-white behind the sheriff and asked in a soft voice, "And yourself, Vietnam?"

The sheriff swiveled his chair around, looked at the picture, and began to answer when his office door flew open. Standing in the doorway was the black female deputy Hilly had seen the night before.

She was out of breath, "Sheriff, we got us a situation."

The sheriff put his reading glasses on the desk and rose from his chair. He followed the deputy into the hallway and, before closing the door, apologized to Hilly, "Give me a moment."

Hilly could hear them heatedly talking to each other in the hallway as she turned back to face the sheriff's desk and relaxed a little in the armchair. The sheriff's chair had swiveled so that the back faced the parking lot window. The unique light blue color of the ribbon in the glass-and-polished-wood display case on the credenza caught her eye. Hilly stood, leaned forward, and caught her breath. The object in the display case was unmistakable with its light blue ribbon—thirteen stars, brass eagle, and five-pointed star.

The office door opened and Hilly stepped back and brought herself to rigid attention. She brought her right hand up to her brow in a perfect salute.

The sheriff came around his desk and raised both hands in protest. "Please, Miss Walker, you don't have to do that. It's not required."

Hilly remained at attention and snapped back in a loud voice, "Sir, give me the honor!"

The sheriff brought himself to attention and quickly returned the salute.

Hilly brought her right hand down to her side and, still at attention, said loudly, "Thank you, sir! It was an honor, sir!"

The sheriff put himself at ease and, as he plucked the handheld radio from its charger on the credenza, said somewhat officially, "You're welcome, ma'am." Then he said, "Hilly, we got an emergency. Big and I are a little shorthanded today, and we'd like you to come along with us if you don't mind."

Hilly relaxed her stance, "Sure, sir, anything I can do."

The sheriff came around his desk, "OK, consider yourself deputized and no more of the 'sir' stuff."

Hilly couldn't stop herself, "Yes, sir...er, sheriff."

She followed him as he made his way to the front door. He stopped briefly to speak to Alice and the woman at the radio console. "Big and I each have a handheld radio plus the Tahoe's radio."

They woman at the console answered, "Yes, sheriff."

He continued, this time speaking to Alice at the counter, "And confirm you've alerted the fire department?"

"Yes, sheriff. But they're all at work and it could be a while."

"Noted. And Scooter?"

The woman at the radio console answered this time, "As soon as I can, sheriff. He's out of radio and cell phone range up Milner's Hollow on that livestock call. And the phones have been out of order up there for a few days because of the rain we've been having and a lightning strike on one of those towers. I'll head him your way as soon as I can raise him."

"Fine." The sheriff turned his back to the heavy glass front door and said to no one in particular as he pushed it open, "Damn it. I keep forgetting about cell phones these days." Hilly followed him through the door.

Outside, the deputy had the idling Tahoe waiting with the roof light bar running. People had stopped going about their business on the square and were watching.

The sheriff heaved himself into the front passenger seat and placed the handheld on the dash. He slammed his door, and the deputy turned on the siren and stepped on the gas. Hilly barely had the rear passenger door shut as she fumbled at first with the shoulder harness while the Tahoe picked up speed.

A metal screen separated the back and front seats. Another metal screen behind her separated the rear bench seat and the cargo area. A standard police vehicle, she thought. And, although this SUV still had its inside rear door handles and locks intact, Hilly was sure there was probably a cutout button for them on the front console.

Next to Sheriff Ferguson's left knee in its brackets was a standard Remington 870 shotgun with a wood stock. A large three–D-cell Maglite rested in its clip and charger on the other side of the console.

The Tahoe accelerated down the block, hesitated at the red light as the deputy cleared both ways, and then turned right past the bank. She was doing fifty or better as she passed the Bluebird.

The sheriff unclipped the hand mike above the Tahoe's console and officially put them in service with the woman back in the office on the town square.

The deputy was doing seventy at the town limits as Hilly finally secured her shoulder harness and seat belt.

CHAPTER 17

The Sink

Dark clouds filled the sky as the Tahoe overtook the slow-moving thunderstorm which had moved through Batavia earlier that morning. The deputy flipped on the high beams.

A few large drops spattered on the windshield. She set the wipers on interval.

A few miles farther and Route 153 made a ninety-degree turn toward the south around the edge of a cornfield. A lesser county road continued straight.

They rode in silence, listening to the wail of the siren, the deputy concentrating on her driving and the sheriff lost in his thoughts, until the sheriff raised his voice and asked his deputy, "Big, how much further to Moon's old store and the sink?"

The rain had picked up; before answering, the deputy twisted the wipers to high. "About four miles, sheriff."

The sheriff frowned, "And those kids rode all that way this morning?"

"Yes, sir. They're young and full of it. School's out for the summer. Time to explore. Weren't you ever young?"

Small hail pellets danced noisily on the Tahoe's hood and roof. The ditches on both sides of the highway filled with muddy water. Lightning suddenly danced across the tops of the trees on either side of the road and a thunderclap rolled over the Tahoe. Visibility dropped. The wipers were not keeping up.

The deputy let off the gas, and the Tahoe slowed as Route 153 dropped into a narrow valley. Hilly glanced out the side window and caught a glimpse through the trees of a stream. It was running high and muddy.

A moment later the Tahoe was in the clear. Sun dappled the dry road ahead. Another mile and the Tahoe slowed. The deputy reached down to the console and silenced the siren.

The sheriff pointed to the left, and the deputy turned across the northbound lane and into what looked to Hilly like a small park or picnic area. The gravel pullout curved back to the right and rejoined the main highway. On the grass in the area between the gravel pullout and the main highway stood a scroll-like, heavily weathered metal sign. The tires crunched on the gravel as the Tahoe rolled past the sign and approached two picnic tables under the trees with a wooden fence just beyond. Hilly was briefly able to read the sign as they rolled past:

SINK OF THE EAST FORK
OF THE SUN RIVER

The Tahoe coasted to a stop by one of the picnic tables, and all three occupants noticed the two small bicycles padlocked with vinyl-covered chains to one of the tables.

Leaving the doors open and the motor idling, Hilly followed the sheriff and his deputy past the bikes and stood on the other side of the table near a trash barrel behind the wooden fence. The drop on the other side of the fence down to the churning brown water was a steep and rocky twenty feet or more.

Hilly caught up with the two and stood near the deputy. The valley at this point was narrow and lined with gray rock ledges. Each ledge was thick with moss and green ferns. As the racing, muddy water swirled in from the left, the current became confused, and, to Hilly's amazement, just disappeared. On one side was a raging river, and on the other side was a rocky, tree-covered, peaceful valley.

The sheriff was the first to speak. He pointed to where the river disappeared below them in a mass of muddy foam and small whirlpools. He raised his voice for Hilly's benefit, "I've never seen the sink so full."

Hilly questioned him, "The sink?"

"Yeah, they call it a sink. The river simply disappears into a cave and reappears again about three-quarters of a mile downstream. Normally, in the summer there's not much water running through here and you can walk easily through the cave with a flashlight." He pointed to his deputy, "Hell, Big here will back me up. If you've grown up around here, you'd walked through the sink at one time or another, isn't that right, Big?

The deputy nodded her head a little, turned, and looked at the bicycles. "Don't look good, sheriff."

"Yeah, I'm thinking the same thing. Messing around in a cave is fun, but you've got to watch the weather. The sheriff turned and jogged back to the Tahoe. "Let's go!"

Hilly and the deputy followed. Doors slammed simultaneously, and the deputy accelerated back onto the highway.

CHAPTER 18

Moon's Store

Route 153 continued for another half mile to a T intersection and a three-way stop. Route 153 continued straight after the stop sign, and another state route, 602, descended steeply to the intersection from the left.

Set back about fifty feet from the highway just before the intersection was an ancient, ramshackle gas station and small store. The weathered clapboard building was more gray than white. A portico extended over the gas pumps and sported a faded round blue and orange Gulf sign. A service bay stood open, with an old Chevy pickup up on jacks inside. Next to the service bay was a store of sorts with a modern Coke machine near the front door. A faded sign above the door advertised "Souvenirs and Postcards."

At the sound of the Tahoe, a man who appeared to be close to eighty stepped out. He wore greasy coveralls and was wiping his hands with a red shop rag. A frightened, wide-eyed boy followed him outside.

The sheriff reported their location over the console mike as the Tahoe came to a stop near the gas pumps, got a reply, picked the handheld off the dash, and climbed out of the vehicle.

Hilly followed but remained next to the Tahoe. She noticed the price of gas in the window of one of the pumps was a mere 79.9 cents a gallon. Super Leaded and 95 octane decals decorated one pump.

The deputy shut off the motor and joined the sheriff. The old man finished wiping his hands with the oily rag, stuffed it in a pocket, and extended his hand to the sheriff. The sheriff shook the old man's hand. The old man nodded at the deputy. "Howdy, Sheriff, what took you so blame long to git here? I'm a taxpayer just like all the rest in this hellhole of a county."

Sheriff Ferguson smiled and cut him off, "Cut the shit, Moon." He nodded at the boy and asked the old man, "What's going on?"

"I was sittin' havin' a cup of coffee, Sheriff, mindin' my own business, taking a break, you know, when this here youngster came a knockin' on my door blubberin' all to hell and disturbin' me. Said he lost his friend. I couldn't make heads or tails out of it."

The boy looked terrified and was wiping his eyes with the palms of both hands. He wore a striped blue-and-white T-shirt, jeans, and red Keds. He was caked with mud from head to toe.

The sheriff knelt in front of him and gently put a hand on his shoulder. "What's your name, son?"

The boy sniffed and sucked in some snot, "Jimmy, Jimmy Lee Bailey, sir."

"Tell me what's going on, Jimmy."

"Well, sir, me and my cousin Ronny was hiking through the cave with our flashlights and the water started to come in fast. We was about midway and didn't know what to do, so we started to run for it. We'd been through the sink before and knew a secret way out, but by the time we got there the water was real deep and over our heads. We thought about swimming out, but the water was too fast so we started climbing. I climbed up one side and got out, but Ronny climbed up the wrong side and got stuck up there against the roof. He didn't dare try to get over to where I was." The boy started to cry again and wiped his eyes smearing mud across his face.

The sheriff asked, "Is Ronny still in the sink, Jimmy?"

The boy nodded.

"Jimmy, can you show me and my deputy where you got out?"

The boy nodded again and pointed across the highway. Sheriff Ferguson took the boy's hand and began walking. The deputy followed. They waited for a large dump truck to pass by and crossed the highway.

———

Hilly waited by the Tahoe. Moon Williams found a toothpick in one of his pockets, started chewing on it, and walked over to Hilly. He looked her up and down, made a half circle around her, and leaned against the front fender of the Tahoe. Hilly had seen crazy before and held her ground.

Moon pulled out the toothpick, examined it closely, and asked, "Yer new here ain't ya?"

Hilly answered as politely as possible, "Yes, sir, from Detroit."

Moon cackled, "I thought you was a Yankee the minute I set eyes on ya and your fancy clothes. Got any kin around here?"

"Not anymore."

"You look like a lawyer to me. Got any word about the injunction?"

The sudden change of subjects was unexpected, but crazy was crazy and he looked harmless. "I don't know anything about an injunction, sir."

Moon Williams pointed a thumb down the highway. "You know, agin that big dam downstream. They say in a few years me and my store will be under three hundred feet of water." He cackled again and continued, "And I don't know how to swim." He slapped his hand against his thigh like it was the funniest thing he had ever heard.

Hilly thought it was kind of funny, too, in a way.

Moon then got serious and said, "Well, ma'am, I hear tell a couple of those 'green' organizations as they call 'em was filing an injunction to stop it. Lookin' at ya, I thought you was maybe important and knew about it." Then he added, "Ya all got the purtiest blue eyes I ever did see."

CHAPTER 19

Squeezed Tight

Hilly and Moon had reached a silent impasse while they waited. Finally, old man Moon, who was leaning against the front fender of the Tahoe picking his teeth and grinning to himself, and Hilly, who was leaning against the rear passenger fender with her arms folded across her chest, studying the parking lot and wondering why this character Moon didn't have anything else to do, heard the deputy huffing and chuffing across the highway.

Hilly turned and walked around the tailgate. Moon went the other way around the front grille.

The deputy had one hand on her black woven gun belt and was doing her best trotting across the parking lot considering the gun belt held her Glock 19, an extra ammo clip, a canister of pepper spray, handcuffs, a handheld radio, and a small flashlight. She was breathing hard when she went past Hilly and opened the tailgate. She reached in the Tahoe and pulled out a large black canvas duffel bag with the word RESCUE stenciled in yellow on each side.

She took a couple of deep breaths and then said, "Ms. Walker, we need help. Sheriff says you gotta come with me right now!" With that she slammed the tailgate, easily hefted the canvas bag up on one shoulder, walked around a perplexed Hilly Walker, and with her free hand opened the driver's door. She leaned across the front seat and snapped the large, black, three-D-cell Maglite out of its clip. The deputy handed the large flashlight to Hilly and shut the Tahoe's door.

Hilly hefted the flashlight in one hand. She had always liked the way a big Maglite felt before they were banned on the beat.

Moon Williams came up behind the deputy. She turned and told him, "Moon, this is real important now, you understand? Me and the sheriff are trusting you to stay right here by the car in order to tell everyone where we are. You got that?"

Moon, who hadn't seen this much excitement since he didn't know when, danced up and down from one foot to another while vigorously nodding and said, "Yes, ma'am, Miss Big, I'll wait right here; don't you worry!"

The deputy asked again, "Are we real clear, Moon? And you leave this car alone? There better not be anything missing."

"Oh, yes, ma'am!"

The deputy hefted the bag again, turned, and headed across the gravel parking lot. Hilly followed holding the Maglite at her side. Both women paused at the highway while two large orange dump trucks passed by. Hilly yelled over the diesel engines, "Deputy, what exactly is going on?"

"First off, call me Big like everyone else."

"Why Big?"

"Short for Big Betty. Been called Big all my life."

The trucks passed in a black cloud of diesel, downshifting for the stop sign.

The two women trotted across the highway and the far shoulder, then made their way into the brush and trees on the other side. Big was quickly running out of breath as they made their way through the small valley. Hilly easily trotted behind her and offered to take the bag, but Big refused.

"It ain't far," Big continued breathlessly. "Sheriff thinks the other boy might still be alive. Thinks the water might still be rising, though. Says you might be that boy's only chance."

Hilly followed, "*Me?*"

"We're almost there. He'll fill you in soon enough."

The terrain began to rise steeply. Big and Hilly pushed the underbrush aside and came into a small clearing. Next to a large tree and a rock outcropping was Sheriff Ferguson. His sport coat and tie were thrown aside on the ground, and he had rolled up both sleeves. The day was starting to heat up as the sun rose over the tops of the trees. His shirt was showing dark sweat stains under both his arms.

As Big and Hilly neared him, the sheriff reached out impatiently for the large Maglite.

The tree was rooted around the gray outcropping. One of its roots ran horizontally across the rock ledge before disappearing underground.

Jimmy Lee Bailey was sitting quietly on the root with one arm around the tree and his feet dangling over the rocky ledge. He was holding the sheriff's badge and turning it over and over.

Big dropped the canvas bag and quickly unzipped it.

Sheriff Ferguson pulled his Glock from its holster, switched on the flashlight, and dropped to his knees in front of the rock ledge.

Deputy Big sat heavily on the ground and began unlacing her boots.

Sheriff Ferguson said over his shoulder as he peered under the ledge, "Hilly, the others are still thirty minutes out, and Big and I are too large to fit. Too much blubber. So I'm afraid it's up to you."

Hilly knew exactly what he meant, but she never had liked tight places. Especially dark, tight places. She uncharacteristically began to twist the gold chain around her neck. She tried to buy a little time and innocently asked the sheriff, "What's up to me?" But she knew.

Big had her expensive Timberland boots and socks off. She got up and tip-toed barefoot over to the canvas bag. Hilly saw her toenails were painted a luscious pink. And she also saw that the deputy, too, was starting to sweat.

Deputy Big brought out of the bag a yellow safety helmet with chin strap and a four-LED headlamp affixed to the front. She quickly examined it and switched it on and off. Satisfied, next she pulled out a coil of nine-millimeter nylon climbing rope and laid it on the ground.

Sheriff Ferguson scooted back a bit from under the ledge and heavily stood up with one hand helping push on his knee. He holstered the Glock and said, "It's tight, but I think you can make it. And I didn't see any snakes."

As the sheriff handed her the flashlight, Hilly thought to herself that this was definitely one of those wrong place at the wrong time moments.

Deputy Big handed Hilly her finely oiled boots and wool socks and pointed to Hilly's feet. "Them pumps will never hold up in there. I think we're about the same size."

Hilly took the boots and socks. She sat on the ground and set the Maglite aside. As removed her shoes, Deputy Big picked up the yellow helmet, switched on the headlamp, and placed it on Hilly's head. Then she maneuvered the elastic strap under Hilly's chin.

Hilly had the left sock and boot on, and, surprisingly, they fit just about perfectly. She started pulling the sock and boot onto her right foot as Deputy Big knelt in front of her and hurriedly laced and tied the left boot.

Hilly finished tying the right boot, handed her sunglasses to the deputy, and then emptied her pockets. Cell phone, change, motel key with the wood block, and wallet. She kept her Timex and Swiss Army knife with her. She picked up the Maglite, pivoted around, and came up on her hands and knees in front of the gray rock ledge.

Sheriff Ferguson, with a hand on the ledge, knelt on her right.

Hilly tipped back the helmet a little and aimed the flashlight beam under the ledge. She had expected a hole of some kind, a cave. There was nothing except a small horizontal crack. Hilly turned to the sheriff. "You're kidding, right?"

The sheriff was now on his hands and knees. "No, I think you can do it." He reached over and placed his hand on Hilly's back. "You're going to have to get down on your stomach, push the rope ahead of you, use your elbows. Kid says it opens up in about thirty feet."

Hilly took another look. "Yeah, I think I'll fit."

Deputy Big laid the coil of rope in front of Hilly, and Hilly lowered herself to her stomach. Ahead of her the opening under the ledge looked to be about two feet wide and maybe seven or eight inches high.

Jimmy Lee Bailey jumped down next to Deputy Big. He had clipped the sheriff's badge to his belt.

With a grunt Hilly pushed the rope and Maglite ahead of her and into the opening. The top of her helmet scraped on the rock as she inched forward into the cave on her elbows. Memories of crawling under barbed wire in basic training came back to her, only she thought this was much smaller.

Progress was slow. Just inches at a time.

The sheriff and the deputy moved closer, and their heads almost touched as they peered into the opening. Big cupped her hand around her mouth and said, "If you see some big scary-looking spidery things, don't worry. They're cave crickets. They're harmless."

Hilly grunted back, "Gee, thanks!"

She developed a rhythm. Push the rope ahead, elbows and feet, elbows and feet. She was completely in the cave now and felt the cooler air. As she inched ahead, if anything, the passage felt tighter. She could barely raise her head now. Her elbows were in tight against her sides. She could feel the rock ceiling behind her rubbing roughly against her butt. Breathe, she told herself, breathe.

The passage became narrower still. Hilly was barely able to stretch her arms out in front of her, and she had to turn her head to one side. Each time she breathed she raised a small dust cloud in front of her and had to spit the dirt from her mouth. Using only her toes she pushed ahead blindly a quarter inch at a time.

Then, suddenly, she was stuck. She had an overwhelming and horrible realization that the ceiling and floor of the passage were immoveable.

Hilly began to panic and told herself she had to remain calm. She blew dust from her mouth and into the headlight's beam. Finally she yelled, "Shit! I'm fucking stuck!"

The sheriff and deputy were only twenty feet away.

Deputy Big poked her head into the opening and yelled, "Exhale!"

Of course, Hilly thought.

CHAPTER 20

Mud, Sweat, and Tears

Hilly exhaled and pushed hard with her toes. She moved forward a fraction of an inch. She took a few more short breaths and exhaled hard. She grunted, exhaled, and pushed again. Again, a little progress. She felt as if the earth was crushing her. She was committed to only going forward. There was no way to reverse. Exhale, forward. Exhale, forward. She was pushing the Maglite and rope with the side of her helmet a fraction of an inch at a time.

Hilly guessed she had now moved forward barely a foot. Not much progress, but she found she could now turn her head a little and look forward at the flashlight and rope. The passage was opening up a bit, just as the sheriff had said it would.

The problem now was her ass. It was in the tightest spot and hopefully would compress easier than her rib cage. Hilly grunted and pushed as hard as she could. She gained another inch, maybe two. She heard some fabric rip. She pushed hard again. Like a cork in a bottle she surged forward a few inches and was through the tight spot.

Hilly rested her head on the rope coil and took a few breaths. The cave opened quickly and soon she was on her hands and knees. The rough passage floor dug painfully into her knees and palms as she crawled forward.

Soon she was able to duck-walk under the low ceiling. She stopped and turned toward the dim entrance. The sheriff was barely fifty feet away with his head under the ledge. She shouted, "I'm through!"

The sheriff shouted back, "ETA of the others is about fifteen minutes!"

Hilly shouted again automatically, "Roger, that!" Her military days. Then she turned, picked up the rope coil, and slung it over her head and one shoulder. Soon she could bend over and actually walk down the passage, playing the flashlight ahead along the gray walls and ceiling. What little daylight there had been from the entrance was completely gone.

The passage continued downward and then intersected a larger passageway that angled down to the right. Hilly could now stand with the top of her helmet just a few inches below the cave's ceiling. She shined the flashlight down to the right along the larger passage, turned, and started forward.

Ledges protruded from each side at waist level, but she could easily negotiate the narrow spots by turning sideways.

Although the passage was still dry, she heard running water ahead, almost a roar.

The passage steepened and the borrowed, nicely polished boots sloshed in an inch of water. The water deepened and came over the top of the boots, soaking her feet as she pointed the light downward.

The passage suddenly intersected a much larger cave almost completely filled with rushing water. Hilly took another step, but there was no bottom. She fell back, almost losing the Maglite, and sat hard in six inches of cold, muddy water soaking her to the waist. Shit! she said to herself. Can this get any fucking worse?

As she stood trying to shake some of the water she heard a small voice over the roar. "Lady, help me!"

Hilly looked up and brought the flashlight's beam with her. The larger cave was perhaps thirty feet wide and filled with rushing dark water to within three feet of its ceiling on the far side. Hilly played the flashlight upstream and then downstream. Then she saw him a little bit downstream, when the powerful beam reflected off his glasses.

The kid was kneeling on a tiny ledge on the other side with his head bent under the rough, flat ceiling. The boy shakily pointed his flashlight toward Hilly. The bulb barely flickered. What was his name? Ronny?

Hilly shined the Maglite's powerful beam upstream and downstream. They seemed to be in a large room along the sink's passage. Upstream a short distance, the cave ended as the muddy water boiled up from below. Downstream, the water frothed against a solid wall of limestone as the cave's roof slanted downward and met the raging water. It was evident the room was filling up.

A few minutes ago, the water was just below the boy's ledge; now it was lapping at his knees. She herself had been standing a few minutes ago in ankle-deep water which was now up to her shins. There was no time to waste.

Hilly brought her free hand up to mouth and yelled, "Stay put, Ronny! Don't move! I'll get you out!"

The boy nodded, lowered his feeble flashlight, and tried to back farther into the wall at his back.

Hilly shined the light up and down the cave once more. Number one, assess the situation. This had been her training over and over again through the years. In other words, don't go off half-cocked. But there was very little time.

She backed up, lifted the coil of climbing rope from her shoulder and placed it and the flashlight on the ledge to her right.. The beam pointed out into the larger cave. She noticed the water near her in the entrance passage was clearly higher and moving closer.

She thought maybe she could somehow tie the Maglite off in the middle with the climbing rope and use the flashlight's weight to throw it over to the boy on the ledge and then pull him across.

Stupid. This was a ten-year-old kid, not an adult. One slip and he would be quickly sucked under. They would recover his body somewhere downstream.

Hilly rejected that idea. She knew what she had to do. She backed up farther into the still dry portion of the passage, lifted off the yellow helmet, and began unbuttoning her blouse. I'm going to have to get him myself. No choice, lady.

She folded the now-filthy silk blouse, her favorite, and laid it on one of the waist-high ledges. She noticed her mother's art deco pin was missing. No surprise after that crawl.

She bent over and unlaced the muddy, waterlogged Timberland boots. She pulled them off along with the heavy, wet wool socks, which she then stuffed into each boot. She placed the heavy boots on the ledge with the blouse. Then she peeled off her once-favorite slacks, noticing a large tear along one of the legs, before also placing them on the ledge.

Hilly was down to her bra and panties. She shivered and thought about the boy over there on the ledge. Kid, she chuckled to herself as she put the helmet back on and adjusted the chin strap, you're about to get a great female anatomy lesson when this half-naked woman rescues you.

She picked up the Maglite and coiled rope. Both the helmet and the light were new LED types. They were powerful, and would remain that way for hours.

She placed a hand on each side of the passage and shuffled forward barefoot in the cold water. Hilly thought, Light is not the problem; time and rising water are the big problems. And finding a place to tie off the rope.

Hilly looked up and down the main cave. The walls were smooth limestone, except to her right, upstream, was a large slab of rock that looked as if it had fallen from the ceiling and landed on the ledge below. The rock looked solid, as if it had rested in its present spot for hundreds, if not thousands, of years. She guessed it must have weighed tons, but, more importantly, it rested against the wall at an angle and would permit her to loop the rope around it. Surely, hers and the boy's weight would not move it.

Before she started forward, she laid the flashlight on the ledge in the side passage next to her clothes with the beam shining out into the cave. Something to shoot for, she thought.

She carefully made her way along the ledge several yards to the slab of rock. An almost-naked woman wearing a helmet. Very fashionable.

Standing in the cold water at the slab, she carefully balanced herself and took the coil of rope from her shoulder. If she slipped or fell now, she was sure the water would take her quickly downstream and under. There was nothing to grab onto on this side before the water disappeared.

She laid the rope down in the water, took one end in her hand, and made a couple of loops. She threw the rope over the slab of limestone so it would hopefully dangle down over the far side. Hilly carefully knelt at the bottom of the slab and reached behind it. Her fingertips just touched the end of the rope. Not good, she thought. She grunted and tried to wedge herself farther behind the slab without the helmet blocking her way.

There! One finger curled around the rope, and she gingerly pulled it toward her. Soon she had two fingers around the rope. The friction of the rope on the rock made it difficult, but in a few moments she had the rope in her grasp and took a breath.

Finally, still kneeling on the small ledge next to the rushing water, she had the end out from behind the rock. She pulled it toward her with one hand while paying it out around the rock with the other. She quickly tied it off.

She tied the other end off around her waist with a bowline knot and shifted the knot around behind her back. Hilly took one last look at the slab of limestone and the coil sitting on the ledge. The coil looked as if it would pay out with no snags or tangles. She hesitated for a few seconds.

She looked downstream. In her helmet's headlamp beam, the kid was now sitting up to his waist in the muddy water, head bent under the ceiling.

She thought, fuck, no choice girl, and pushed off with both legs as hard as she could while trying to keep her head above water.

The cold was the first shock. Then the realization of the absolute power of the flowing water. Her momentum brought her to midstream quickly, but then the current took her.

The rope paid out behind her as she swam hard for the other side. She hoped to reach the far wall upstream from the boy, but she was moving downstream like a runaway freight train.

The current had taken her quickly, but she was a strong swimmer and with a few hard strokes she touched the far wall quickly. She grabbed the ledge, now underwater, brought her feet in under her, and began to walk down the side of the cave toward the boy, with just her head and the helmet above the waterline. The current seemed less powerful along the cave's walls than it had been in the middle.

The wall was slick, and one problem she had was the weight of the rope as it bowed out downstream and pulled at her waist; but so far she could manage it. This energy might work in her favor on the trip back.

Hilly inched along the ledge and reached the boy in a few moments. He was still sitting on the ledge with his head bent under the ceiling. She could see he was shivering badly in the water, which was now up to his waist. They didn't have much time, she thought. Not only because the cave was filling up completely, but soon they would be dealing with hypothermia. Ironic, she thought. On a hot July morning.

As she came opposite him, Hilly looked up. Her headlamp lit up his face. She spit some water out, raised her voice over the rushing water, and asked, "How you doing, kiddo?"

Ronny Henderson squinted into the headlamp. His lips were blue. Not a good sign. His lips quivered as he answered her, "I'm real scared, ma'am!"

Hilly noted the politeness even under these circumstances. She tried to keep her voice calm, "Yeah, I know you are, honey, but I'm going to get you and me out of here in a second."

Ronny asked, "Is Jimmy OK?"

"Yes, he is, honey. He's waiting for you outside."

The boy's spirits rose a little. "Great!"

"Now, Ronny, we don't have much time, and you have to do exactly what I say. Have you ever rode piggyback?"

He nodded, "Yes, ma'am!"

Hilly spit out some more water, bobbed up and down in the water, and continued, "OK, that's what we're going to do, only piggy-front."

Front or back? Afraid he might let go and be swept away, Hilly had made the decision to have the boy in front of her instead of behind, but it would make it much harder for her to reach around him and handle the rope. She told him, "You're going to put your arms around my neck and your legs around my waist in a second. You think you can do that?"

Ronny's lips quivered again and he cried a little, "Yeah, I want outta here!"

"OK, first drop that flashlight."

The boy nodded and did what he was told. He let go of the flashlight, it rolled off the ledge and disappeared under the swift, muddy water.

Hilly clung to the ledge with one hand, reached down with the other, and pulled the climbing rope's knot around her waist on the downstream side to her front. "Are you ready, kiddo?"

The boy inched forward and placed both hands on the ledge in anticipation.

"OK, on three. One, two, THREE!"

The boy jumped with his arms out and landed perfectly against her chest. As he landed on her, his weight pushed her backward into the flowing water and they both went under and were pushed quickly downsteam by the swift current. Treading water as hard as she could, they both surfaced again as the rope played out and tightened, spinning them both around so that they faced upstream toward the Maglite's beam.

The boy was holding on tight around her, almost choking her. She felt his legs around her and his tennis shoes dig into her back as she pulled hard, hand over hand, on the climbing rope, making slow progress against the current. At the same moment, the now-taught rope was pivoting both of them toward the other wall, just as Hilly had hoped.

Hilly pulled hard on the taut rope and made progress inch by inch as the unrelenting current tried to push them downstream; but at the same time it was still also rapidly pushing them toward the far wall. The heavy current midstream streamlined their bodies until only their heads and shoulders were above water. Hilly knew she dare not lose her grip as she reached forward and advanced on the rope.

Suddenly, with a sharp impact that careened them sideways and almost loosened her grip, they went hard up against the far wall and the current lessened somewhat.

Hilly made more progress. Her grip was strong as she doubled the rope around each hand and pulled hard. The flashlight's beam was only ten feet away; then five; then two; and then they were at the water-filled entrance to the side passage.

First her knees felt the rock under her, and then her feet as she gained her footing. Crawling breathlessly into the shallow water, she backed up into the side passage, dragging the boy under her. She planted her feet and put both hands up on the rock ledge on either side. The boy, Ronny, still had a tight grip around her neck and waist.

Coming up on her knees coughing and spitting, she felt her heart pounding and her arms shaking. She reached up with one hand and pried one of his hands loose while looking down closely at him. Miraculously, his glasses had survived and his eyes were wide behind them. His lips were blue now and quivered. He was shaking and some tears rolled down his cheeks. She continued to pull hard on his arm. "OK, honey, we're safe.

You can let go and we'll get out of here. The hard part is over. You done good. That was a brave thing you did. I'm proud of you."

He sobbed a little. "I'm still scared, lady!" But his grip on her eased, and he began to slip down into the water beneath.

Hilly now straddled him and came up quickly to her feet. "I know, honey. My name is Hilly, by the way." She bent over and brought him out of the water to his feet. Hilly put her arm around him. Both were soaked and dripping as they scooted up the side passage until they reached a point where the floor was dry. Both were shaking in the fifty-degree cave air, but they were safe.

Hilly set Ronny down on the dry floor. No doubt about it, the water was farther up the side passage. They had to be fast. She quickly checked him over for any injuries. Aside from being scared and wet, the boy seemed in good shape. No broken bones; not a scratch that she could see.

Hilly picked up the bright flashlight and gave it to him. "Here, honey, you take care of this for me and we'll get out of here in a second."

"Yes, ma'am." he said as he clasped the heavy flashlight to his chest and stared up at her.

Hilly reached for her filthy clothes and the deputy's Timberlands and realized her underwear was soaked through and practically transparent, showing more to the kid than he had likely seen before. She laughed inwardly. Something to tell his buddies tomorrow. The naked lady who saved me. Well, she thought, at least there would be a tomorrow for both of them.

CHAPTER 21

Daylight

As the boy fiddled with the big flashlight, Hilly pulled on her wet, muddy slacks. She shrugged into her battered, silk blouse thinking it was too bad there wasn't a mirror in this cave. It would have been fun to look at the train wreck she had become.

She took off the helmet and tried to brush back her hair. More of a habit than anything. She put the helmet back on and pulled the strap back under her chin. Then she stepped into the waterlogged Timberlands and tied them as best she could. The rawhide laces were spongy. She left the socks on the ledge. Someone can come back for those and the rope when the water's down, she thought.

The boy seemed to be much better, but they were both were wet and cold. Daylight and summer heat were just a hundred feet away through that terrible squeeze. Hilly helped him up, gave him a hug, and aimed him up the side passage. "OK, honey, do you know the way out?"

He nodded and pointed the flashlight's beam up the passage way. "Yes, ma'am, that way."

She laid a hand on his shoulder. "You lead the way, Ronny." Hilly turned back briefly and looked toward the main cave. The water was higher now in the side passage, inching toward her and the boy quickly.

The cave was filling up, and the flowing water was within inches of the ceiling in the main passage. It had been a close call for both.

Together they walked up the side passage. While the boy walked straight through, shining the flashlight ahead, she had to turn sideways here and there to negotiate the narrow spots between the ledges on either side. Ruefully, she thought small was good in a cave.

She checked her Timex and was surprised to see she had been in the cave barely thirty minutes. Help should be on the outside by now if the sheriff had been right.

The boy came quickly to the narrow outside passage. As Hilly came up to him, he was bent over picking up something and examining it in the flashlight's beam. He handed it to her. "Is this yours?"

It was her mother's art deco gold pin. She was thankful it had been found. "Yes, thanks for finding it!"

She put the pin in one of her pockets, noticing his voice was pretty normal now and thinking how fast ten-year-olds recover. Hilly pointed at the smaller passage. The air felt warmer. They were almost out. "You first, kiddo!"

The boy shrugged and started walking up the smaller passage. Hilly followed, her helmet just below the cave's ceiling. The passage quickly narrowed, and soon both were crawling forward on their hands and knees. They heard excited voices at the other end and could see daylight ahead in the small opening.

Soon both were on their stomachs, with the boy shining the Maglite ahead and Hilly close behind.

The voices were nearby but still somewhat muted. Someone shouted, "Here they come! Stand down!" Suddenly, a powerful beam of light was pointed in their direction down the tiny passage.

Inching forward using their toes and elbows, the small boy was having an easier time of it. The passage fit him perfectly. All Hilly could see were the bottoms of his Keds pivoting up and down in front of her as he came to the smallest portion of the passage—the portion Hilly had been secretly dreading. But what choice was there? An elevator?

A little daylight now outlined the boy as he quickly opened up the distance between them and she could sense movement around the small entrance barely thirty feet ahead. The boy had no trouble, but then it was her turn in the tight spot, with her head and helmet bent to the side and her hands uselessly lying on the passage's dry floor ahead of her. She grunted and pushed as hard as she could with her toes as she exhaled. It felt hopeless. She was stuck fast and felt she couldn't breathe as the floor and ceiling of the cave pressed in on her.

The daylight ahead of her suddenly brightened. Hilly heard cheers and clapping but with her head bent to one side she couldn't see ahead. She deduced that the boy had crawled out of the cave.

Like she had done going into the cave, she exhaled again and pushed hard with her toes—but to no avail. She spit dust from her mouth and got ready for another push.

The passage darkened again. There was a scraping sound, and she sensed someone inching toward her. A rescuer for the rescuer? A man's voice said, "Ma'am…er Hilly, hang on a second. The sheriff thought you'd have some trouble so we're going to pull you out of this here rabbit hole. They voted me the smallest, so here I am. I'm small and wiry, but this is as far as I can go." The voice was familiar.

She just couldn't raise her head. "Is the boy OK?"

"Yes, ma'am. They're looking at him now, but he don't look none the worse for wear. You done real good."

Hilly gave a sigh of relief and said, "I'm pretty well stuck!"

"I'm going to push a rescue pike with a hook on the end of it toward you. I can see you plain, ma'am. I'll git it right next to your right hand in a second. When you feel it, grab on." He laughed. "If this don't work, they're talking lard or motor oil." He continued, "I've got a rope tied around my ankle so those outside will pull on the rope when I give a yell. They'll pull me, and I'll pull you. How's that sound for a plan?"

"Sounds half-ass to me."

The man laughed again at her remark, "OK, here comes the pike."

Hilly could hear scraping sounds on the floor of the cave and suddenly felt the hook nudging her right hand. She hooked her fingers around it. She gripped the pike above her right hand with her left hand.

"Ready?"

"Ready."

"On three. One, two, THREE!" The man signaled the others outside the entrance.

Hilly exhaled hard and held her breath. Although she felt as if she was suddenly being stretched to twice her height, she felt herself slowly pulled forward a fraction of an inch at a time.

The pull was relentless. There would be scrapes and bruises, but in just a few feet she could raise her head again and look right into the man's blinding helmet-mounted light.

The pace forward increased, and that's when Hilly let go of the fiberglass pole. She was past the tightest section and she was determined to exit the last twenty feet on her own.

The people on the other end of the rope sensed less weight on the line and stopped pulling. Her rescuer asked, "Why'd you let go, Miss Hilly? We're almost there."

She spit some dust and answered, "I'm coming out under my own power."

He answered as he backed up with the pike, "Sure, I understand. We're almost there."

Elbows and toes.

The man who had crawled in after her was coming into daylight. He was only a few feet away and grinning at her as he reached up and turned off his headlamp.

Without the glare of his headlamp she recognized him instantly. It was Billy, the flagman, from the day before. He also wore a yellow helmet with a chin strap. He was dressed in a dark blue T-shirt with an embroidered badge over his left breast in the shape of a Maltese Cross with the letters BVFD in the middle, a fire department badge. Red suspenders rode up over his shoulders and down to his tan, heavy turn-out pants. He wore heavy black rubber boots.

Relieved, Hilly grinned back as she inched forward. "Billy, we gotta stop meeting like this."

He slid the pike behind him and out the opening and answered as he inched back, "Good seein' you agin, Miss Hilly. Keep goin'. We're almost out."

"Shouldn't you be directing traffic or something?"

"Exactly what I was doin' until my department pager went off and then we drop everything."

Hilly nodded and blew some more dust out of her mouth. In her years on the police force and in the army she had never seen more dedicated, professional humans than firefighters. She knew without a doubt when she had seen that Maltese Cross on his shirt that she was in good hands.

Billy inched out of the small opening into the daylight. He came up on his knees in front of the opening and, although he came to his feet, he bent over the entrance and waited.

Hilly's head came out of the opening, and she blinked in the bright sun. She walked forward on her arms and raised her torso.

A crowd of people moved in and formed a semicircle around the opening. The sheriff was at the front with Big and another deputy whom Hilly hadn't met. Most of the people behind the sheriff were firefighters in heavy turn-out gear. Two other firefighters were in plain blue uniforms standing by a gurney. The two boys, Jimmy and Ronny, were standing to one side of the gurney, Ronny swathed in a gray wool blanket. There was a photographer and another with a large video camera on his shoulder.

Behind everyone, the old man, Moon, was dancing up and down swinging his arms. Hilly noticed Big was wearing her dress pumps.

Billy reached down, gently took Hilly's arm, and brought her to her feet. Hilly stood and squinted in the bright light and instinctively brushed the dirt from her ruined clothes. A loud cheer and clapping came from the crowd as one of the firefighters came forward and wrapped a blanket around her.

CHAPTER 22

Return To Town

Sheriff Ferguson, Deputy Big, Hilly, and the two boys pulled out onto the highway and turned north behind the other deputy, who was also driving an identical Tahoe. Hilly had met him briefly and just knew him by his nickname, Scooter.

The Batavia Volunteer Fire Department, meanwhile, were still stowing gear in their two red-and-white fire trucks and ambulance parked in front of Moon's store.

Big was driving the Tahoe, with the sheriff riding again in the front passenger seat. Hilly sat between the two boys in the backseat. Hilly and Ronny had BVFD gray wool blankets wrapped around them. The large Maglite was back in its charger on the console, and the sheriff had his badge clipped back on his belt.

A half mile north of Moon's dilapidated store, Deputy Big pulled into the sink's picnic area to retrieve the two bicycles. The other Tahoe continued north

The East Fork of the Sun River was still running high and muddy, piling up against the cave's opening, but the water was lower than it had been even thirty minutes ago.

Ronny shrugged off his blanket and the two boys jumped out of the car along with Deputy Big. The three of them walked over to the picnic table, and the boys began to unlock their bicycles.

In the Tahoe, Sheriff Ferguson turned around in his seat and faced Hilly for a moment. "You don't look so good."

Hilly glanced at herself in the Tahoe's rearview mirror and tried to wipe some dirt from her cheek. "Tell me about it. It'll be a long time before I go into a cave again."

"No, I meant you look a little sick."

"I'll be all right in a little while, Sheriff. Don't worry about me."

The sheriff hesitated for a moment and then spoke. "That was a very brave and selfless thing you did back there."

"Thanks. High praise coming from someone like you."

"No, I mean it. I haven't seen anything like that in forty-five years. You didn't hesitate."

"Vietnam?"

"Yes." He waved his hand in the air. "I'll tell you about it sometime, but I always remember I was one of the lucky ones who got to come home. It was a long time ago." Then he added quietly, "Times and people change."

They sat in silence for a moment. Jimmy was having trouble unlocking his bike.

The sheriff continued, "Hilly, I'm curious, you dove right in that hole without any hesitation."

"To serve and protect."

"There's that, I guess. You never lose it. But I think it was more than that. Am I right?"

Hilly looked down at her hands, "I had a nine-year-old brother once…nobody could save him…cancer…I'll never stop wishing he was still around…little boys should live to grow up."

The sheriff nodded and turned back around in his seat.

Deputy Big and Jimmy had freed the bike. She and the two boys walked to the rear of the Tahoe and she popped the tailgate. She lifted the bikes into the SUV and arranged them on top of the rest of the gear. Satisfied, she shut the tailgate, and she and the boys climbed back into the Tahoe each one again on each side of Hilly.

Deputy Big put the SUV in gear. Ronny gave Hilly a hug as they pulled back onto Route 153. Sheriff Ferguson unclipped the Tahoe's hand mike and called in service. After receiving an acknowledgement, he replaced the mike in its clip. The five drove north in silence, the two boys looking out their windows and no doubt beginning to wonder what was facing them motherwise back in town.

Deputy Big had left the air-conditioning off for the time being, and the windows were open. The radio came alive with the sheriff's call sign and a woman's voice. "Victor One."

Sheriff Ferguson again pried the SUV's hand mike from its clip and pressed the transmit button. "Victor One, go ahead." He released the transmit button and waited.

"Hate to bother you, sheriff, but I got *Mr.* Rice here. Says he understands why Ms. Walker missed their ten o'clock appointment but says it's imperative they meet today and could he reschedule at two." She had put the emphasis on the word *Mr.*

The sheriff sighed, turned in his seat toward Hilly, and raised his eyebrows as he waited for an answer. Hilly had dropped the fire department blanket around her waist. She didn't speak but instead nodded quickly at the sheriff.

The sheriff turned back around and depressed the mike button. "Affirmative at two."

Although most law enforcement agencies had adapted what was called clear speech, some habits were hard to break.

The woman on the radio said, "ten-four."

Deputy Big slowed the Tahoe as they came to the intersection east of town where Route 153 made a ninety-degree turn to the west. Hilly reached out, tapped Deputy Big's shoulder, and quickly asked, "Can you pull over for a second?"

The deputy hit the brakes and stopped on the gravel shoulder on the north edge of the intersection. She left the Tahoe idling. Hilly reached over Ronny on the passenger side and hurriedly opened the door. She left the blanket on the seat, climbed over the boy, and jumped out into the bright July sunshine. Clear of the SUV, she bent over with both hands on her knees and vomited onto the roadside gravel.

Deputy Big and Sheriff Ferguson sat quietly in the front seats. Concerned, Jimmy leaned forward and asked, "What's wrong? Is she sick?"

The sheriff turned, shook his head, and put a finger up to his lips.

Hilly straightened up, took a breath, then bent over and vomited again onto the roadside.

The two fire trucks and the ambulance had caught up and approached the intersection, their diesel engines clattering and their stacks spewing black exhaust as their drivers downshifted for the turn.

Hilly straightened again and took another breath.

As the fire department convoy came around the Tahoe, the drivers each hit their air horns and blipped their sirens much to the two boys' amusement. As they passed, several arms protruded from the trucks with a thumbs-up sign as Hilly watched them disappear ahead. She took the handkerchief that the sheriff offered her and climbed back into the Tahoe. This time the two boys scooted over and she sat next to the window. She kept the sheriff's handkerchief and held it in her lap.

Deputy Big put the Tahoe in gear. As the SUV picked up speed, Hilly faced the window and felt the fresh air on her face. As they approached the outskirts of town, Hilly leaned forward and asked, "If you don't mind, Sheriff, just let me off at the Bluebird."

"Sure, Hilly, we can do that, but I think you'd be putting off the inevitable. There's sure to be some kind of reception brewing at the office. I'm sure the press will be there, if nothing else. If you don't talk to them now, they'll find you at some point. I don't want to disappoint anyone." He turned and pointed a thumb over his shoulder at the two boys, "And these two characters have mothers to face. I'm sure the families will want to thank you personally at some point and it might as well be now. What do you say?"

Deputy Big looked up in the rearview mirror and added, "And I sure wouldn't want to be them." The two boys crouched down in their seats and tried to find something of interest out the windows.

Hilly knew how much public officials liked to strut their stuff in front of the press. As much as she just wanted to shower and relax, she knew the sheriff was probably right. Either the limelight now or later, she thought. She sighed, "OK, Sheriff, you win. Big, dump me out at the courthouse."

Big nodded and drove past the Bluebird, stopped for a red light at the corner bank, and then drove down the west side of the square. As they turned in front of the courthouse, everyone in the Tahoe saw a small crowd in front of the Sheriff's Department Annex. Hilly easily spotted the two men who had been at the entrance of the cave when she had crawled out. One was holding his still camera, a Nikon, and the other was busy hoisting his large video camera up on his shoulder.

Deputy Big parked in one of the spaces reserved for sheriff's office vehicles. The small, early lunchtime crowd closed in on the passenger side of the Tahoe as the sheriff opened the rear passenger door.

Hilly was the first out. She had again wrapped the fire department's blanket around her to cover her tattered and filthy clothes. The two boys slid over the seat and jumped out after her.

Two women and a man brushed by the sheriff and Hilly. The women tearfully hugged Jimmy and Ronny while the man shyly stood a few feet away. Hilly figured the man, dressed in jeans with a rag hanging from one of the rear pockets, a work shirt, and a farm implement hat, was one of the fathers.

The photographer with the Nikon moved in and clicked away. The man with the heavy video camera worked his way forward, green light glowing on front of the camera.

The woman hugging Ronny released her son and turned to Hilly. She wiped a few tears from her cheek and smiled. "Oh, Miss Walker, they told me what you done for Ronny in that cave. How can we ever thank you?"

Hilly pleaded, "Please, ma'am, you don't…"

Her words were cut off as the woman burst into tears again, squeezed Hilly in a bear hug, and sobbed on Hilly's shoulder. "My boy means everything to my husband and me. God bless you!"

Hilly, embarrassed, relaxed a little and placed a hand on the woman's back. She spoke softly into the woman's ear and shed a few tears herself. "Thank you. I'm glad I could help your family today." The woman released her grip, backed up, smiled at Hilly, and wiped her tears again.

Hilly looked at the man standing nearby. Ronny's mother laughed at the implication and said, "No, this ain't my husband. This here's my brother and his wife. My husband been working the dayshift at the dam site and should be here in a little bit."

With this, the man hesitantly stepped forward, took off his hat, offered his hand, and pointed at the other boy, who was still clinging to his mother. "I'm Jimmy's dad, Ralph Bailey. From what I hear, you did a heck of a thing, Miss Walker. The whole town thanks you and welcomes you."

As if on cue, the man with the Nikon moved closer. He had parked the camera below his left armpit for now. He held a small spiral notebook and pen at the ready. "Ms. Walker, I'd like a few words with you."

Sheriff Ferguson moved in quickly, arms outstretched. He had no trouble gently pushing both of the men back onto the sidewalk. He smiled and personally addressed the man with the notepad. "Now, Rolly, Ms.

Walker has been through a pretty harrowing experience in the past couple of hours and has no comment right now. Maybe I can arrange a meeting later. But for now maybe a couple of photos of Ms. Walker and me?" The sheriff stood next to Hilly and smiled as the reporter raised his Nikon and snapped a few more pictures of the two together. Hilly shook her head. Politicians. The sheriff had simply wanted her to come to the courthouse for a photo opportunity.

The reporter weighed maybe 130 pounds to the sheriff's 250 plus, and Hilly could see he was somewhat cowed by the bigger man but managed to hang in there. The reporter pulled a business card from his pocket, and, even as the sheriff was pushing him back again, he held the card out to Hilly over the sheriff's shoulder. He waved the card. "Please, Ms. Walker, give me a call. I'd like to talk to you."

Deputy Big suddenly reached in and snatched the card out of his hand. She said, "Now, Rolly, where's your manners?" Then she handed the business card to Hilly. It read: Roland Harrington, *Walker County Eagle*.

Sheriff Ferguson smiled and thanked the crowd before he and Deputy Big ushered Hilly, the mothers, the one father, and the two boys through the glass doors into the annex's lobby. Before the doors slowly closed, a battered blue Ford F-150 pickup truck pulled up behind the Tahoe, half on and half off the sidewalk. A man leaped from the truck, left the door wide open, and rushed into the lobby.

He wore dusty blue jeans, a bright yellow safety vest over a worn tan canvas work shirt, scuffed work boots, and a yellow safety helmet matching the vest. He was rail thin, wiry, and had a deep tan.

The woman who had been working at the radio console had taken off her headset, turned the volume knob up, and had joined the crowd. Hilly found out later her name was Elsie, another fixture at the Walker County Sheriff's Office.

Alice, the other stalwart of the office, had also moved around her counter into the middle of the lobby.

The man from the pickup truck drew up short when he saw the sheriff. "Hello, Sheriff," he said politely. "Looks like you had to give my boy Ronny there a ride home." He stared at the boy who was trying to hide behind his mother.

Sheriff Ferguson stepped forward and, with slight sarcasm in his voice, said, "Nice to see you again, Emery. They keeping you busy?" The sheriff moved in close, put a hand on the man's shoulder with a hard squeeze and shook the man's hand with the other.

"Yeah, Sheriff, if those greenies don't shut us down soon."

The sheriff turned the man around to face Hilly, who had sensed the bad blood between the men. "Emery, this is Hilly Walker. She just saved your son's life. Volunteered. Took him out of a very bad situation down at the sink."

The man's demeanor changed quickly as he took off his hard hat and held it in front of him. He offered his hand to Hilly, and she took it, noticing the hard, calloused grip. "Much obliged, Miss Walker. I heard what you done. My wife and I will keep you in our prayers forever."

"You're welcome, Mr. Henderson."

"Please call me Emery, Miss Walker."

Hilly nodded toward Ronny, still hiding behind his mother and casting fearful glances at his father. "I'm glad your boy's OK."

"We can never repay you, ma'am."

Photo opportunity over, the sheriff stepped in and interrupted. "Folks, I think Ms. Walker wants to clean up and relax a little. Deputy, why don't you unload those bikes, we'll let everyone go on their way, and then you can take Ms. Walker back to the Bluebird."

The two families followed Deputy Big out to the Tahoe. She opened the tailgate and lifted out both bicycles onto the sidewalk.

Alice took a moment to squeeze Hilly's hand before she went back behind the counter. Elsie returned to her radio console and telephones and donned her headset. The Sheriff faced Hilly with a smile. "Big will take you back to the motel. Lucky for that boy you came into town when you did. I can't thank you enough myself for saving that kid." He stepped back. "Stop by later today and I'm sure Alice will find some petty cash to buy you some new clothes. And a word of warning."

"Yes."

"You strike me as someone who can take care of herself, but keep an eye on old L. T. Rice this afternoon. He's an old buzzard and plenty tricky."

"I'll do that, Sheriff. And I just might take you up on that clothes money."

The sheriff opened the heavy glass door for Hilly. Deputy Big was waiting in the Tahoe with the engine running. As the Tahoe turned the corner at the bank, Deputy Big hit the steering wheel and laughed, "You know, I think it's about time me and the sheriff need to lose some weight!"

The deputy dropped Hilly at her room at the end of the Bluebird. Hilly got out, closed the door, and leaned into the window. "Thanks for the ride, Deputy."

As she put the Tahoe back in gear, Deputy Big pointed a finger at Hilly and said, "You're welcome. I'll see you soon, Hildegard Walker." Then she laughed, "And you owe me a new pair of boots, girl!"

Hilly unlocked her door and entered the room, noticing that Miss E. had turned the air conditioner on low. She shrugged off the blanket and pitched it on the bed. Turning to shut the door, she was surprised to see Miss E. in the doorway holding a brown paper bag and a can of RC Cola. Handing Hilly the bag and the can of pop, she exclaimed, "My Lord, you're a mess. I won't detain you any longer, but I thought you'd need some lunch. Here's a tuna fish sandwich and a can of cola. I've got a police scanner. Looks like you're a real hero."

Hilly held up the brown bag. "Thanks for your kindness. This'll hit the spot, Miss E."

Miss E. turned and headed back to the office. Hilly shut the door, leaned against it for a moment, and let out a breath. Then she straightened up and headed for the bathroom mirror. Her clothes were torn and caked with mud. She stood in front of the mirror and felt proud for a private moment. You done good, girl, she thought. Then she laughed as she put a hand on her throat. Sure she was a mess, but the gold earrings and the matching necklace were still in place!

Hilly sat on the edge of the bed. She looked at her Timex Indigo, still ticking like the old ad, and thought, Shit, I haven't even been in this town twenty-four hours and look at me. She popped the tab on the RC and pulled the tuna sandwich from the bag. She decided to at least see the lawyer in a little while, probably sign a paper or two, and then make tracks for Detroit in the morning after a good night's sleep.

CHAPTER 23

The Rightful Heir

Locking her door at the Bluebird, Hilly walked around the motel, and started up the alley to the town square. It was five minutes until two, and she had plenty of time to make her appointment with the lawyer, Rice. The July sun beat down on the alley. The temperature was in the low nineties with humidity to match, just as it had been yesterday.

Hilly felt good after a long, hot shower. She adjusted her fanny pack to the rear. She was dressed in some of her last clean clothes: tan cargo pants, leather belt, yellow pocket T-shirt, and her Ray-Ban aviators. She was hoping that Miss E. had a washer and dryer, because she had not spotted a laundromat. If Counselor Rice expected dress-up clothes, he would be disappointed. Those clothes had been trashed in the cave.

Hilly had checked herself out in the shower, and except for some small bruises and scrapes front and back, she had come through the rescue pretty well intact.

Halfway up the alley, she spotted the cook from the café leaning against one of the post office Dumpsters. He wore a stained white apron and hair net and had one foot braced against the metal side of the Dumpster. As Hilly passed by, he took a drag on his cigarette, flicked the ash, and nodded in her direction.

Once more she came out of the alley between the sheriff's office building and the post office, noticing there was now a brown Ford Crown Victoria parked in front.

Turning right along the sidewalk, she noted that the crowd was gone and the square looked just as it did yesterday afternoon when she had first arrived. People were coming and going as usual on this Tuesday. A car pulled up to the drive-up mailbox next to her as she walked along. A few older men occupied the wooden benches near the tall monument.

Hilly stopped in front of the Worm Café and looked up. Just as she had remembered on her drive around the square yesterday, one of the second-story windows was stenciled with gold letters:

L. T. RICE

ATTORNEY AT LAW

In the other window she now noticed for the first time, the same gold letters declared:

FREDERICK RICE

DENTIST

A heavy, wooden door with a large beveled window was up three steps from the sidewalk between the Worm and the Victory movie theater. As Hilly mounted the steps, she noticed the cook from the café had followed her and was now leaning in the doorway of the Worm.

He took a final drag on the cigarette, flicked the butt into the street, and went inside.

The heavy door had a brass escutcheon with a thumb latch. Hilly pulled the door open and started up the worn wooden steps in the dark, cool stairway. She pulled the front of the T-shirt away from herself and was glad to be back in the air-conditioning.

At the top of the stairs a long, dim hallway with a wooden floor and a strip of carpeting down the middle ran the length of the building. Two milk glass light fixtures hung from the ceiling, barely lighting the area. Hilly figured forty-watt bulbs.

Signs hanging from brackets over the doors indicated the occupants. The sign over the first door to her right had L. T. Rice's name on it and was labeled simply 101. The door farther down the hallway must be the dentist's office, she thought. The building was silent. Apparently no drilling down the hall at the moment.

Hilly turned and faced 101. There was another large brass escutcheon with a thumb latch. As she opened the door, it tripped a brass bell mounted inside on the upper door frame.

Although somewhat darkly furnished, the lawyer's reception area was brightly illuminated by the two large windows facing the square. Between the windows stood a tall, ornate grandfather clock. A large, brass pendulum swung slowly back and forth behind a beveled glass door. As Hilly closed the door behind her, the clock played four sets of Westminster Chimes and then chimed twice to acknowledge the hour.

An open door to her left led into another room. To the right of this door stood a matching heavy wooden desk and swivel chair. On the desk stood what appeared to be a genuine Tiffany desk lamp. Except for the front wall with the windows, bookcases lined the other three walls.

Sitting on the desk, next to a computer monitor and keyboard, was a calico cat. As Hilly entered the cat jumped down from the desk, strolled nonchalantly over to her, and arched its back as it wove back and forth in between Hilly's ankles.

A plump white-haired woman who Hilly guessed might be in her late sixties quickly entered the room through the open door at the sound of the bell. She was nicely dressed in a white blouse and gray skirt, with a string of pearls around her neck and a pair of reading glasses dangling over her bosom. She smiled, approached Hilly, and picked up the cat in one arm. "Hello, you must be Hildegard Walker. I'm Fran, L. T.'s secretary. This is Zoe. I hope she didn't bother you. Nice to finally meet you. We've been expecting you for a few days." The woman offered her free hand.

Hilly took the woman's hand for a moment while thinking here was yet another resident of Batavia, Kentucky, who knew her without introduction. For all she knew, maybe she had a dental appointment down the hall.

"Pleased to meet you, Fran. Please call me Hilly." Then she couldn't help but reach out and scratch the cat's head. "I have a two o'clock appointment with Mr. Rice. I spoke to him on the phone a few days ago in Detroit. He insisted it was important I drive down here for some reason and meet with him in person."

Fran put one hand on her pearls and said enthusiastically, "Yes! Indeed! Mr. Rice was quite excited to have finally found you." Then she reached out and squeezed Hilly's shoulder. "It was so brave what you did for that Henderson boy! The whole town is talking about it!"

"Thanks."

Fran turned, still holding the cat in one arm, and motioned Hilly to follow her toward the open door. "Just follow me, Hilly. Mr. Rice is right in here."

As Fran walked through the door dividing the rooms, she bent over and let the cat drop to the floor. It ran a few steps, then stopped, sat on its haunches, and nonchalantly licked a paw.

This room was dark. There were two windows on the south wall, but the "view" was a two-foot gap between the Worm Café building and the adjacent post office's brick wall.

Similar to the outer office, the walls in this room were lined with wooden bookcases with horizontal glass doors. Above the bookcases were what appeared to be dark colonial-era oil paintings. A brass floor lamp sat in one corner and provided some light. A large wooden desk stood in front of the windows. A brass, green-shaded desk lamp with a pull chain sat to one side on the desk, and an old dial phone sat on the other. In front of the desk was a straight-backed wooden arm chair with red leather inserts on the seat and back.

Behind the desk was a white-haired man sitting forward in an ancient wooden swivel chair reading a large volume with a six-inch magnifying glass. He was wearing a neatly pressed blue-and-white striped dress shirt with a white collar. The sleeves were rolled up past his elbows. Dark blue suspenders and a red bow tie completed his ensemble.

The man had not noticed the two women who had entered his office. The secretary, Fran, cleared her throat.

The old man looked up and said, "Oh, yes, I'm sorry. How rude of me." He set the magnifying glass on the desk, picked up a thick set of wire-rimmed glasses, and carefully put them on one earpiece at a time. Then he stood up and came slowly around the desk with his right hand extended. Hilly noticed a cane leaning against the wall behind the desk.

He cleared his throat, looked Hilly up and down, and smiled, "Ms. Hildegard Leona Walker, I presume." He chuckled at his small joke.

Hilly stepped forward and took his leathery hand. He was about her height, thin, and she guessed somewhere on the other side of eighty years old. His blue-and-white striped seersucker trousers were worn high, as older men sometimes did. On his feet were highly polished brown dress loafers with tassels. "Pleased to meet you at last, Mr. Rice."

He let go of her hand and motioned her toward the chair in front of the desk while he retreated back around the large desk. "Please have a seat, Ms. Walker."

"Thank you, and call me Hilly, sir."

The secretary cleared her throat again. "L. T., I have some work to do."

Rice waved his hand in dismissal. "Oh, yes, Fran. Take that damn cat with you and please shut the door when you leave." Fran turned and the cat followed her.

Rice sat down stiffly in the swivel chair and leaned back. "OK, Hilly it is." Then he waved a finger at her. "And none of this 'sir' business, young lady. I go by L. T. to everyone in this town." He chuckled again as he laced his fingers across his chest. "Although I'm sure a few townfolk have some other names for me. I've been watching over this town for more than fifty years now."

Hilly smiled back at him. Rice rocked forward, pushed the volume aside, and put his elbows on the desk. "You and I have quite a bit of business to conduct, and I'm sure we'll get to know each other quite well, Hilly. By the way, I've heard all about that rescue this morning. Quite a brave thing you did saving that Henderson boy. I know the town is fixing to reward you later."

"The truth, sir…er, L. T., is the sheriff and his deputy didn't give me much choice. And here's a little secret: I was the only one who would fit in that hole. Time was running out."

"Oh, I've seen your resume, so don't act shy with me."

Hilly continued, "As for the town of Batavia, I'm sorry but I want to leave for home tomorrow morning."

Rice sat back and waved a finger again. "Oh, you'd better change your plans, Hilly, because you won't be leaving soon, I'm afraid."

Hilly crossed her legs and folded her hands in her lap. "Oh?"

Rice continued, "Well, before we get started and I start explaining, Hilly, first things first. Oh my, I hate to be official. Do you have the identification I requested?"

Hilly reached around and brought her fanny pack in front of her. She unzipped it and brought out her passport and wallet. She laid the passport on the desk; then she opened her wallet and fished out her Michigan driver's license and laid it next to the passport. "Right there, L. T."

Rice leaned forward and drew both documents across the desk toward him. He picked up the driver's license first and held it in front of him. He looked at the driver's license then Hilly then the driver's license again. He made a note on a pad of paper. "Looks like the big five-oh's coming up fast."

"Don't remind me."

Laughing under his breath, Rice said, "Believe me, Hilly, fifty is looking pretty good to me!" Hilly smiled.

Rice scrutinized Hilly's passport in the same way, made another note, and then handed both documents back to her. He eased back in his chair again. "Sorry to be so official with you. It seems rude, but it's necessary from my viewpoint. Now let's get down to business."

Hilly placed both documents back in her fanny pack and zipped it shut.

Rice tented his fingers in front of his face.

Hilly waited.

Rice asked, "Do you know who Charles McHenry is, by any chance?"

"Yes, sure, he's my great-grandfather on my mother's side of the family. I met him once when I was a little girl. I think I was about eight years old. He seemed like an old man even back then. My grandmother left home when she was young and went north. The only other time I was down this way was over twenty years ago, and I don't think he was around. I don't know much about him."

"Yes, all that is correct. He was an interesting man. He died about a year ago at the age of a hundred and five. Were you aware of that?"

"No, my mom died some years ago, and I've lost all contact with any family down here."

"Well, Hilly, be prepared for a lot of good news and bad news, I'm afraid. The truth is he was the last family, blood kin if you will, you had down here as far as I can tell."

"What's some of the good news?"

"You seem to be the only heir old Charlie had."

Hilly leaned back. Although she had dismissed what the sheriff had said that morning—in fact, almost forgotten about it—she felt some goose pimples form along her arms. Hilly asked, "And...?"

"Well, you've inherited over nine thousand acres of land. Nine thousand two hundred sixty-seven acres to be exact. And a farmhouse and outbuildings."

Hilly felt a little lightheaded.

"That's some of the good news. There's more."

"What's some of the bad news?" She asked.

"Some of the bad news is that Kentucky is one of the worst states in the Union in which to inherit anything."

CHAPTER 24

Last Will and Testament

Rice rose stiffly from his swivel chair, closed the volume that had been in front of him, and placed it on a bookcase to one side of his desk. From the same shelf, he picked up a thick file and carried it the few feet back to his desk. He sat down again in his chair and opened the file in front of him. "Your great-grandfather Charlie was quite a character in his later years in this and other parts of Kentucky. Before the war, and I'm talking World War II now, he was a farmer just like his father before him on the outskirts of town with a few hundred acres of land he inherited. Mostly corn and soybeans. And, I might add, he was an only child."

Hilly interrupted, "Yes, I'm familiar with the house."

Rice nodded and continued, "He and your great-grandmother, Lil, also an only child, lived in what was then a simple three-room farmhouse with some outbuildings. They had two daughters, your grandmother and your great-aunt. I guess Charlie was always a frugal man and saved his little bit of money. A strict man. Had a temper, too. I suspect that was one of the reasons your grandmother got married and headed north during the war to work in the defense plants at the time and never came back."

Hilly nodded. It made sense from the stories her mother had told her.

"Anyway, after the war, things got to booming again, especially the pent-up desire for new cars. Charlie had a friend in town by the name of Ralph Kingston who owned the local Ford dealership, and Charlie loaned him some of his savings near the end of the war in exchange for a percentage of the business. Pretty shrewd, as it turned out. Kingston Ford is still in business. You might have noticed it on the way into town."

Hilly, beginning to be fascinated by this family history, simply nodded.

Rice continued, "Charlie was always the silent partner, but Kingston turned out to be a real go-getter. During the late forties and fifties, Kingston bought up other dealerships around the state and some in Ohio and Tennessee. He eventually became the biggest car dealer in three states. In fact, his grandsons are still in the car business. Kingston expanded into furniture, too. And all this time your great-grandfather rode his coattails, so as to speak, with his small percentage. A few hundred grew into millions."

Rice paused. "How rude of me. Where are my manners? I get caught up in things. Would you like some coffee? Tea? Maybe a can of pop?"

Hilly answered, "Maybe a Coke would be nice. I'm not much of a coffee drinker."

Rice spun the dial on the old phone and spoke into the handset. "Fran advises me that the Worm is a RC Cola place. Will that be OK? She'll be back in a minute."

"Sure, but before we get started again, how much are we talking about? Roughly?"

Rice cleared his throat. "The land, the house, and the outbuildings in today's market, between me, the court, and the state, we figure somewhere between fifteen and twenty million."

Hilly felt a little faint and hesitated, "You did say 'million'?"

"Yes, probably closer to twenty million, even twenty-five million, depending. It's one of those good news side of things."

"What's the bad news side?"

"Well, I'll get into that part in due time, but some of the bad news is that there is no more money left after twenty years in a nursing home, I'm afraid. But let me start where I left off."

Hilly leaned back and thought, Shit, twenty-five million bucks?

Rice continued, "I grew up in Lexington and eventually went to law school at the University of Kentucky. I say 'eventually' because I bummed around a bit after my high school graduation. Too young for World War II and too old for the Korean War. I even worked as a lumberjack for a little while in Oregon. In those days, a guy could hitchhike around the country fairly easily. Anyway, after some adventures, I graduated from the University of Kentucky's law school in 1958. With honors, I might add. Married soon after. My wife passed away a while back, but I've got two sons and a daughter and a passel of grandkids. Then I was offered a job here in Batavia by a lawyer by the name of Higgins. Smart man, and not just because he hired me. Started to work for him in this very office and never left. Some fifty-three years ago."

Rice removed his glasses, put an earpiece in his mouth, and reflected. Then he put his glasses back on an earpiece at time. "Anyway, Higgins was your great-grandfather's lawyer back then. He eventually died at the relatively young age of forty-five of a heart attack, and I took over as Charlie's lawyer."

They were interrupted as Fran and the cat entered the room. Fran was carrying a tray with a coffee mug, a can of RC Cola as promised, and a glass of ice. She set the tray on a corner of Rice's desk, set the steaming mug in front of the lawyer, and handed the cola can and glass to Hilly, who took one in each hand.

Fran picked up the tray and placed it under one arm. She looked at both of them. "Anything else before I leave?"

Rice shook his head, and Hilly thanked her. Fran closed the door behind her. The cat sat in the middle of the room and apparently decided to stay this time.

Rice took a sip of his coffee and continued, "Charlie used his money in those early years to buy up as much land as possible here in Walker County. Cheap in those days. You've inherited a lot of acres of corn and soybeans. Charlie's original farm and more west and south of town on either side of the highway. And there's a lot of acreage out by the interstate, too. It's all farmed with a share for you, of course. And there are the farmhouse and outbuildings you're familiar with. Charlie expanded the house over the years. Quite a place. But the biggest holding you've got is roughly the west half of Worm Ridge and somewhat north of it to the county line. Prime timberland. Some of it actually virgin. Hardwoods. Oak, maple, walnut. Your share of the ridge extends from just north of town all the way west to the Sun River fork."

Hilly, still fascinated, took a sip of RC and interrupted, "May I ask who owns the eastern half of Worm Ridge?"

Rice tented his fingers again, "I was going to get to that soon. But the other half is owned by the man downstairs."

"The man downstairs?"

The lawyer pointed at the floor, "Camas Worm. That land has been in the Worm family for over two hundred years, Hilly."

"I see. So it's true."

"What's true?"

"Nothing, go on."

Rice continued, "Charlie lived a long life, but, unfortunately, the last twenty years or so were spent in a nursing home. First the one here in town and later in a fancier one up in Lexington that could meet his needs better. He was good until his mideighties." Rice chuckled, "Just like me, huh?"

"He was an ornery old coot at the end. Kept his mind mostly. Was the oldest person in Kentucky for a while, too, but he finally gave out last year. Besides all the land, he had had considerable savings, too. He had sold his percentage in the Kingston empire in the early eighties for a tidy sum, and what he didn't use to buy still more land around here, he invested in bonds and so forth. The farming took care of itself. It's more of a break-even proposition to tell the truth. But he had used up most of what he had, except for the land—your land, it seems—on the day he died."

"Still sounds pretty good to me."

Rice waved a finger at her. "Not so fast, young lady. I'm about to get into some of the bad news."

Hilly slumped a little in her chair, took another sip of RC, and waited.

"Well, I should say it's not all bad, and I think you'll make out OK, just OK, in the long run." He drew a piece of yellowed paper from the file and handed it to her. She leaned forward and carefully took the sheet of paper. "You're holding Charlie's actual handwritten will. What we call 'holographic' in that it is entirely in his own handwriting and dated and signed by him. In Kentucky no witnesses are required, only someone to testify that it is indeed the deceased's handwriting, and I did that. No one has contested the will at present, and I don't foresee that."

Rice sat back. "Give it a quick read and I'll continue." He took another sip of coffee while Hilly read.

She saw that the first lines were pretty standard. It seemed to read like a proper will. The only other one she had actually seen was her mother's long ago. Hilly looked up.

Rice continued, "Like I said, nothing wrong with the will itself. It hasn't been contested, and Judge Winslow over at the courthouse has accepted it. Pardon me, but I guess I have neglected to tell you that I'm Charlie's executor." He waved it off and collected his thoughts. "The problem came from the line where he leaves everything to his wife Lillian, and if he should outlive her—and, boy, did he—then he leaves everything to his 'family.' There was no family until I finally found you and you drove into town yesterday."

"Lucky me, I guess."

145

"Pissed off some people around here, to be honest with you." He continued, "Another one of those good news for you and bad news for others."

"What exactly do you mean by that?"

"You've got to remember that it's not the state's responsibility to find heirs. Oh, the state might make a halfhearted attempt to find an heir. Local newspapers, advertisements, things like that. But by no means is the state going to hire an investigator like I finally did."

"An investigator?"

"Yes, a guy out of Lexington who was recommended to me. Couple of hundred bucks an hour, but obviously worth it as you are now sitting in that chair in my office. He knew his stuff."

"You went through a lot of trouble, L. T., when it seems you really didn't have to."

Rice smiled. "You don't know the half of it yet, Hilly. You've got to remember I knew Charlie for a long time and that with no heirs, his entire estate, all that land, would have gone to the state of Kentucky to do with as it as it saw fit, and I couldn't see that."

Hilly took another sip of her RC. "Why not?"

Rice waved his finger again. "Don't think for a moment those politicians up in Frankfort wanted to make a nice state park out of Charlie's land, which is more or less what he wanted. I started hearing things. Payouts, maybe some bribes even. Stuff under the table. There's a Korean car company rumored to want the land out near the interstate for a big development. A big home improvement company apparently wants a big chunk of land just west of town, and one of the big-box stores wants some of it, too. Just because of the car company's interest. When they finish that dam, there will be lakefront property. Big vacation homes. Despite the fact it'll ruin a couple of the best smallmouth bass fishing streams in the nation, not to mention some of the best canoeing and kayaking in Kentucky, too. One of my favorite places. And worst of all, I hear an Atlanta concern wants Charlie's half of Worm Ridge for its timber."

Suddenly, Hilly remembered the Asian men in the Worm Café yesterday and the other businessmen, including the Elvis Costello lookalike and his two friends. No doubt they all somehow knew she was on her way to Batavia.

Rice continued, "No, Hilly, I've lived here practically all my life now, and I didn't want this area ruined, so I just had to start looking for an heir myself."

Hilly took another sip of her cola and set the glass on the floor. She spread her hands. "What makes you think I'm any different?"

"No guarantee, but I'm beginning to like my chances."

"I have a feeling some more bad news is coming."

"Not everyone in town feels the way I do. That's the bad news. There's lots of folks want what they call progress and want the land developed. The mayor and city council for one. They want to talk to you and soon. Good for the town and county and all that."

"So that is one of the reasons everyone in town knows who I am?"

"Yes, there's a raging debate on just what you will do. You're going to hear from all sides, I'm afraid. Even the old guys on the benches out there are talking about it."

"It seems I've been escorted here and there by members of the Worm family. Do you know anything about that?"

"They're a mysterious bunch. You'll have to ask them, but I would guess they have some kind of agenda, too. No doubt they'll let you know at some point in their own way."

Then Rice backtracked, "Took only about a week to find you, by the way, and that's when I called."

"What if I had hung up?"

"The investigator, name of Charles Forsyth by the way, was still tailing you and would have persuaded you."

"Like a ride in his trunk?"

"Nothing quite that dramatic." Rice laughed and added, "At least I don't think so. But I hope you now understand why I needed you to drive down here."

Hilly nodded, "I sense you've got some more bad news."

"Before I get into some more really bad news, I've got to warn you that Forsyth reported he was pretty sure some other people were trying to locate you, too. We don't know who they are quite yet, but Forsyth reported it to me before I paid him this morning and he left for Lexington. Some of the people he questioned in our search for you reported some other men asking them the same questions." Rice scratched his head. "It's puzzling. But he reported that as far as he could tell no one else followed you down here, but he added that maybe they were behind him a day or so."

"He followed me?"

"Yes, I think he drives an old Ford Taurus. And, by the way, Forsyth told me you drive too fast and that he felt a woman your age shouldn't be flirting with young flagmen."

Hilly sat back and was, for a moment, at a loss for words. She had sensed the man in the old Ford pickup was tailing her, but although she now remembered the white Taurus behind the truck, she had never sensed the tail. The guy was good. She told Rice, "Yeah, he's good. I never suspected."

"Yes, he had his eye on you all the way. Said we saved some money with him staying at that Super 8 in Cincinnati instead of a Hilton or something."

"Any idea of who the other people looking for me are?"

"No, he just said people up in Detroit recalled some men in a red car. Out-of-state plates. It's in his report."

Hilly sat back, "You said red car. Interesting."

"What's that."

"Oh, nothing."

"Well, let me continue."

"OK." Hilly picked up the RC and took another sip. She was starting to like this stuff.

Rice continued, "I'm going to start to get into some of the really bad news. Taxes."

"Taxes?"

"Yes, taxes. You'd better grab hold of that chair, and after I'm done, you might just want to drive back to Detroit in the morning like you've threatened to do."

"Oh, boy."

"Hilly, remember when I told you earlier about Kentucky being a terrible state to inherit anything?"

Hilly nodded.

"Well, some of the bad news is that you're what the state of Kentucky designates as a 'class C' beneficiary. There's three classifications, A, B, and C, depending on how distant your relationship is with the deceased. The more distant the relationship, the more Kentucky inheritance tax you must pay. Being Charlie's great-granddaughter, you're a class C."

Hilly said slowly, "What exactly does that mean?"

"It means your inheritance tax is two hundred thousand dollars plus sixteen percent."

Rice paused, and Hilly did some quick calculations in her head. "That's over three million dollars!"

"Yes, and it gets worse. That's just the state's take. The feds get their share, too. The federal estate tax has an exemption of the first five and a quarter million, and then for 2013 a forty percent rate for everything over that." Rice opened a desk drawer, pulled out a small calculator, and handed it to her.

Hilly took the calculator and concentrated on it for a few moments. She looked up wide-eyed. "So, assuming we're talking about twenty million dollars, I could be on the hook for taxes on my great-grandfather's estate for close to nine million!"

Rice nodded, "Although I spoke to Charlie about this and some other possibilities for his estate to avoid these taxes as much as possible, he would never hear it. Wanted to keep things simple. I'm sure he told Higgins the same thing. And it's more like a seven million tax liability."

Hilly reminded him, "You're talking to someone with a doubtful pension now, a fifteen-year-old car, a Detroit condo with an underwater mortgage, and maybe, just maybe, a few grand or so in savings."

Rice countered, "You don't have to inherit anything. It's up to you. Indeed, pack it up and head home tomorrow. But after you speak to some others, I think you'll stay. There's more than I'm telling you. There's some people here in town that want to talk to you and show you a few things. Then make up your mind. It's all we're asking."

"We? What others?"

Rice raised his hands. "All I'm asking is just be patient, Hilly. The important thing right now is you and I must appear at the Walker County courthouse before Judge Winslow, Courtroom 160, at nine o'clock sharp Thursday."

"Thursday?"

"Yes, Thursday. It's the date and time set for the judge's final report. Everything with the estate has been done in the last year. Probate was started. An inventory has been taken. The judge has set Thursday as the final report. That's when you and I show up and file a motion for the court to accept you as the rightful heir. You have until Thursday to decide."

"The judge must know I'm in town. Everybody else does."

Rice chuckled. "Yes, he does, but the final report date has been set by him for some time, and his hands are tied."

"What if I don't show?"

"Then I'm afraid Charlie's land will go to the state of Kentucky to do with as it pleases."

Hilly finished her cola and set the glass on the floor next to her chair. Rice rolled his chair back and stood stiffly. He reached for his suit jacket and shrugged into it. He said to Hilly, "I have two suggestions."

Hilly came to her feet. "Yes."

"First, stay around. This past hour was just a start. Take a look at the area and Charlie's land, your land. I know for a fact you'll be contacted by some very dedicated people with some great ideas. They'll be pinning some hope with you. I think you'll be interested in what they say."

"What's number two?"

"We've been talking for a while. He looked at his watch. Why don't you help me down those damn stairs and let an old man treat you to a late lunch downstairs? The Worm has a very good chicken-fried steak."

Hilly smiled. She was beginning to like Rice despite all the warnings. "Sounds good, if you answer one more question."

"What would that be?"

"What's the L. T. stand for?"

Rice laughed as he shuffled toward the door with his cane, "Leonard Theodore. But keep it under your hat. Not many people know that. I'm too old to be called Lenny."

Rice had some words with Fran on the way out. The cat escorted them to the door.

The Worm Café was crowded. Hilly and the lawyer were escorted to the same booth she had been seated in the evening before. There was a lone occupant this time. He was the older man who had been with all the younger people the night before. Hilly had the feeling he had been waiting for her and L.T..

As she and Rice walked with Camas Worm toward the back of the café, all heads turned toward them. When they were halfway to the booth, everyone in the café put their utensils on the tables and began to applaud. Uncharacteristically, Hilly felt blood rushing to her cheeks as she nodded to them.

As Worm continued to escort them to the rear of the café, the man in the booth stood. He appeared to be in his mid to late fifties and possessed a certain handsome ruggedness. He was wearing a khaki, short-sleeve safari shirt and cargo shorts. He wore tan desert boots and sported gold wire-rimmed glasses.

As Rice and Hilly slipped into one side of the booth, Worm laid a plastic-covered menu in front of each person. Hilly sat on the inside.. Rice sat on the outside with his cane leaning against the table. The other occupant slipped back into the booth and sat down opposite Hilly.

As Worm turned to return to the cash register and a waiting customer, he gave Hilly a smile and a discreet thumbs-up. Hilly noted that, although his shirt was pulled over it, the .38 Colt was again in his waistband.

The man now seated across from them offered his hand to Hilly and introduced himself. "I'm Dr. Stephen Cunningham of the University of Southern Kentucky's geology department. Pleased to meet you at last Ms. Walker!"

Puzzled, Hilly took his hand. She detected a British accent. Yet another person who knew her without introduction. "Pleased to meet you, Dr. Cunningham."

Rice had said nothing yet, and it became obvious that he and Cunningham already knew each other. As if to answer her question, Cunningham released her hand, sat back down, and said, "L. T. and I have already met."

Hilly turned to Rice. He smiled slyly and said, "This is one of those people I told you about in the office."

Trish the waitress approached, holding two newspapers to her breast with one hand and carrying her order pad in the other. This afternoon she was dressed in a pair of jeans, a white T-shirt, and a clean, white apron. She had a pencil stuck above one ear. Before anyone could speak, she laid the two newspapers on the table in front of Hilly and rotated them so Hilly could read both. One newspaper was the *Walker County Eagle* and the other was the *Lexington Herald-Leader*.

The waitress slouched, held her pad in one hand, and squeezed Hilly's shoulder. "Great job, girlfriend, I knew you were something special."

Hilly drew in a breath. Both papers sported a head shot on their front page of her emerging from under the ledge after the rescue. She was wearing the yellow helmet with the headlamp. Her face was painted with mud. It was also obvious that she was still wearing her gold earrings and necklace.

The waitress pointed at the headlines of both papers with her pad while still squeezing Hilly's shoulder. They read in one-inch black letters, FASHIONABLE RESCUE!

Hilly laughed and covered her face with both hands. The other joined her. This was certainly one for the scrapbook.

Cunningham leaned forward and exclaimed, "Oh, Ms. Walker, how I envy you!"

Hilly took a breath, lowered her hands, and looked up from the newspapers. "Envy me? How?"

Cunningham brought up a topographical map from beside him, unfolded it on the table, and smoothed it out. He said with a grin, "Let me explain, Ms. Walker."

CHAPTER 25

Cop Talk

Hilly lay in bed with her back propped up against the headboard with two pillows behind her back. The air conditioner was on low. On the TV across the room TBS was showing a rerun of Seinfeld. It was the episode wherein George gets into an argument with the Bubble Boy. A glass of ice and a can of RC Cola were on the bedside table again courtesy of Miss E. Hilly reached over, popped the tab, and filled the glass.

As she took a sip, she thought, had anyone else had quite a day like this? First the cave rescue in the morning and then learning she was about to inherit over 9,000 acres of land worth maybe $20 million. Then there had been lunch a little while ago with Dr. Cunningham. He had some very interesting things to say about her inheritance, too.

Hilly took another sip of the cola. This stuff was pretty good. She had had another glass of RC with lunch. Rice had been correct; the chicken-fried steak and mashed potatoes at the Worm had been delicious. She wondered if Worm had thought of a franchise like another Kentuckian, Colonel Sanders, but the name of his café would probably ruin any attempt at expansion. And Colonel Sanders had probably never carried a loaded gun in his waistband as he served his customers. No, the name Worm Café wouldn't be very catchy.

Hilly was sure of another thing: She was beginning to see that sides were clearly being taken in this town, and she was clearly in the middle. On one side, she was beginning to discover, were the people who wanted progress, and on the other side were the people who liked the town and county just the way it was and wanted to preserve the status quo. She was also beginning to sense a third factor, too. Something dangerous and sinister at the very edge.

Rice had become the go-between and had scheduled some appointments in the next few days for her. There were the Koreans, the Shop Here! big box store people, the mayor and the city council, and something new—people from the Sierra Club and the National Parks Conservation Association wanted to speak with her.

As Hilly was watching George argue with the Bubble Boy about the spelling of the word Moors and thinking that all this was rapidly becoming a big deal, someone knocked on her door. She rolled from the bed, pulled the window curtain back an inch, and saw the brown Crown Vic parked near her door.

Hilly peeked through the security peep hole. Deputy Big was standing on her doorstep holding Hilly's dress pumps in one hand. What now? she thought. The deputy had already opened the screen door and was holding it open with her shoulder.

Hilly retrieved the deputy's battered boots and opened the door. Sounding as cheerful as she could, Hilly asked, "Deputy, to what do I owe the pleasure of your visit?"

Deputy Big smiled. The two exchanged the shoes. The deputy frowned at the battered boots and hitched up her gun belt. She looked past Hilly into the interior of Room 15.

Hilly turned her head and looked into the room with the deputy until she realized it was just an old cop habit.

Deputy Big asked, "Are you busy?"

Hilly laughed, "Not really."

"I know it's been a long day for you, but how about taking a ride with me on a call I think you'd be interested in?"

Hilly looked at her watch. Nearly six o'clock. "Are you still on duty?" she asked.

Deputy Big sighed, "Yeah, until twenty-three hundred. I'm pulling a double shift today."

Hilly knew firsthand about long hours. It had been one big factor in her retirement. "OK, sounds good. I have some questions for you."

"Yeah, no doubt."

"Hang on a sec, I'll gather some things."

Deputy Big stood in the doorway while Hilly went back in the room. She put a few things—wallet, cell phone, sunglasses, and room key—in her fanny pack and reappeared in the doorway. The deputy had turned and was standing under the awning, looking over the other parked cars and pickup trucks.

Hilly pulled the door shut behind her and tested the knob. "OK, let's go."

Deputy Big looked at the fanny pack. "The sheriff let me see some of his notes. Knowing kind of who you are now myself, I'm betting you have some type of weapon around." She pointed to the Honda. "Either in your car or in your room."

Hilly didn't know how to quite answer. Finally, she said, "Well, yeah, I do."

"Why don't you just gather it up and bring it along."

"I don't understand."

"Let's just say I'd feel a little better if you were armed, too. It's no problem. You're no doubt more qualified than me."

"OK." Hilly turned, unlocked the door again, and disappeared inside. A moment later, she appeared on the porch again, locked the door, and once again tested the lock. This time Hilly was carrying both the blue fanny pack and on top of it a black nylon holster with the butt of a dull black automatic pistol showing on one end.

"I knew you had to have a gun somewhere, girl." Deputy Big pointed to the holster. "Loaded?"

"Yes, ten in the magazine. Chamber's usually empty until just before I turn off the lights."

"A Beretta 92?"

"We called it an M9 in the service."

Deputy Big nodded. "Looks new. I thought those held 15 rounds."

"It was a retirement present from everyone." Hilly shrugged. "You're right, but it's the clip it came with, haven't had time to shop for a bigger one, and I didn't know the laws down here." She looked at the Beretta.. "Haven't even fired it yet to tell you the truth."

Deputy Big said with no explanation as she headed around the Crown Vic, "Put one in the chamber and strap it on. I'd feel a lot better if you rode with me armed this evening. I've heard some things."

Puzzled, Hilly set the fanny pack at her feet, loosened her belt, and threaded it through the holster. Then she pulled out the Beretta, chambered a round, checked the safety, and slid the gun back in the holster. She snapped the flap over the gun's butt. It had been a while.

Deputy Big slid into the driver's seat and shut her door. Hilly opened the passenger door and hesitated. The deputy felt the other woman's discomfort. "Don't worry, you're with me, probably still deputized from this morning, and Kentucky is an open-carry state."

Hilly placed her fanny pack on the front floor and climbed into the passenger's seat. As she shut the door, she wondered just how often a law enforcement officer rode with an armed civilian. But she had to admit that the Beretta at her side felt good.

Although out of production now, the Ford Crown Victoria was still the first choice of most cops as a patrol vehicle. It had been in production for twenty years, and tens of thousands had been sold and a high percentage were still on duty despite efforts to replace it by the Big Three car manufacturers. The Crown Vic was long and wide, with a huge trunk for equipment and a wide console to accommodate radio and computer equipment. It was a solid rear-wheel drive car with a large, powerful V8 engine that gave thousands of miles of reliable service. It was a tough vehicle that almost every cop had driven at one time or another.

Big and Hilly strapped in and the deputy started the car. Before she put the car in gear, Big did the required briefing with Hilly. Hilly had done the briefing herself many times herself and listened patiently. Big swept her hand over the dash and said, "I'm sure you've got plenty of hours riding around in one of these."

"A few," Hilly said as she checked out the interior. Like the Chevy Tahoe they had used earlier in the day, the Crown Vic had the same basic equipment. There was a lockable sliding steel mesh screen between the front and rear seats. It was painted a dull black. As Hilly twisted in her seat, she could see that, unlike the Tahoe, the standard Remington Model 870 shotgun rode in its holder along the cross brace above the mesh screen behind their heads.

Big leaned forward and pointed to the area just to the left of the center console and under the dashboard. "There's a yellow button just under here that releases the locks on the shotgun. It's a twelve-gauge with four shells in the magazine." She leaned back. "None chambered."

Hilly nodded. Standard.

Big continued, "Over here under the armrest is the trunk release button, the one with the key slot. There's also a trunk release button on my key fob."

Hilly nodded again. She had given her ride-alongs the same basic briefing herself many times. Most had nervously told her that if it came down to them, a civilian, actually unlocking the shotgun in the car, they were probably in pretty big trouble.

"In the trunk is a Colt AR-15. Semiautomatic only, I'm afraid. It's got twenty in the clip, none chambered. I'm sure you're qualified on it and my Glock 17."

Hilly nodded again. It was true. She had qualified on the civilian version AR-15 and the military version M16 many times. She had shot expert in both services. "I've shot the Glock a few times with friends, but our standard Detroit PD sidearm was the Smith and Wesson M&P40. And I'm real familiar with the AR-15 and the Remington."

Big answered, "I'm sure you are." She continued, "I'm not familiar with the Smith and Wesson. Just remember I've got one chambered, and there is no external safety on the Glock. Just pull the trigger." Big put the Crown Vic in gear. The tires crunched on the gravel. The deputy smiled, "Remember I'm in charge. Any questions?" Big plucked the mike from the dash with one hand and steered out of the parking lot with the other. She reported "en route" to her call and hung up the mike. She got a curt "ten-four" in response.

Hilly replied, "I've got it. Got another question."

"Shoot."

"Where's your backup gun?

Deputy Big made the right turn on to Route 153. She pointed her thumb at Hilly.

She smiled, "You my backup gun tonight, sister."

Past the town limits, Hilly finally asked, "What's the call?"

"It's a vandalism call down at the dam site. I'd thought you like to take a ride down there. Some spray-painting of equipment. It's been happening a lot lately. Nothing serious yet."

Hilly countered, "Sounds like some monkey-wrenching going on."

"Monkey-wrenching?"

"You know, like the book."

"What book?"

"*The Monkey Wrench Gang* by Edward Abbey."

"Never heard of it."

"It's a novel. Came out in the nineteen-seventies. I first read it in college. It's about a small gang of environmentalists trying to stop the Glen Canyon Dam on the Colorado River in Arizona, I think. They vandalize equipment like bulldozers and earth movers. You know, throw a monkey wrench into the works, so to speak, to stop progress."

"Never heard of doing nothing like that, but I do know there's a lot of people opposed to this here dam. And not just people in Kentucky. I've heard of national groups, too."

Hilly thought of Dr. Cunningham, what he had said, and her strange date early in the morning. She asked Big, "How long has the dam been under construction?"

"Just started, really. A few months. In fact, there's supposed to be some kind of protest at the site this comin' Sunday. Sheriff's goin' to put a few of us down there. Supposed to be some press, too." Deputy Big made the right angle turn a few miles outside of town as they retraced the route south they had made that morning.

Hilly thought for a moment. "I don't want to tell you how to run things around here, but I'd be expecting some trouble with that protest. A lot of people don't like the Corps of Engineers and what their dams do to rivers. They're pretty passionate. These kind of protests can escalate, if you know what I mean."

"Yeah, some people around here call them 'greenies' and 'tree huggers.' See them as takin' away jobs."

———

The two women rode in silence for a few minutes. They approached the small park again at the sink. Deputy Big pulled the Crown Vic into the sink's small parking lot. She braked to a stop near the same picnic table to which Jimmy's and Ronny's bicycles had been locked that morning. She threw the car into park, opened her door, and left the engine running. "Thought you'd like to take a look now."

There was an old faded red Volvo wagon parked next to the cruiser. Both women stood just beyond the picnic table and looked down at the now docile East Fork of the Sun River. What had been a raging torrent that morning was now a gentle stream.

As they looked upstream, the East Fork ran from riffle to pool to riffle in and around large boulders and under overhanging trees. A lone fisherman a few hundred yards upstream, no doubt the Volvo's owner, tried his luck with a spinning rod casting a lure at the base of a rocky riffle.

The evening sun was in the tops of the trees on the opposite ridge above the river. Downstream a few yards from the overlook, the East Fork fell into a blue pool and disappeared into the sink under a sheer cliff face.

Hilly commented, "Way different than this morning, and beautiful."

Big turned to her, "Yeah, and they say this is one of the last of Kentucky's free-flowin' streams from source to mouth. Excellent smallmouth bass fishing everyone says. Maybe the best in the state. It gets better downstream." She looked up at the sky and continued, "I'll wait if you want to walk through the cave to the other end. Don't look like any rain tonight."

Hilly laughed, "Like I told your boss this morning, no more caves for me."

Big pursed her lips, "Mmmmmm."

Hilly asked, "What's that supposed to mean?"

Big started back to the cruiser, "Oh, nothing. By the way, Scooter was in there with another deputy and retrieved our climbing rope, and my socks. Had to climb up nearly thirty feet. He was up against the ceiling, he said. Said you and the boy couldn't have had much more room left."

The two women climbed back into the Crown Vic. Big pulled back onto the highway. Soon they passed Moon's old store, stopped at the three-way intersection, and continued south on Route 153. Big relaxed behind the wheel and turned to Hilly, "I don't see no ring. Been married? I don't mean to be nosy, but I've been meaning to ask."

Hilly slouched in her seat, "I was married a long time ago. Two years to another cop about a year after I left the army and joined the Detroit

PD. Big mistake, as I soon found out. Partly my fault. I'm just not suited to living with anyone full-time I guess, and he couldn't stop fooling around. We broke up after two years. Best for both of us. That was a long time ago. I still know him. He got married again, and this time it stuck. Three grown kids and a grandchild at last count. He retired before me. Big beer belly. Probably still fooling around."

"So, no kids?"

"No kids. Too late for that now. How about you?"

Deputy Big twisted her wedding ring as the Crown Vic dropped deeper into the East Fork's shadowed valley. "A husband and two kids, and I love them all to death, believe me."

"Your kids with your husband now?"

"Yeah, he's a mechanic at Kingston Ford there on the west side of town. Gets home at five or so. When I pull these long double shifts, my mom has the kids until then. She loves them like crazy."

Hilly sat quietly for a moment. "Sounds good, Big."

The road continued to descend gradually along the East Fork in its shadowed valley. The cruiser passed a few cars parked along the road. One man, standing near his open trunk and breaking down his fishing rod, waved to the deputy as they passed by. Big waved back. Hilly spotted a few more fishermen here and there wading or sitting on rocks trying their luck.

Then Hilly asked Big, "What about Sheriff Ferguson?"

Big turned to Hilly, "What about him?"

"I saw the Medal of Honor in his office this morning when he went out into the hall to talk to you. *The* top honor, in my opinion. How did he earn it?"

Big shook her head, "He displays it but doesn't talk too much about it. Says it was a long time ago and people shouldn't make a big fuss about it. Or Vietnam, for that matter. All in the past."

"You've got to know a little."

"Only time he opened up to me and another deputy was at a two-day law enforcement seminar we attended a few years ago in Louisville. He'd had a few with us at the hotel bar that evening. The other deputy, Harland, who you haven't met yet, asked him about it. Said it was in 1968. The war was at its peak. He'd been drafted right after college. Army made him a warrant officer and taught him how to fly a helicopter."

"I saw the picture."

"Said he and his crew and some other crews were ordered to rescue some other soldiers at a forward base that was being overrun by the Viet Cong. Everybody got shot up pretty bad, but the sheriff kept going back. His helicopter was damaged, but he took another one. Last two times in he was flying solo, he said. And he was wounded twice. In the arm and the leg but he kept flying back and forth in that overloaded helicopter. Called it a Huey."

Hilly nodded. She had ridden some hours herself in one of those models in her day.

Big continued, "In all, and I looked this up, they say he saved over fifty men. And they put him up for the Medal."

Hilly let out a low whistle, "That's really something."

"Some of those men still keep in touch with him. They're all getting up there. A few stop in and see him from time to time over the years with their wives or grandchildren."

"Wow, that must be nice. Is the sheriff a local boy?"

"Yeah, born and raised here in Batavia. Except for the military, he's never left. Been the sheriff as long as I can remember."

"Is he a good boss?"

"Yeah, overall, we get along. He's fair. But he's got problems. Life hasn't been too good for him in recent years. He's taken some hits and had some bad luck."

"Bad luck?"

"Well, I shouldn't be blabbin' so much. He had a son and still has a daughter. The son was pretty much the star. He was an all-star quarterback here in Batavia for the high school team, the Wildcats. Made all-state twice. Did really well scholastically, too. Every college in Kentucky wanted him and even some big-shot national universities. But he elected to go to West Point. Maybe you know about sons and daughters of Medal of Honor winners?"

Hilly nodded, "Practically automatic admission, I've heard."

"Yeah, star quarterback there, too, in the late eighties and early nineties."

Hilly thought for a second. "Ferguson? That Ferguson? You're kidding? Sure, I remember him."

Big hesitated and took a breath.

Hilly asked, "Don't tell me, Iraq?"

"No, Afghanistan. He stayed in the army instead of going pro after his first hitch was up."

"Sure, now that you mention it, I remember. It was kind of a big deal that he turned down a pro football career. And, of course, I remember the news that he had been killed but can't remember exactly how."

"Died in some kind of crash. Was a colonel by that time. It's been about ten years now, I think. The sheriff and his family never got over it, although his wife and daughter probably don't even remember."

The two women sat in silence for a moment. Hilly was about to ask what Big had meant by that last remark when the cruiser rounded a bend and approached a large iron truss bridge. Big let off the gas, and the Crown Vic rolled onto the bridge. Big pointed to the left and explained, "This is where the West Fork meets the East Fork and becomes just the Sun River. The dam site is just down the road a little ways."

Hilly looked upstream through the bridge trusses as they passed by. The West Fork resembled the East Fork. Pools and rapids between high limestone bluffs. But the West Fork was larger and deeper.

A large, yellow tandem dump truck drove onto the bridge northbound, causing the bridge to shake under its weight. Two cars with roof racks were pulled over on the left shoulder just beyond the bridge. Two couples stood by four colorful kayaks near the cars, drinking from water bottles. Orange life vests were scattered on the ground next to the kayaks. All four people were dressed in shorts, T-shirts, and light canvas shoes.

They waved at the cruiser, and two of them raised their water bottles in mock salute.

Hilly said, "That looks like fun!"

"Yeah, they start upstream about ten miles where Route 287 crosses the river. Where they're putting in that new bridge."

"I got stopped there for a few minutes while they hauled off an old Civil War monument or something."

"Yeah, while you was in the cave getting' that boy, Billy said he probably knew who you were. He's a looker ain't he?"

"Yeah, if I was just twenty years younger. Hell, a year younger."

Both women laughed.

Hilly continued, "He mentioned something about a lost treasure?"

"That old legend has been floating around here for over a hundred years. Ain't nothing to it, in my opinion." Then Big continued, "If you stay here any length of time you ought to see some of the West Fork before it's flooded. A lot of people around the country are making the trip here before the dam is completed. It takes all day to get to this point. I've lived here all my life but never done it." Big thought a moment and laughed. "I sure wouldn't fit in one of those little boats anyway! But people say it's a nice way to spend a day, though. Lots of people do it in the summer. There's a guy back in town makes a living renting canoes to people."

"I took a float trip once in upper Michigan and loved it."

Big bit her lip, "Yeah, do it while you can. In a year or so, they say there'll be four hundred feet of water here."

Hilly thought Big was the third person to tell her this. First it was Billy the flagman, and then it was the crazy old man, Moon, who owned the old store.

Shortly after they crossed the bridge, the valley narrowed even more and they encountered a long line of opposite-direction traffic made up of mostly pickup trucks, both new and battered. Hilly thought she recognized a few of the trucks from the motel parking lot.

Big commented, "Must be end of shift."

They passed two large signs. Both were copies of the signs that Hilly had seen yesterday at the site of the new bridge construction over the West Fork. One warned to keep cell phones and radios off, and the other advertised the Sun River Dam site with the requisite Corps of Engineers symbol. Big left her radio on, Hilly noticed.

After they passed the signs, the highway became gravel, and the road became rough. Big slowed the cruiser to a crawl as they bumped along the uneven surface. Big leaned forward and pointed through the upper portion of the Crown Vic's windshield. "Right here is actually where the dam will sit. This is the narrowest part of the valley."

Hilly powered her window down, leaned out, and looked up. It was evident where the dam would be built. She could see that her side of the valley had been denuded for a few hundred yards from top to bottom, and large areas of rock had been blasted away.

Ahead, a short distance beyond the dam site, the valley suddenly widened. A large gravel parking lot to the right was full of heavy earth-moving equipment and a few white trailers converted to offices. A guard shack sat just to the left of the parking lot entrance. Big pulled the Crown Vic up to it in a cloud of dust, just as a man stepped out its door.

The deputy put the cruiser into park, picked up the mike, called in her arrival at the scene, and got a reply. She replaced the mike in its holder. Then she shut off the engine, grabbed a clipboard with paperwork from the center console, and climbed out. She hefted up her gun belt with her free hand and used her rear to slam the cruiser's door.

Hilly climbed out and stood by the passenger's door.

The guard was in his early sixties, wearing blue jeans with a belt that cut beneath his overhanging belly. He wore a white short-sleeved shirt with dark blue epaulets and pocket flaps. A small gold badge pinned to his right breast announced SECURITY GUARD in black letters across the bottom. His baseball cap was also dark blue with an embroidered badge on the front. His face, especially his nose, neck, and arms, were red and creased. It was clear the man had spent a lot of time both in the sun and behind a bottle, and not in a guard shack. He was chewing on a wooden toothpick, rolling it around in his mouth.

He shot a glance at Hilly, then walked right up to Big with his right hand extended while taking the toothpick from his mouth with his left. "How's it going, Deputy Big? It's been a while."

Big shook his hand, "OK, Elmer." She released her hand and pointed to Hilly. "Elmer, I want you to meet Hilly Walker. Hilly, this here's Elmer Anderson."

Elmer walked around the front of the Crown Vic and offered his hand to Hilly over the top of the passenger door. He and Hilly quickly shook hands. Elmer put the toothpick back in his mouth and began chewing on it once more. He looked Hilly up and down. "So you're the one inheriting all old Charlie's land? I heard about you today. Rescued that kid this morning. Whole town's talking about it."

"Pleased to meet you, Elmer."

Elmer pulled a soiled red handkerchief from one of his rear pants pockets, took off his hat, and mopped his forehead and neck as he walked over to Big's side of the car. He looked at Big while pointing at Hilly with his thumb. "Not only pretty but armed." He laughed and slapped his knee with his hat. "Dang! I sure like that in a woman!"

Big looked at Hilly and winked, "C'mon, Elmer, don't be a flirt. Leave Ms. Walker alone. Besides, word just might get back to Mildred you carryin' on a bit."

Elmer laughed and put his baseball cap back on. "Dang guard shack! AC ain't working. Cheap-ass company!"

Big countered good-naturedly, "C'mon, quit complaining and wasting my time, Elmer. Some of us have to actually work for a livin'. You got some business for me?"

"I'll bet this nice car you drive around the county has some good AC."

Big took a breath and asked again, "You got some business for me or not, Elmer?"

The man was still looking at the hood of the brown Crown Vic.

Big asked again louder, "Elmer!"

The man snapped out of his trance and looked up, somewhat confused. Then he remembered. "Oh, yeah, Big, we got some vandalism to report from last night. Discovered it during the start of the day shift. Course that's the *only* shift right now due to government cutbacks." He proudly pointed at his chest. "That's why they got me here at night. I told 'em I sure didn't hear anything."

Big pointed to the equipment yard with her clipboard. "Elmer, why don't ya just show us."

Hilly and Big shut their doors and Big locked the cruiser with her key fob. Standard procedure even out here, Hilly thought.

Elmer led the way across the gravel lot to one of the white prefab trailer offices. "The boss chewed my ass before I went home this morning, but I swear I didn't hear or see nothin' last night. You know I told 'em they need some chain link fence topped with razor wire around the whole yard, I did."

Big said, "Good idea."

They came to the first trailer, and Elmer pointed to the side of the building. "There's a part of it." Someone had spray-painted in black paint

ALL GOOD THINGS ARE WILD AND FREE! Big took a small digital camera from her pocket and began to take pictures.

Elmer took off his cap and mopped his forehead again. He asked the two women, "What the hell is that supposed to mean anyhow? Pardon the language."

Hilly said quietly, "It's a quote from Henry David Thoreau, I think."

Elmer put his hat back on and stuffed the handkerchief back in his pocket. "Henry who?"

"Thoreau. You know. Walden Pond and all."

"Ain't never heard of the man. He sure ain't local."

Big stopped taking pictures and made some notes on her clipboard. "Where's the other damage, Elmer?"

Elmer walked them farther into the yard through rows of heavy equipment and stopped at a large yellow dump truck. Spray-painted on the driver's side of the hood in the same black paint was STOP THE DAM! And below this SAVE THE SUN RIVER! Big pulled the camera from her pocket again and snapped some more pictures.

As Big took the pictures, Elmer shook his head. "This here dam's goin' to be good for this county. They've been wantin' to build it since the middle fifties I think. Lots of jobs. They tell me when it's finished in a few years it'll be the highest dam east of the Mississippi. Almost five hundred feet high! Supposed to back up the West Fork all the way to Beasley and beyond."

Big finished with her camera and made a few more notes on her clipboard. "Anything else, Elmer?"

"No, ma'am. One guy had a broken windshield in his truck and was tempted to go after some insurance, but on second thought he was sure his kid had done it. No, ma'am, just the spray paint."

The trio turned and began to make their way back to the guard shack.

Elmer complained again, "Like I said, they need a fence around here. It's a big yard, and there's only one of me here at night. I can't be walking around all night. I got somewhat of a bad knee. And it's only goin' to get worse. I hear some fuckin' tree-hugging group filed another injunction or some such legal thing again up in the federal court in Lexington to stop construction. Oh, pardon the language again, ladies. And we got some kind of protest here next Sunday they say."

"Two deputies will be here for that, Elmer, and some state police."

"Well, I just don't want any trouble you know. Can we paint over those signs?"

"Yeah, go ahead, Elmer, no problem."

They approached the Crown Vic. Big clicked the locks, opened her door, and threw the clipboard on the seat. She turned to Elmer as Hilly walked around the cruiser to the passenger side. Big said, "Elmer, there's really nothing we can do now about that spray painting."

"How about takin' some fingerprints or something?"

Big let out a breath. "Your company can stop by the courthouse and get a copy of my report in a day or two for insurance purposes from the front desk, but that's about it for now. Just keep an eye out and be careful here at night, you hear, Elmer? Keep your eyes out for suspicious vehicles and such. So far no real harm." She hesitated as she climbed in the Crown Vic. Before she closed the door she finished, "Yet."

Big started the car, pulled the mike from its clip, and called in service and en route back to the courthouse. As she waited for a response from the dispatcher, she put the Crown Vic in gear, looked over her shoulder, and made a one-handed U-turn back onto the highway. She got a response from the dispatcher and replaced the mike in its clip. The Crown Vic bounced and rocked back and forth on the gravel.

Hilly looked across the river at the east side of the dam site, where the trees had also been cleared from the valley. She said quietly, almost to herself, "Big Yellow Taxi."

Big fought the steering wheel on the rough road and glanced over at her passenger. "What'd you just say?"

"Nothing. Just thinking." Then Hilly added, 'You know, the Joni Mitchell song? Paved paradise? The tree museum?"

Big shook her head. "Never heard of it."

When the road smoothed out, Big stepped on the gas and said, "Old Elmer's not one to work hard. I suspect there's a flask or two stashed somewhere, too."

Hilly replied, "Seemed a little nervous to me. Maybe with some good reason. I don't think it was any local people did the spray painting."

"The Monkey Wrench Gang you mentioned?"

"Could be. Something like that. He was right about the fence. Whoever it is could probably go after the equipment next if construction continues."

"Thanks, I'll put that in my report."

———

After riding in silence for a moment, the women came to the truss bridge over the West Fork. The tire noise changed as they crossed the bridge. Both women noted the two cars carrying the kayakers were gone.

Hilly asked Big, "What did you mean about the sheriff's wife and daughter on the way down?"

Big drew a breath, opened the console, and brought out an opened pack of gum. She offered a stick to Hilly, who refused, before unwrapping a stick for herself. Big chewed thoughtfully and then replied, "I shouldn't be telling you all this."

Hilly nodded in agreement but Big continued, "The sheriff's pushing seventy now. A man like him really should be retired by now and doing some fishing, but sadly his wife, who was a real nice woman, started suffering from Alzheimer's about five years ago. It started slowly with little things and then got worse. Not a good thing to see. The sheriff took care of her as best he could for a year or so but couldn't handle it after a while. She's now in a nursing home in town, and it ain't cheap on his salary. But it gets worse. His daughter, she's in her upper forties now, is in some fancy institution down in Atlanta, and the sheriff pays some of that. I hear it was drugs over the years helped fry her brains, but who knows. Between you and me, she was whatever her brother was not. The sheriff's got to be strapped moneywise. Don't let his cheerful demeanor fool you, Hilly. It's got to be hard on him, his family and all falling apart. And on top of everything, he's going to have to start a reelection campaign soon if he wants to keep his job. And next year it looks like he's got some younger competition in the form of one of the city councilmen."

"Doesn't sound good."

"No, it doesn't." Then Big asked, "You think we're going to have more trouble here because of the dam?"

"Seems to me the people who live here are pretty much in favor of that dam."

"Yeah, the people who count here and in Washington and Frankfort for sure are, but there's some up in these valleys who are going to get flooded out and have to move. People who have been living there for generations and they're not happy."

"Like the Worms?"

"Yeah, probably some of them, too, are affected by the dam in this county and elsewhere. Up in the hollows that'll be flooded. I hear some of 'em tried to stop the government from using eminent domain to flood the land some years ago but lost every case that came to court. People are appealin' I hear, and no money's been paid out, but it don't look good. The government always seems to win in the end." Big turned, smiled, and winked at Hilly. "Those government folks think we're all just a bunch of ignorant hillbillies who don't know nothin' about nothin', right? Nobody can beat the government, right?" Then she chuckled to herself with an inner joke of some kind, turned forward, and continued, "Heck, lawyer Rice told me they even used eminent domain to seize some acres of your great-grandfather's land a while back to build that new bridge over the West Fork." Big added, "That Worm family's been around here for a couple of centuries at least. Kind of a legend. Keep to themselves mostly."

"Some of them have been following me around the last two days. Sort of like bodyguards." With this thought, Hilly glanced in the passenger's rearview mirror, but the road behind was clear. She guessed the Worms trusted Deputy Big.

Hilly looked in the mirror again as they passed Moon's old store. Still nobody following. The store was shut tight, and there were no lights in the fading light.

Big thought for a few moments, "First I've heard of that. Like I said, they mostly keep to themselves. Take care of their own business. Our department has little or no contact with them." She shrugged, "They solve their own problems I guess."

"They've been friendly. I've got a feeling they'll let me know when the time's right. I'm pretty sure it's got something to do with the land I'm supposed to inherit."

"Maybe they want to buy some of that land."

"Not unless they have some millions of dollars, according to L. T. Rice." Hilly continued, "I've had a few words with Mr. Worm. So far he's treated me nice at the restaurant. I'll have to say, the food there is delicious."

"The Worm's been around for generations. As long as I can remember. Most of the town eats there at one time or another."

"I've also had words with Mrs. Worm. She's a lot younger, isn't she? Seems on the ball. Well both of them do. I don't know about the Worm that works in the kitchen, though." Hilly laughed at the way she used their name.

———

The cruiser was approaching Route 153's right-angle turn to the west when the radio came alive. Hilly had been thinking about the Bluebird, a shower, and a good eight hours of sleep when they received the call.

"Charlie 3?" Charlie 3 was Big's call sign that evening. Hilly had heard her use it at the dam site.

Big picked up the mike and answered after the squelch. "Charlie 3, go ahead."

"Charlie 3, we've got a report of a family disturbance at the Henderson residence. 343 North Ninth Street. Neighbors report the husband's drunk and is outside with a knife."

Big replied, "Charlie 3's en route. What's Charlie 2's location?"

The dispatcher answered, "He's here with me doing some paperwork, but he's en route to the location now."

Big rogered the dispatcher and put the mike back in its clip. She turned on the red and blue grille lights and roof bar, hit the siren, and stepped on the gas. The Crown Vic's V8 roared into action. As she concentrated on her driving, she told Hilly, "It's not far. Just a few blocks north of the Bluebird."

Hilly's dream of stretching out on Room 15's queen-sized mattress faded, but the rush of running hot again in a police car quickly replaced it.

Big hardly had time to get the Crown Vic up to eighty when she slowed at the eastern edge of town. Traffic was light. Big turned off the siren just as she turned right on Ninth Street, just to the east of Johnnie's Market. As they drove north, Big slowed at each four-way stop to clear the intersection until they pulled up in front of a small, white frame house on the east side of the street. There was a battered blue Ford F-150 in the driveway.

Hilly recognized the last name, Henderson, from the radio call a few minutes earlier, the pickup truck in the driveway, and now she recognized the man standing in the yard waving the knife in one hand and an almost empty vodka bottle in the other. It was Emery Henderson, Ronny's father.

Big reported her arrival at the address to the dispatcher and got a reply. She left the Crown Vic idling and exited the car, leaving her door open. She walked around the front of the car, unsnapped her holster, and drew the Glock, leaving her finger alongside the trigger guard.

Hilly also opened her door and exited the car but remained standing behind her door as she unsnapped her holster.

One of the sheriff's department Tahoes pulled in behind Big's cruiser. A deputy climbed out and walked up beside Big. He had also drawn his Glock but kept it at his side.

The sun had set, shrouding the neighborhood in twilight. The red and blue flashing lights from the sheriff's vehicles reflected off the white house, Emery Henderson, and the three people standing near the Crown Vic. Some neighbors had gathered on the sidewalk opposite the Henderson house to watch.

Emery Henderson staggered a few feet in each direction. He was still dressed in his work clothes from that morning. Work boots, blue jeans, and a tan canvas shirt.

Big yelled, "Put the knife down, Emery, before anyone gets hurt. We don't want any more trouble tonight, do we?"

Emery Henderson waved the knife around in another circle with his right hand and took a swallow from the vodka bottle from his raised left hand. He tried to wipe his mouth, but the bottle's neck interfered. He cried out, "They docked me a half day's pay is what they done! That ain't right. My boy cost me a half day's pay!"

Big yelled again, "Mrs. Henderson, are you and Ronny OK?"

The screen door opened with a protest squeal from its spring, and the woman and the boy stepped out. Both seemed uninjured. The door swung on its spring and shut behind them. The boy quickly hid behind his mother, clapped his hands over his ears, and shut his eyes tightly. The woman hesitated and then nodded at Big.

As Hilly listened, Big quietly asked the other deputy over the idling engine of the cruiser, "Harland, how do you want to handle this?"

Harland answered, "Christ, we was here just a few weeks ago. Same thang. If you ask me, we just shoot the son of a bitch."

Big turned from the other deputy and yelled again, "C'mon, Emery, put the knife down and we'll talk."

Emery Henderson waved the knife around again and pointed with the bottle to his family on the porch. "It ain't fair. I lose pay because of that little shit!"

Hilly quietly said to herself, "Fuck this." But it was loud enough for the two deputies to hear. She walked forward and slammed the cruiser's door behind her. She turned and marched across the grass toward Henderson.

Harland, the deputy, stepped forward, but Big held him back with a hand to his chest.

Hilly walked across the yard until she was three feet in front of a surprised Emery Henderson. Not expecting such a confrontation, he swayed a little and stepped back a foot as she concentrated intensely on his right hand, which held the knife. The knife was a folding type, had a four-inch shiny blade, and a bone handle. There was an empty leather holster for the knife on Henderson's right side. To Hilly it looked like a cheap Shop Here! model, but it was deadly enough. She saw there was no blood on the blade.

Henderson dropped the near-empty vodka bottle on the grass. Hilly followed his movement and stepped forward. Her legs were apart and bent slightly. Most of her weight was on her left leg. She held her arms apart and low in front of her.

Henderson leaned forward and studied her for a moment, and then his eyes widened with recognition. He relaxed somewhat, blinked, and slurred his words, "I…know…you. You're the lady from…this…mornin', ain't…ya?"

Hilly replied in a normal voice, "Drop the knife, Henderson, I'm not going to ask you again."

Henderson slashed the knife back and forth. His eyes got mean again. Hilly followed the movement of the knife. "Or what, lady?"

Hilly lowered her voice and hissed in a taunting manner, "Or I'm the *lady* that's going to kick your ass, you piece of shit." She waited.

Henderson suddenly thrust the knife at her.

Hilly stepped quickly to her right and forward. In one fluid motion, she grabbed Henderson's wrist with both her hands from the top, stopped the thrust, lifted his right arm, and applied upward pressure to his right wrist. Simultaneously, she kicked up hard into his groin, toe first.

Henderson's eyes opened wide. He dropped the knife onto the lawn. Hilly released his wrist, and he grabbed his crotch with both hands and sank to his knees. He opened his mouth and wailed something that sounded like "Ahhhhh!"

Hilly was so fast that both deputies just had time to flinch a bit by the time Henderson was on his knees. Big made an O with her mouth, and the other deputy started to say "shit" but only got the *sh* part out.

Henderson was still on his knees, moaning, as Hilly stepped back a foot, put all her weight on her left foot again, and roundhouse kicked Henderson in the gut hard with the top of her right foot. He made a loud "OOF!" and fell onto his back, still holding his crotch with his knees folded back over his stomach. Then he rolled over onto his right side in a fetal position and continued to moan.

Henderson was still trying unsuccessfully to get a breath as Hilly picked up the knife by the blade in her left hand and flipped it quickly so she held it by the plastic bone handle. She knelt next to Henderson, bunched his shirt collar in her right hand, and squeezed before she brought the tip of the knife a fraction of an inch below his right eye. She lowered her face next to his and squeezed the shirt collar harder, choking off all his air. His face turned red and his eyes bulged. He brought one hand from his crotch to his throat and pawed harmlessly at her hand.

Hilly leaned her head over and whispered directly into his ear, "Listen to me carefully, you fucking asshole, or I'll pop your eyeball right out on the ground in front of you. Understand?" She put some pressure on the knife tip.

Henderson, wild-eyed, nodded quickly.

She continued to whisper even lower into his ear. "No matter where I am on this planet, if I ever hear of you abusing that woman or that boy again, I swear I'll come back and kill you."

Henderson's tongue came out of his mouth.

Hilly shook his head hard with her right hand and asked, "Is that clear, you miserable, fucking prick? Do you understand me?"

Henderson, nearly unconscious now, managed to look at her and nodded.

She suddenly let go of the man's shirt collar and slammed his head into the grass. She drove the knife into the lawn a fraction of an inch from the side of his head but still in his view. He rolled away from her onto his left side, kept the fetal position with both hands back on his crotch, coughed, and continued to try to draw a breath.

Hilly rose to her feet and watched Henderson as the two deputies surrounded him. He was plainly defeated, and the pair holstered their Glocks.

Hilly knew it was traditional to bow to an opponent, but not in this case. The man deserved no amount of respect.

Big pulled her handcuffs from the case on her belt with one hand as the two deputies rolled the groaning Henderson over onto his stomach. Hilly watched as Deputy Big pulled the man's arms behind his back and snapped on the cuffs. He continued to groan loudly as they pulled him to his feet. Deputy Big reached down, pulled the knife from the lawn, and folded it shut with both hands.

Deputy Harland led the stumbling Henderson across the grass to the Tahoe, pushed him into the rear seat, and shut the door.

A few of the neighbors still stood on the sidewalk across the street as Hilly and Big made their way back to the Crown Vic. One of the neighbors, an old woman in a bathrobe, still showed astonishment with both hands clasped on either side of her head. Another neighbor, a middle-aged man, put his arms out in front of him and clapped his hands as the two women approached the cruiser. A few others joined in.

Hilly smiled at the people on the sidewalk and then reached into the cruiser and pulled her fanny pack out. "If it's all right with you, Big, I'm going to walk back to the Bluebird alone. It's been one hell of a day, and I want to get my head straight a little." Then she added, "I want you to do me a favor, though."

Big nodded, put Henderson's knife on the cruiser's roof, placed both hands on her gun belt, and looked at Hilly. Before she answered, she stepped back and appraised the other woman for a moment. "Jesus, that was something! What you just did! I've never seen anyone move that fuckin' fast!" She snapped her fingers. "Just like that and that asshole's down!" Then she asked, "What would that favor be? I think this town owes you one after today."

Hilly fastened her fanny pack. "Yeah, well…men like him need to be taught a lesson once in a while. I was thinking about that poor woman and boy."

"We've had nothing but trouble from him over the years, and I was glad to see he finally got some trouble back. Boy, did he!"

Hilly nodded toward the house. The woman and the boy were still standing on the porch, watching the Tahoe drive off toward the courthouse. "I really didn't hurt him much, didn't break anything……this time." He'll be sore, though. I just want you to put him in a cell overnight and let him sober up. No charges. I want him released in the morning so he can go back to his job and support those two over there. But keep him away from them for a while."

"Yeah, I guess we can do that tonight. He's got a sister here in town he can stay with, if you answer a question."

"What's that?"

"You got to tell me what you told him when you were up close with him on the ground."

Hilly smiled and shut the car door. "I told him to have a nice day."

Big laughed, shook her head, and started across the yard to check on Mrs. Henderson and Ronny. Hilly turned and began walking south on Ninth Street.

CHAPTER 26

Kentucky Blu

The tan, late-nineties Buick LeSabre passed under the dark railroad bridge on Kentucky Route 287 and continued west toward the brightly lit I-75 interchange.

The sun had set a while ago, but a streak of orange still glowed on the horizon. The weather had been clear and hot most of the day, in the mid-nineties, except for a band of thunderstorms that had moved through the area in the early morning.

Sheriff Ferguson pressed the off button on his cell phone as the Buick passed over the interstate and approached the businesses just east of the main highway. I-75 was the major north–south artery between the Deep South and the Midwest. Even this late on a July evening it teemed with traffic divided between truckers and vacationers. Because of the railroad right-of-way on the east side of the highway, most of the businesses at the interchange were on the west side.

Sheriff Ferguson came down off the interstate overpass and smiled. He had just received two reports, the first one from Deputy Harland and then one from Deputy Big. Sheriff's departments were political, and, as with most of them, the most grievous mistake an employee could make was not keeping the sheriff immediately informed of all cases or happenings of any importance. If a mayor, city council member, or any other politician spoke to the sheriff about something and the sheriff had not been informed and appeared ignorant, there was hell to pay. It was even worse if the press was asking the questions. So both deputies had dutifully spoken to the sheriff on his cell phone when they had arrived back at the courthouse and jailed Henderson.

Sheriff Ferguson flipped the cell phone shut and laid it on the passenger seat next to his department portable radio. His deputies, especially Big, had been excited in their account of Hilly Walker kicking the shit out of that dirtball Henderson. God knew the man deserved it, the sheriff thought. Sheriff Ferguson shook his head as he thought of the Walker woman as he passed the Super 8 and then the Best Western, Burger King, and McDonald's. First, the cave rescue that morning, and now this evening she had taken out that troublemaker in, according to Big, a couple of seconds. But it was not surprising; the sheriff had read her bio.

The sheriff had agreed to let Henderson go in the morning as long as he was going to stay at his sister's house for a while. But before being released, he was to be detained so the sheriff himself could speak to him. He intended to tell the man that the next time he would see to it that Henderson would do serious time. After the "Come to Jesus" meeting, one of the deputies would escort Henderson to his house to pick up some things and his truck.

The Waffle House was on the north side of Route 287 and one of the last businesses of the interchange area. Ferguson turned into the asphalt parking lot. He noticed there were just four other vehicles in the lot: a red Buick Regal, a muddy, dark green Range Rover, a blue Jeep Cherokee, and a white Lincoln Signature Town Car with the shorter wheelbase. All four cars were facing out and had Georgia license plates.

Ferguson nosed in next to the red Regal, noticing four men standing between the Regal and the Range Rover. One of the men was leaning on the Buick, and the other three, in rough clothes, were leaning against the filthy Range Rover. Ferguson recognized one of the men from the previous night's meeting but not the other three. They appeared to be tough-looking Mexicans. As he walked around the front of the Regal, he also noticed another man sitting in its backseat smoking a cigarette, the same man who had been sitting there last night. As the sheriff walked past, the man took a drag on the cigarette and flicked the ashes out the window.

The man in the rear of the Regal nodded toward the sheriff and took another drag. The other men kept quiet and looked silently in his direction as he started across the lot.

Ferguson was dressed in civilian clothes: Levis, a green polo shirt, a faded blue Bass Pro baseball cap, and a worn pair of Nikes. The sheriff pulled out his shirttail as he approached the Waffle House's door to cover his badge and gun.

It could have been any Waffle House. They were all the same. As he entered, he faced a counter with revolving stools and to one side an area of booths. A waitress, who looked to be about eighteen, stood near the cash register reading a *People* magazine and chewing gum. Ferguson thought there had to be a lone cook at this hour, but he was probably out back taking a cigarette break or in the john taking a leak.

Seated in one of the booths toward the rear was a distinguished-looking man in his seventies with a full head of silver hair. He wore expensive tan slacks and a blue-and-white striped shirt with a button-down white collar. Both his pants and shirt were immaculately pressed. An expensive blue summer-weight blazer hung on a hook at the end of the booth. He wore a pair of silver-framed glasses and had a napkin pressed into the open collar. A large ceramic plate in front of him was piled high with waffles slathered with maple syrup and two sausage patties and a coffee cup on the side.

The waitress looked up from her magazine as Ferguson entered.

Another man was seated on one of the counter stools reading a newspaper with a cup of coffee in front of him. As Ferguson walked by, the man placed the newspaper on the counter and rotated on his stool to follow him. Ferguson recognized him as the man named Phil with the Elvis Costello glasses.

The waitress clutched a stainless coffee pot from the warmer and followed the sheriff to the booth, where the older man sat eating his waffles with apparent relish. The Sheriff slid his bulk into the booth opposite the silver-haired man.

The waitress stopped at the end of the booth and lifted the coffee pot a little higher. "What can I git ya?"

Ferguson turned over a ceramic cup and simply pointed at it. The waitress dutifully filled it and left.

The older man, Alex Kingman, swallowed a mouthful of sausage patty, put his knife and fork down, and patted his mouth with the napkin around his neck. Kingman was the CEO of an Atlanta company by the name of the Atomic Furniture Warehouse. Although the company headquarters was in Atlanta, his furniture warehouse empire enveloped the entire Southeast and parts of the Midwest with over a hundred stores. The store chain had been started by his father in the early 1950s; hence the name. Recently Kingman had started to expand in the Western portion of the country. The company's TV ad that most of the Southeast knew featured a man in a bear suit dressed as an astronaut yelling at viewers about low, low prices. Sometimes Kingman himself did the ads. Most importantly, the Atomic Furniture Warehouse imported many goods in containers from South America and had a fleet of some 400 trucks that were familiar to everyone on the interstate highways.

Kingman held out both hands in a friendly manner, smiled, and asked, "Roscoe, how are you doing?"

Ferguson shrugged, took a sip of his coffee, and said, "I've got a problem with what's going on, Mr. Kingman."

"Yeah, we have a problem, Roscoe."

"If it's about that Walker woman…"

Kingman laughed, "Yes, we have a problem with her, but what I'm talking about is much worse."

Ferguson looked up, puzzled. "What's that, Mr. Kingman?"

Kingman pointed at his plate. "That Walker woman is nothing, Roscoe, compared to the fact that if my wife finds out I'm eating this shit she'll kill me. I've tried to be good after my bypass operation a couple of years ago, but, what the hell, a man's got to stray once in a while. Am I right? I've got to swear you to secrecy about what's on my plate, OK? Sure you don't want to order something? It's on me tonight. Sky's the limit."

Kingman picked up his knife and fork, cut a chunk from one of the maple syrup-soaked waffles, and stuffed it into his mouth.

While Kingman chewed, Ferguson waved his hand in front of him, "No thanks, Mr. Kingman, I had a big meal a little while ago at the Worm."

Kingman swallowed, "Ah, the Worm. Best damn restaurant for a couple of hundred miles. That man should franchise. Not a very appetizing name, though."

Kingman took another forkful of waffle. While he chewed, he raised a hand and motioned to the man at the counter. The other man stood up, picked up the newspaper he had been reading, and walked over to the booth. He folded the paper neatly with both hands, laid it on the table beside Kingman, and said, "Here you go, boss."

The other man, Phil, continued to stand at the end of the table and purposefully unbuttoned his sport coat. Ferguson caught a glimpse of the automatic pistol in the holster under the man's left arm. The gun appeared to be a small model stainless Colt.

Waiting for Kingman to finish with his waffle, Ferguson looked up and said, "I suppose you've got a permit for that gun?"

Phil smirked and nodded his head toward the parking lot. "I thought the county line was the median of that interstate down the road a bit, Sheriff. And, yes, I've got a permit. You want to see it?"

Ferguson ignored the man and turned back to Kingman. Kingman finished chewing, laid down the knife and fork again, and picked up the newspaper. As he began to leaf through it, he dismissed Phil with a wave of his hand. Phil smirked once more at the sheriff and walked back to his counter stool.

Kingman folded back the newspaper and said, "Ah, here it is." He rotated the newspaper, laid it in front of the sheriff, and tapped an article. It was in the Region section and contained a paragraph and a two-inch picture, the head shot of Hilly Walker coming out of the cave after the rescue that morning. Ferguson read the paragraph.

Kingman said, "This is the afternoon edition of the *Atlanta Herald*. By now maybe a few million people have seen it."

Ferguson nodded. Rolly Harrington at the *Eagle* must have put it out on the wire. The sheriff pushed the paper back across the table. "Yeah, she was a real hero this morning. Saved the kid when no one else could."

"Why did you let this happen for Christ's sake?"

"She was in my office when the call came in. I was introducing myself to her. Trying to get a feel for who she is. I don't think she suspects anything, Mr. Kingman."

"This complicates things. We started out with an anonymous person in a big city who wouldn't be missed much among millions of people, but now we have a hero in a little Kentucky town."

The sheriff stated, "It was your men who missed her up in Detroit, Mr. Kingman." He added, "I want out of this deal. I won't have anything to do with a murder."

Kingman laughed, "Out? Oh, no, you're in way too deep now, Roscoe. The only thing I can figure you have to do now is to stand aside and let us solve the problem and handle things."

"Us?" Ferguson asked.

"You've got to remember I have bosses, too, Roscoe. They wouldn't be too happy with either of us if that old lawyer and the Walker woman show up in court Thursday."

There were a few minutes of silence. The waitress returned, refilled their coffee cups, and returned to her magazine.

Kingman continued, "Everything was in place for Thursday, Roscoe. The seed money has all been distributed. To the judge. To the legislature. Everyone's satisfied. The Koreans, the Shop Here! big box store people, and the cartel. It was all in place. By the way, we have decided to call our product Kentucky Blu. Catchy, don't you think? Like bluegrass. Get it? Then that old lawyer throws a wrench into the works and finds that woman up in Detroit who nobody knows and gets her to drive down here yesterday to screw everything up. There's a lot riding on all this, and, like I said, if she and the lawyer show up on Thursday…Well, we can't have that happen, can we?"

Ferguson replied, "You're talking about Rice now, too?"

"He kind of sealed his fate, too, when he found the Walker woman, don't you think?"

"But he's over eighty years old."

"Yeah, well, I hear he still likes to go fishing by himself. And I hear the Walker woman likes to jog along country roads in the early morning. Could be a farm truck on the road that early, too."

Ferguson spread his hands, "I don't like this one bit." Then he whispered, "We could all get the death penalty."

Kingman took another bite of waffle, chewed, and swallowed. He washed it down with another sip of coffee. "You worry too much, Roscoe."

Ferguson looked over his shoulder at the waitress. He noticed the cook had returned. He whispered again, "You'll worry, too, when they put that needle in your arm."

Kingman patted his mouth with the napkin, leaned back, took another look at the sheriff, and suddenly changed the subject. His voice took on an edge. "By the way, Roscoe, I visited your daughter last week." Ferguson looked up. "Yeah, that's right. To tell you the truth, she looked a little better to me. She didn't seem to be staring off into space as hard.

That hospital must be pretty expensive, huh? I'd sure hate to see her back on the streets."

Both men stared each other down for a moment. The color rose in Ferguson's cheeks.

Kingman glanced toward the man sitting at the counter. "Phil over there's been snooping around a little, too. Told me that nice nursing home in town is going to probably raise its prices maybe fifteen percent next year. Phil thought the place was pretty nice, from what he saw, and the only one in town. He said someone offered him a doughnut. Seemed a lot better place than some of those cheap, shoddy places upstate, from what I know. Patients lying in their own shit and piss. A lot of them die from infections, I've read."

Ferguson suddenly realized he was gripping the edge of the table hard. He relaxed his grip. The sheriff calmed himself, reached out, and tapped the newspaper. "Do you know anything about Ms. Walker?"

Kingman replied, "No, the article doesn't say much. Just know she's from Detroit."

Ferguson smiled, "I had her in the office this morning. You probably know that. She's a retired schoolteacher. Taught school for almost twenty-five years. Should be a pushover for your guys. Told me she recently took up jogging in her spare time." The sheriff tapped the paper again, "Wasn't much of a rescue either. Kid had almost found the way out on his own accord. Newspaper made a bigger deal of it than it was. Yeah, I can't see her giving you guys much trouble. And the lawyer, Rice, is in his eighties and can hardly make it up his office steps most mornings."

Kingman leaned back, "Glad to see you're finally coming around, Roscoe."

Two cars came off the highway and into the Waffle House's parking lot. Both had Ohio plates. One was a green Volvo wagon with luggage strapped to its roof rack and the other was a late model Chevy Malibu. Doors slammed. Four adults and five kids. Two of the kids started punching each other. It was obvious they were all traveling together. The excited children ran ahead of the two sets of parents. One boy held the door open for the others, except for the small girl at the end of line. He purposely entered ahead of her, making sure the door shut in front of her. No doubt, his sister, who got even by sticking her tongue out at him as she manhandled the heavy glass door herself.

Warm, summer night air rushed into the restaurant. The waitress grabbed a handful of menus, and the cook readied the grill. As voices filled the restaurant, Kingman pulled the napkin from around his neck, wiped his mouth, and then dropped the napkin next to his empty plate. He slid out from the booth and draped his coat over his arm. Ferguson also slid out from his side of the booth.

As Kingman shrugged his coat on and glanced at the two families across the restaurant, he said, "Time to go. I don't like kids. Never liked to be around them." Before he turned for the door, he left a twenty dollar bill on the table. "Don't worry, everything will be fine. I'll be in touch, Roscoe."

As Kingman walked to the door, Phil left his counter stool and followed his boss. Before the man with the Elvis Costello glasses went out the door himself, he turned and pointed his thumb and forefinger toward the sheriff, winked, and then dropped his thumb like the hammer on a gun.

Sheriff Ferguson shook his head, let out a breath, put two dollars on his side of the table, and followed a few minutes later, when the cars in the tough-guy convoy had followed one another onto the highway. He thought about Hilly Walker and hoped he had given her some kind of an edge. He was reminded of the old short story by O. Henry. "The Ransom of Red Chief."

CHAPTER 27

Worm Cave

The bedside digital alarm began its electronic beeping. Hilly opened one eye. It was 4:50 a.m. She silenced the alarm, rolled over, put one forearm over both eyes, and groaned. She had drifted off at about ten o'clock. It had taken her a while to come down. She would feel better in a while, after a solid seven hours. She brought her knees up under the covers and groaned again. Despite being in good shape she thought, the previous day had certainly tested her.

Hilly had no doubt lost her temper the previous evening. That, she thought, hadn't happened for some years. But to look on the plus side, she hadn't actually killed the man. And she could have done so pretty easily. One jab with the base of her palm would have driven the bones from his nose into his skull with deadly results. Lights out for Mr. Henderson. So she had had some control and just taught him a lesson and wouldn't hesitate to do it again. And, after all, he had made the knife thrust first. Her martial arts training had been mainly defensive. But she had taunted him. There was that. And he was drunk. Not much of an opponent. The two deputies had not heard the taunting or the threats afterward. These were the things running through her mind on the walk back to the Bluebird. She turned on the bedside lamp, groaned again, and rolled out of bed.

Hilly had quickly walked the three blocks back to the Bluebird. Faster the first block, bile rising in her throat, and then slower the last two blocks as she had somewhat calmed herself. She knew that adrenaline built up quickly and then was slower to dissipate. The surge of adrenaline had certainly been greater in the cave that morning. She had begun to relax by the time she was crossing the Bluebird's parking lot to her room. Miss E. had been standing outside the office and gave her a small wave. Hilly remembered that the woman had a police scanner. The old lady had kept to herself, though. Hilly thought Miss E. was probably worried about being taken down herself if she uttered a word.

Hilly had entered her room and bolted the door. She had quickly stripped down and taken a long, hot shower. By the time she was toweling off, she was actually smiling to herself. It *had* felt good to take the scumbag down, and she had been in control. Maybe she had put the fear of God into him, although she doubted it. Her whispered threat had been real, though. She had acted with perfection, although it had been some years since her last match. Martial arts were all about discipline, practice, and fitness, but rarely used in real life like last night. Hilly smiled as she reached for her clothes. She still had it.

She had slept in the nude and slipped on her running bra and panties, then the pocket T-shirt and cargo shorts. She was running out of clean clothes and would have to definitely do some laundry this afternoon. As she was buttoning her shorts, she walked barefooted over to the window and pulled the curtain back an inch. It was still dark. The parking lot was lit by a few spotlights and the porch light of every room. No one was moving about yet. All the workmen's pickup trucks and utility vehicles were still.

Professor Cunningham, who preferred to be called "Doc" she had learned the previous evening, had insisted on five in the morning. He had impressed her as being punctual and businesslike. The early hour was still a mystery to her. On the plus side, he was kind of handsome with the gold wire-rimmed glasses and British accent in a college professor way—or was it Indiana Jones?

Hilly was sitting on the edge of the bed tying her Nikes when she heard the low rumble of the V8 engine and the crunch of tires in the gravel parking lot.

She parted the curtains and saw the university's white Chevy Suburban in the parking lot parked crossways behind her Accord. She glanced at the bedside clock. It was five o'clock exactly. Very punctual. Although still dark, the sky had lightened somewhat in the east. It appeared that there were three people in the Suburban, two in front and one in back. The professor had probably brought along two of his students, she thought.

Hilly straightened the bed covers, although she knew either Miss E. or the girl who worked for her would make up the bed later. It was an old habit. She took one look at the bathroom and flipped the light off. The towels were straight on their racks. Another old habit, probably from her army days.

Everything she needed for the day, including the Beretta, was in her backpack. It was in its nylon holster trucked just under the top flap. Hilly hefted the pack onto one shoulder, made a final visual check of the room while turning off the lights. She wondered briefly if there was time to grab a couple of Johnnie's doughnuts and a cup of coffee from front office.

Professor Cunningham was standing on the stoop with his right hand in the air, poised to knock quietly. He stepped back and whispered, "Sorry, I saw a light but didn't know if you were ready to go or not."

She smiled, set the lock, stepped out, and whispered back, "That's OK, I've been ready for an hour. Got my five-mile run in, too, Doc."

"Exceptional, Hilly!" He whispered back.

She put her hand on his firm shoulder as they walked to the Suburban, "Just joshing you a little bit, Doc. I just rolled out of the sack ten minutes ago."

Professor Cunningham grinned nervously. He had yet to understand American humor. He opened the rear door for Hilly. Hilly held her pack in front of her and climbed in. While she situated herself and placed the pack on the floor in front of her, the professor quietly shut her door and climbed into the front seat himself. The dome light went out as he clicked his door shut.

As her eyes adjusted to the dark interior and she raised her head, she was surprised to see not a student behind the wheel but Camas Worm. Hilly tensed as she realized the Worm Café's cook was sitting to her left and holding a Colt AR-15 with a telescopic sight across his lap.

Worm put the car in gear, and, as they pulled out of the Bluebird's parking lot and briefly under one of the flood lamps mounted outside at the corner of her room, she could see that the Colt assault rifle was set on safe but also had a full auto setting. Hilly reach for her pack, but the cook leaned over, put his hand lightly on her arm, and said, "We're friends, Captain."

Hilly straightened and looked at him. No one had called her by that rank in decades. He removed his hand from her arm and held it out to her. She reached across with her right hand and took his firm grip. He introduced himself, "Leroy Worm, former army ranger. Pleased to finally meet you, Miss Walker."

Hilly released his hand and nodded at the Colt assault rifle.

Camas Worm turned left onto Main Street while Leroy Worm explained the rifle, "A necessity, ma'am. Your life's in grave danger, Miss Walker. I believe you're beginnin' to learn that or else you wouldn't have put that Beretta in that thar pack."

Hilly answered, "First of all, Leroy, call me Hilly, OK?" Then she asked him, "You were in the four-by-four pickup truck that followed me into town on Monday weren't you?"

"Yes, ma'am. Mr. Rice insisted when he learned you was going to drive down here. Told me what you were driving, make, model, color, plates, everything. I waited up there on 153 near the county line most of the day.

My cousin Todd was sittin' out on 287 just east of the interstate most of the day, too, until I called him on my cell phone that I had ya in my sights. Only two ways for you to come into town." He laughed and added, "By the way, Miss Walker, you and Billy shouldn't have been flirtin' that much. He's married, and his wife's expectin.'"

Hilly remembered Rice asking about her car on the phone now. She thought it was kind of strange at the time, but now it made sense. She also remembered the flagman, Billy, talking to the pickup driver behind her. It all made sense now. "So the Worm family's been my bodyguard so to speak for the last two days?"

"Yes, ma'am."

The traffic lights were flashing yellow this time of the morning. Camas Worm slowed as he approached the bank on the corner, then accelerated past the church on the north end of the square.

Leroy Worm sensed some of Hilly's puzzlement. He pointed to Camas Worm. "Camas is my older brother, Trish is my sister-in-law if'n you didn't know that already, but there were other Worms watchin' out for you, like Miss E. She's kind of an aunt."

Camas Worm kept his eye on the road but interrupted, "That's enough for now, Leroy." He looked at Hilly in the rearview mirror and said, "Don't worry, Miss Walker, we're goin' to explain everything. It'll become right clear soon."

Leroy Worm bent over the assault rifle and carefully picked up a large white Styrofoam box from the floor at his feet.

He handed it to Hilly. "Here, Miss Walker, Camas and Trish thought you might like some breakfast. The rest of us already ate at the Worm. We would've invited ya and all but after that rescue in the mornin' and taking out ole Henderson on his front yard later, we thought you might need that extra hour of sleep."

Hilly balanced the box on her lap, punched the tabs, and opened it. Inside were three fluffy pancakes covered in syrup, two sausage patties, and a large helping of hash browns, each in its own compartment. The sudden, delicious smell made her stomach rumble.

Camas Worm accelerated out of town on Route 153.

Leroy handed her a set of metal utensils wrapped in a cloth handkerchief. Doc Cunningham turned and offered her a large, lidded Styrofoam coffee cup. Hilly ate her breakfast as Camas Worm drove west on Route 153. As she finished the second sausage patty, he slowed, doused the headlights, and pulled onto the shoulder near the mailbox that marked the long gravel drive running north to the house and barn at the base of the Worm Ridge.

The professor powered his window down while Camas Worm opened his door, slid from his seat, and stepped out onto the asphalt carrying a pair of binoculars from under the seat. He quickly closed the Suburban's door just enough to switch off the dome light and leave Hilly, Doc, and Leroy in darkness. Camas Worm braced his arms on the hood of the car. He peered through the binoculars at the area near the farmhouse a half mile distant. The sky was clear, the air was cool, and sunrise was still an hour away, but the eastern sky continued to lighten. This and the starlight gave him somewhat of a view.

After a minute or so, Camas lowered the binoculars, took a few steps back, and slid back into the Suburban. Everyone sat in the dark vehicle listening to the rumble of the engine. Hilly sensed a decision was being made.

Finally Leroy Worm leaned forward and whispered to his brother, "See anything, Camas?"

The other man answered, "Nothin' I could see. Couldn't make out any other vehicles. Course it's pretty dark under them trees and all around the buildings."

"How many men did cousin Linda say came into the Waffle House?"

"She told me there was two inside when the sheriff showed up. That furniture guy from Atlanta you see all the time on the TV. Said he was a good tipper. And that asshole with the thick glasses. Five more outside with the cars. Two of the dumbshits we already know and three, new, tough-looking beaners. She said besides the sheriff's wife's Buick there was the red Regal, the Range Rover, a Jeep Cherokee, and the Lincoln. All Georgia plates, according to her."

Camas put the Suburban in gear but left the headlights off. The professor powered his window up as they turned into the farm lane. Leroy leaned forward over his brother's shoulder as they idled along between the rows of corn. Hilly held onto the coffee cup as she dropped the empty Styrofoam box at her feet. She opened the top flap of her backpack.

Soon they were alongside the farmhouse. Camas pulled into the lane leading to the barn and backed around, parking the Suburban facing back toward the road. He turned off the ignition as the three men slid out. Hilly dropped her empty cup on the floor near the empty food container, grabbed her pack, and followed.

The three men walked to the rear of the Suburban. Leroy, cradling his assault rifle, walked a few yards beyond. He stood facing the woods and listened.

Camas Worm stood by for a moment as Professor Cunningham busied himself with opening the tailgate, then walked over and stood with his brother.

As Hilly joined the professor at the rear of the vehicle, she could make out a dirt track in the darkness that climbed the ridge diagonally behind the farmhouse. Her surroundings began to look somewhat familiar despite the fact that it had been almost thirty years since she and her mother had last visited the place.

Camas walked back to the car holding a flashlight while the professor dragged equipment from the rear compartment onto the lowered tailgate.

Hilly turned her attention from the dense woods back to the Suburban. She noticed that Worm had the old Colt .38 in his waistband. Professor Cunningham stopped what he was doing, brought one hand up to his cheek, and said to himself, "Hmmm." Then he abruptly leaned into the car, grabbed a stack of clothing, and held the clothes out to Hilly.

Hilly's eyes widened in surprise, she dropped her pack at her feet, and almost automatically took the stack from him. The clothing appeared to be a worn but clean pair of coveralls made of tough gray material in a herringbone pattern and a University of Southern Kentucky sweatshirt. Balanced on top of the clothes was a black nylon climber's belt, a pair of wool socks, and a pair of well-worn brown boots with Vibram soles. The boots started to fall, and Hilly brought the stack of clothing and gear under her chin while she tried to balance everything.

It was hard to speak, but she asked the professor, "What's all this?"

Professor Cunningham replied over this shoulder as he drew even more equipment out of the rear compartment, "Well, Hilly, you certainly can't expect us to go spelunking in that summer outfit you're wearing, can you?"

"Spelunking?"

"Yes, spelunking, cave exploring."

"I know what spelunking is…Now wait a minute. I thought we were taking a hike on the ridge. You said last night at dinner we were going to look at my property."

"Yes, indeed, I said we were going to look at your potential inheritance. And that's what we're going to do. Now hurry up a bit. It's going to be light soon. Julie, one of my students, felt you and she were probably the same size, so everything should fit."

Hilly protested, "You didn't say anything about cave exploring. After yesterday, I've just about had enough cave exploring for a lifetime, Professor Cunningham. With that map you had last night, I thought we were going for a hike this morning."

"Well, we certainly are going for a hike, Hilly, just underground. I wanted to surprise you. And we're not going to actually do any real exploring."

He placed a well-worn red fiberglass helmet on her head as she ducked under it. Similar to the helmet she had used the day before, with an LED headlamp mounted on the front and a chin strap, it was covered with scratches and a few, actual deep cuts.

Hilly knelt and laid the pile of clothing on the ground. She swiped the helmet from her head and placed it next to the clothing. She straightened up and looked through the trees at the star-filled sky. Professor Cunningham tried to catch her attention while handing her a mini Maglite in a black nylon holster and two packages of batteries. He also added a pair of black nylon kneepads to the clothing pile.

Cunningham followed her gaze upward and gently put a hand on her shoulder. "I take it you're worried about the weather?"

She nodded.

"And well you should be after yesterday. Every caver should. Very prudent of you. Not to worry about where we're going, but, of course, I did, in fact, check the weather report not an hour ago. A Canadian high-pressure ridge has moved into this area bringing fine weather, what you Americans call good weather. Lower temperatures today, I might add. It's been so horrendously hot this past week. No chance for thunderstorms today, Hilly. No flash flooding."

He smiled at her while handing her the small flashlight and batteries. "The triple As are backup for your headlamp, and the double As are backup for the flashlight. There are fresh batteries in each unit. An experienced caver always has three sources of light. Today, in fact, we will have four sources of light."

"Four?"

Professor Cunningham reached back in the Suburban and handed her a thick white wax candle and a waterproof match container. "Put these items in your backpack with the batteries, and then clip the holster with little Maglite to your belt, Hilly."

"A candle? Sounds a little old-fashioned."

"You'll be surprised just how much light a candle gives off. In fact, I plan to show you." He chuckled, "And not much can go wrong with a candle and a match, can it? I'll be carrying the same equipment as you, with one exception."

He reached back in the Suburban and brought out a large six-volt flashlight. It was the type with a big battery pack below a large handle and a four-inch spotlight. He explained, "Spelunkers usually don't carry such a bulky or heavy thing like this, but where we're going and for what I'm about to show you, I'll need this. It's the latest model with LEDs and has a bright beam of over four hundred feet. They say it will burn for twenty-four hours, not that I plan to do that." He looked at the large flashlight and sighed, "When I started exploring caves, Hilly, a longer time ago than I care to admit, we actually used carbide lanterns, just like the old-time miners. A small acetylene flame in the middle of a reflector. My, have times changed!" he said as he set down the big flashlight. Then he pulled a large tan pack from the rear of the Suburban and placed it on the ground behind the truck.

Cunningham clasped his hands together and said quietly, "Right. That should do it, Hilly. Mr. Worm was kind enough to make some sandwiches for us, which should be reason enough for you to tag along with me today. And I have a couple of bottles and some plastic bags for our garbage and waste."

Hilly hadn't moved. "Waste?"

He clasped his hand together again and answered with some excitement, "We should be inside for some time, I should think. Maybe go where no one has ever tread. Think about that for a moment, Hilly. There's an old saying. Take nothing but pictures and leave nothing but footprints."

"Yes, I think I've heard that one."

Professor Cunningham waved his hands at the stack of clothing on the ground in front of her. "Right. Now let's get dressed, Hilly. I promise this experience will be much different than your show yesterday. It's absolutely crucial you accompany me today."

Hilly still had some reservations about the spelunking but, being far from timid, bent down and unlaced her Nikes.

Professor Cunningham sat on the tailgate and unlaced his desert boots.

Camas Worm turned, walked over to Leroy, and had a few words with him.

Hilly sat on the ground and pulled her Nikes and socks off. Then she stood and pulled the university sweatshirt over her head. It fit perfectly. Next she unfolded and unbuttoned the coveralls, stepped into them, and shrugged them up and over her shoulders. The coveralls also fit well.

Professor Cunningham was doing the same a few feet away, as Camas watched silently beside his brother.

Hilly buttoned the coveralls up the front but left the neck open. As she sat down to pull on the wool socks, she asked the professor, "I'm starting to sweat already. Is all this necessary?"

Cunningham buttoned his coveralls and replied, "Very much so, Hilly. The cave, as we've measured it, is a steady fifty-one degrees."

Hilly noticed the nylon kneepads the professor had placed on the ground, thinking they were the kind she had seen airline baggage handlers wear. She wished she had a pair of them yesterday morning at the sink and dutifully pulled one over each foot and left them hanging around her ankles before she tugged on the leather boots and tied them tight. She noticed a GORE-TEX tag on one of the boots. Waterproof. Then she looked down and noticed the name Shelley embroidered in red thread above the coverall's left breast pocket and thought, hopefully, she wouldn't ruin someone else's boots for the second day in a row. She stood and adjusted the kneepads.

Camas Worm came back to the Suburban and continued to watch them dress.

Hilly cinched the nylon belt around her waist and drew it up tight before clipping the flashlight and its black nylon holster to it. The red helmet came next. Hilly adjusted the chin strap. She turned to Professor Cunningham. "How do I look, Doc?"

He replied, "Very professional, Hilly. I say fantastic. I dare say you'd make the cover of *Spelunker Today* magazine." He chuckled, "Just what the fashionable cave explorer is wearing these days."

Camas Worm cut in, "Quit the bullshit and keep it down, you two. It's almost daybreak."

Hilly frowned in Worm's direction and quickly whispered to Professor Cunningham, "I feel like a combatant in a paintball contest, to tell you the truth, or part of a SWAT team."

Cunningham hefted his large pack onto his back and picked up the big flashlight.

Hilly put the candle, match container, and extra batteries into her pack alongside the Beretta in its nylon holster and cinched the pack. She stood and hefted the pack onto her back.

Camas Worm quietly shut the Suburban's tailgate as Leroy Worm backed up, still keeping his eye on the dirt track behind the house. He nodded at his brother.

———

Professor Cunningham led the foursome toward the barn. It was almost daybreak now, and Hilly could make out a narrow path angling downward between the barn on the left and the dense woods on the right. As Hilly passed the barn, she suddenly became suspicious and took a few sideways steps, looking it over. She walked backward a few steps, looked at Camas Worm, who had followed her, and touched her nose. In response to her stare, he simply nodded slightly. Hilly turned and trotted a few steps to catch up with Professor Cunningham.

Beyond the barn, the path continued to descend below the dark green field of corn in densely planted rows. The humid summer air began to feel much cooler.

Ahead, now that it was light enough to see details, Hilly could make out a dense, white patch of fog hanging in the air just above a small ravine.

Professor Cunningham descended ghostlike into the fog, then stopped and waited impatiently for the others to catch up. As Hilly caught up to him, she saw that the professor was standing at the edge of a small, grass-lined stream perhaps a foot wide and a few inches deep. The clear water made pleasant gurgling sounds as it ran over and around its bed of smooth stones and sand. The banks rose steeply on each side and were thick with brush and deep green waving ferns. The moist air now had a definite chill to it. Hilly began to remember being here as a little girl.

The Worm brothers caught up with Hilly and the professor. Camas Worm stepped up to them and pulled the revolver from his waistband. As if to answer Hilly's unasked question, he simply said, "copperheads" as he stepped over the tiny stream and took the lead, pointing the gun and flashlight ahead of him. He pushed the wet overhanging branches away from himself as he slowly made his way upstream in a brushy tunnel.

The professor followed the senior Worm in the narrow ravine, with Hilly following and the other Worm bringing up the rear with his assault rifle. Hilly found herself inspecting the area around her boots closely after Camas Worm's comment.

After a few minutes, Camas and Professor Cunningham came to a halt. Hilly caught up and realized in the growing light that both men were standing in front of a large gray limestone ledge under which the tiny stream they had been following flowed from a clear, mirror-like pool. On top of the ledge grew a few large trees rooted in a bed of almost fluorescent green moss and deep green ferns. Several small, brown tendrils dangled over the ledge.

Leroy Worm joined them. Cold, moist air wafted from under the ledge at the foursome.

Hilly now remembered standing at this very spot with her great-grandfather and mother when she was a little girl and being warned never to come here alone. Then, as now, she thought it was one of the most beautiful—no, enchanting—places she had ever seen.

After a moment, the spell was broken as Camas Worm, pistol at ready, shined his flashlight around. Hilly could see that the stream continued well under the ledge at the rear of the pool.

Finally, Camas pronounced, "Don't see none. I hate them snakes. Don't do anybody any good as fer as I'm concerned."

The professor dropped his pack, and Hilly did the same. Hilly was now glad for her sweatshirt and coveralls. The Worms were only dressed in white T-shirts, jeans, and farm implement caps.

Professor Cunningham picked up the large six-volt light next to his pack and switched on its powerful beam. He squatted down and aimed its beam under the limestone ledge.

Hilly bent over and, with the powerful light, could see that the cave under the ledge just beyond the pool tapered to a waist-high opening from which the spring emerged. Unlike the cave opening the day before, this one thankfully looked to be large enough for a person to at least be able to crawl on hands and knees. There appeared to be some sort of metal gate or screen across the cave's opening a few yards into the cave.

Professor Cunningham stood and turned off the light. Hilly also straightened up. The professor turned to the Worms and clasped his hands together. "Right! Well, Camas and Leroy, thanks for breakfast from both of us; it was delicious, as usual. We both appreciate your help, but we'll take it from here."

Camas Worm squinted at the two cavers and pointed a finger at the ground in front of them. "You have your cell phone, right, Doc? And the café's number?"

"Yes, of course, old boy, not to worry."

"There's lots to worry about. I want you two to stay right here when you come out til Leroy and I git here. Understand?"

The professor brought both hands up in protest, "Yes, yes, as ordered, sir."

Both Worms turned to leave. "C'mon, Leroy."

Hilly stopped them, "Wait a minute, please. I have a question for the three of you."

The Worms had only gone a few feet and turned around. The three men waited for her next words. Hilly hiked her thumb over her shoulder. "Does this cave have a name?"

Camas shook his head. "I don't reckon it does officially, ma'am. Not on any map I ever seen. Those that knew about it over the years just called it Old Man McHenry's Spring or some such thang like that."

Hilly raised her arm in front of the men and glanced at her Timex. "And I guess it's true that in about, hmmm, twenty-seven hours or so this cave will be all mine, as L. T. Rice says?"

All three men nodded with puzzled looks on their faces. Camas Worm said, "Yes, ma'am, true enough."

"Then as the future owner I hereby officially name this cave. From now on it will be known to everyone as Worm Cave. It's settled." She added, "If that's OK?"

Hilly saw Camas smile for the first time in two days and turn to his brother, who nodded.

The professor laughed and repeated, "Worm Cave?" He slapped his thigh. "So be it! We'll enter it in the register. Got kind of a ring to it, I dare say."

Camas Worm, still smiling, walked up to Hilly and gave her an uncharacteristic hug, which pinned her arms to her sides. He backed away, and said, "Mighty nice, ma'am. Thank you. I'll let all our kinfolk know."

Hilly reached up, switched on her headlamp, and turned to the professor. Trying to imitate him, she clasped her hands together and said, "Right! Let's see what this cave of mine is all about!"

CHAPTER 28

Exploring

Hilly and Professor Cunningham waded through the clear, shallow pool and ducked under the limestone ledge. Cool air poured from the cave's entrance, which was perhaps four feet high and almost the same wide. The narrow stream ran close to the right wall, and the remaining floor of the cave was sand and gravel.

Six feet into the newly named Worm Cave was an ancient iron gate blocking the entrance. It consisted of what looked to Hilly like rusty rebar. Two crude hinges were on the right over the stream, and a simple latch was on the left. The steel supports had been cemented into drilled holes on each side. The rectangular openings in the gate were large, six inches square. Large enough for small animals but not a human, Hilly thought.

Although the gate appeared old and rusty, Hilly could see by the change in color and sheen on the metal that oil had been applied recently to the hinges and the latch. A large, brand-new, shiny brass padlock hung from the simple latch.

Professor Cunningham bent over as he stepped out of the entrance pool. He took his pack off and laid it and the large flashlight on the tiny sandbar. He reached up and snapped his headlamp on as Hilly crowded in behind him. The professor crawled forward on his hands and knees and palmed the padlock in one hand. The padlock did not require a key; instead, it had four rotating digits in its base.

As Cunningham thumbed the numbers, he said over his shoulder, "Hilly, the correct combination is simply one-two-three-four. Not very original for an ATM PIN number, but it is perfectly adequate for this purpose.

Hilly sank to her knees in the soft sand and replied as both of their headlamp beams danced over the steel bars. "One-two-three-four; got it, Doc."

He pulled the brass padlock open, removed it from the latch, and pushed the gate inward. It swung smoothly on its crude hinges. The professor picked up his pack and threw it ahead into the passageway past the gate. Holding the large flashlight in one hand, he crawled past the gate and turned toward Hilly. "When Camas and I came here two weeks ago, everything was rusted badly. We had to cut the old padlock off with a hacksaw, which took some time, and even then we couldn't move the gate. But with some time and liberal amounts of lubrication, it eventually moved. Judging by its construction, this gate has probably been here for over a hundred years and certainly locked most of the last fifty years.

He motioned Hilly forward and she crawled past him. "Why the gate and lock, Doc?"

"A lot of caves in Kentucky are gated, Hilly. Remember, most caves such as this one are on private property. Although this gate's older, there was a boom in cave exploring and tourism back in the nineteen-twenties and -thirties. People trying to make a tourist buck during the Great Depression. Then, in the last fifty years, there has been a boom in recreational caving. Cave owners wanted to protect their property, and, today, of course, there is the liability problem. I believe you saw for yourself what can happen with curious little boys." The professor closed the gate behind them, hooked the padlock through the latch on the opposite side of the gate, and snapped it shut.

Hilly was sitting on her knees and asked, "So no one's been in here much?"

"My limited research says just occasional visits by permission but not for decades and decades, maybe well over a hundred years or more. Worm Cave is virtually unknown to the world. Completely forgotten, that is, until two weeks ago, when Camas and I cut the lock."

"How did Mr. Worm know about it?"

"Oh, Hilly, there is not much the Worm family doesn't know about this area."

"I'm beginning to sense that, Doc."

"Camas told me when he visited my office, his 'granddaddy' told him about a great cave under this ridge when he was a little boy himself, and 'great,' as you'll see, doesn't even begin to describe it!"

Hilly certainly sensed the professor was getting excited about what was ahead..

As he crawled past Hilly on his hands and knees to his pack, he laughed and said, "Sorry to be crude, Hilly, but this cave up ahead, Worm Cave as you named it, is a spelunker's wet dream. It's what every caver dreams of finding, and I'm proud of being part of it." He added with enthusiasm, "Words fail to describe it." He shrugged his pack on. "And, as far as we can tell so far, this is the only entrance. On what will be your land! Damn!"

Hilly could hear the excitement in his voice rise again and echo off the walls as they crawled forward. He continued, "This is a big, big discovery, Hilly. Bigger than the Mammoth–Flint Ridge connection in 1972, bigger than Lechuguilla in 1986, and probably bigger than that of Son Doong a few years ago. And it's all yours. Like I said last night at dinner, God, how I envy you."

Hilly shook her head. Their headlamps bounced and reflected off the floor, walls, and ceiling. The cool air persistently blew past them toward the entrance, now one hundred feet behind them. There was a smell of damp limestone. She was suddenly thankful for the kneepads and again for the heavy coveralls. Lechuguilla? Son Doong? She had no idea what he was so excitedly talking—no, almost babbling—about.

The passage continued straight as they crawled along the sandy floor in silence for several more minutes. Gradually the ceiling rose until they were able to awkwardly duck-walk sideways. Hilly felt this was more difficult in some ways, but progress under the ridge was somewhat faster for them this way.

As the two made progress along the passage, Hilly scraped her helmet several times against the ceiling and was thankful to be wearing the red helmet, understanding just how it had suffered so much damage. Tired of the awkward duck-walking, she finally asked the professor, "How much farther like this, Doc?"

He turned toward her and shuffled sideways a few steps, "Just a little bit more and it opens up a bit. Do you need a break, Hilly? We can stop now and rest a little."

"No, Doc." Hilly said this while feeling how awkward it was to walk on your toes, knees bent, and with your head to one side. Despite being a runner and fitness buff, she knew her legs—hell, her whole body—would be stiff again tonight.

Finally, after some more long minutes, Hilly sensed the cave's ceiling had risen, and the professor had stopped a few yards ahead. She caught up to him, stood up, and took a few deep breaths, feeling her heart rate elevated somewhat. She could feel sweat breaking out on her forehead under her helmet's headband. She twisted her head back and forth to loosen her neck muscles and placed both hands in the small of her back as she straightened up.

She looked back down the passage. Her helmet's LED headlight was more of a wide beam and not a spot. It only illuminated about fifty feet of the passage behind them; after that was nothing but a black void with no sign of the entrance. The professor handed her an open water bottle. She took a big gulp and handed it back to him.

"If you're wondering," The professor said, "we're in about a couple of hundred yards. I'd estimate we're a good five hundred feet under the ridge by now."

Hilly looked up at the gray limestone ceiling, now barely an inch above her helmet.

The professor screwed the cap back on the water bottle and slid it into one of his pack's outside pockets, "Don't worry, Hilly, unlike mines, cave-ins in a natural cave such as this one are a rarity. I shouldn't worry about it if I were you."

They continued to walk up the passage without having to duck. Hilly asked, "Does anything live in a cave like this?"

The professor answered, "Not too much past the entrance, but there are some animals. There is some evidence of bats in this cave, but in our other few visits so far we've only seen one. It's disappointing, to say the least, as there's been a fungus going around in the Midwest the past few years decimating the bat population. Contrary to what most people think, bats are not harmful. In fact, they do much good." Then he added, "You and I shouldn't even be in here, Worm Cave, until it has been surveyed. I'm breaking some protocols, but Worm and I decided someone—namely, me—had to bring you in here. Camas Worm, by the way, does not like caves."

The passage narrowed and began to wind a little bit. The professor suddenly stopped and pointed to a small ledge on their left, which he illuminated with his headlight. "May I introduce, *Hadenoecus Subterraneous*, the common cave cricket."

Hilly jumped back. "Oh, shit, spiders!"

The two brown cave crickets were barely a foot from her arm. They were about three inches long. Two large antennas sprouted from their foreheads and flicked back and forth. The cave creatures had six long, thin legs, four in the front part of their bodies and two large jointed legs in the rear on either side of a short tail.

Professor Cunningham caught her as she jumped back and laughed. "Completely harmless, Hilly, I assure you; although they won't win any beauty contests."

The headlamps or the presence of two humans seemed to have no affect on the creatures as they flexed their antennas. Hilly remembered being told about the cave crickets when she entered the cave at the sink yesterday but didn't recall seeing any of them. But then she was concentrating on finding a ten-year-old boy.

Hilly, fascinated by the two crickets, leaned forward until she was just a few inches from them. "Pretty laid-back, huh?"

"Yes, harmless. Not much for them to fear." He looked around the passage and shrugged. "What's interesting is that these crickets aren't usually found so far into a cave. Could be they have some sort of way to the surface."

Hilly and the professor continued their hike deeper and deeper into Worm Cave. Then he suddenly stopped and took off his pack. He sat down on a wide, low, sharp-edged ledge that slanted down from the left.

Hilly caught up, "I don't need another break, Doc, if that's what you're thinking."

"No, Hilly, this is where we make a turn and leave this passage."

Hilly looked ahead into the passage they had now been walking along for, she estimated, a quarter mile. Nothing had changed. The tiny stream still trickled along the right wall, but now there was a difference in the airflow. It had increased in velocity and was flowing from beneath the ledge onto her ankles.

The professor caught her looking past him with a question on her face. "The passage we've been following dead-ends in breakdown in about fifty yards."

"Breakdown?"

"Yes, the ceiling has collapsed into the passage, and that's as far as we can go, not being a cave cricket, of course." He snapped on the powerful six-volt flashlight and played the beam down the passageway ahead of them. Just as he had said, the cave ended in a pile of large limestone slabs from floor to ceiling. On the right, the slabs glistened in the light as water trickled over them in tiny waterfalls.

The professor turned off the powerful light and set it on the sandy floor near his pack.

"I thought you told me that caves were safe."

"What I just showed you probably occurred thousands, perhaps tens of thousands, of years ago."

Hilly pointed her chin down the passageway. "So this is it? Not much of a cave. What's all the excitement about anyway?"

The professor removed the water bottle from one of his pack's pockets, unscrewed the cap, and took a gulp. He handed the open bottle to her with a smile. When she took the bottle from him, he pointed between his legs. "We're going to continue under here."

To Hilly, as she looked down, the opening under the ledge seemed to be barely two feet high. The professor rose from the ledge, sank to his knees, and then onto his stomach. His head disappeared as he peered under the ledge. "Take a look for yourself, Hilly, it's a bit of a squeeze for about fifty feet or so but not too bad."

Hilly removed her pack, took a gulp, capped the bottle, and dropped both items on the dusty floor. She sank to her knees, then her stomach, and stretched out next to the professor. She rested her head on her hands and looked ahead. She could see the dusty passage was much wider than the one at the sink. In her headlamp's glare, she estimated that it stretched a good twenty feet wide under its rough ceiling, maybe two feet high in the middle, and it tapered to an inch or so on either side.

She blew some dust from the floor, and it blew back into her face as the air came from the passage. She coughed and said, "You and Mr. Worm didn't mention this part."

The professor turned and said cheerfully, "It's elbows and knees for about seventy-five feet; then it begins to open up a bit. We'll have to push our packs ahead of us. Worm and I didn't know how you'd feel about this sort of thing again after yesterday."

"So you lied to me?"

"Well, we withheld some truth."

"You know what, Doc?"

"What's that, my dear?"

"You and Worm and everyone else underestimate me."

The professor pointed into the passage, "I'm beginning to believe that, Hilly. Ladies first, I dare say."

"No, you go first."

He reached behind for his pack, the water bottle, and the flashlight and pushed them ahead of him a few feet. "Piece of cake, Hilly."

"Yeah, piece of cake. You Brits always say shit like that. Stiff upper lip and all." Hilly answered with little conviction.

Hilly would remember this moment as the first time she actually felt curious about the cave—her cave, apparently—and where the crawl would take her. Maybe she had some spelunker in her after all.

They had been crawling in the low passage for fifteen minutes. Doc had been correct, Hilly thought, as she moved forward inch by inch. The crawl on her elbows and knees brought back long-ago memories of basic army training again. Barbed wire above, mud below, and live ammunition being fired over her head as she cradled the M16. Now the only view ahead was her dusty pack and the professor's Vibram soles. The only sound was her helmet occasionally scraping the rough ceiling and the pair's labored breathing. On either side, the wide, low crawlway's ceiling tapered steeply down to meet the dusty floor. Unlike the tight crawlspace at the sink yesterday, Hilly today felt the luxury of actually being able to turn around. It would take some effort, but she felt it could be done. Caving wasn't for the obese.

The professor was raising some dust in his forward progress, and she had to spit every few minutes as his dust blew back in her face. The professor had explained to her and the Worms that the cave was breathing when they were feeling the air exiting the cave at the entrance. Had he known this when he offered to let her go first into this crawlway? Was it cave etiquette of some sort? She was learning.

Hilly heard him grunt ahead and then saw him raise his torso. Then his lower body as he stood up, and then she was just looking at his boots and coverall-covered ankles. She inched forward and realized they were emerging from under a ledge into a passageway similar to the first one. She cleared the ledge and came to her knees. The professor offered her his hand, and she came to her feet.

She looked up and down the new passageway with her headlamp as she dusted herself off. She saw detail in her light's glare. This passageway contained no water and had perhaps had an inch of fine dust on its floor. She quickly noticed there were footprints in only one direction. Puzzled, Hilly pointed down the unmolested passageway and asked, "What's this way?"

The professor answered, "Ah, Hilly, we'll make a spelunker out of you yet! The fact is, we don't have a clue what is in that direction just yet. A caver always likes to ask the one important question, 'Does it go?' meaning how far and if he or she might be the first."

"Does it go?"

"Yes, that's the question generally."

She laughed and pointed down the passageway, "No, damn it, does it go, Doc?"

"Oh, forgive me, I misunderstood. Like I said, we don't know just yet. Perhaps you'll find out yourself some day. After all, it's to become your cave soon, Hilly." He turned, hefted up his pack, picked up the flashlight, and walked the other way.

Hilly walked a few feet in the other direction until she stood exactly where the footprints stopped near where she had crawled out from under the ledge. She put one foot in the smooth dust, withdrew her boot, and looked at the footprint she had left. She whistled in amazement to herself as she turned, put on her pack, and followed the professor.

They walked along the passageway for another ten minutes, edging deeper under the ridge overhead, before the second passageway, too, ended abruptly like the first in a pile of large limestone slabs that Hilly now knew as "breakdown."

The professor knelt on the dusty floor of the passage and looked under a huge, slab of limestone that slanted down toward them from the left side of the cave. He turned toward Hilly, "Sorry, only one more tight spot, I promise. We can squeeze through here with our packs on no problem. Height less of a problem than width. I'll go first, but this time I want you to wait here until I call, OK?"

Hilly looked back the way they had come and then at the opening under the slab of limestone. She had the feeling they were now a long, long way inside the cave. "Shouldn't we leave some bread crumbs or something, Doc?"

"Bread crumbs? Oh, I see. Hansel and Gretel you mean?" He chuckled. "The cave is not too complicated after this, I promise. In the old days, when spelunkers used carbide lamps like the miners did, they would draw arrows on the rocks with the soot of their flame pointing out at any questionable junction. Mind you, always pointing out. But this arrow drawing defaced the cave. Now everyone uses electric lights, so that habit went away. What we've done so far is pretty simple. I dare say, you could find your way out. And remember caves look different going the other way. Nowadays we use colorful flagging tape to mark the way out. I have some here in my pack and would've used it if I knew you were becoming uncomfortable."

"Don't worry, Doc. I'm OK, I guess."

The professor said, "Right!" and went forward on his hands and knees. He started crawling forward, looked over his shoulder, and reminded Hilly, "Wait here until I call."

Hilly sat down on the dusty floor, leaned her pack against the rough rock wall, and stretched her legs out across the passageway. She wondered what the professor had in store for her now, and started to think maybe she should have stayed in Detroit.

In a few minutes, she heard the professor's muffled call. "OK, your turn!"

Hilly came up on her hands and knees, ducked under the limestone slab, and crawled forward. Her headlamp revealed that she was not in a cave passage, as before, but actually crawling under huge blocks of limestone that had fallen across each other. Nervous, she wondered whether the professor had been correct about caves being stable and that these rocks had indeed been in place for thousands of years.

She took a turn around yet another large chunk of limestone and now could see the professor ahead in her headlamp. Cold air was now pouring through the blocks of limestone and around her. She could see that he had taken off his helmet and turned the headlamp off. He had switched on the big six-volt flashlight and was playing it around in front of him. As she crawled yet closer, she saw that he appeared to be sitting on a ledge of some kind.

She emerged from under the last slab of limestone to one side of the professor. He switched off the six-volt and placed it next his helmet. She saw he was indeed sitting on a ledge with his feet over the edge.

He turned to her and said, "Be careful now, it's quite a drop."

She came alongside him still on her hands and knees and stopped. Then she sat up and rocked back on her heels. Her headlamp was now the only light for both of them. Hilly looked from side to side and up and down. She was speechless. She couldn't comprehend. Everywhere she looked beyond their tiny rock ledge was absolute darkness. The silence was deafening.

CHAPTER 29

Concordia

The professor broke the silence. "Impressive, isn't it?"

She was still sitting on her heels next to him trying to make sense of it all. She answered in a whisper, "Impressive? An understatement. I can't find words, Doc. It's awesome. Breathtaking."

"That's what all my students said, Hilly. Awesome."

She looked to the left and then to the right with her helmet's headlight. Nothing appeared in its suddenly inadequate beam. Then she looked up where there should have been a ceiling. Nothing. She pointed the beam downward and still nothing. There was nothing to focus on. She suddenly felt dizzy and put her hand on the professor's shoulder to steady herself. He reached up and held her hand.

He said, "We call this place the Opera Box."

"The Opera Box?"

Still holding her hand, he replied as he switched on the more powerful six-volt light with the other hand, "Most appropriate. Cavers are always giving names to things."

The powerful blue-white beam shot out in front of them over the abyss. He played the beam upward, and Hilly could see there was indeed a smooth, gray ceiling at the limit of the beam. As he aimed it downward, she could make out a jumble of rocks and slabs far below them.

She withdrew her hand and he turned toward her. All she could say was, "*Wow!*"

He turned back toward the cave and continued to point the beam in all directions. "Yes, Wow! I dare say, that word doesn't cover it. We undoubtedly are looking at maybe the largest cavern in the world!" He hesitated, turned back to her, and added in a conspiratory tone. "And it soon will all belong to you."

Hilly took a deep breath and let it out.

"Of course, it hasn't been properly surveyed yet, but we estimate that the ceiling up there," he pointed the light beam upward again, "is three or four hundred feet above us." He played the beam downward. "And the floor down there is roughly another three or four hundred feet below us, making, we think, this cavern roughly eight hundred feet high. The same as an eighty-story building!"

The professor leveled the beam. "And we can't even see the far side from here. My students and I estimate this cavern—no, passageway—to be roughly a quarter of a mile wide. Just think of that! Yes, my students all said, 'Awesome!' almost in unison when they first crawled out here."

Hilly was still in awe. She whispered to him again, "Better than awesome, Doc. Words can't describe this."

"An eighth natural wonder of the world, in my opinion. And there's more."

"More?"

"You noticed I said, 'passageway'?"

Hilly shook her head, "Don't tell me…"

"Yes, it seems this is a gigantic passageway running under the ridge over us." He played the powerful light to their left. "To the left, or west, is one of the world's largest areas of breakdown. We don't know how high that mountain of rock is yet, even if it fills the cave in that direction, or if a person can actually climb to the top and continue."

Hilly asked, "So you don't know if, in caver jargon, 'it goes'?"

"So right, Hilly. We figure if it goes, the cave will end in that direction in a few miles where this ridge, Worm Ridge, ends at the West Fork of the Sun River."

"And to the right, or east?"

"No one knows quite yet. We think this incredible passageway, cavern, could go for miles in that direction under the ridge. We, my students and I, have only been roughly a half mile in that direction yet. To a place we've named Concordia."

Puzzled, Hilly asked, "Concordia?"

"A very special place." He would not say more.

Hilly looked around the ledge. "Sounds interesting. I feel like Dorothy. Show me how we get to Oz, Doc?"

The professor smiled and answered, "I'm very pleased you said that, Hilly, although, believe me, there's no Yellow Brick Road. It will take some effort. To tell you the truth, before everyone met you a few days ago and, ah, saw the things that have followed so far, I was prepared to take you only this far. Yes, we underestimated you." He paused and pointed, "First, we have to climb down to the floor."

He stood carefully and brushed the dust off the seat of his pants. He offered Hilly his hand, and she came to her feet next to him, carefully keeping some distance from the edge of the Opera Box. He picked up his pack, threw it onto his back, and put on his helmet. He adjusted the elastic chin strap, snapped on the headlight, and picked up the six-volt. With that, he brushed by her, stooped, and ducked back under the slab of limestone slanting down behind them.

Hilly followed closely.

The professor came to his knees then sat with his legs stretched out in front of him. He worked his way forward and downward in a sitting position while ducking under the slab. This time he went to the right instead of back along the initial crawlway that had brought them out to the Opera Box. Hilly did the same and began to understand the reason for the coveralls.

He grunted as he spoke to her. "Here to the right a bit, or to the left as we were sitting on the ledge, is a very large piece of limestone leaning out from the cave wall. We couldn't see it from up there on our perch. Don't worry, it's probably been leaning for hundreds of centuries. The space between it and the wall has filled in over the eons, creating somewhat of a stairway for us. In fact, one of my students, Shelley, whose gear you're using, named it the Giant's Stairway."

The professor came out from under the slab and stood, bracing himself with one hand on the cave wall and holding the six-volt flashlight in the other. The Giant's Stairway angled down in front of him between the cave's south wall and the gigantic piece of limestone. The space between was perhaps four feet wide.

Hilly stood, brushed off the seat of her coveralls, and came up behind him. She placed both hands on his shoulders, and peered down the gigantic crack.

He switched on the powerful light and shone it down ahead of them.

Hilly looked down past his shoulder at the supposed stairway. Jammed into the narrow space were rocks and slabs of limestone of all sizes. The stairway slanted steeply downward into the darkness. She also noticed what appeared to be two lengths of climbing rope. The first began just below them and ran down along the left side of the stairway, at which point another rope began on the right and disappeared into the darkness beyond the flashlight's powerful beam. "Some stairway, Doc."

He answered, "The ropes are an aid. We rigged them up a couple of days ago. Nothing technical, I assure you. I'm not a big fan of rock climbing, rappelling, and all that. We'll descend here some two hundred feet vertically and then things level out somewhat until the floor."

"If you say so, Doc."

He looked over his shoulder at her. "Ready?"

Hilly gave him a slight push. "You first, I'll be right behind you."

He made a small Catholic cross gesture across his chest. Hilly's eyes widened. The professor saw her expression, laughed, and said, "Just kidding, Hilly." She balled up a fist and hit him square on top of his helmet. He made a small jump to a rock below and descended along the Giant's Stairway.

The gigantic limestone slab loomed higher and higher on their right as did the cave wall on their left, as the pair descended in the narrow space between. Mostly the descent involved squatting and then jumping down to a lower rock. Both Hilly and the professor used the affixed climbing ropes to balance themselves. The careful descent of the Stairway took them twenty minutes.

At the base of the Giant's Stairway, the professor stopped, leaned back against the limestone, and waited for Hilly to catch up. He checked his watch. They had been in the cave some ninety minutes. He switched on the powerful six-volt light as Hilly landed nearby and brushed off her coveralls. In the beam Hilly could see that the remaining distance to the cave's floor was at a much shallower angle over a jumble of large limestone slabs that she guessed at one time had crashed down from the ceiling or calved from the cave's wall. To Hilly it looked almost like a pathway in a flower garden. As they rested for a moment, she pointed ahead and asked, "Can I name the rest of the way down the Giant's Stepping Stones?

The professor smiled and answered, "Sure, why not? It's almost your cave after all. You can name it anything you want, Hilly. So now we have the Giant's Stairway and the Giant's Stepping Stones. Right-O!"

Hilly started to move forward but halted when the professor didn't move with her.

He switched off the six-volt and placed the side of one hand at chest level against the huge limestone rock he had been leaning against. He said, "I was hoping you would want to continue beyond the Opera Box, Hilly, because I wanted to show you something."

She answered, "Yes?"

"We had Deputy Big pick you up and show you the dam site last night on purpose, Hilly."

Hilly shook her head, "We? On purpose?"

"Yes, to show you where Corps of Engineers is building the highest dam east of the Mississippi for billions of taxpayer dollars." He sawed his hand back and forth on the rough limestone rock next to them. "Right here, give or take a few feet, is just about where we estimate the water level to be in this cave when the dam is completed in about three years."

Hilly looked at his hand in her headlight, then up toward the ceiling, and finally down toward the floor of the cave. The ride with Big had been planned all along, she realized now. They did have the vandalism call, but Big no doubt would have taken her there anyway on a routine patrol most likely. Now, gazing around, she was beginning to realize for the first time that the dam was not only going to affect families living up in remote valleys, or fishing, or kayaking, and all the other things that are eliminated when a free-flowing river simply disappears forever, but that Worm Cave—her cave; no, she was beginning to think of it as everyone's cave now—would be flooded and lost forever.

She was speechless for the second time in an hour but finally managed to whisper, "Shit, half the cave will be flooded."

"Yes," the professor answered, "to a depth of almost two hundred and fifty feet. Maybe deeper. Right now it's just a rough estimate."

"Does anyone else know this?"

He waved his hand around, "Not yet but I'm sure the Corps will be delighted in a twisted way to know about all this additional 'reservoir' for flood control." The professor turned and continued downward toward the cave's floor. "Follow me. It's not all I have to show you, Hilly."

They continued to descend, hopping from one giant boulder to another. Hilly noticed that, although the gaps between the Giant's Stepping Stones were not wide, at the most three feet and easy to jump over, she had to be careful as the black depths between the steps were sometimes over twenty feet.

The last step was a large flat slab of limestone tilted on its side. It acted as a ramp down toward what appeared to be a pile of sand and gravel. The professor stopped at the edge of this last step and jumped down the last two feet to the cave floor, landing with both feet onto the sand. Hilly followed. Coming up behind him, she was surprised to see in the light of their headlamps that they were actually standing on a small sandbar that sloped down into the small riffles of a stream of very clear water. The water was so clear that when Hilly looked upstream at the small pool above the riffles, she only saw the sandy bottom in her light. She knew the water was there, but it had simply disappeared as if by magic. If she hadn't known better, she would have simply stumbled into it. The pool could be inches or feet deep, she thought.

They stood and listened to the sound of the small stream for a moment. Then the professor switched on the flashlight. The stream at their feet was barely four feet wide as it ran between its sandy banks. Beyond the tiny stream on its far side, the cave's floor was flat, smooth limestone, unlike the side they had just descended, and was littered with large boulders scattered here and there.

He swept the beam upward. The far wall appeared smooth, sheer, and somewhat concave, as high as they could see, hundreds of feet. Hilly thought it looked like the inside half of a giant pipe. She placed a hand on the professor's shoulder once again and said, "I hate to keep saying this, but, *wow!*"

He replied, "Yes, very impressive. And it gets better." With that he made a leap across the stream and landed with a crunch in the gravel on the other side. He turned and offered his hand as Hilly made her own leap.

She suddenly asked, "Is the water in this stream drinkable? It's so amazingly clear."

The professor took off his pack, opened a large pocket along the side, and handed Hilly the now half-full water bottle. "Usually a stream of this size in a cave is referred to as a river, believe it or not." He pointed down. "This one is still unnamed, so put your thinking cap on." He continued, "I suppose the water is safe, but keep in mind we don't know its source and it hasn't been tested. But in a pinch I'd drink it. Good Lord, it's probably been filtered quite enough!"

Hilly took a few swallows and handed the bottle back. She laughed, "I'll think about a name, but I think we've sort of overdone it with the word *giant*, and it's pretty small."

The professor set the water bottle next to his pack, walked upstream, and stood by the edge of the nearly invisible pool. He motioned for Hilly to join him while shining the flashlight into the apparently depthless water. "Come this way, I want to show you something interesting, Hilly."

She walked upstream to where the professor was standing, while still marveling at the clarity of the water. In her headlamp it was still difficult to know where the stream bank ended and the water began. Every rock, pebble, and grain of sand on the pool's bottom was crystal clear. The pool could have been five inches deep or five feet deep. If a person didn't know it was there, Hilly felt it would have been possible to walk into the water with no warning.

And, in fact, the professor stopped her from going farther for just that reason with his free hand. "Now halt right there," he said as he played the six-volt's beam around the pool. There was a large, square boulder on the far side of the pool that the water had undercut somewhat. The professor squatted and aimed the beam in the water and under the rock as Hilly watched.

Suddenly he whispered excitedly, "There's one, no two!"

Hilly squinted but saw nothing. Then she saw the two small, white creatures move on the pool's bottom. "Oh! I see them, too!" she said under her breath.

The professor said, "*Cambarus pellucides*, the blind crayfish. A very rare and endangered species, but from what we can tell in such a short time, we think they thrive here in…er, Worm Cave."

Hilly asked, "Completely blind?"

"Yes, they live all their lives in complete darkness. No need for eyes."

She watched the two small crayfish. "What do they eat?"

"Mind you, I'm not a biologist, but I've been told by colleagues they eat organic matter washed into the cave, which gives me the idea there must be hundreds of surface openings for a cave this vast. Openings for all kinds of small animals but not large enough for a human except one."

The professor played the light to his left. He whispered excitedly again, "Look, Hilly, we're in luck, a blind fish, too, *Amblyopsis spelaea*, and in the same pool! And there, another one!"

Hilly squinted at the upper end of the pool just downstream from another series of riffles. "Yes, I see them, too!" The two small, completely white fish were darting back and forth and coming in their direction. Hilly observed, "The light doesn't seem to bother them or the crayfish."

"Nor should it, but they would sense something immediately if we were to disturb the bottom or raise our voices. But in reality they have no natural enemies or predators but humans."

"Us?"

Unfortunately, yes. Both these animals are on the endangered species list. Pollution mainly. And dams, of course."

"I'm beginning to understand." Hilly replied.

The two watched the small white creatures in silence for a few minutes. As the professor turned to retrieve his pack, he slyly asked Hilly, "Do you think creatures as small as those crayfish or fish have the might to stop a two-billion-dollar dam?" Then he winked and added, "Maybe we just might find out, if their existence in this cave becomes known, of course."

Hilly walked upstream with the professor along the underground river. They occasionally stopped at one of the nearly invisible pools to look for blind crayfish or fish. They spotted a few more of the rare creatures.

To Hilly the underground river seemed to divide the huge cavern's floor into two distinct areas. Her helmet's headlight was limited, but to their right or south of the river, was a rugged landscape of huge boulders and blocks of limestone that rose steeply above them to the distant wall, just as it had in the area they had climbed down from the Opera Box. To their left, the cave's floor was fairly smooth and flat and seemed to rise gradually to meet the north wall somewhere in the distant darkness.

Hilly and the professor kept to the north river bank, where the walking was much easier. A short distance ahead, the professor stopped and waited for Hilly to come alongside him. She noticed a tiny rivulet of water nearby running out of the darkness to their left and emptying—no, dripping—over a small ledge into the river.

He pointed into the darkness toward the north wall and said, "We'll leave the river here for a side excursion, Hilly, but we'll come back eventually."

Hilly pointed with her chin at the clear pool near where they stood. "I've been thinking and I want to declare this body of water to be named henceforth the Invisible River."

The professor laughed, "Good show! Henceforth and everything. Sounds official to me. The Invisible River it is!" Then he added, "Follow me up this tributary; I have something to show you!" He started for the north wall, and Hilly followed.

For a while they walked in silence along the smooth, gray limestone floor, each in the small pool of light at their feet from their headlights with absolute blackness and silence now surrounding them in all directions. Now, more than ever, Hilly sensed the vastness of Worm Cave. She hurried a few steps to keep the professor within her headlamp's range. He had quite a stride, she was discovering, and he hiked along swinging his arms with the six-volt in one hand.

Suddenly, he stopped and held his hand up. She almost ran into him. "Do you hear that, Hilly?"

Hilly listened for a moment. "Hear what? I don't hear anything."

"Exactly. Now look around." Hilly turned completely around and then looked up and down. The almost-level floor slanted away into the darkness toward the river. The ceiling above was more invisible than the blackest night's sky.

The professor reached up with his free hand and switched off his headlight. He nodded at her, "Now you do the same and then hold your breath for a moment."

She did as he asked. The blackness and silence were absolute. Hilly held her breath. No sound except maybe a little ringing in her ears. The sound of her heartbeat? Blood rushing through her arteries? She held one of her hands in front of her face and slowly brought it toward her. She saw nothing, even as she touched her nose. Amazing! Finally, she said, "Doc?" No answer. Then, "Professor Cunningham?" Still no answer. She reached up, fumbled a bit finding the headlight's switch, and turned it on. After the darkness, the sudden blue-white light hurt her eyes.

There was no professor.

Hilly turned quickly. Her heart was pounding with a little uncharacteristic panic. He had moved quietly when their lights were out and was now standing to one side.

"Not funny, Doc."

He switched his headlamp back on. "An old commercial cave trick I'm afraid. Tour guides all turn the lights off at some point in for the tourists."

"And you're no exception on this tour, right?"

"Had to be done. Tradition and all." He turned and continued along the small rivulet toward the north wall.

Hilly followed and asked, "How do you know where you're going? I'm afraid I'm a little turned around now for some reason. Right now I sort of feel I'm walking on a different, distant planet."

He stopped and took a rectangular object from his pocket. At first Hilly thought it might be a cell phone. "It helps," he said, "to have a sense of direction and recognize landmarks. Or to leave colored tape at critical junctions, as I explained before." He held up the object. "But I do have this compass with me."

He held it out and Hilly took it. She was familiar with compasses from her early days of army field exercises and held it flat in front of her, aligning north with the tip of the compass's needle. Sure enough, it pointed in the direction they were walking, which made sense—the north wall of the cave. As she handed it back to him she said, "I would never have thought of using an old-fashioned compass or even that it would work in a cave."

"Of course the compass works! A compass works anywhere on earth for the most part. A compass is one of the tools we use to map a cave, along with a measuring tape of some kind and a notebook. The method for mapping a cave has not changed in centuries."

"I hate to ask, but what about GPS?"

The professor looked up and asked, "See any satellites?"

"Of course not!" She answered.

"There's your answer!"

"Point taken, Doc."

They continued along the flat surface of the cave as it slanted ever so slightly up toward the north wall. Hilly looked around but could see nothing outside the pool of their headlamps. She commented again, as she walked behind the professor, "Except for a lack of a spacesuit and some stars, I still feel I could be walking on the surface of some distant planet."

"Yes, good comparison, actually. We're in a very alien environment on the planet Earth. Not what we're used to certainly."

Hilly yelled, "Beam me up, Scotty!" The professor looked back at her and pretended to frown.

Their path suddenly steepened, and Hilly sensed they were reaching the north wall of the cave, which would have to tower above them. The professor stopped and again switched on the more powerful flashlight.

Hilly looked around with her helmet's headlamp. Extending in front of them and perhaps fifty feet to each side was a smooth, wet, multicolored—mostly browns and whites—magnificent waterfall of stone. Breathtaking. She had never seen anything like it. Hilly quickly leaned forward to touch the front edge of the stone waterfall, but the professor grabbed her wrist to prevent it. Puzzled, Hilly turned and looked up at him.

He said, "Mustn't touch it. Very sensitive. The oils from the tips of your fingers will divert the tiny film of water from the area you just touched, and growth, the slow deposit of minerals over centuries, will stop."

She straightened, and he released her wrist. "Sorry, I didn't realize. What is it? It's beautiful!"

It's called flowstone. He aimed the powerful flashlight's beam upward.

Hilly followed the light and caught her breath. The flowstone clung to the immense north wall in what looked like hundreds of feet of brown draperies or curtains or even what looked like slices of stone bacon, even beyond the range of the light. She whispered in awe, "It's breathtaking!"

"One of my students, Jeremy, found this a few days ago. He named it Angel Falls.

"Named after the highest waterfall in the world, obviously."

He looked up, "Yes, the rest of us thought the name very appropriate."

"What is it?"

"You mean the composition?"

"Yes."

"Over thousands or even millions of years, rainwater seeps though the limestone layers above us and ever so slowly dissolves it. That process, of course, is what makes a cave, but to make the flowstone," he played the flashlight's beam up and down the immense formation again, "the water carrying the dissolved limestone from above seeps slowly down the wall and deposits it to form the flowstone or calcite, a stable form of calcium carbonate." He paused and continued, "At a rate, I might add, of about an inch every hundred years."

"But we're looking at hundreds of feet here."

"Yes, indeed."

"Incredible. Just the base of this formation is a hundred feet wide."

"It's hard to contemplate geologic time, Hilly." The professor turned off the six-volt. "Follow me, Hilly, I want to show you something else Jeremy found on his detour. After that, I know a perfect spot where we can eat some lunch."

They skirted the north wall in silence as Hilly tried to wrap her mind around just how long Mother Nature had taken to make a cave the size of this one. The professor took a detour to their right around a jumble of massive boulders as the cave floor rose higher. They climbed for another hundred yards, and then, just as the cave's floor plunged steeply, the professor turned left around one of the last massive limestone boulders and began to pick his way along the slope back to the north wall.

Suddenly he stopped and Hilly caught up with him. He appeared to be standing in front of a tree trunk—a very large tree trunk perhaps ten feet in diameter. In the limited light from their headlamps, Hilly could dimly see more of these formations to their left in a scene reminding her of something from a fairy tale illustration or perhaps a Hobbit movie. She quickly realized the massive tree trunk was also flowstone of a type like Angel Falls, only an immense column.

The professor again switched on the light. "Welcome to the Redwood Forest." He shined the six volt's beam up and down the massive column in front of them, and then played the light to the left, revealing three similar massive columns. He explained, "This one and the other three columns have the same basic makeup as Angel Falls, but instead of flowing down the wall of the cave and depositing the minerals in that manner, these massive stalagmites, or columns, were formed over eons by a slow, steady drip from somewhere above. Remember an average of a cubic inch per century, Hilly. They haven't been officially measured, but we estimate these columns to be eighty to hundred feet high. And remember somewhere above us are probably their counterparts, stalactites, hanging at this very moment over our heads."

Hilly stood quietly in front of the magnificent column for a moment, smiled, and said, "Good thing we're wearing helmets!" Then she asked, "No touching again?"

The professor shook his head in the negative.

She commented, "Hard not to, it's so beautiful!"

The professor looked at his watch. "We've been at it for a few hours, and I don't know about you, but I've worked up an appetite. So if you'll follow me, I know a perfect spot for an early lunch." He switched off the large flashlight, rounded the massive column, and started to pick his way down a rocky slope.

Soon the slope leveled out and they were again standing near another smaller, clear stream or cave river. Hilly said, "This river doesn't look the same. Much smaller."

The professor stopped. "Yes, this is the North Fork. I guess it's now the North Fork of the Invisible River. We'll follow it downstream to the confluence of what is for the time being the North Fork and the East Fork, which form the Invisible River, as you named it. It's that special place I told you about before we descended from the Opera Box that we call Concordia."

Once more, Hilly asked, "Concordia?"

He continued walking. "I'll explain in a minute. Not much farther."

They followed the tiny stream of water and soon came to a large, thigh-high block of limestone in front of which the small stream flowed into a larger one. The professor set the six-volt on the limestone block and shrugged off his pack. He picked up the flashlight and turned around.

Hilly took off her pack and leaned it against the block next to the professor's.

He switched on the powerful light and said nothing. Hilly turned and gasped as she followed the beam upward. Rising above them hundreds of feet appeared to be the sharp prow of a gigantic ship. On either side were massive passageways angling into the darkness.

The professor whispered, "Welcome to Concordia."

They stood in silence. Finally Hilly shook her head and said, "Words fail me. I don't know what to say, Doc."

The professor switched off the light. "Don't say anything, but imagine if suddenly we could light everything up." He thumbed back over his shoulder. "We could take it all in at once, Angel Falls, the Redwoods, Concordia here, and who knows what else we haven't seen. This is as far as we've come." He sat on the limestone block and began pulling things from his pack and laying them on the flat rock beside him.

She asked, "Why the name Concordia?"

"It's the name of the Roman goddess of harmony. I'd never heard of it either in any other context, but one of my students had been to one of its namesakes on a trek. It's apparently the name given to the junction of two huge glaciers in Pakistan near the mountain K2. We thought it seemed appropriate." The professor continued, "This is truly a UNESCO World Heritage Site and then some, Hilly."

Hilly sat on the block next to him. "I've heard of World Heritage. I took a trip one summer to Norway when I was in the army. There's a fjord…"

"Geirangerfjord. Yes, I've been there, too. A dramatic sight, a world-class view. I've been as well to some of the others such as Yosemite, the Grand Canyon, the Great Barrier Reef, Yellowstone, Carlsbad Caverns, Machu Picchu, and some cathedrals such as Chartres…there are almost a thousand sites, and I'm sure your Worm Cave will eventually join them, Hilly."

"Yes, I've been to Chartres, too." Hilly hesitated and then swept a hand in front of her, at Concordia. "But this is better than any cathedral, most cathedrals."

The professor nodded into the darkness. "Yes, I agree. These two passageways could go on for miles yet…who knows what wonders we'll find…

Hilly whispered to herself, "One person just can't own all this." Then she gave the professor a sharp look of understanding.

The professor said nothing but just nodded. "I was hoping you'd say that, Hilly, or something similar." He smiled as he pulled a fat, white candle from his pack and fished a waterproof match container from his pocket. He placed the candle between them on the rock, struck a match with his thumb, and held its flame to the candle's wick until it caught. He blew out the match, pinched it between his thumb and forefinger, and carefully placed it back in the waterproof container. Next he brought out two large sandwiches wrapped in wax paper, two small plastic containers with blue snap-on lids, and two plastic forks. He placed the containers and forks between them and handed Hilly one of the wrapped sandwiches.

The professor held his sandwich with one hand and reached up and switched off his headlight with the other. Hilly followed his lead. She was surprised at the amount of light the single candle put out. It easily illuminated the area around them.

The professor busied himself with unwrapping his sandwich. "I hope this is what I think it is. Ah, yes!" He took a bite, smacked his lips, and exclaimed, "A Worm Café lunch specialty!"

Hilly unwrapped her sandwich and peeled back the top slice of bread, revealing a thick slice of meatloaf nestled in mayonnaise under a thick slice of cheese and slices of hard-boiled egg.

The professor gently spread out the wax paper wrapping next to him and laid his sandwich on it. Then he fished in his pack and brought out a full water bottle.

Hilly took a bite of her sandwich and caught a slice of egg on her lip with a finger as it fell from her mouth. With her mouth full, she mumbled, "Mmmm, a heart attack waiting to happen, but delicious!"

The professor picked up a fork and tapped one of the containers as he passed the water bottle to her. "Some of the very best potato salad you're ever going to sample, I dare say. Mouths full, they sat in silence as the Invisible River gurgled over its pebbles at their feet in the candlelight.

Hilly placed her sandwich on its wrapper and picked up the potato salad container and plastic fork. She pried off the lid, laid it next to the half-eaten sandwich, and put a forkful in her mouth. She mumbled again with her mouth full, "Mmmm, delicious. Mr. Worm knows how to run a restaurant. Nice of him to fix lunch for us."

The professor swallowed, "You need to know he's no saint. Food is not all he has a recipe for, Hilly."

"Meaning what exactly?" She asked.

"Meaning moonshine. White lightning. Hooch."

"Moonshine?"

"Yes, alcohol. I guess we can call it moonshine for lack of a better term. Camas Worm and his family are probably some of the biggest producers of illegal whiskey in the state—maybe the whole South, I've been told from anonymous sources."

"Whiskey?"

"Maybe you know, but a lot of counties in Kentucky are dry, meaning no liquor sales. Even in counties where it is produced legally. The Worm family has been filling the demand for over a hundred and seventy-five years. In fact, your great-grandfather, the man you're an heir to, actually supplied the Worm family with corn for decades before he died. Still does, in fact, even in death, through the farm's caretaker, as I understand it. Half that corn you see out there is destined for the Worm family's stills."

Hilly put down her fork and sighed. The professor chuckled and read her mind, "Yes, you're not only inheriting this fabulous cave on Thursday, but you're going to be in cahoots with a sort of moonshine cartel."

"How many people know about this?"

"Just about everybody but you, Hilly."

"Everybody?"

"Oh, yes. Your lawyer Rice, the judge presiding Thursday, and the sheriff. It's no secret in Batavia."

"Even the sheriff?"

"Especially the sheriff. A long tradition in this county. Like I said, goes back a hundred and seventy-five years or more. Everybody gets a little cut of the action."

"I met him. He seemed honest enough. Shit, a war hero."

"You have to understand that making whiskey illegally here is not exactly viewed as particularly bad by a lot of people."

"Who buys it?"

"Well, the locals for sure out the back door of the Worm Café most likely."

"Right next door to the courthouse?"

"I'm sure some regular customers work there, too."

Hilly shook her head.

The professor continued, "A lot of it I understand goes north. As you probably know firsthand, there's still a lot of strong ties with people up there."

That's for sure, Hilly thought. Including myself. Big time in this case.

"I've even had a little taste myself. Pretty good, but kind of a higher proof than I'm used to."

"You, too?"

The professor waved a hand in front of him in the candlelight. "My involvement all started about three weeks ago when Mr. Worm paid a visit to the university. I usually keep my office door open. I was reading a student's paper when he knocked. I looked up, and there was Camas Worm himself standing in the doorway all spruced up and dressed in his Sunday finest holding his hat in one hand. He introduced himself and asked if I was Dr. Cunningham. I have to admit, I had never heard such a surname as Worm. I've since found out it is German. I said I was indeed Dr. Cunningham. He then asked me if I knew anything about caves."

"So this cave, this sure-thing of a World Heritage Site, was some sort of secret between the Worms and my great-grandfather? How could this have been kept hidden from the world?"

"I've since started to do a little research, and there is indeed a mention here and there in the early 1800s, long before the Civil War, of a great cave in this area of Kentucky. It became sort of a legend in this area. But as the interest in caving grew and cave tourism became popular, no one had apparently been able to find anything in this area, and it was soon forgotten as the area around Mammoth Cave to the northwest of here got everybody's attention. Just as there's a legend in this area about buried treasure but nothing's ever been found." He thought for a moment, "Hmmmm, just had an original thought that maybe the two could be related?" He shook his head and said, "I don't see how, but it's an idea."

Hilly said, "I interrupted you."

"Oh, well, yes. Mr. Worm came to my office those weeks ago to tell me about this cave, Worm Cave, as we're calling it now. With your great-grandfather's death and the beginning of the dam construction, the Worm family's hand was forced so to speak, and they had to show someone—me, in this case—the cave."

Hilly replied, "How's that? I sense they like to keep to themselves. For Camas Worm to come to your office?"

"Yes, they are clannish."

Hilly looked around in the darkness. "There are groups, 'greenies,' the locals call them, who oppose the dam because they want the river to remain free-flowing. When they find out about this cave, it's a no-brainer. That's why you brought me here to see it for myself."

"Yes, indeed."

"Well, it worked, Doc."

"There's more to it, I'm afraid."

"More?"

"Remember I told you the Worms are no saints?"

"Yes."

"Well, I'm sure one of the factors that brought Camas Worm to my office is the cave. Nobody wants it flooded, even them. Kind of ironic they're on the side of the greenies, as you call them. But the Worms were starting to branch out a few years ago into, ah, another product line, so to speak. It apparently can be grown quite well up in these hills and hollows. The climate is very conducive."

"Let me guess, marijuana?"

"Good guess, Hilly."

"I smelled it as we walked by the barn this morning."

"Well, yes, I guess a policewoman like yourself would know a little about that, er, product."

"So the Worms are growing pot now besides the moonshine business?"

"It's a bit more complicated at the moment. I'll explain." The professor paused and looked up toward the cave's ceiling. "Hilly, don't forget that the Worm family owns the eastern half of Worm Ridge up there." He pointed in front of them into the darkness. "You have the only entrance, but somewhere down those passages the cave becomes Worm property. A 1933 ruling of the Kentucky courts states that the owner of any land owns it to the center of the Earth."

"So my great-grandfather was in cahoots with not only moonshiners but pot growers in and around Worm Ridge?"

"Well, not quite. That's where it begins to get complicated, I'm afraid, according to Camas Worm."

"Complicated?"

"Your great-grandfather didn't mind the moonshining, tradition and all, and he had somewhat of a taste for it himself, but he wouldn't allow the marijuana growing on his land."

"But the barn…?"

The professor took a bite of his sandwich, swallowed, and continued, "After your great-grandfather died—as I understand it, after what Mr. Worm told me in my office that day—it became known that apparently there was no heir to his thousands of acres of land, including his portion of Worm Ridge and beyond to the north. Thousands of acres of private forest land, which is much less susceptible to DEA searches from what he told me than public lands, and in a county wherein the sheriff might look the other way in exchange for a 'donation,' would come up for a public auction after a few rulings. Money has changed hands with other public officials, too, of course."

"So it's not the Worms' pot I smelled."

"No, about a year ago this other faction which even the Worms fear moved in and set up shop in anticipation of being able to buy the land when it was auctioned. According to Mr. Worm, a lot of the deep pockets and muscle comes from south of the border, if you know what I mean, although everything seems to be based in Atlanta at present. According to Mr. Worm, the marijuana business is booming. Recreational marijuana is now legal in Colorado and Washington State, with more states on the way to legalizing it. The demand will only increase according to Mr. Worm."

"So basically there are squatters on my great-grandfather's land above us growing pot."

"Yes, according to Mr. Worm, they are starting to harvest their first crop as the Worm family looks on and is powerless."

"Using my great-grandfather's barn for storage."

The professor took another bite of his sandwich. "And don't forget the Atlanta people are not the only interested party. There's a Korean car company that wants the land out by the interstate and railroad, a big-box discount company, and developers who want the land in and near what will be lakefront property when the dam is completed in a few years, to name a few. Apparently who gets what in the future auction appears to have been settled some time ago. The judge, who's in on it, too, is to rule your great-grandfather's land goes to the state of Kentucky this Thursday at nine o'clock."

Hilly ate another forkful of potato salad and paused to think. She mused, "And then along comes Hildegard Walker as the heir apparent thanks to L. T. Rice, and suddenly a big wrench has been thrown into the works."

The professor finished his sandwich and licked his fingers. "Yes, exactly!"

Hilly thought for a moment and reached in her pack. The Beretta was still there. "If I had to guess, I'd say offhand that it's not the lakeshore developers or the Koreans who want me out of the way, huh?"

"No, I would guess lakeshore developers maybe aren't violent people as a whole, or the Koreans, but would certainly not mind if somehow you disappeared."

Hilly looked at the professor. "Hence, my bodyguards, the Worm family."

The professor looked down and picked a crumb from his coveralls. "Yes, of course. It's in their best interest to keep you alive."

Hilly spread her hands. "So the Worms' ulterior motive is pot and moonshine, not me. They have to protect me so I inherit the land. And they have to join the greenies to stop the dam by finally making Worm Cave public after a hundred and seventy-five years. By giving me your guided tour today, they figure I'll be so impressed that I'll help do that."

"Well, partly, Hilly. I'm convinced deep down they really don't want this cave flooded as a by-product of that big dam."

"But it all fits together, doesn't it, Professor?

"Yes, Camas Worm is certainly a cagey fellow."

"Besides the cave, all those hollows and woods won't be flooded either if the dam is stopped and will remain just the way they are for the moonshine and pot growing in the rosy future if I stay alive."

"Yes, if you are killed, it kind of ruins things."

She said with irony, "Thanks a lot." Then she asked, "How about the Atlanta 'organization'?"

The professor sighed. "That's why I'm showing you all this this morning, Hilly. After seeing this magnificent cave, Mr. Worm, Mr. Rice, and I were quite hoping to convince you that after you inherit the land, you just must donate your portion of Worm Ridge, which includes this great cave, to the National Park Service, the US government, and Camas Worm will do the same with his portion of Worm Ridge.. Incidentally, Hilly, I overheard what you whispered to yourself and what you said to me a few moments ago about the cave and its ownership. I dare say I know which way you're leaning."

She said. "Let me guess, Doc, Rice is also the Worm family lawyer."

"One of their legal representatives, certainly."

Hilly took another forkful of potato salad and muttered to herself, "Win-win. The feds take over the ridge, get rid of the other pot growing competition, and the Worms can go back to business as usual elsewhere in their empire. And the dam building will certainly be stopped making other people happy including the Worms again."

The professor answered, "Yes, everything you said is correct. Win-win. The feds will certainly not want pot growers on national park land! And no one will want to see this cave flooded when it is revealed. Rice says you will get a huge tax break. So you win, too. And don't forget, the very best part, a new national park will be created for all, Hilly."

"All I have to do is stay alive until tomorrow morning."

The professor nodded.

CHAPTER 30

Locked and Loaded

With the evening sun slanting outside, Hilly and the professor sat in the gloom just inside the cave's entrance and just outside the locked gate waiting for the Worms to pick them up. After securing the gate, Hilly and the professor had left the cave ten minutes earlier, walked up to the barn to get some bars on his cell phone, and called the Worm Café.

Camas Worm, according to the professor, had sounded upset that they had left the cover of the cave and told him to return to the entrance to wait. He had asked the professor if there were any vehicles parked in the vicinity, and the professor had replied that there weren't any in sight. Camas Worm said he would leave immediately and would honk his horn three times to signal them to leave the cave. He emphasized that when they heard the horn, and only the horn and not the sound of a vehicle or motor, were they to leave the cave entrance. The professor had expressed his opinion to Hilly that Camas Worm was getting just a touch melodramatic.

After finishing their lunch the professor had been scrupulous about picking up and transporting literally every crumb from Worm Cave. They had explored a little here and there on the way out which had unexpectedly consumed more hours than the professor had initially planned but the pair hadn't been able to help themselves. The difficult portion had been the climb from the cave's floor along the Giant's Stepping Stones and the Giant's Stairway from the Invisible River to the Opera Box. This had taken over an hour itself.

Now they sat in the sandy entrance by the pool and waited with their backs against the entrance's west wall and their boots just short of the flowing spring. They had both removed their helmets. Hilly had placed hers by her side. She had put a few fresh scratches in its finish. The professor had placed his helmet between his legs. It, too, had some fresh scratches and gouges here and there in the fiberglass.

Hot, mid-July evening air blew into the entrance, in contrast to early that morning, when cool air had been exiting the cave. The bushes, grasses, and ferns just outside the entrance trembled in the breeze. The professor had explained again that the cave was 'breathing' as pressures tried to equalize. Sometimes the gigantic cave took air in, and sometimes it blew it out its only entrance.

In the heat, both had unsnapped their coveralls down to their waists, and they were sharing the last of the water. There had been quite a bit of exertion in the past hours, Hilly realized, as she ran her fingers through her sweaty hair. Miss E. had assured her she would tend to her laundry today. She could hardly wait for the Bluebird's shower, air-conditioning, and some clean clothes.

Hilly drained the water bottle with a big gulp, sighed, and passed it back to the professor. He placed it in his pack.

She reflected for a moment, then said, "Worm Cave National Park. World Heritage Site. Sounds good to me."

The professor responded, "Yes, it has a certain ring to it."

"Won't help with my condo payment at the end of the month, though."

"Look at it as a huge tax deduction."

Hilly laughed, "I'm sure L. T. Rice has it all figured out and the paperwork filed somewhere in that office of his. You and L. T. and Mr. Worm are sure some cagey fellows."

The professor pointed into the cave. "We had to get you in there to see it for yourself, Hilly."

"And to think last week at this time I knew nothing about it." She arched her back, "It's been a hell of a couple of days, Doc."

"I'm sure you are going to come out OK on everything. Something left over after the taxman."

"There's that." But Hilly had begun to wonder whether Worm Cave itself would have any value and increase her inheritance when its discovery on her great-grandfather's land was made public. L.T Rice hadn't mentioned Worm Cave at all. How do you value a cave? Yet more taxes to pay? A huge deduction? She had some questions for him.

Besides the change in the wind direction at the cave's mouth that evening, there was another evident change. Hilly had her nylon holster clipped to the climber's nylon belt around her waist. She was now holding her Beretta 92FS in her right hand with the gun resting on her right thigh. She had worked the slide on leaving the cave for the walk up to the barn. There was now one in the chamber and nine more rounds in the clip. She checked the safety once again. As she did so, the professor looked nervously at the dull pistol in her hand.

Hilly was beginning to believe that Camas Worm wasn't being melodramatic at all.

Soon they heard the horn three times and rose stiffly to their feet.

CHAPTER 31

Back to the Farm

Tis time the ride back to town was with Trisha Worm in the old Ford
four-by-four pickup with the primered fender, Leroy's truck. Trisha made
a U-turn between the old farmhouse and the barn, reached over, shoved
open the passenger door, and left the engine running. After stowing their
helmets and packs in the bed, Hilly slid to the middle of the front seat, and
the professor climbed in and shut the door. He rolled down the window.
Trisha was smoking a Lucky, and there was no air-conditioning in the old,
battered Ford. He rested his arm on the sill while Trisha put the truck in
gear and started down the long driveway with one hand on the wheel and
the other holding the cigarette off to one side.

Trisha noticed Hilly's holstered Beretta, and Hilly noticed Camas
Worm's old Colt .38 tucked into Trisha's waistband. In addition, Hilly had
taken note of an ancient Winchester lever-action rifle behind their heads
in a gun rack that hung across the back window.

They rumbled down the long driveway in silence, and Trisha, putting
the cigarette back in her mouth, manhandled the old truck with both
hands onto the paved highway without the aid of power steering. She
found fourth gear a moment later, flicked an ash out the window, raised
her voice above the engine, and, after she got a nod from the professor,
asked Hilly, "Well, Ms. Walker, what'd you think of that there cave."

Hilly answered, "Fantastic! It's definitely hard to take Worm Cave in all at once."

"Camas said this mornin' when he and Leroy returned you decided to name it Worm Cave."

Hilly nodded, "Just seemed right."

"Well, the news spread, and the whole family thanks you for that, Ms. Walker."

Hilly said to no one in particular over the roar of the truck, "Yes, Worm Cave National Park."

Trisha leaned back and gave a knowing look at the professor behind Hilly's back and smiled. The professor did the same and smiled back. Hilly caught it all and shook her head. Cagey people. They had planned most of it before she hit town on Monday.

As they passed the town limits near the Ford dealership, not one of them noticed the white Lincoln Town Car and red Buick accelerating in the other direction.

Trisha dropped the professor off at the Fireside Motel. As he exited the truck, Hilly stopped him with a hand on his shoulder. "Thanks for the tour, Doc. It was wonderful. I'd like to see some more of my cave eventually."

"So would I, Hilly. So would I. Count on it." Then before he shut the door he said, "Return the clothing and other equipment at your leisure, Hilly. Maybe we'll see you at the Worm Café later."

Hilly winked, "Count on it, Doc."

After he pulled his pack and the two helmets from the bed, Trisha reversed and pulled out onto Main Street. Hilly turned and watched the professor walk stiffly to his room through the rear window as Trisha observed her.

Trisha teased, "I think I heard maybe a little middle-aged flirting going on just now, Ms. Walker. He is kind of good lookin' if'n you ask me."

They accelerated past the church on a green light and a block later turned down the alley leading to the rear of the Worm Café. Trisha parked the truck, stepped out, and toed the cigarette butt into the asphalt. "I hope this is OK, or I could take you all the way to the Bluebird."

Hilly answered as she climbed out, shrugged back into the coveralls, and lifted her pack from the bed, "Yeah, it's fine. I can walk the rest of the way. Can't wait to get out of these coveralls and under that shower. And I told you to call me Hilly and not this Ms. Walker stuff."

Trisha teased again, "Sure thang, Ms. Walker."

As Hilly walked down the alley, Trisha yelled to her as she climbed up the loading dock steps, "You all keep that fancy gun ready, you hear. Clean yourself up some and relax. Someone'll check on you later." Hilly kept walking and gave Trisha a wave as she walked along the back of the post office and its Dumpsters and loading docks.

As she neared the crossing alley that cut over to the Bluebird, Hilly suddenly decided to forgo the shower for a while and instead turned toward the town square. The Worm Café seemed crowded even at this early evening hour. The Worms were busy serving and didn't notice her walk by. She passed the café, opened the heavy outside door leading to its second floor, and climbed the steps. Hilly entered L. T. Rice's office, the brass bell rang, and the door closed behind her. The air-conditioning felt heavenly.

Rice's secretary, Fran, sat immobile behind her desk with a surprised expression on her face. The cat lounged in the middle of the floor licking a paw.

Hilly realized she must be quite a sight in her dirty, sweaty spelunking coveralls, the heavy boots, and the holstered Beretta on her hip.

The secretary was the first to speak, "Oh, Ms. Walker, we were working late and not expecting you. Is everything all right?"

Hilly asked quickly, "Is Mr. Rice in? I need to talk to him. It's not urgent but I have a question or two about my inheritance."

"No, he just left about ten minutes ago with two men, potential clients I think. If you ask me, they were in some kind of hurry. Didn't seem to be treating him very well in my opinion. He's an old man."

Hilly asked, "Did one of them have thick glasses with heavy black frames and long sideburns?"

The grandfather clock chimed the half hour just then, and the secretary waited a moment to answer. "Why, yes, and the other man was older, silver hair, quite handsome, and dressed quite well. I'm sure I've seen him somewhere before. He said something about going to the farm."

Hilly turned, opened the door—setting off that brass bell again—ran down the hallway, and took the stairs two at a time to the sidewalk. She ran past the Worm Café and the post office. The Worms were too busy and, again, didn't notice. She entered the sheriff's office. The lobby was empty. Alice was in her usual place behind the counter and looked up. She, too, had a surprised look on her face at the spectacle that was now Hilly Walker. The radio operator turned from her console.

"Why, Ms. Walker, you're a sight!"

Hilly cut her off. "Is the sheriff in?"

"Why, no, he suddenly decided to take a long weekend down at his cabin on Lake Cumberland. Left about an hour ago. Should be back on Monday."

"Shit! Is Big on duty?"

"No, she comes in later for the midnight shift."

"Is there any deputy on duty?"

"Why, yes, but both are out on calls. Frank, the jailor, is around somewhere. Maybe he can help you."

Hilly turned around, pushed both glass doors open, and ran out onto the town square. People were going about their business at the end of the day. She turned right and ran the two blocks down the alley around the end of the motel to her Honda in the Bluebird's parking lot.

Reaching inside the coveralls, she fished her keys from the pocket of her cargo shorts. She thumbed the fob, unlocked Lilly, threw her pack into the backseat, and jumped in. She jammed the key into the ignition and twisted. The starter caught on the second try—thank God, she thought—and Lilly roared to life.

Hilly drove north on Ninth, and turned west on Main Street. She caught the lights at the bank and drugstore and continued west toward the town limits, not noticing the blue Jeep Cherokee driving in the opposite direction, with three men—two in the front and one in the rear.

Hilly looked down, and realizing she was doing seventy-five as she passed the town limits, backed off. She slowed more in a few miles at the mailbox and turned up the long driveway. Dust billowed behind her as she drove between the rows of corn. She pulled into the area between the barn and house, reversed toward the barn, and parked nose out next to the white Lincoln and red Buick, both of which were parked in the opposite direction facing the forested ridge.

Hilly locked the Honda out of habit, walked quickly behind her car where the rough track, almost a trail, started up the ridge between the two red and black NO TRESPASSING signs but not before putting a hand on the grilles of the other two cars. Both were hot and she knew for a fact that both cars were not there thirty minutes ago, but it was an old cop habit. She pulled the Beretta 9 mm from her holster, checked the load and the safety, and holstered it.

She jogged silently up the track as it angled steeply up Worm Ridge. Hilly kept to the raised center of the primitive road on the vegetation, because the tracks on either side were still muddy from the thunderstorm the day before. Deep tire tread marks indicated that a vehicle had recently been up or down the road.

Hilly estimated she had gone roughly a half mile when the track turned sharply and steeply to the left as the primitive road switchbacked. Her strides shortened as she rounded the corner and continued up the ridge, slipping here and there on the wet vegetation despite the Vibram soles of the boots.

The forest had grown dense on either side of her. Her pulse had risen and her breathing had increased, but her legs felt strong as she climbed. She had plenty left.

The grade increased even more and the road narrowed as it angled up the ridge, causing her to shorten her steps even more. Only a four-wheel drive, high-clearance vehicle could negotiate it, she thought. No wonder the cars had been left below. No bulldozer—not even one from a hundred years ago—had made this road. She figured it had probably been constructed before the Civil War by horses, hand tools, and human muscle.

The road switchbacked again. This time to the right. Hilly stopped suddenly, her pulse pounding in her temples. She estimated she had run about a mile in the last eight or nine minutes. She bent over with her hands on her knees as her breathing slowed and listened.

Yes, there it was. Directly above her through the trees and thick undergrowth was the sound of a motor running, the putt-putt of its exhaust barely audible through the forest growth. Then she thought she heard a distant voice, a man's voice.

Leaving the track, Hilly clambered up its steep bank and stood at the edge of the forest above the road. She listened again. There definitely was the sound of a motor running somewhere on the ridge directly above her.

She walked slowly uphill, pushing aside wet bushes and low-hanging branches. The thick forest canopy was a good forty feet overhead and blocked the late evening sun.

The undergrowth suddenly changed. Hilly walked a few yards and stopped. The vegetation was now shoulder-high, dark green plants with the characteristic seven leaflets on each stem and unmistakable smell. She had walked into what certainly was a marijuana plantation between the oaks, maples, and ash trees.

Hilly quickly drew her Beretta, checked the load once more, flicked the safety off, and held it two-handed in front of her. She walked slowly forward brushing aside the marijuana plants with her gun while at the same time looking carefully up and down and side to side for trip wires and booby traps.

The slope declined dramatically, and she sensed she was reaching the broad top of Worm Ridge. She realized that the huge cave, Worm Cave, must be somewhere beneath her below hundreds of feet of solid limestone.

The engine grew louder and now she knew for certain it was probably a single-cylinder four-stroke, probably powering a generator of some kind. She crept forward another ten yards and saw through the marijuana plants some kind of structure, maybe a tent, in a large clearing. Hilly edged closer using a large tree for cover. She lowered the Beretta but kept it in a two-handed grip.

She counted three large tents in the clearing—the kind with high walls made of slick plasticized fabric and supported by round metal poles, the kind favored by big-box stores for spring nursery sales in the parking lot. Hilly saw there had been an attempt to throw camouflaged netting over the tops. Two of the tents were set end to end. The third tent, parallel to the others, was the closest to her with its open end toward her right. The solitary tent also had a metal stack protruding from the top near the closed end. Some kind of cookstove, she guessed. The gasoline motor was louder and seemed to be on the other side of the clearing.

A dark green Range Rover with mud-caked tires and undercarriage sat near the open end of the solitary tent. Beyond the Range Rover on the far side of the clearing were three dogs tied to a crude plywood shelter. Food and water dishes were set out in front of the shelter. Two of the dogs, a pit bull and some kind of shepherd mix, were lying down with their heads on their paws and panting with their tongues hanging to one side. The third dog was sprawled on its back twisting its body back and forth. She couldn't tell its breed, but it was larger than the other two.

Just inside the tent opening, a man sat in a blue webbed nylon folding lawn chair. He was dressed in faded blue jeans, a blue pocketed T-shirt, an unbuttoned red checked shirt, and a baseball cap. The cap was black with a white front panel. He had a lever-action rifle across his lap and an aluminum beer can in his right hand.

Another man sat across from him in an identical folding lawn chair. He was partially hidden by the tent. All Hilly could see was his left leg. He was dressed in blue-and-white seersucker trousers and brown leather tasseled loafers.

Hilly stood and listened. The Lincoln and the Buick parked at the bottom of the ridge surely indicated more men somewhere. But where? There was no movement or conversation in the tents. Were the other men out somewhere inspecting the pot plantation? If so, now was the time to move and not hesitate. The odds were in her favor; she decided to act.

Hilly slowly backed into the shade, still holding the Beretta in front of her in a two-handed grip. She moved quickly and quietly to her left until she was opposite the closed end of the tent. She stood for a moment listening, but all was quiet except for the putt-putt of the gasoline engine.

She left the forest and in five strides had her back up against the tent wall. She slowly made her way along the wall, the Beretta held in front of her, finger just outside the trigger guard. She noticed that both her breathing and pulse were becoming elevated. She stopped for a moment and took a few deep breaths to calm herself. She was not casting a shadow on the tent wall that she could see.

The noise of the generator hopefully covered any sound as she slowly came to the open end of the tent and the galvanized metal pole that supported it. A quick glance confirmed that the man with the rifle was still in the lawn chair. He was just raising the beer can to his mouth. The pit bull across the clearing had noticed something, though, and rose to its feet and stretched with his nose in the air.

Hilly struck as she quickly rounded the tent pole with the Beretta raised high in both hands. The man was just touching the beer can to his lips with his head tilted back when she brought the gun's butt down as hard as she could and hit him just behind his right ear just below the ball cap. There was a dull thud as metal met bone. The man dropped the beer can, a Budweiser Light she noticed, and before she could hit him again, he toppled over, taking the chair with him.

Hilly holstered the Beretta and moved quickly as the other two dogs scrambled to their feet, barking and howling and straining against their ropes with their heads in the air.

Rice, who had been staring down at his lap, raised his head in surprise as Hilly bent over the unconscious man. The lawyer sat up and said quite calmly, "Why, Ms. Walker, where did you come from for Christ's sake?" His wrists were bound by a large plastic tie-wrap. Hilly put a shushing finger to her lips, immediately realizing it was a useless gesture with the dogs making an ungodly noise across the clearing.

She turned from Rice and picked up the rifle. It was an old Winchester Model 94 carbine. She worked the lever, jacking the shells out of it until it was empty, and then pitched it to the other end of the tent. Hilly walked quickly over to the old man while reaching inside her coveralls to her cargo shorts and extracting her Swiss Army knife from one of her pockets. She knelt in front of Rice and unfolded the larger blade. She cut upward through the plastic strip binding his wrists. Hilly saw Rice suddenly look up at the same time she felt the muzzle of a gun touch the back of her head.

She tightened her grip on the red-handled knife, but the gun was forced harder into her head. A man's voice said, "Don't kill her yet! I want a bit of that! I haven't had a schoolteacher since high school!"

The man with the gun spat nervously, "Shut the fuck up, Frank!" Then he turned back to Hilly and pressed the gun harder. "Let go of the knife, honey."

She opened her hand, and the pocket knife dropped to the ground. The man with the gun reached down, picked the knife up, and closed the blade with his free hand. "OK, let me see your hands, and stand up very slowly."

Hilly raised her hands until they were even with her shoulders and stood up slowly one leg at a time. The dogs continued to pull on their ropes and bark. The generator exhaust continued to putt-putt. The man on the ground by the lawn chair groaned but didn't move.

The first man continued to hold the gun to her head. Ignorant move keeping the gun so close to your victim and letting her stand, she thought. He should have kept her on her knees and backed away. Amateurs. She knew she could take him, but the second man was a problem, and he was no doubt armed, too. Hilly faced Rice and winked to try and put him at ease and give him some confidence.

The first man put her Swiss Army knife in his pocket, quickly reached forward, and drew Hilly's Beretta from her holster. Keeping the gun on her he whistled and said, "Nice gun, lady. Big weapon for a schoolmarm. Looks brand new. I'll bet it's never been fired." He put the Beretta in his belt and backed away. "Now you put your hands on top your head, honey, and turn around slowly."

Hilly followed his command just as a third man walked up putting a cell phone away and drawing some kind of small automatic, probably a .32, from his inside coat pocket. The third man was much older, taller than the other two, and had a beautiful head of well-groomed silver hair. He was dressed in an expensive blue blazer and gray wool slacks. His dress shoes were caked with mud. He waved the man with the gun away from Hilly. The first man, the guy with the Elvis Costello glasses she had seen in the café, eased around Hilly and stood behind her. Another mistake, she thought. Both men were now in each other's line of fire.

The second man, Frank, took up position about fifteen feet away and to her left, between her and the dogs. He wore some grubby work clothes, ball cap, and was armed with some variety of Colt AR-15 assault rifle. It hung in front of him, supported by a black webbed strap over one shoulder and around his neck.

The man by the lawn chair groaned again but didn't move. The man with the assault rifle laughed and yelled across the clearing, "What's wrong, Alvin? She get the drop on you?"

The man standing behind Hilly—he of the Elvis Costello look, the one she had seen that evening in the Worm—said, "I told you to shut the fuck up, Frank!" The man named Frank had also been in the booth, but there had been a third man and it wasn't the old guy.

The older man walked up to her holding his automatic out in front of himself with only one hand. Mistake number three, she thought.

She lowered her head, trembled, and pled for her life. An act. Her training took over. "Please don't kill me and Mr. Rice. I'll leave and never come back. I promise."

The silver-haired man chuckled and stepped closer, still holding the gun out in front of him. The man behind her laughed when he heard the older man chuckle. So did the man holding the assault rifle. The silver-haired guy was no doubt the boss.

Then the man with the assault rifle said, "Good one, huh, Mr. Kingman? 'Don't' kill me.' What a joke."

The silver-haired man said, "Frank, I told you never to use my name. We'll let the Mexicans do it and get rid of the bodies. Unmarked graves in the woods or something. And shut those fucking dogs up!"

Frank turned, put two fingers in his mouth, and whistled. The dogs froze. Then he yelled, "Shut the fuck up!" The three dogs stretched, sniffed the air a final time, and quietly lay down.

Kingman said, "That's better. Where's Stu?" Then he turned back to Hilly.

Frank answered, "He should be along. Said he had to use the latrine down the ridge to take a shit, Mr. Kingman."

Kingman edged closer holding the small automatic in front of him. He said politely, "Well, Ms. Walker I presume. Too bad we couldn't have met under better circumstances." He waved his gun at the old lawyer and continued, "But counselor Rice over there just couldn't leave things alone. Mind his own business. Isn't that right, counselor?" Rice continued to sit quietly.

Kingman edged closer to Hilly obviously enjoying himself. As he came closer, Hilly continued to hold her hands up and her head down. She trembled more, backed up a step, and turned her head to one side as if trying to avoid the menacing silver-haired man in front of her. She whimpered again, "Please don't kill us, Mr. Kingman. Show some mercy."

Kingman laughed and edged closer. He smirked and looked at the other two men. "Oh, don't worry, Ms. Walker. None of us are actually going to kill you and the old man. Like I said, we've got three experts for that on the way. You and counselor Rice are simply going to disappear."

Elvis Costello behind her, laughed and asked, "How long before the Mexicans get here, Mr. Kingman?"

Kingman stepped closer. "Oh, probably fifteen minutes or so. They were watching the motel when I called. Ms. Walker got past them somehow I guess. That Jeep they're driving should be able to get up here, OK. No need for us to drive down and pick 'em up."

The man with the assault rifle laughed and pointed his gun at Hilly, "Plenty of time for all of us to get some of that!"

Elvis Costello said again, "Shut up, Frank!" But he was thinking the same thing himself.

Hilly could now see Kingman's feet and muddy dress shoes in front of her and smell his breath and aftershave. He was close. She knew she had to be patient and to stay submissive with these men for a few seconds more. The elderly man in front of her wasn't the problem in her mind; rather, it was the man with the glasses behind her, whatever his name is, and the other man, Frank, to her left about fifteen feet away. She needed the man in front of her to actually touch her forehead with his gun so she would know exactly where it was without looking up when she made her move.

Rice sat quietly with wide eyes watching the scenario play out. The man by the lawn chair groaned again.

Hilly let her voice tremble along with her whole body. She ducked as Kingman took a last step toward her. She cowered even more, wished she could produce some tears, and with barely a squeak said, "Please, I'll do anything you say."

The man with the assault rifle yelled, "That's the spirit, bitch!"

Kingman stepped forward the final foot and touched his gun to Hilly's forehead as he told Elvis Costello to get a tie-wrap to bind her wrists. Mistake number four. All he got out was something like, "Sorry, Ms. Walker. Phil, get…

Phil! That was the Elvis Costello guy's name! He made an O with his mouth as if to probably say "OK" as she made her move. Hilly quickly grasped the barrel of Kingston's automatic with her left hand. The three men would be dead in less than five seconds as she first pushed the silver-haired man's gun aside with a firm grip on the barrel and slide while ducking to her left. Then she brought her right hand to the rear of Kingman's wrist and pulled forward while twisting the gun farther back in the opposite direction.

Kingman cried out as the bones in his wrist snapped and the small .32 automatic dropped from his hand neatly into Hilly's. Simultaneously, the man behind her, Phil, instinctively had fired his .45 automatic as she had grabbed Kingman's gun and dropped to her left. Hilly felt the supersonic crack of the heavy bullet as it passed by her ear and hit Kingman directly in the forehead. The powerful bullet exited the back of his head, along with a portion of his brain.

Hilly twisted and fell to the ground to face Phil, who had just killed his boss. She worked the slide on Kingston's gun, pulled the trigger, and hit the second man between the eyes before he could react, splitting the nose bridge of his glasses in the process. The less powerful .32 bullet penetrated his brain some four inches but did not exit.

Kingman and Phil faced each other with surprised expressions on their faces. They both collapsed to their knees. Kingman pitched forward onto the ground while Phil fell backward and landed face up in front of Rice. His eyes stared up into nothingness.

Now prone, Hilly turned and took quick aim at the man with the assault rifle as he was bringing it up from his waist and put two quick shots into his chest. The man lowered his chin and stared at the two bullet holes in his shirt, which were beginning to ooze blood. He fell onto his side with his dead eyes staring at the three dogs.

Hilly came to her knees and, still holding the small automatic with a two-hand grip, pivoted behind the gun. None of the three men was moving.

The smell of cordite was heavy in the air. The gunfire echoed along the ridge. Her ears were ringing. She hardly heard the three dogs begin barking again. They sprang to their feet and began pulling on their ropes in a frenzy to attack her.

Hilly came to her feet and walked to the man with the assault rifle. Holding the automatic on him, she put her boot on his chest and rolled him onto his back. He lay still with his dead eyes staring upward. She muttered, "Bitch, huh? Looks like you won't be getting any of this, huh, pal?"

Blood was now spreading down his chest. His finger was still inside the rifle's trigger guard. She pried the finger away and worked the nylon strap from around his arm and neck with her free hand.. She checked the firing lever on the rifle and saw that he had never taken the gun's safety off. What an idiot, she thought as she slung the rifle over her shoulder, let it hang across her chest, and walked back to the tent.

She stood over the other two men. The silver-haired man was no doubt dead as the back of his head was gone thanks to his trusted employee. Shouldn't have gotten so close old man, she thought. The third man had a neat hole between his eyes as he stared up at her. She saw the shattered glasses frames on each side of the dead man and whispered, "Sorry about the glasses, Phil." She pried his automatic from his hand and put the .32 she was holding on the ground next to it. She bent over him with the assault rifle hanging under her and inspected the bullet hole. OK, maybe a lucky shot, she thought but smiled a little anyway.

She fished her Swiss Army knife out of his pocket and opened the blade. With her free hand she fished her Beretta out of his waistband and saw that the dead man had never put the safety on. She shook her head. Amateur boneheads. Pretty risky and stupid when you stuff a loaded gun in the front of your pants. She holstered the Beretta with the safety on and stepped over the dead man to attend to Rice.

She cut the tie-wrap binding Rice's hands. After closing the knife and pocketing it, she pointed at the two small automatic pistols on the ground a few feet away. "Do you know how to use either of those guns?" she asked the old lawyer. Her voice sounded distant. Rice was in shock but was able to shake his head back and forth in the negative. He uttered weakly as he looked at the bodies, "Jesus Christ!" Hilly could hardly hear him and more or less read his lips.

She picked up the two automatics, ejected the clips, and emptied their firing chambers. She threw the guns in one direction and the clips in the other. The guns landed among the marijuana plants near the tent, and the clips landed near the dogs, making them angrier.

Hilly put a hand under each of Rice's arms and helped the old man out of the lawn chair. He stood but put two hands on her shoulders to steady himself. "Ms. Walker, we've got to call the authorities!"

"First things first, L. T." she said as she started him toward the Range Rover. She was hoping the keys were in the ignition; otherwise, she would have to search the bodies, and there was no time for that. "We've got to get out of here. There's at least one more man up here who wants to kill us and more on the way down below."

As they neared the Range Rover, the old man confessed, "I don't understand any of this too well, Ms. Walker."

She opened the driver's door and leaned into the car. The keys were in the ignition. She withdrew the assault rifle over her head and set it on the leather passenger's seat. Then she turned to Rice and opened the rear door. "Look around, L. T. Those are marijuana plants. These guys had some kind of deal to buy the ridge from the state and make a huge pot plantation. Now get in and lie down on the seat."

Rice nodded and stiffly climbed into the vehicle as Hilly gave him a boost. He sat upright behind the driver's seat.

Hilly climbed into the front, slammed the door, and twisted the key. The Range Rover's V8 roared into life. She looked in the rearview mirror and saw that Rice was sitting up in the backseat. She shook her head and grabbed the gear selector. The Range Rover was an older model with an automatic transmission. She assumed it was in four-wheel drive, but there was no time to read the owner's manual. Along the shifter were the familiar letters P, N, R, and D. Below the D were the numbers 3, 2, and 1. Hilly guessed and clicked the car into second gear, stepped on the gas, and began a turn to start down Worm Ridge. Rice wasn't prepared for the rough ride and his head slammed into the window.

Hilly quickly discovered that the Range Rover had the turning radius of a battleship as she ran the front end into the marijuana plants at the east end of the clearing. She was braking to reverse when the right rear passenger window exploded with a quick burst of close shots. She left the car in drive and stepped on the gas, taking out four marijuana plants and lodging two in the front bumper. At the same time, she felt the Range Rover lean to the side and realized a bullet must have taken out the left rear tire.

She turned in her seat. Rice was now lying prone and cowering on the rear seat. He had not been hit. Another volley of shots peppered the car with metallic pings. The back window exploded in a shower of glass.

One bullet tore through and took out the inside rearview mirror and a portion of the windshield. Hilly ducked instinctively as she steered the Range Rover away from the clearing. Automatic fire, she thought. The car suddenly lowered even more as she started down the track. She knew she had lost the other rear tire.

The firing stopped as she and Rice slid down the steep, rough track and gained ground, with the forest and terrain now between them and the shooter. The Range Rover was, not surprisingly, handling badly with two flat rear tires. Hilly could hear the undercarriage scraping on the raised middle of the track.

Rice sat up and clung to Hilly's seat back, leaning forward. His head was near hers as they careened diagonally down the ridge. Hilly sensed his presence next to her. She yelled over the engine noise, "You OK, L. T.? You're not hit are you?"

He raised his voice and answered, "No, I'm fine. Never been shot at, though. It's enough to get the old juices flowing again, I'll tell you."

It sounded like he had collected his wits somewhat and was actually maybe enjoying himself. The old coot. "If this piece of shit makes it down the hill, we'll get in my car. So be prepared to move, OK?"

The Range Rover bottomed out for a moment, and both Hilly and Rice were thrown in the air. Rice said weakly, "OK." but Hilly was concentrating again on the muddy track ahead and fighting the wheel.

At the first steep switchback Hilly let the engine brake the Range Rover and then downshifted into first, the lowest gear. The engine protested by revving loudly, and the vehicle slowed quickly enough that Hilly had to brace herself with the steering wheel. Rice pitched forward.

She feathered the brakes a little and made the sharp, steep turn, the rear of the Range Rover sliding a bit downhill toward the forest. The sounds were disconcerting, to say the least. The slapping of the ruined rear tires against the fender wheel wells added to the engine howling in the lowest gear and the mud and rocks hitting the undercarriage. The Range Rover was swerving and handling badly as Hilly fought the steering wheel. She upshifted to third gear, and the car jumped ahead.

Rice raised his voice again and asked, "Is it going to make it, Ms. Walker?"

Hilly continued to fight the wheel and said, "Sure, L. T., we'll pretend it's just a rental!"

Rice smiled. The old man's getting into it, Hilly thought, just as they hit a large rock with the right front tire and the car rolled to one side, almost hit a tree, and came close to rolling down the ridge. Hilly steered against the skid and brought the vehicle back up onto the primitive road. Close, she thought, real close.

At the second switchback Hilly selected second gear and then first. The engine revved loudly again in protest as the Range Rover slid down the muddy turn. The rear tires had by now been ruined and were just pieces of rubber and tire casing along the road behind them. The Range Rover was now dragging itself along the track by its front wheels.

Hilly smelled the sweet smell of antifreeze as a small trace of white mist jetted from under the hood and she saw that the temperature gauge was pegged at the hot end of its range. In addition, the red oil pressure light was beginning to blink. Never had she treated a vehicle so badly.

The barn and the cars were now visible ahead in the evening light. The Range Rover was a smoking ruin as it dragged itself to a stop just behind Hilly's Honda and to one side. It died in a flurry of engine knocks as Hilly switched off the ignition.

She helped Rice out of the vehicle, noting that it was easier now that the car sat much lower than it had at the top of the ridge. She helped him to her car, fished out her keys, and unlocked the doors. She helped him into the front seat. As she came around the front of the car, she quickly checked the long drive out to the main highway. It was clear.

She quickly inserted the key into the ignition and twisted. Nothing. She tried the key again. Still nothing. The red and orange warning lights had come on and dimmed as usual, but the starter did not engage. She twisted the key back and forth. The steering wheel had become unlocked. She rocked it back and forth, then tried the key again. "C'mon, Lilly!" The warning lights dimmed but only silence from the starter.

Hilly pounded the steering wheel with both hands and simply yelled, "Fuck, fuck, fuck!"

Rice quietly added, "Maybe we can push it, Ms. Walker. I had an old Model A once…."

She replied sharply, "No, L. T., it's a fucking automatic."

She told herself to keep calm as she stepped out of the car.

She went over to the white Lincoln and the red Buick and tried the doors. Both cars were locked. The interiors were dark, but she remembered the mini Maglite in the holster near her waist. She walked from car to car with the flashlight. Both ignition switches were empty. Of course, she told herself. You idiot, both cars were locked. In a last-ditch effort, she felt the top of all four front tires. Sometimes people left keys there. Nothing. The keys were obviously in the pockets of two very dead men with holes in their brains a mile back up the ridge.

She didn't want to leave Rice by himself, but maybe she could run down the lane to the highway and flag someone down. Someone who wouldn't mind stopping for a filthy, crazy woman dressed in coveralls.

As she walked back to the Honda, Rice was still sitting stoically in the front seat. Then she noticed some movement in the corner of her eye. Two headlights were turning into the lane, and it appeared as if they belonged to a blue Jeep Cherokee. The Mexicans in a Jeep that Kingston had mentioned.

Shit, shit, Hilly thought as she ran for the ruined Range Rover while yelling for Rice to get down. He still sat stoically in the Honda's front passenger seat. She reached into the Range Rover and pulled out the assault rifle. Holding the rifle with one hand under the forestock and resting the buttstock on her thigh, she pulled back the bolt to be sure again there was one round in the chamber. She removed the clip, tilted it toward her, and checked that there was at least one round on the top. The clip was shorter than she was used to in both the military and the police department. Those had been twenty rounds as a standard. This clip was probably ten rounds, she thought, but it felt even lighter than that. She jammed the clip home and ran around the rear of the Honda and came up on its right side where the line of fire down the lane was better. She opened the front passenger door, powered the window down, knelt, and rested the assault rifle on the window sill. She flipped up the small fire control lever on gun's receiver from "safe" to "fire." This gun was a semiautomatic, unlike Leroy Worm's no doubt illegal automatic model, and had only two settings, not the third "auto" setting. It would fire only one round with each trigger pull.

She estimated the Jeep was about halfway—maybe 250 yards—down the lane. It didn't appear to be in a hurry and was coming directly at her and Rice. The best possible shot at a moving vehicle.

Hilly took aim and tried to control her breathing. The light was dim, the assault rifle had open sights, and she had no idea how the gun was sighted in previously. Not good. She calmly told Rice, "Cover your ears, L. T." He dutifully brought both hands up alongside his head.

As the Jeep came closer, she shook her head and wondered for a moment what her fellow DPD retirees had been doing these past two days. Bitching about the bankruptcy and their pensions? Bingo? Coffee at the nearest McDonald's? Cutting the lawn?

The Jeep was about 200 yards away. She had to give herself and Rice some time. She slowly let out her breath and held it, put the driver's side of the Jeep's windshield on top of the sights, and pulled the trigger three times. The three hot brass casings landed to one side on the grass. Rice jumped in his seat at the sound.

One of the Jeep's headlights exploded in a shower of sparks. A trail of white steam rose from under the front grille on the driver's side. Where the third bullet hit was anybody's guess, Hilly thought as she raised her head for a better look. The brake lights painted the corn red on either side of the drive as the Jeep came to a sudden halt. Both front doors and one of the rear doors flew open.

The assault rifle was shooting low at 200 yards, she decided, as she lowered her eye to the sights again and raised the barrel a fraction of an inch. Hilly fired three more times as the men dove into the corn on either side of the lane. She thought she saw the man behind the driver grab his leg.

The bolt on the assault rifle had locked back, indicating there was no more ammunition. Hilly dropped the clip, empty. There had been only six rounds in the rifle. She stood and quickly pitched the gun and the empty clip over the Range Rover into the undergrowth.

Rice still sat in the front seat with his hands over his ears. Hilly crouched again behind the Honda's passenger door, duck-walked back a few feet, and opened the rear door. She pulled her pack from the backseat, shut the rear door, and put her pack on the ground. She rummaged through it until she found her cell phone, a simple flip phone and not a smart phone. She opened it and the screen and keypad lit up. There were four bars. "Quick, L. T., what's the number of the Worm Café?"

The old man didn't move. Hilly put an arm on his shoulder. He looked at her hand and then her and seemed to come out of it a little. She raised her voice and asked again, "Quick, L. T., what's the number of the Worm Café?"

He answered this time, "Three-one-six-W-O-R-M."

Hilly looked at her phone. She hated it when businesses used catchy letters instead of numbers. "Shit, L. T., what's the area code?"

Rice said calmly as if correcting a child, "Why, it's eight-five-nine, Ms. Walker."

Hilly punched in the numbers, cursing under her breath as she slowly found the last four letters.

There were three rings, and then it went to voice mail. Hilly cursed and left a short message, flipped the phone shut, and put it in one of her cargo shorts pockets.

Then she reached into the Honda, put an arm around the old man, and helped him from the car. In a moment, they were both crouched behind the passenger door. "C'mon, L. T., we gotta get out of here and try to get lost in the corn. It's the only plan I can come up with right now." Then she asked him, "When was the last time you rode piggy-back?"

Rice's eyes widened a little bit.

Hilly turned around and said, "C'mon, climb on."

Rice self-consciously put his hands around her neck, Hilly grabbed each of his legs, and began to stand. Then she heard the dogs barking faintly high on the ridge. Hilly stood for a moment with Rice on her back and listened. The barking continued and was getting louder by the second. Clearly, the dogs had been let loose either by the man who had shot up the Range Rover or the man who had been guarding Rice.

She bent down again. She and Rice might have had a chance in the corn losing the men in the Jeep, but they wouldn't be able to lose the dogs that way. Even though she was armed, she felt the odds would favor the three vicious animals. She patted one of the old man's hands in front of her. "C'mon, L. T., get down. They've let the dogs loose. Time for Plan B." She stooped and helped Rice stand behind her.

Hilly powered up the front passenger window, shut the Honda's front door, and took his hand. She opened the rear door and put an arm around the old man's shoulder. "L. T., you're going to have to lie down on the seat back here and keep quiet. Don't move. I'll try to decoy everything away from you."

As Rice climbed in the backseat, he asked, "What about the dogs, Ms. Walker?"

"You can't hear them that well yet I guess, but they're headed down the ridge. I could probably take care of one or two of them, but I don't know about three."

Rice was lying across the backseat, and Hilly leaned in and said, "Please lie still and don't get up or get out of the car. Can you do that for me, L. T.?"

The old man nodded and said, "I'll be real still, Ms. Walker."

Hilly said OK and shut the door. She jogged behind the still-smoking, ruined Range Rover and stood between the NO TRESPASSING signs where the primitive road started up the ridge and waited. The barking was louder. Even Rice probably heard the dogs now.

One of the dogs tumbled out of the undergrowth and onto the muddy road barely a hundred yards above Hilly. The dog had cut the switchback in its frenzy. It was the pit bull. The leader. The dog picked itself up and saw her at the end of the road. The other two had followed the road and were not far behind.

Hilly drew the Beretta just as a bullet took a splinter out of the tree to her left just above her head. A loud report followed a fraction of a second later from somewhere down the lane behind her. She instinctively ducked, turned, and started running for the barn.

Another shot rang out, something high powered. As she crossed to the barn, she saw two men coming up the lane with rifles trying to use the corn as cover. She stopped, crouched, brought up the Beretta in a two-handed stance, thumbed the safety off, and fired two rounds at the men in the lane. The range was ridiculous for the nine-millimeter handgun, at least one hundred yards still, but she was satisfied to see the two men dive for cover. It bought her a little time.

Hilly ran down along the barn with the Beretta still in her right hand. The barking was even closer. The dogs were at the cars now as she came to the spring below the barn and the edge of the cornfield behind it. She turned toward the cave opening and splashed along the tiny stream between the undergrowth on either side. In seconds, she waded through the pool in front of the cave and ducked under the limestone ledge. She sank to her knees and crawled forward to the metal gate a few yards inside the cave in the shadows. She carefully placed the Beretta on the dry sand to one side and pulled the mini Maglite from its holster. She turned the flashlight on, put it in her mouth, and palmed the heavy brass padlock.

The dogs snarled and barked and followed her scent down the path along the barn. Hilly flicked the digital numbers at the base of the padlock until they showed 1-2-3-4, as the professor had told her. She pulled the padlock's brass body down, and, to her relief, it clicked open. She removed it from the gate's latch and pitched it into the cave. Then she turned the old latch up and to one side and pulled the heavy gate toward her.

The dogs had now made the turn and were splashing up the narrow stream toward her and the cave. Hilly picked up the Beretta and, still holding the mini Maglite in her teeth, crawled quickly around the rusted gate. She slammed it shut and lowered the latch just as the first dog, the pit bull again, splashed through the pool at the opening and lunged at the gate, taking the old rebar in its powerful jaws.

CHAPTER 32

Cornered

The other two dogs joined the pit bull at the metal gate, snarling and barking. The pit bull now had its brown and white snout forced into one of the squares that made up the gate's frame. Baring its teeth, it was pushing its head hard against the rusty rebar on either side. The squares in the gate, though, were just a little smaller than its blunt head, and it could only push its head in as far as his eyebrows. The fur was tight around its eyes as it growled and snapped at Hilly, desperate to get to her throat.

The second dog, perhaps the smartest, growled and dug furiously next to the pit bull with both front paws at the base of the gate in frenzy to tunnel under the lowest rebar. Just to the right of the second dog, unnoticed, was a small gap under the gate where the spring ran. The third dog, the big one, danced in circles behind the other two, raising its head and barking and slobbering on the sand.

Hilly had no time to think about what came next as she picked up the Beretta in her right hand. She thumbed off the safety, placed the muzzle a few inches from the pit bull's ugly snout, and shielded herself with her left hand. The white in the dog's eyes grew wide as it looked up at her a fraction of a second before she pulled the trigger. The vicious dog went silent and dropped into the sand as what was left of his its head came free of the gate.

She quickly leveled the gun at the other dog and pulled the trigger a second time, four inches from the top of its head. The dog's head exploded, spraying blood and brain matter on the gate before it dropped limply into the sand next to the pit bull.

At the sound of the gunfire, the big dog stopped suddenly and looked at Hilly with a curious expression, its ears suddenly up in the air. Hilly quickly fired again. The round hit the big dog in the neck, but he didn't go down. Muttering under her breath, "Sorry, boy, it's you or me," she fired again. This time the shot was lethal, and the large dog went down on its front legs and then rolled over on its side in the pool of water at the cave's opening. It was still, its tongue lolling out of its jaws.

Hilly holstered the Beretta and the mini Maglite, which was still in her mouth, and threw open the gate. Two sudden loud shots rang out from near the barn. One bullet hit the limestone ledge above her head, showering her with splinters of rock; the other bullet hit the gate to her left, fragmenting the bullet on the rebar and causing a bullet fragment to ricochet and hit her in the left forearm. She cried out instinctively and hugged her wounded arm to her side. She rolled back into the darkness of the cave, slamming the gate shut with both feet and throwing the latch. She turned onto her stomach, trying to use the dead dogs for cover, and brought the Beretta out of its holster, aiming it through a square in the gate with her right hand while her left arm, cupped under her, dripped blood into the sand. She grimaced with pain as she looked over the barrel of the Beretta and sought movement. Her arm hurt like hell.

Hilly spotted the brass padlock in the sand next to her, and she transferred the gun painfully to her left hand. She picked up the padlock, raised herself a few inches, and twisted the shackle through the latch. She quickly pushed the shackle against the rebar until there was a satisfying click and then sank back onto her stomach. She transferred the Beretta back to her right hand. She remembered the professor's cell phone showing no bars that morning in the cave's entrance.

CHAPTER 33

Retreat

In the dim light Hilly examined her left arm. The coverall sleeve along her left forearm had been ripped by the bullet fragment. The bleeding seemed to have lessened somewhat, but she couldn't be sure. She could move her arm and wiggle her fingers. A good sign. Hopefully, a flesh wound. But this wasn't the time or place to perform first aid, as another shot rang out. She ducked instinctively again and was rewarded with a mouthful of sand. This time the bullet passed through the metal gate unobstructed just above Hilly's head and went into the darkness of the cave. She heard the bullet ricochet a long way down the passageway behind her. A test shot or most likely to keep her pinned down. From the sound, it was a heavy rifle of some sort and seemed to have come from the undergrowth near the pathway along the barn.

Spitting the sand out, Hilly knew there were at least four, maybe five, armed men outside the cave. The man she had hit guarding Rice could have recovered by now, found his rifle and ammunition, and would be really pissed. There was the unseen man who had shot up the Range Rover as she and Rice had escaped down the ridge. There were three men in the blue Jeep Cherokee. She thought she had wounded one of them but not mortally. By now they could be anywhere around the cave's entrance, to the side, or above and ready to rush her.

She had four rounds left in the Beretta and at some point she had to tend to her wound. She decided the cave entrance was not the place to be as some fine dirt sifted down over the ledge into the pool in front of her. She started slowly backing up using the palms of her hands and her toes and knees. She grimaced each time she had to use her left hand and tried to keep the Beretta out of the sand when she pushed with her right hand.

Another shot rang out from the undergrowth near the barn. The bullet hit a piece of rebar and ricocheted off the cave's limestone wall just above her head. She ducked again but continued making progress deeper into the passageway.

Hilly was sure now that the random shots were to keep her pinned down and provide the other men with cover. They would soon rush the gate. Her only cover in the long passageway was at the breakdown, the low side passageway near the end that she and the professor had crawled through that morning on their way into Worm Cave.

Hilly knew she had to buy time. Where were the Worms? she thought as she turned and duck-walked up the long passageway with no cover.

Soon the outside light faded completely, giving some scant cover. She holstered the Beretta and brought out the mini Maglite. Grateful for its blue-white light, she made progress and was soon able to stand up, her unprotected head just below the ceiling. She stopped to take a breath and heard men's voices, distant but still echoing up the passageway. They were speaking in a mix of English and Spanish. She thought she heard the Spanish word for dogs, *perros.*

Hilly jogged along the left side of the passageway, making progress in the sandy soil. The beam of her small flashlight jumped up and down in front of her as she tried to shield most of the light with her body. The voices faded as she jogged still deeper into Worm Cave, but the sound was replaced by a metallic clanging, no doubt the men attacking the padlock with an ax or sledgehammer. Maybe one of them had found the tool in the barn, she guessed. The brass padlock, although a good brand, was only intended to keep the curious little boys from town out of the cave, not five men. It would soon give way, and they would be in the cave behind her!

The ledge she and the professor had crawled under to find the second passageway would have been deceiving, but she had been there that morning and their tracks in the soft soil helped Hilly find it easily. As if to reassure herself, Hilly shined the light up the passageway. The beam faintly illuminated the pile of rocks that marked its end, what the professor had called breakdown.

She knelt in the sand and ducked under the ledge, playing the light around the low crawlway. Then she lay on her stomach and crawled forward. Unlike this morning, though, she pivoted around and then scooted sideways as far as possible until she was pressed against the crawlway's south wall, her head an inch from the ragged ceiling. She inched forward just a bit until just the top of her head showed in the entrance passageway. Hilly set down the flashlight in the dirt and switched it off. She reached along her side and took the Beretta from its holster and held it in front of her. Better cover. She blew some dirt from her lips and waited in the dark.

Hilly waited thirty long minutes in the darkness. The only sound was her breathing and the tiny stream swirling and gurgling nearby. She was tired, filthy, and now becoming chilled after all the exertion. The adrenalin was leaving her body, and she was becoming a little nauseated like yesterday when she had had Big pull the Tahoe over. What was the cave's temperature? She thought she remembered the professor saying it was fifty-one degrees Fahrenheit or close. She felt the breeze in the passageway on the back of her neck. The cave was breathing out. Glad now for the dirty coveralls as she lay in the dusty, low passageway, she tried to pull them around her closer, but she didn't have much room to maneuver. She lay still with her chin resting in the dust waiting. For what?

She heard distant voices. She wriggled forward two inches. Faint light beams played around on the dull cave walls and occasionally reflected off the tiny stream of water and onto the ceiling. She had good cover now but only four rounds left. Not good. There was an enormous cave behind her. The professor had been adamant that, as far as anyone knew—even the Worms—this was the only entrance. No back door. Time for a Plan B she thought. No, wait a minute; driving the Range Rover down the ridge had been Plan A, leaving L. T. in the backseat of the Honda, the gate, and decoying the dogs was Plan B. Now she needed a Plan C. Damn!

Hilly moved forward another few inches and aimed the Beretta painfully left-handed down the dark passageway. She could now make out the individual flashlight beams coming toward her. Two of them were strong and bright, much like the professor's six-volt model. The third was much smaller and dimmer. Just a regular flashlight. Three men, she decided, but maybe a fourth tagging along behind without a light? Three, maybe four, armed men walking single file, well spaced out. Smart.

Crouched under the ledge, Hilly believed she was still invisible to them. A deep voice suddenly said, "*Alto. Silencio.*" Hilly began to squeeze the Beretta's trigger with the sights lined up on the first man when the men came to a halt and switched their flashlights off in unison, plunging the cave into total darkness.

Hilly decided on Plan C. She needed time. Time for the cavalry hopefully to arrive. She fired two rounds down the passageway and prepared to turn and crawl farther into the cave. The muzzle flash gave away her position, but she had inched back into the low passageway and had decided she wasn't going to be there much longer.

There were two pistol shots in return from down low. The men had been crouching or lying on their stomachs, and she had missed completely. Smart. She inched forward and looked down the passageway. Then she heard a metallic click, and there was a small flame thirty yards away. It faintly illuminated a big, dark-haired man with a large backpack.

Hilly brought the Beretta up again, but before she could fire, it appeared as if someone had lit a Fourth of July sparkler. In a split second she realized it was a lit fuse and it was now arching toward her in the darkness, lighting up the passageway. The man had thrown too high, and the sparking fuse hit the cave's ceiling and landed short in the sand as she scrambled backward in the crawlway and covered her head and ears. A stick of dynamite!

There was a bright flash and then the explosion. Hilly felt the heat roll for an instant up the passageway. The stick of TNT had luckily landed short of her crawlway in the deep sand, and the limestone walls around her hiding place had shielded her. She crawled forward and, painfully using her left hand again, fired her last two rounds from the Beretta in the darkness, this time aiming low. Working by practiced feel in the dark, she quickly transferred the pistol to her right hand, let the empty gun's slide snap forward, and lowered the hammer with her thumb. It was time for Plan C. She would move deeper into the cave.

She holstered the Beretta and felt for the mini Maglite in the dirt in front of her as she pivoted around on her stomach. She flicked the small flashlight on, put it in her mouth and crawled as quickly as possible deeper into the cave using her elbows and toes before the men threw another stick at her, this time with more accuracy.

Soon she was out in the second dusty, larger passageway. She stood and tried to brush herself off with her right hand. Ridiculous, she thought, as she ran to the second crawlway, which led to the Opera Box, while cradling her left arm with her right and still holding the mini Maglite in her mouth.

At the correct place, she came to her knees, then her stomach. As she crawled forward, she heard a distant thump far behind her. They had thrown another stick of dynamite. What would the professor have thought, a man who hadn't even wanted to leave one single crumb in Worm Cave? Now there were men throwing sticks of dynamite. She halfway hoped they had somehow collapsed the first crawlway. That would certainly put a stop to the men apparently hired to kill her at any cost, but the outcome would be the same as she became truly trapped in this gigantic cave with only one entrance. Trapped in her own cave, Worm Cave. Sitting in the dark for who knew how long hoping to be rescued somehow like a Chilean miner.

She crawled out on the Opera Box, being careful to stay back from the edge. It was time to tend somehow to her wound. Still holding the flashlight in her mouth, she gingerly was able to see her wound as she peeled back the tattered fabric of the coveralls. The wound ran six inches along her left forearm in a straight purplish-red line. The bleeding had stopped, but it still hurt like hell. Even now she could see that the edges were showing signs of clotting as the wound went from a dark red in the middle to almost black along the edges.

All these years, she thought, the active service in the military police in Europe carrying a weapon, twenty years in the Detroit Police Department carrying a weapon, and really never a scratch until now in a cave in the middle of Kentucky. Technically, she guessed, she had been shot, wounded by a bullet fragment. A flesh wound, she thought as she inspected it closely with the small flashlight's bluish-white light. She probably needed stitches. How many times had she heard that term, *flesh wound*, in countless war movies and Western dramas. "Ah, just a flesh wound, Festus," Matt Dillon might have said. Well, she knew now that even a flesh wound was bad news and very painful.

But Hilly didn't have the time to dress the wound. She had to keep moving. There wasn't time yet to feel sorry for herself. There were men behind her who wanted to do more than give her another flesh wound. They wanted to kill her.

She unsnapped the coverall's left cuff. Grimacing, she gingerly rolled the tattered sleeve up past the wound and above her elbow. Maybe later she could strip down and cut a strip from her T-shirt or shorts and bind it when she was deeper into the cave under Plan C. At least nothing was touching the wound now, and it was in the air.

Hilly scooted backward carefully off the Opera Box and crawled to the left, the way she and the professor had done that morning, until she stood at the top of the Giant's Staircase. She started carefully down between Worm Cave's massive gray limestone south wall and the huge slab of limestone that had split from the wall eons ago.

Progress was slow as she climbed down from one limestone block to another. The ropes were still in place, and she clung tightly to them. When she came to the bottom on the first rope, she took her Swiss Army knife from her pocket, cut the climbing rope, and pulled it down from the rocks above her. She did the same with the second rope, hoping to make any descent that much harder for the men following her.

She came to what she had named the Giant's Stepping Stones in due time and descended even farther. Finally she was hopping from the last stepping stone across the tiny Invisible River to its sandy north bank, her goal for the last hour. She dropped the mini Maglite in the sand, knelt, and scooped the cold, clear water with both hands. God, she thought, this tastes wonderful! Hilly stood and let the water drip from her hands. The water had revived her somewhat, and, although she would have liked to stay in this spot and stretch out on the sandy bank of the tiny stream until help arrived, it was too exposed. There was a direct line of sight from the Opera Box, and a powerful flashlight beam could cover the distance. So could a bullet from a high-powered rifle. She would have to keep moving, but somehow, although her thirst had been slaked for the time being, she felt she had to remain near this tiny river.

She shined the flashlight around the area. Absolute blackness surrounded her, and there was no sound except water gurgling over the smooth, round pebbles in front of her. Upstream, the way she and the professor had walked, she decided was out of the question. The walking was too easy. It was the obvious choice to the men following her. Hilly turned and aimed the flashlight downstream, the direction she and the professor had not attempted. She walked a few yards. The Invisible River continued for yet another several yards ahead of her and disappeared into a wide crack under a huge vertical block of limestone, the base of the gigantic pile of breakdown that the professor had said lay in this direction.

She walked up to the gray wall of rock and played the light down into the crack. She was surprised to see the cave river flowed over a rock ledge into the crack and splashed onto the rocks many feet below, creating a waterfall perhaps sixty feet high. The sound of splashing water echoed around the large chamber. It then disappeared under a jumble of rocks and, she guessed, continued through the cave. Following the stream was out of the question now. There was no way down that she could see and no way out, even if she could climb down.

Hilly came to her feet and pointed her light upward. The huge pile of breakdown the professor had spoken about rose above her farther than the beam of the tiny flashlight could reach. She walked back a few yards, knelt down, and again drank several more handfuls of water before she stepped around the large block of limestone under which the stream disappeared. She wore her Timex Indigo on her right wrist and, with a push of a button, checked the blue lighted dial. She was surprised to see that it was a little after ten in the evening. She had been in the cave almost two hours. She selected a route, put the flashlight in her mouth again, and began to climb.

Some time later, the breakdown leveled out, with just piles and blocks of limestone ahead of her. The cave's ceiling was still invisible hundreds of feet over her head in the darkness as she sat down on a convenient block of limestone and caught her breath. The climb hadn't really been too bad, just steep from one boulder to another higher one. Her legs ached, her left arm still hurt, the climb had been painful, and she was drenched with sweat even in the cool air of the cave. Not good but she had apparently conquered Breakdown Mountain.

She pushed the light button on the Timex once again and saw that it was now a little after eleven o'clock. She decided she was going no farther and that it would be almost impossible to find her now, a single person in this huge, perhaps the world's largest, cave. She lowered herself onto another larger block of stone and stretched out full length. Some joints popped. She pulled the coveralls as best as she could around her, starting to feel chilled. Before she turned off the mini Maglite, she inspected the wound on her arm. It was pretty much scabbed over, and the pain had lessened now that the climb was over. There was no sign of any infection or swelling yet. As she lay on her back, she imagined the cave's ceiling hundreds of feet above her head. The professor had said that he thought the cave was largely unexplored. There was a good chance from what he had said that no human in the history of the Earth had ever been in this very spot she occupied. Something to think about later.

Just before she turned off the mini Maglite and closed her eyes, she wondered if it was her imagination or had her flashlight dimmed a little?

CHAPTER 34

Tracker

In her dream Hilly heard men's voices. They were arguing, not loud but distant. She opened her eyes, shook her head. Complete darkness. Had she gone blind? Then she remembered she was in Worm Cave. She checked her Timex. A little after midnight. She had been asleep for about an hour.

More voices. She sat up. She was cold, but this thought disappeared when she turned and looked behind her. She caught her breath. Three men with flashlights were standing on the Opera Box and closer than she would have thought, perhaps 100 yards in a straight line. It had taken a long time to climb down to the Invisible River and then up to her position, but in the dark with the small flashlight, she didn't realize how close the Opera Box actually remained to her hiding place along the cave's wall.

One of the men was gesturing. There were two big men with powerful flashlights and backpacks with some type of automatic rifles slung over their shoulders. The hired assassins. The third and smaller man who was gesturing wore a red checked shirt she recognized and carried a lever-action rifle she also recognized. Alvin, the man she had hit over the head up on the ridge. It looked like he had recovered and found his rifle and ammo.

One of the men played his light around and directed it for a moment in her direction. She ducked down before the powerful beam swept over her position. Hilly knew that, although they seemed close, in reality they were hours from where she knelt and would have to find the way. She was safe for now.

After the light flashed by, she rose again. Who were these men? She suspected they were Mexican cartel enforcers of some type sent to oversee the new marijuana plantation and the people she had shot. Crawling forward a bit, she took shelter behind a waist-high block of breakdown. The two Mexicans seemed to be arguing with Alvin in broken English. It was hard to make out all the words at this distance, but she thought she heard the third man, Alvin, say, "ain't goin' no further" as she peered over the rock.

Suddenly, Alvin backed away a few feet and pointed his rifle at the two Mexicans. One of the Mexicans laughed, stepped forward in an instant, grabbed the rifle barrel, and pushed it to the side. Alvin pulled the trigger, but it was too late. The rifle shot echoed up and down the huge cave.

Both of the powerful men grabbed Alvin. The Winchester and the flashlight clattered onto the rock ledge as he tried to resist. He screamed as they walked him toward the edge of the Opera Box and then easily threw him off the ledge. He screamed for the seconds it took for him to fall almost three hundred feet in complete darkness. Then there was a distant thud, and the screaming suddenly stopped.

One of the Mexicans knelt at the edge and played his light down as they both laughed. Big joke, Hilly thought. The other lit a cigarette. Then the one kneeling reached behind him, picked up the dead man's Winchester and flashlight, and threw them over the ledge. The lit flashlight pinwheeled down with the rifle for a terrifying amount of time before they both clattered onto the rocks far below near Alvin's torn body.

Both Mexicans were carefully peering over the edge and laughing. The one smoking dropped his cigarette on the Opera Box and crushed it out. They both ducked back under the entrance to the Opera Box and disappeared. The cave again plunged into darkness.

Hilly had never witnessed such casual brutality. Clearly they were hired killers. She stood, stretched, and arched her back. She felt for the flashlight in its holster on her left side, the empty Beretta on the right. She felt her way back a few feet until her hand felt the block of limestone and sat down. She dare not turn on any light.

Something bothered her. She thought she had been climbing up from the Invisible River pretty much in a straight line, but in actuality she had been angling to the left and approaching the cave's immense south wall considering the angle from which she had just watched the two men murder the man with the Winchester, Alvin, at the Opera Box.

A compass would be nice, she thought, as she sat in the darkness atop the mountain of breakdown. Hey, Breakdown Mountain would be an excellent name, she thought to herself, if I ever get out of this nightmare alive. She realized that, with the immensity of the cave and no landmarks, it would be easy to get completely turned around. She knew from what the professor had said that Worm Cave ran in a general east–west direction under the ridge above. Following the tiny river might help, but for now it had disappeared underground.

There were voices again. She stood, edged forward until she felt the boulder in front of her, and leaned on it, bracing herself with her elbows. Suddenly beams of light played up and down behind the huge slab of limestone that had partly detached from the south wall. The two men had not left the cave, as she had hoped. They were apparently driven to find and kill her and had found the Giant's Staircase.

Without the ropes Hilly knew it would take a long time to climb down to the cave's floor. Chilled and tired, she leaned on her rock and waited a long time for the men to descend. From the lights and voices she knew the men were almost down the stairway and would then turn down the stepping stones to the river.

Taking a chance, Hilly bent over, shielded her left wrist with her right hand, and pressed the button on the Timex. The blue glow indicated 1:35 a.m., Thursday, July 18. She was tired and desperately needed to sleep but dare not close her eyes. Even on a rock bed in a chilly cave she might sleep now for hours and be discovered, however unlikely. No, she said to herself as she shifted her feet and yawned, there was no one else to stand watch.

A Plan D began to form in her thoughts as she watched the men's lights and listened to their voices. They were confident and not a bit stealthy, probably thinking they would catch her quickly.

Suddenly, she jerked upright. The Timex. It was the Explorer model. She had completely forgotten about the tiny compass on the band! Cheap, no doubt—but it might actually work and had not been attached for decoration.

She drew the mini Maglite from its holster as she ducked behind the block of limestone, turned it on, and placed it on the ground in front of her. She unbuckled the watch's strap and set it in front of the light. The tiny compass was barely over a quarter inch in diameter. The little blue metal arrow was pointing to her left. There were only four marks around the dial, N, S, E, and W. She slowly rotated the watch in a full circle, but the small metal arrow didn't budge but instead kept pointing to her left. She rotated the watch again until the N was under the tip of the needle. The needle was indeed pointing to the north wall of the cave. Timex had actually put a working compass on the band and not a fake for looks! God bless the Timex Corporation and its $39.95 watch!

The voices were louder now. The men had reached the bottom of the staircase and were out from behind the huge slab of limestone. She turned off the light and holstered it. She felt slightly better about her situation and fastened the watch back on her left wrist.

The two men were visible below her and were shining their lights down the Giant's Stepping Stones. Hilly watched their progress from the summit of Breakdown Mountain until they, too, jumped from the last stepping stone over the Invisible River to its sandy bank. She carefully cupped her hand around the Timex and lit the dial. The glowing blue light indicated just a few minutes past three in the morning now, which reminded her that she had to be in that courtroom in less than six hours, or, dead or not, the two men hundreds of feet below her would have accomplished their mission. As she watched them from above, she wondered what had happened to L. T. Rice. She hoped the old man had somehow made his escape to the main road as a result of her decoy and had met the Worm family somehow on their way from town.

As Hilly watched, the two Mexicans slipped their packs off, then their rifles, and set them at their feet. Though a long way below her, the cave was silent, and she could hear they were speaking in Spanish. A few times Hilly recognized the word *mujer* and laughter floated up to her perch. They left both powerful flashlights on and the scene was partially illuminated far below her.

One of the men sat on a convenient rock, set down his flashlight, and pulled a pack of cigarettes from his shirt pocket. The pack was red and apparently new. Probably Marlboros, Hilly thought. He tapped the pack hard against his other hand, unwrapped the cellophane ribbon sealing the cigarettes, then threw the cellophane ribbon nonchalantly at his feet in the sand. Hilly shook her head and muttered to herself. He put the cigarette between his lips, pulled a silver lighter from his front pants pocket, lit up, and took a deep drag. The burning ash was bright, a glowing beacon in the darkness. Then he blew a lungful of smoke across the flashlight beam at his feet and held the cigarette to one side.

The other man was walking up and down the sandy bank playing his light here and there. It looked to Hilly as if he was studying the footprints in the sand. He reversed direction and walked along the tiny river until he was almost directly below her hiding spot. He knelt down at the spot where the Invisible River disappeared under the large slab of limestone and fell in a delicate waterfall. Hilly thought Murderer Falls might be good name now if she made it out.

The man stood and shined his light around the area. He walked to the place where Hilly had started her climb, picked up some of the dust, sifted it between his fingers, and put it to his nose. Then he looked up directly at her and suddenly aimed the beam upward. Hilly ducked as it swept over her hiding place.

He walked back to where the other man was taking his cigarette break, put his flashlight on the ground, and took out his own pack of cigarettes from his shirt pocket. He placed the cigarette in his mouth and leaned over, letting the other man light it. He took a drag, held it, and exhaled. Then he held the cigarette European style between two fingers and spoke softly in Spanish to the other man. They were exposed and not worried. Confident. Just your everyday hunt for a crazy *mujer* in the world's largest cave. They remained in a discussion for a while longer and smoked their cigarettes, one sitting and one standing, gesturing here and there with their lit cigarettes.

Then it appeared the break was over. The man sitting on the rock stood up and took a final drag on his cigarette and exhaled. Hilly watched the tip glow brightly. He casually flicked the cigarette butt into the Invisible River. The other man did the same and then stepped up to the edge of the tiny stream, pulled his fly down, and took a long piss in the river. The other man did the same, but instead stood casually beside his cohort and pissed a long stream onto the sandy bank. As Hilly watched, both men hiked up their flies simultaneously. Before they shrugged on their packs, each took a small object from a side pocket, then picked up their powerful flashlights.

———

The beginning of Plan D would begin in a few moments Hilly thought. She would watch as both hit men would disappear toward the area the professor had called Concordia, the easier path. She would climb back down to the Invisible River and then out of the cave. Simple. If her luck held, she'd be out of the cave by sunrise.

The two men raised something to their mouths. Hilly heard what she thought was a radio squelch. Each had a walkie-talkie! She was puzzled about this until one of the men gave the other a wave as he began to walk upstream toward Concordia while the other walked to the base of Breakdown Mountain and looked up. Shit! she thought. They had split up!

The man below her, the one who had examined the tracks, began to climb carefully and slowly. Worm Cave all of a sudden didn't seem so big and vast to her. Hilly turned and sank back to her hands and knees. She had to give herself some distance before standing up and turning on her flashlight. Put some Breakdown Mountain between her and the man climbing. The killer would see the light if she stood. She turned on the light and crawled forward until she was certain she was out of the line of sight from his perspective at the bottom of the huge pile of rocks. Then she stood and made her way as quickly as possible over the top of Breakdown Mountain.

There was no path and the way was difficult through the litter of large and small limestone rocks that had fallen from the ceiling eons ago. She stopped frequently and shined her light at the tiny compass on her watchband to keep her bearings. She was making her way to the west.

Farther along she felt almost sure she was losing some elevation as she climbed over a seemingly infinite number of rocks. She stopped again and oriented the compass. Still to the west. The professor had said he was certain the vast cave followed the general east–west orientation of Worm Ridge above.

As she started off again, something caught her eye and she glanced over her shoulder. Had she detected some light behind her? If so, the Mexican was closing the gap between them more quickly than she had thought. In a few moments she definitely was starting to climb down off the vast pile of breakdown. This side was somewhat steeper than the east side. She lowered herself down from block to block feeling the pain in her left arm, still holding the mini Maglite between her teeth.

Fuck, she thought, the Mexican was pushing her deeper and deeper into a cave with no entrance except the one behind them. She had to come up with another plan soon.

Quicker than she expected, she came to the cave's floor again, stopped, and caught her breath. She played the light around and listened, but there was no sound of water that she had expected. Was the Invisible River somewhere below like the sink a couple of days ago? Her light was now noticeably dimmer—not much, but noticeable. Unlike lithium batteries, alkaline batteries slowly lost their power. LED bulbs, she knew, took very little power, but, still, not good. The professor had stressed and preached three sources of light that morning for this very reason. Her only source was giving out. Not good at all.

The cave floor ahead of her was flat and dusty. Good news and bad news. She could move faster, but she would leave tracks. As she set off at a jog she knew she had to find some kind of hiding place. She could feel hotspots now on both feet, the start of blisters. Her knees and back were starting to ache, and she desperately needed some sleep. She had counted on encountering the river again to slake a growing thirst.

She stopped and oriented the compass again. Standing in the middle of what seemed a vast, dusty plain, she turned again and saw a faint beam against the rocks at the summit of Breakdown Mountain. She shined the light behind her and saw that her footprints were as plain as day in the dust. The only footprints. Ahead the cave's floor was completely smooth and unmarked. Not even any animal tracks. The professor would have been thrilled to be in this virgin section of the cave, she thought sarcastically as she began to jog and put more distance between the Mexican and herself. Her tracks would be a piece of cake to follow.

A hundred yards farther, the cave floor for the time being was smooth and an easy jog, but Hilly noticed it had begun to descend. She picked up the pace a bit, her flashlight shining ahead perhaps twenty yards. She stopped frequently to check the tiny compass on her wrist.

She looked over her shoulder. The Mexican, from his distant light, looked to be descending down Breakdown Mountain and making progress. The jog over this portion of the smooth floor had certainly widened the gap between her and her pursuer, but, of course, she had no idea what lay ahead in this apparently unexplored cave.

As she turned back, it appeared that the cave floor had disappeared in front of her. Her flashlight beam disappeared into black nothingness with no warning as she half slid to a stop at the very edge of the precipice, her feet inches from the drop. Unbalanced, she fell backward and caught her breath.

Hilly came to her hands and knees, crept to the cliff's edge, and played her light down. The precipice was undercut somewhat like the Opera Box, and she dared not go any closer. Her small flashlight beam failed to reach the bottom. To be safer, she lay on her stomach and peered over the edge into the chasm. Far below she heard water splashing into a pool of some kind; the Invisible River it seemed had emerged from its subterranean route beginning back at the base of the mountain of breakdown. Sweeping the flashlight from side to side, she realized that she had almost jogged right off the edge of a large, deep canyon. She could see layers of rock on each side and below, which reminded her of a past visit to the Grand Canyon years ago but on much smaller scale—but, on second thought, maybe not so small for a cave.

She picked up a pebble and dropped it over the edge. Many seconds later she heard the *kerplunk* as it landed far below in the water. Hilly carefully stood up and found another large, sharp-edged rock. She backed away from the edge and heaved it as far as she could and watched it arch through her feeble flashlight beam and disappear. Again, many seconds later there was a substantial splash far below. So, Hilly, told herself, there was a body of water of some sort many hundreds of feet below, and she had almost done a nice swan dive into the canyon because she wasn't being careful.

But there was no time to sightsee. The deep, dark chasm—the Grand Canyon was a good enough name for now, she decided—was right in her way, and she had to somehow skirt it. The Mexican would soon be on the smooth floor, following her tracks, and rapidly closing the gap. At this thought she looked back and he appeared, indeed, to be almost down and probably a half mile away. His powerful flashlight was too far away to outline her, but that didn't mean he couldn't spot her miniature light now. Humans can see even a tiny light miles in the distance, she knew from her military training.

But which way? Right or left? Hilly turned it over in her mind, shrugged her shoulders, and decided to walk to the right along the rim of the Grand Canyon. In barely a hundred yards, she realized that she had made a mistake. The Grand Canyon was apparently closer to the north wall of Worm Cave than to the south. The north rim of the canyon she was following tilted up and was becoming steeper and steeper. It became apparent that it was merging into the steep north wall, and if she continued, she could easily slip on the loose rocks and slide over the rim to her death hundreds of feet below. The north rim of the Grand Canyon, as it fell off into the chasm, had quickly become impassable for anyone but an experienced climber.

She turned around and was soon back at her starting point, having lost time and muttering to herself about the bad choice. Hilly jogged left. The Mexican was at the base of Breakdown Mountain. She could see his powerful flashlight moving up and down in a definite rhythm as he jogged along her path in the dust in what she now thought of as the Flatlands.

CHAPTER 35

Impressive

While Professor Cunningham and Leroy Worm waited behind him in the narrow passageway with the weapons and equipment in the early morning hours, Camas Worm crawled carefully out of the opening onto the Opera Box using just the shielded light of his penlight. He was well aware of the drop ahead of him. He reached the edge, switched the tiny light off, and let his eyes adjust to the absolute darkness. He gazed into the blackness and listened carefully for a few moments. There was only silence and darkness all around him in the great cave. Satisfied, he flicked the penlight back on and motioned for the other two men to join him on the ledge.

All three men were outfitted in spelunking gear, helmets, coveralls, kneepads, and, at the professor's insistence that caving was serious business, three sources of light. The Worms had objected. That had been some hours ago, but the equipment had been rounded up back at the Fireside courtesy of Cunningham's students.

The professor was next to crawl out onto the Opera Box next to Camas. He immediately spotted the crushed cigarette butt and inspected it. He frowned at the black mark the crushed cigarette had left on the limestone and the shreds of tobacco. He muttered to himself about littering the cave. He inspected the butt while Leroy Worm brought up the equipment and joined them. Leroy had his assault rifle and two extra thirty-round clips. Camas had taken the old Winchester lever-action from the gun rack in the pickup to add to his venerable .38 Colt revolver.

When all three men were in position, lying prone at the edge of the Opera Box, Camas turned off the penlight again and they stared into the darkness, searching for any other sources of light but there were none. Camas whispered to the others, "I reckon she has to be in here somewheres, boys."

Leroy, who had never been this far into the cave, added, "She's in here somewheres with someone chasing her, I reckon, judging from that thar cigarette butt and those spent shell casings back thar. Judging from them nine-millimeter casings, she's armed I figure with her own gun, Camas. But it don't look good considering those 7.65-millimeter rifle casings we found, too."

Camas countered, "Or out of ammo. I'm of the belief she would have made a stand back thar and held her ground if'n she still had some ammo, Leroy. No, I reckon she bein' chased right now with a good head start considerin' there's no lights to be seen."

The professor spoke up, "She and the ones after her have been in here long enough to be deep into the cave by now, but which way did she go?"

Camas, in a normal voice, said to Leroy, "Pass me one of them big lights, brother. It's time for some illumination, I reckon."

———

Earlier the Worm Café had been particularly busy that evening, and Camas, Leroy, and Trisha had thought Hilly was safely ensconced in her room and spending the evening there. After all, Trisha had last seen her turn down the alley toward the Bluebird Motel.

The café's cell phone was on a shelf in the kitchen with the amber blinking message light facing the wall, so no one had noticed it for some time until near closing time. Trisha had seen the blinking light first when pulling a large commercial can of ketchup from the shelf to routinely refill all the red plastic squeeze bottles on the booth tables and counter. The yellow mustard squeeze bottles were next.

As she listened to the messages, her eyes opened. She slipped the phone into one of her front jeans pockets and hurried into the dining room. Her husband, Camas, was at the cash register. He was talking with a regular customer, "Tiny" Mitchell, a retired farmer with large pink cheeks, who was leaning his considerable weight against the counter, when Trisha approached Camas and whispered in his ear. His eyes widened, too, and he quickly untied his apron as he asked his customer, Mitchell, "Tiny, we got us some kind of a personal family emergency, and have to leave. Can I count on you to stay a bit and lock both front and back doors?"

Mitchell was puzzled for a moment; the Worms practically lived 24/7 at the café. He stood for a minute bobbing his toothpick up and down, looked at Trisha and Camas, knew Leroy was always back there somewhere and asked, "All three of ya?"

Camas nodded as he locked the cash register and gave the other man a knowing look, something Mitchell noticed as he took the toothpick from his mouth, "Sure, Camas, but it'll cost you one of those rib-eye steaks of yours and maybe a jar or two of you-know-what from the back.."

Camas threw the apron on the counter, "Thank ya, Tiny, the steak'll be on me but keep yer mitts off that stuff in the back. Hear what I'm a sayin'?" Mitchell nodded. Then Camas turned to the remaining customers. "Folks, family emergency, we got to leave; go ahead and finish up, yer meals are on the café."

Trisha followed her husband to the kitchen. She hesitated while her husband went out the back door to make sure that all the stoves and appliances were off, but Leroy had taken care of it. Leroy was waiting near the loading dock in his old four-by-four pickup with the engine running when Trisha piled into the middle seat next to him while pushing his assault rifle out of the way. She had to duck as Camas slammed the door and reached around to take the old Winchester lever-action from the gun rack. He levered a .30-30 round into its chamber.

Leroy gunned the old truck up the alley, swung around the town square in front of the church, blew a red light, and headed west past the town limits on Route 153.

Five minutes later he slowed at the mailbox and swung into the drive to the farmhouse. The Worms all saw him at once in the headlights, and Leroy braked to a halt. He doused the lights but left the truck running as all three jumped from the cab. L. T. Rice was sitting on the ground leaning against the mailbox post. His seersucker suit coat was folded in his lap. At the sight of the Worm's truck, he was attempting to stand.

Trisha reached him first, knelt, and coaxed him back to a sitting position. She immediately checked for injuries. She said in a soothing voice, "L. T., just lean back agin the post and take it easy whilst I check you over a little." The skinny old man was a mess. One side of his face was caked with mud, and his clothes were rumpled and dirty. When she was satisfied there were no injuries, she sat down and put her arm around his shoulders. She could feel his heart racing. The two men stood in front of them on the gravel drive. Trisha asked Rice, "Where's Ms. Walker? Is she OK?"

Tears formed in the old man's eyes. He pointed down the drive toward the dark, looming ridge. He spoke haltingly, taking a breath between sentences, "She's in the cave…Two men chased her in there…Lots of gunfire and dead people…She saved my life."

Trisha spoke gently, "L. T. how did you wind up here?"

Rice pointed over his shoulder and answered, "I came through the corn like I think she wanted me to. Followed the rows to the road. Last time I saw her I was in her car and she was running down the path by the barn."

Camas and Leroy looked at each other. Leroy nodded. Camas handed the cell phone to Trisha. "Stay here with L. T., Trish, whilst Leroy and I check it all out. Call the Fireside and git Professor Cunningham out here. Then take L. T. to the hospital, leave him thar to be checked out, and both you and the professor come back here, you hear?" He pointed a finger at them. "The two of you don't go any further than this here mailbox. Understand, Trish?"

Trisha nodded. Camas motioned to his brother to get into the truck. "C'mon, Leroy." Then he turned to the two people sitting by the mailbox post before shutting the old pickup's door. "Me and Leroy will check it out and be back."

Trisha nodded, "Sure, Camas, what about the sheriff?"

He gave his wife a knowing look and said, "Not yet. We'll keep the law out of it for a while longer. Me and Leroy will handle it for now."

With that, Leroy put the truck in gear and they started up the drive toward the house and barn with the headlights off. Camas Worm had the Winchester barrel pointed out the open window with the gun butt on the transmission hump, and Leroy drove with his assault rifle across his lap and its barrel pointed out the window.

Halfway up the drive, Leroy, whose night sight was better than his brother's, put a hand on his brother's shoulder, then lowered it slowly palm down. Leroy put the truck in neutral and let the truck roll to a stop behind the blue Jeep Cherokee so as not to activate the brake lights.

Leroy let himself out but left the door open an inch. Camas did the same. Both men stalked silently to the front of the Jeep Cherokee, guns at the ready. They took note of the broken grille, the bullet hole in the windshield, the sweet smell of antifreeze, and the dead man on his back with his upper torso hidden in the corn with his legs stretched out onto the gravel. Leroy prodded the man with his gun barrel and knelt next to the body. Camas came up behind his brother with a flashlight from the truck. He cupped his hand over the lens as they studied the body.

Leroy said in a low voice, "Looks like a serious leg wound. Small caliber but powerful. Tore it up pretty good. No doubt got the artery and then some judging by all that's soaked into the ground. Seen it before." He lifted a belt lying near the body with his gun barrel. "My guess, he didn't get the tourniquet on before he passed out." Then he looked around. "And his buddies didn't stay around to help him none."

All Camas Worm said was, "I reckon, Leroy. Big fella. Looks Mexican."

Leroy, in almost a whisper, said, "Wait here in the truck, Camas. I'll do some scoutin." Then he disappeared silently into the corn rows with his rifle. .

Camas climbed back into the truck, this time into the driver's seat. He badly wanted a cigarette but knew a lighter and glowing cigarette butt could be seen a mile away. Ten minutes later he heard a pop in the distance, and a few minutes later he saw his brother double-timing down the road toward him.

Camas put the truck in gear, pulled into the corn, drove around the disabled Jeep, and met Leroy halfway. Leroy climbed in the truck only slightly out of breath. "One guy sitting near the spring made the mistake of raising his gun. I checked, bullet went clean through him. I seen him a few times in the café. Looks clear up there but a lot of carnage."

Camas parked head on to Hilly's Honda, and both men climbed out. It was now almost totally dark. Camas took the flashlight from Leroy in one hand and his Colt revolver in the other. He noticed Hilly's pack on the ground. Leroy had attached a flashlight below the barrel of his assault rifle after disappearing into the corn.

Camas inspected the wrecked Range Rover, noticing the marijuana plants in the grill, and made a low whistle. Both men turned and walked down along the barn to the spring, stepping over the latest body as they made their way upstream to the cave entrance. They played their lights into the cave entrance, taking note of the three dead dogs and the ruined gate and lock. Camas whispered to his brother, "I got me a bad feeling Ms. Walker's somewhere in Worm Cave and she ain't alone. Damn. We should've protected her a might more, Leroy."

Leroy said, "We all thought she was at the motel, but she sure is headstrong. Didn't count on how much."

"Let's check up on the ridge first."

Leroy nodded and followed his brother back along the barn to their truck. Camas pointed a light at Hilly's Honda as he walked to the rear of the car, "C'mon, help me push it out of the way."

Leroy opened the driver's door to make sure the car's parking brake was off and it was in neutral. "Wait a minute, Camas. The keys are still in it."

Leroy climbed into the front seat, made sure the car was in park, and twisted the key. The starter caught, and the Honda roared to life. He pulled it around and to one side of his truck. Leroy locked the front hubs on the Ford, and the old truck, with its high clearance and four-wheel drive, handled the road and switchbacks and came to the crest of Worm Ridge with no problem.

The marijuana farm with its tents, lights, and generator was no surprise to the Worms. Unknown to the men working there at the fledgling plantation, the Worm family had secretly scouted it during the previous month and, if truth be told, admired the setup.

Camas pulled the truck into the clearing and backed it around until it faced back down the rough track.

Leroy, with his rifle ready, jumped out of his truck. Camas followed with the old Colt revolver in his right hand. The generator still putt-putted in the background. The two Worm brothers walked over to the three bodies. All the men had been customers at the Worm Café. Leroy squatted, waved the flies away that had begun to gather, and studied the dead men. He stood and gave another low whistle. He spoke a few words to this brother, "That thar woman is mighty impressive."

Camas took off his implement hat and wiped his brow with a handkerchief. "Looks like she got the drop on three of them here. The one along the road makes four. Why don't we just make it five counting that other fella you just took care of. Bullet went clean through like you said. They'll never find it. No use makin' it any of our business more'n it is, Leroy."

Leroy nodded, "It'll be hard to believe that woman took out four men, much less five, but sounds good to me, Camas."

Camas pointed to the truck, "Can't do much for these fellas. They's in God's hands now. Looks like we're goin' need that cave professor guy and some of his equipment. Looks like to me that Walker woman's been chased into the cave."

Leroy said as he climbed back into the truck, "I ain't never been in that thar cave, or any other in fact, Camas. Never liked the idea of a cave, but I guessin' there's always a first time."

Camas climbed in the other side, "I think you're about to find out what it's like. Trish is goin' to be pissed when she gets the news about these here three though."

Puzzled, Leroy asked, "Why's that, Camas?"

Camas answered, "That old guy with the silver hair over yonder was a good tipper, she always said." Both brothers laughed.

———

They braked to a stop fifteen minutes later at the mailbox next to the university's Suburban, which was parked across the drive with its parking lights on. The professor was behind the wheel, and Trisha Worm and L. T. Rice sat in the roomy backseat.

Coincidentally, moments later Deputy Big arrived and pulled her Tahoe onto the shoulder nearby and activated the blue-and-reds on the roof. She exited the Tahoe, put her county mounty hat on, hitched up her gun belt, and strolled nonchalantly to the front of the Suburban, where she faced the Worm brothers before motioning for everyone to exit the Suburban, too. She politely greeted everyone. "Camas, Leroy, Trish, Professor, L. T."

The five murmured a greeting back to the deputy.

"I must say this seems very peculiar, folks," Deputy Big said. "Mind telling me what's going on?"

———

Camas Worm switched on the powerful light, and the blue-white beam shot out into the darkness.

Leroy, who had never been in Worm Cave or any cave, whistled softly, "Lord Almighty."

As Camas played the light around, the professor looked at his watch. Deputy Big had given them the rest of her shift before she would call the staties and the feds. He asked, "How do we know she's in here somewhere?"

Leroy answered him, "We're pretty sure someone's tryin' to kill her, professor, and, judgin' from the spent casings we found, she's givin' 'em a fight." Then he added, "She's already kilt five of 'em and three dogs. They's havin' a tough time of it with that thar woman."

Camas pointed down, "Six now, I reckon, boys. She's in here somewheres and I reckon now it's goin' to take more'n the three of us to find her. I'm guessin' it's time for us to back out of this here cave and call the authorities." The other two men followed the flashlight beam downward to the crumpled and torn body far below.

CHAPTER 36

Dead End

Hilly guessed he could see her flashlight now as she took the only option along the south side of the Grand Canyon. At first she was able to easily walk along the rim of the canyon, but soon her way was blocked by breakdown that had tumbled from the cave's wall and ceiling right to the edge of the canyon. She found herself climbing upward to the left in an attempt to clear it. One slip and she might tumble into the deep chasm.

Some distance later she had climbed back down onto the rim again after the detour and made more forward progress. She constantly checked for a way down, but the rim still overhung the canyon's sheer wall with nothing but blackness below. Twice she picked up a rock and dropped it over the edge, only to hear a splash long seconds later in the darkness below. Three more times in the next hour she had to climb high above the rim in yet more detours around breakdown that had tumbled onto the rim and into the canyon far below.

Finally, she drew to a stop and faced the largest pile of breakdown yet. It blocked her path completely and rose higher than the weak beam of her flashlight could reach. She also heard the sound of falling water far below her to the right. Stepping along the flat, overhanging rim, she carefully approached this next huge pile of breakdown that spilled over the rim and was surprised to see in her flashlight's beam that the huge, ancient avalanche of rocks spilled into the darkness of the canyon and seemingly created a ramp that filled the canyon's south wall. As she heaved herself atop the first boulder that blocked her way, it looked like a way down to the river. As she climbed down the huge ramp of rock, she knew that she had to somehow follow the river far below to save herself.

Hilly climbed block by block down the ramp created by the huge pile of breakdown, again holding the small flashlight between her teeth and glancing frequently up and to the right for any evidence of the hit man's light. She was stymied at one point by a nasty drop that looked impossible until she found a spot where she estimated the drop was about eight feet. She dropped to her stomach, backed over the edge until she held herself only by both hands on the sharp edge, and let go. The three feet to the rocks below felt like an eternity before she landed, lost her balance, and came down roughly on one knee.

Soon the breakdown ramp leveled and a large, sheer wall of limestone rose to her right. The hollow sound of water increased dramatically, the wall to her right suddenly vanished, and she realized that the wall had been replaced by a large, very black, and perfectly still lake. Hilly knelt and aimed her flashlight down into the water, submerging the mini Maglite a few inches before she realized where the water's surface began. It was *that* clear and *that* invisible. The Invisible Lake fed by the Invisible River she thought.

Looking back up the way she had just struggled down, she realized this tremendous ramp of rock had spilled down eons ago, creating a dam in the Grand Canyon, and she was now walking across that dam. Hilly walked along the shore and soon came to the outlet. She knelt again, set down the flashlight, cupped both hands, and drank deeply. Then she stood, shook the water from her hands before wiping them on her filthy coveralls, and picked up the flashlight.

To her left she could see the Invisible River tumbling and splashing at least fifty feet from rock to rock in still another waterfall along its course.

She looked back up into the dark, steep canyon and desperately wished the whole area could somehow be lighted. How magnificent it would be to see the huge, gray walls of the cave curving up each side to the ceiling hundreds and hundreds of feet far above her. In between the Grand Canyon, itself two hundred feet high but dwarfed by the scale of Worm Cave, cradling this immense lake of pure water with a beautiful waterfall at its end dropping to the cave's floor. Had anyone but her seen this in human history? Ever? She shook her head at the thought.

———

As she began the climb down alongside the waterfall, a beam of light flashed in the distance. It played down into the canyon at the far end and then back and forth between the walls. The light flashed off the lake's surface and gave Hilly some idea finally of the scale of the cave she had only been imaging. It was breathtaking but at the same time signaled danger. The Mexican had arrived at the head of the Grand Canyon and surely saw her light. With his powerful flashlight he would quickly see the way around the canyon and not make the mistake she had made.

Hilly climbed with little difficulty down to the bottom of the waterfall, where it formed a clear, deep pool. She noticed another waterfall tumbling into the pool on the far side in the increasingly feeble beam of the mini Maglite. She paused to kneel and drink again, noticing two blind fish suspended nearby in the nearly invisible water.

She stood and aligned the tiny compass on her watchband with north. The Invisible River flowed out of the pool, still running in a generally westerly direction. She also noticed it was 6:17 a.m. on the Indiglo dial. Somewhere above the sun was rising on a warm July morning and the birds were singing, but nothing had changed in Worm Cave. Night or day, it didn't matter. Timeless. She was becoming chilled and had begun to shiver.

Hilly made her way along a narrow ledge to the pool's outlet. The Invisible River continued to gurgle and dance along its bed between sheer banks in her light. She also noticed that there seemed to be considerably more water flowing here than there was back at the area below the Opera Box.

She continued to make her way gingerly along the small ledge above the stream until it narrowed and she realized she would have to actually walk in the little river to make any more progress. Hilly stepped off the ledge and was surprised to find the water much deeper than it appeared. It came up to her knees as her feet found the sandy bottom. The cave water was frigid and numbing as she splashed forward, keeping the flashlight in one hand and balancing herself with a hand on the sheer rock wall to her left..

The river continued seemingly forever in a series of riffles and pools between its vertical rock walls. Some of the pools were merely ankle deep, but wading through a few involved water nearly thigh deep and holding on to limestone ledges with both hands for balance, flashlight clamped once again in her mouth. As the Invisible River ran in its mini canyon of sorts, Hilly fervently hoped she would not have to swim.

It was hard to judge distance, but she continued slowly in this manner for what she estimated was at least a half mile. Her legs were numb, and she could barely feel her feet on the sandy bottom when she caught a small glint in front of her, a reflection of some sort, in the near distance and above the river. She stopped in the thigh-deep water and raised her head. There! Something shiny in her light. Hilly took the flashlight from her mouth and walked forward.

As she put her foot down there was no bottom! Her right foot went down and her left knee buckled as she tried to back-pedal and regain her balance. Her left hand still had a tight grip on the ledge above and took most of her weight. She brought her right hand across and gripped the ledge with her fingertips, careful not to lose the flashlight. Hilly regained her balance as she finally brought her right leg back under herself and transferred the flashlight back to her mouth.

Standing in the thigh-deep water, she was breathing hard and shivering. It had been close, she had made a similar misstep rescuing the boy and at the other end of the Grand Canyon, and, although she was an excellent swimmer, being submerged suddenly in the cave's cold water could have been a disaster. A fall into the water and hypothermia would begin to be a problem in just a few minutes.

As she caught her breath, she realized the pool widened in front of her and was obviously much deeper than she had anticipated. The ledge she was gripping continued as far as the flashlight was able to illuminate. She started forward, facing it and gripping it tightly hand over hand with her body bent so that her submerged toes also provided some traction against the limestone wall.

As she went slowly along in this manner, the pool continued to spread out around her. A slip now into the deeper water and she would just have to swim for it. But where? She didn't want to backtrack. Hilly's arms and legs ached as she worked her way along the edge of pool. Her fingers were beginning to cramp. She tasted the aluminum flashlight between her teeth. Then she noticed the ledge beginning to rise at the same time the angle lessened, and soon she could pull herself out of the water. In a moment she found she could put most of her weight on her feet and just use the ledge to balance herself. She could walk along the pool as the cave finally gave way and opened out around her.

Hilly found a convenient rock and sat down heavily as water dripped from her coveralls and boots. She let her arms and legs relax, caught her breath, and played the light around her perch. She had arrived at a tiny, sand beach at the edge of the water. There seemed to be no outlet that she could see or hear for the Invisible River to flow from the large, quiet pool in front of her. A small whirlpool in the middle of the pool quietly twisted round and round.

She stood and walked along the edge of the dark pool. She didn't walk far, because tons and tons of gray limestone rose steeply everywhere and blocked her path. As she made her way back to the tiny beach and sat wearily down on the rock again, Hilly knew almost for certain that she had found one end of Worm Cave.

—

Looking upstream from where she had come, she saw no light in the distance yet. The chill was even worse now that she was wet and not exerting anymore. She was shivering and tried to bring the dirty coveralls closer around herself.

Never one to give up, Hilly was thinking it was time for a Plan E when a piece of dull metal caught her eye at the base of a nearby rock. Hilly rose and then knelt next to the rock. She brought the flashlight down near the object. It looked to be a tarnished utensil handle of some sort. Digging in the dirt at the base of the rock with her fingers, she pried the object loose. As she turned it over in her hand she could see it was a very tarnished and bent spoon. The first manmade object she had yet to see in Worm Cave. She studied it closely, but there were no markings other than a simple design on the handle. From the tarnish, it appeared to be made of silver and very old.

She continued to turn it over and over in her light, and then it registered. The fact that this spoon just could not logically be this far into the cave except for one reason hit her. What if where she sat wasn't far into the cave at all? She couldn't imagine someone else coming this far, hours and hours, miles even. What if, despite what the professor had insisted upon, there was another entrance close by?

Hilly stood and climbed the steep slope up the rocks above the pool. She came upon a flat area among the rocks and saw what looked like the remnants of an old, tattered pot and nearby what looked like the remains of a fire pit with pieces of burned charcoal. The reflection she had seen in the distance.

Nearby she picked up an old fork, which looked to be the mate of the spoon. And there were the remains of a small barrel, its staves and hoops scattered about. Her spirits soared! Someone had cooked here at some point a long time ago, but they had come here from another direction, she just knew, by some other way. There had to be a way out. Other men had been in the cave at least as far as the whirlpool.

She played the mini Maglite on the steep rocks above her and immediately saw what appeared to be a well-worn path climbing upward through the jumble of breakdown. The dirt was packed between the rocks. Someone had walked there. No doubt a way out, no matter what the professor believed. With her first optimism since she had fled into Worm Cave many hours ago, Hilly stood and started to climb above the whirlpool. But with her first step, the flashlight failed as its two AA alkaline batteries reached their life limit. The darkness was complete.

Hilly froze. She tapped the flashlight against the palm of her other hand to no effect. The Coppertops were finished. She whirled around but could see nothing. She brought her hand up to her face but could not even see a finger even when it touched her face. The only sound was a distant murmur of water, really just a echoing drip, near the whirlpool.

Hilly cursed and tried to remember what she was seeing when the mini Maglite had given out. She crouched and felt around the area like a blind person until she was somewhat sure there was a rock to sit upon. She slowly lowered herself onto it.

She cursed again. The spare batteries were back in her pack. She just knew she was close to an entrance given the old utensils, pot, barrel parts, and the fire pit. All evidence pointed to it. She just needed fifteen minutes of light. She thought if she was the crying type this would be a good time. The sound of a rock falling in the near distance broke the pity spell. The noise seemed to have come from above her and some distance away in the direction from which she had come. She remembered the professor telling her it took hundreds of years for rocks to fall in a cave when she had been worried about the breakdown around them. It didn't make sense, given what he had said and the odds, that she had just heard a rock fall.

Hilly continued to listen intently in the darkness. Hearing, smell, touch, and—what was the other one?—yes, taste were the only senses that still worked. Sight had been taken. She heard nothing but the occasional murmur of the whirlpool and the hollow drip of water below. She remembered the professor's admonition that a spelunker should always carry three sources of light. Well, most spelunkers are not chased into caves by dogs and armed hit men. Excuse me, Professor. Right now she'd give a lot for two spare AA batteries or even a candle and a match as she sat and twisted the useless flashlight around in her hand, feeling its knurled surfaces.

Suddenly she sat upright. She reached around her waist until she felt the flashlight's nylon holster and slipped the mini Maglite back into its pouch. She reached inside her coveralls with one hand and carefully pulled her cell phone from one of the pockets in her cargo shorts, where she had stashed it. Simple, her cell phone. Source of light number two. How's that, Professor?

Her Samsung 400 was an inexpensive flip phone. Hilly had yet to graduate to a more expensive and capable "smart" phone unlike almost everybody else it seemed to her on planet Earth, but right now, as she felt it in her hand, her cheap phone was priceless even though no cell towers or Internet existed deep within Worm Cave.

By feel, she righted the phone and opened it. She felt for the keyboard and realized she was holding it upside down. She quickly turned it 180 degrees so the keyboard was on the bottom. She needed to push the end button near the upper right of the keyboard to activate the phone. She fumbled for a moment, thought she had located the correct button, bent and shielded the phone, and pushed. The Samsung name appeared in the upper half of the phone followed by the Sprint symbol and jingle a long moment later. Too late she had forgotten about the jingle! Jesus, it sounded loud in the silence of the cave and could certainly give her away! Soon after, the multicolored screen came to life with the time in the middle, 6:51 a.m., along with the backlit keyboard. There were no bars, of course. She also noticed the little battery symbol in the upper right of the screen was empty and the battery outline was red. Bad news.

Hilly stood and held the open cell phone in front of her. Actually, she thought as she tested it, since she was in total darkness, the light seemed sufficient to guide her and follow the rough path. She started to climb. Realizing the size of the cave, she knew she still might have hundreds of feet to climb. The cell phone had buoyed her spirits. Then it automatically dimmed and she was plunged back into almost total darkness. She pressed the end button again and the phone brightened. So this is how it will go, she thought as she guided herself upward looking for an entrance.

She held the cell phone in front of her. The brighter mode lasted five seconds before she had to push the end button or open and close the phone to get another five seconds of brighter light. The climb steepened. Her heart pounded, her legs ached, she felt her wound throbbing, and was certain she now had a number of blisters on her feet. She saw an occasional dusty footprint, which lifted her spirits. She was now sure there was a way out above her somewhere.

Hilly fell into a rhythm with the phone as she climbed, afraid to rest, afraid the battery would suddenly fail. She had no idea what the red outlined battery icon really meant other than she was running out of juice. The climb steepened even more and became near vertical. She held the Samsung in her left hand and used her right hand to help climb, having to halt her progress every five seconds to open and close the phone. The display's relative brightness indicated nothing. The phone's internal lithium-ion battery would fail suddenly, unlike the gradual loss of power with the mini Maglite's alkaline batteries.

Hilly estimated she had climbed two hundred feet or more when the grade suddenly decreased and, to her surprise, she crawled onto a wide, flat ledge. She went forward on her hands and knees until she felt she had the strength to stand. She opened and closed the cell phone. Something was at her feet. She worked the phone again and realized she was standing at the edge of another fire pit. She refreshed the phone again and played it around. There was quite a bit of trash, some old wooden crates, a broken china cup, and some wire, but nothing to start a fire.

She caught her breath and stepped over the blackened pit. In the dim light on the other side, there appeared to be an opening under a ledge. She walked carefully, sank to her knees, and refreshed the phone. It was a passageway, an opening nearly five feet high with a dusty floor. Dozens of footprints led into the darkness. What did spelunkers say? Does it go?

Hilly ducked and entered the passageway. She walked along working the phone, only having to duck a little after a while. The floor was soft and dusty. The dry passageway turned to the right, and soon she was able to walk upright. The only thing that slowed her progress was the necessity of working the cell phone for light. She would have preferred to jog. Her only disappointment was the absence of daylight—or any light—ahead.

The passageway angled a little more to the right. When not working the cell phone, she let the fingers of her left hand drag lightly on the cave's rough limestone wall. Hilly had the sense that the passageway was opening up even more when the lithium-ion battery in her phone failed with no warning and plunged her back into complete darkness—her second source of light gone. Hilly cursed again under her breath and worked the phone a few more times but to no avail. It was finished. She slipped it back into her pocket by feel. Time for plan F she thought. Or was it now Plan M, or even Z?

She was careful not to move. She reached out and touched the left wall again. She would have to go forward by touch now, a slow go for sure. She sank to her hands and knees and moved forward, her left hand feeling the wall and her right hand probing the dusty floor ahead so she wouldn't just drop into a pit like she had almost done when she had suddenly come upon the Grand Canyon. Progress was slow as she inched forward into the darkness, hoping for daylight.

Suddenly, the passageway was bathed in a brilliant blue-white light so intense that after the complete darkness it hurt her eyes and caused her to squint and tear up. She noticed that the passageway ahead took a sharp left turn, and a large object of some type, it appeared to have wheels, blocked the cave. As her eyes adjusted, she turned but could only make out the silhouette of a large man holding the light on her from behind. He was well over six feet tall, broad, and had to duck his head in the passageway. She caught her breath. He was barely fifty feet away.

Instinctively, she reached for her red Swiss Army knife, came to her feet, opened the three-inch blade, and held it in front of her in a defensive stance.

A deep voice with an accent boomed out, "Ah, señorita, you did well, but I finally caught you, eh?"

Hilly stood her ground trying to keep her hands from shaking as the man inched closer. She had been taught to stay silent, not return any taunts. All business. Somehow she knew it would all end here. She also wondered if the man knew about the professor's law of three sources of light as she concocted yet another plan.

The man shined his light on her right hand, "Ah, but I am disappointed by that tiny knife, señorita."

Hilly stood her ground. The man was still silhouetted behind the light, but she saw him move his right hand in the unmistakable movement to holster a pistol of some type. He had been holding a gun on her. Why didn't he just shoot? Ego, she figured. One strike against him already. Hilly thought of the old joke about bringing a knife to a gunfight. In this case, a pocket knife with a three-inch blade, a screwdriver, toothpick, tweezers, scissors, and a corkscrew.

She saw him move his right hand behind his back and, with another unmistakable motion and sound, pull a large knife from a sheath in the small of his back. He brought the knife into the light and turned it over a few times to show her. She estimated a serrated ten-inch blade.

He chuckled, "Now this is a knife!"

Hilly thought as she worked on her plan, you and I are going to find out you're no Crocodile Dundee, asshole. You're forgetting we're in a very dark cave.

The man was barely five feet away now, holding the knife in his right hand and the flashlight in his left. She crouched and got ready. She feinted to her left as he thrust his knife forward. He wasn't expecting what happened next. The knife sliced through her coveralls, cutting the fabric and just missing her left side as she spun quickly to her right and delivered a hard kick to his right knee. He screamed, but it wasn't the knee she was after. As she spun past him, she thrust her small knife blade as hard as she could squarely into the front of the man's large flashlight. The lens shattered and the bulb popped, throwing the passageway into darkness once more as her pocket knife lodged itself in the flashlight.

Hilly was up and running blindly in the soft dirt. She felt the man reach out and try to grab her leg, her foot, anything, and, as she broke free, she tripped and came to her knees. She regained her footing. The darkness was disorienting. She went to her left, extending her fingertips, and found the wall. If only she had a light of some kind. The third source. Then she remembered her Timex Indiglo. As she stumbled forward, she unbuckled the watch and lit the dial. The light was faint. She fell to her knees and held the watch in front of herself as she crawled forward. Behind her she could hear the killer slashing the air with his knife and cursing. She had another advantage, she had seen the passageway ahead, and she doubted he had paid any attention. As she crawled forward she held the watch close to the surface, but it barely illuminated four inches of the dusty floor. But it was light, her third source. The man behind her had none.

Hilly inched forward on her knees and her left hand while holding the watch in her right hand near the dusty floor. As with the cell phone, she had to stop every few seconds and refresh the luminous blue dial, then crawl forward again. Every third time before she refreshed the dial she reached to her left to touch the cave's wall with her fingertips to orient herself; then it was back to her awkward crawl.

She suddenly heard a familiar sound. It was the unmistakable sound of a cigarette lighter opening, then steel striking a flint. She turned and saw the sparks and then the small flame. The man had discovered his second source of light, what looked to be a Zippo lighter that he was carrying. He was barely thirty feet away and waving the lighter in front of him as he limped toward her. She could see his face now with its large black mustache as he grimaced in pain at each step.

Hilly stood and began to jog forward but had hardly taken a step when she ran hard into a solid and unmovable object. She was knocked backward. The watch flew out of her hand and landed ahead of her out of reach in the soft dust. It glowed blue for a few seconds and then was lost in the darkness.

The collision had knocked the breath out of Hilly, and she saw stars for a few seconds. She came to her knees and groped blindly about. What had she hit?

The man was barely twenty feet away now, and she could hear him breathing. She felt something, and her hand closed around a round object. It was wood and maybe two inches in diameter. There was an identical object just above the first, then another, and she used them to bring herself to her feet. Then she felt the wooden rim and the steel tread and realized it was a large wheel of some sort. The round wood objects were spokes. She worked her way to the right and quickly bumped into a large, flat wooden surface. A wagon? It confirmed what she had seen in the distance before she had broken the man's flashlight.

The breathing was heavier. She turned, crouched, and came into a defensive stance once again.. The man was barely five feet from her. She could smell his putrid breath as he faced her. She had struck the first blow but this was no skinny drunk on a front yard. He took a step forward, wincing when he used the knee. Then he held out the lighter in his left hand, inspecting her while holding the large knife in his right. He laughed and with a deep voice. "Ah, there you are again, señorita. Let me get a good look at you." Then he pointed his knife at her, "Don't worry, I plan on fucking you before I kill you." Then he slipped the knife back into the sheath at the small of his back.

Hilly backed up until she felt the wagon's tailgate at her back. The man edged forward holding the lighter in front of him. In an instant, she dived under the wagon.

The man growled and dived forward. The lighter flew from his hand and was snuffed out in the dust. The complete darkness returned. Neither of them had light. She crawled forward breathing hard, but the man was fast and was able to blindly grab one of her ankles before she had gone two feet. He dragged her out from under the wagon, laughing his deep laugh all the while. She tried to kick with her free foot, but she was on her stomach. She tried to twist around to fight him, but the man was strong and she couldn't break his grip.

Hilly reached out and was able to grab one of the spokes on the right wheel with both hands. She hung on with all her strength. The man pulled harder with one arm but could not dislodge her. A tug-of-war using her body. She was panting loudly now and fighting for her life, and he was growling with his effort.

In desperation, he groped in the darkness with his free hand and was finally able to grab her other flailing leg by the ankle. He pulled her toward him with all his considerable strength. The fight to the death would now be in total darkness.

Hilly lost her grip on the spoke with one hand and then the other. She dug her fingers into the dirt but was being pulled backward little by little. In a last effort, she grasped the wagon wheel's wooden rim and its iron tread and locked both arms around it. This slowed him somewhat, but he broke her grip once again.

He pulled her toward him in the dark, past the wheel. Hilly screamed.

There was a loud, heavy thud. The cave's floor seemed to rise a few inches, buckle, then settle quickly once more. Dust filtered down from the ceiling of the passageway and choked them both. The man coughed loudly, hesitated, but did not release his grip on Hilly. There was a loud screeching noise as rocks ground together. Then there was silence for a moment. Then more screeching. A brilliant, large shaft of sunlight filled the space just ahead of the wagon as the large limestone blocks choking the passageway ahead of the wagon parted.

The change from absolute darkness to daylight was quick. The killer, who had been facing the wagon, released his grip with one hand to shade his eyes with the other.

Hilly blinked in the sudden brilliance. Next to her she saw clearly the large wooden wheel and its metal rim in detail—the grain in the wood and the imperfections in the metal. Puzzled, she raised her head. On the other side of the wheel lay a large silver revolver with dull yellow grips in a skeletal hand. Carved into each grip was a prancing horse.

The killer had recovered from the disturbance, the choking dust, and sudden light. He coughed and laughed at his seemingly good fortune. With a fierce roar he grabbed her free leg again and began pulling her toward him by her ankles, now bringing each of her feet on either side of him. Faster than she could respond, he released his grip on her ankles, reached forward, and grabbed the coverall material around her waist.

Hilly snatched the big silver revolver from the bony hand by its grip just before it would have been out of reach. The hand came apart and finger bones scattered in the dust as she dragged the revolver toward her with both hands.

She cleared the tailgate, and the big man forced her over on her back by twisting one leg over the other. He screamed at her in his rage, "Now I will fuck you and then kill you by cutting your heart out, whore!"

Hilly forced herself to sit up in front of him as he parted her legs around his waist. She felt his hardness. The gun was heavy. She brought it up in front of her with both hands and cocked the hammer with both thumbs. There was a metallic click as the cylinder rotated and the hammer locked.

The man stopped spreading her legs and stared at the gun with the large, black bore in the end of its barrel just a few feet in front of his eyes. Hilly would always remember with satisfaction the surprised look on his face as she pulled the trigger and said, "Fuck you, asshole!"

There was a loud, deafening report. A large, white-hot flame leapt from the barrel, and she felt a satisfying kick. The distance was point blank, and the .36 caliber bullet hit him square in the chest.

She pulled back the hammer again with both thumbs. The man looked down at this chest and put a hand over his wound, a black circle on his shirt with a hole in the middle. Blood was starting to seep from the hole. With a roar he moved forward again. Hilly raised the revolver a few inches and pulled the trigger again. The same loud report. A flame leapt again from the barrel, and she felt a satisfying kick again in both hands. This time the killer's head jerked back and then forward. A large hole in the middle of his forehead was surrounded by dark powder residue. He remained on his knees in front of her for a few moments, his eyes registering surprise in their final seconds. Then he toppled forward, pushing her to the ground under his weight.

CHAPTER 37

Daylight

Hilly coughed. The air was thick with acrid black powder smoke and dust as she tried to breathe. The man's heavy, massive body lay on top of her and was squeezing the air from her lungs. Her ears rang from the two gunshots in the enclosed passageway. Her right hand was free, and she gently lay the silver revolver on the cave floor next to her.

After many hours of almost complete darkness even the dim sunlight that filtered from the hole in the ceiling beyond the wagon seemed a blessing. She pushed his shoulder with all her strength and used her legs in an effort to roll him off her. The body moved a few inches, and she was able to free her left arm. Again, she grunted and with all the strength she had left she was finally able to roll him over on his back so she straddled him. His lifeless eyes stared at the ceiling as she came to her knees over the body.

In the dim light she saw that the front of her tattered coveralls and pocket T-shirt were now smeared with the blood from his chest wound. She looked down at the body and quietly said, "Whore, huh? Yeah, fuck you again, asshole." Then she rolled off him and turned toward the rear of the wagon. She picked up the heavy revolver, opened her coveralls, and tucked it in at an angle in her waistband. She noticed her watch under the wagon. Nearby was the man's lighter. It was a Zippo. She put the watch back on her wrist, noticed the time, and cursed. It was eight thirty. The Timex was still ticking.

Hilly crawled on her hands and knees around the wagon wheel, then stood and stared down at mummified remains leaning against the wheel. He was still wearing his gray clothing. His parchment-like skin was stretched over his skeletal remains. His skull had tipped forward onto his breastbone and yet he was still wearing his wide brim hat with what looked like a feather in the band as well as his pistol belt, holster, and tattered leather boots. His bony left hand rested on the cave's floor, like his right hand had—the one from which she had pulled the revolver. Hilly noticed a cracked leather pouch with a rawhide drawstring in the bones of his left hand as she studied the remains.

She knelt on one knee in front of the mummy and carefully extracted the pouch from the skeletal fingers. She held in it in front of her and gently bounced it up and down in her hand appraising it and feeling the weight. There appeared to be a round object inside somewhere between the size of a plum and an apple. Holding the pouch in one hand, she carefully undid the drawstring, which fell into pieces. She carefully widened the mouth of the pouch and peered inside while holding it up at an angle to the sunlight pouring in the opening twenty feet away. Her eyes widened and she whistled under her breath.

She heard men's voices coming from outside as her hearing returned. She carefully folded over the old leather and quickly, gently stuffed the pouch into a pocket of her cargo shorts. She stood while self-consciously trying to pat the dust from her coveralls. Hilly worked her way sideways along the wagon hand over hand using the sideboards for support. She peered into the wagon and noticed a number of heavy wood-and-metal strongboxes in the bed. A shaft of bright sunlight created by the dust and smoke angled down from the hole and illuminated the wagon's tongue and the jumble of rock in front of it. She stepped onto the wooden tongue and looked up. The hole was more a horizontal crack about six feet long and three feet wide and maybe eight feet above her head. Hilly tightroped sideways along the wagon's tongue until it disappeared under the rock rubble. She looked up at the blue morning sky above her and started climbing.

The men's voices were closer now. One was saying, "Ed, that was a good test, but it looks like we're going to have to use a lot more TNT to get all this material small enough to haul off and get down to bedrock."

She heard the other man reply as she climbed, "Yeah, I reckon, Don. It's kind of unusual to see limestone broken up like this." She heard him drop a rock. "Almost like someone blew it up before us."

Hilly climbed as high as she could but was still crouched atop the loose rocks a good four feet below the opening. Her footing was precarious as she slowly and carefully came to her feet and reached up. She carefully grabbed one edge of the hole for balance. Slowly, her head and shoulders, then her chest emerged into the humid, summer air. She breathed deeply as she balanced herself on one side of the opening. She was on a steep, rocky hillside. Then she recognized the old bridge and highway intersection below.

Two older men with their backs to her were standing on a large boulder. Both wore rugged work clothes with bright yellow safety vests and matching yellow hard hats. One had a clipboard and the other was kneeling with a camera. Both were peering down at something between the boulders. A similarly dressed younger man with a handheld radio was making his way up the rocky hillside toward the other two men.
Hilly could have yelled for some help but she was determined to leave the cave on her own just as she had done after the rescue. She put a forearm on each side of the hole and lifted herself from the hole like a gymnast using parallel bars. She swung one leg to the side, then the other, and rolled onto the limestone slab, feeling its warmth. Hilly pushed herself up and stood on weak legs. She breathed deeply and coughed again. The warm morning air felt delicious.

At the sound, one of the men quickly looked up, turned, and was so startled to see her that his helmet did a back flip off his head. The other man was still preoccupied with something below. His partner punched him in the shoulder and made a twirling motion with one hand. The other man looked up and twisted around. His helmet also came off at the apparition before them barely twenty feet away.

As she faced the men, Hilly self-consciously tried to tidy herself up a bit by brushing her thighs and then rubbing her hands together, but it was futile. The front of her coveralls and T-shirt underneath were smeared with fresh blood and mud. Her hair was matted and tangled. She had the big silver revolver stuck in her waistband along with an automatic pistol in a holster on her belt. One missing coverall sleeve displayed a bad wound on her forearm that was clotted black and now with small red streaks around the edge.

One of the men placed his hands on his hips, "What the fuck…"

Hilly interrupted him by looking at her watch and asking, "Can one of you please loan me a car or truck? I have to get to town in a hurry."

The men stood with their mouths open when the third man with the radio hopped up onto a nearby rock, pushed his helmet back, and studied her for a moment. Then he said, "Holy Jesus! Is that you, Ms. Walker…er, Hilly? It's me, Billy!"

Hilly nodded her head quickly, yes, turned, bent over, and vomited onto the rocks below her.

CHAPTER 38

Courtroom 160

Billy's work car turned out to be a faded maroon '94 Buick Roadmaster he claimed he had inherited from his grandmother. It was missing a front hubcap, had a blanket thrown over the torn front seat, and a quarter of a tank of gas.

The three men had quickly gotten over the shock of seeing Hilly almost magically emerge from the cave opening and were eager to help her. They peppered her with endless questions, but Hilly hurriedly waved them off. Especially when they had insisted she needed an ambulance and medical help. Instead, she insisted she had to get into town and again asked if she could borrow someone's car or truck.

Billy had helped her down off the rocky hillside to the main road and then jogged with her to the construction crew parking lot, where he had offered to drive her into town himself. When she adamantly refused his offer, puzzled, he had handed her the keys to the battered Buick.

The two demolition engineers had remained behind on the hillside, and the last Hilly had seen of them, they were kneeling, peering down into the exit hole, and scratching their heads.

The old Buick roared up and out of the West Fork of the Sun River valley, stopped once along the shoulder at the top of the grade, and then accelerated again spraying gravel behind it as Hilly kicked the Roadmaster up to a steady seventy-five, then eighty, as the road ran straight toward town and the rows of corn and soybeans flashed by on both sides. But at eighty, the car's worn front suspension and steering wheel began to shake violently, so she backed off a bit. The sun was still low in the east, and she noticed Billy's wraparound sunglasses hanging from the rearview mirror. She took one hand and lifted the pair off, slipped them on, and quickly glanced at herself in the mirror. What a mess! She took another quick look and thought, real chic look now with the shades, babe, a person could almost forget the dried blood and guts on me.

Three minutes later she slowed as she neared her great-grandfather's farm. The gravel lane near the house and barn was lined with service vehicles. Red fire trucks, yellow rescue trucks, unmarked and marked cop cars, a couple of school buses, and one truck with a large satellite dish on its roof. A white tent was pitched between the house and the barn, and next to it were a white canteen truck with its side down and yet another ambulance. At least two dozen people were milling around the area. Hilly looked at her watch and guessed what all the hoopla was certainly about—her—and thought to herself, it's going to get a lot bigger in just a few minutes, folks, when everyone quickly finds out she was above ground and there was another body or two. A real shit storm was brewing.

A gray Kentucky state trooper Ford Crown Victoria was parked across the lane, blocking it where the drive ended in Route 153. A trooper in a gray uniform leaned on the hood eating a sandwich. A white Styrofoam cup perched next to him on the hood. As Hilly roared by at seventy-five, the cop straightened up, spilled his coffee, and began talking excitedly into the radio mike clipped to his shoulder.

Hilly pressed the car to eighty anyway, and the steering wheel whipsawed back and forth. She glanced at her watch again. 8:52.

She slowed again at the town limits, passed a pickup truck, and nearly T-boned an old Pontiac pulling out of the Lasso and Go! Passing the Fireside Motel, she saw four cars waiting for the red light at the town square by the old Rexall drugstore. Wishing for lights and siren but using the Roadmaster's horn instead, she pulled into the opposite lane, ran the red around the first car, and hurtled into the town square. She braked hard at the crosswalk midway down the square, but two pedestrians saw the Roadmaster coming and jumped back up on the curb.

Hilly came around the square, passed the Subway and the firehouse, locked the brakes in front of the courthouse, and ran the right front tire up over the yellow curb. She threw the Buick into park and hit the ground running, leaving the driver's door open, the engine running, and the car chiming.

Hilly ran up the short flight of gray limestone steps. The heavy brass doors opened into a long hallway tiled in a diamond design flanked by a stairway on each side. Each door opening in the long hallway had a sign hanging at a right angle over the door. Hilly looked right and left. Surprisingly, no one seemed to be in the courthouse. The black-and-white tiled hallway in front of her was empty. And also to her surprise, there was no security checkpoint that she could see. No metal detector archway, no tables, and no gray plastic tubs. Then she noticed to her right an ancient man in some kind of blue uniform. He sat behind a wooden podium on which a desk lamp had been mounted, and a handheld radio sat upright in front of him. Hilly saw him as she skidded to a halt on the tiles. She glanced at her Timex Explorer. It was 8:58 a.m.

The old man picked up the radio at the sight of Hilly, and she turned toward him. She unconsciously put a hand on the butt of the ancient revolver in her waistband, and he carefully set the radio back down. Before he could say anything, Hilly cut him off and shouted, "Courtroom 160, Judge Winslow, where is it?"

The old security guard glanced at the big Colt pistol again and now noticed the holstered Beretta. He pointed nervously down the hall with a quivering finger. "Third door on the right, just past DMV and the county clerk."

Hilly resumed her sprint and heard the man excitedly shouting into his radio something about an insane armed woman loose in the courthouse. Outside a state trooper with coffee stains on his pants pulled up behind the Roadmaster in his Crown Victoria.

The sign over the polished wooden double doors with brass hinges and latches said Courtroom 160. Hilly pushed both doors open, entered the courtroom, and stopped in her tracks ten feet down the central aisle.

The courtroom was packed. Every seat had been taken. People stood along the back wall. Some sat in the jury box. Everyone turned in unison and was suddenly looking at her. Midway down the aisle she recognized the three Korean men from that night in the Worm Café. Near the front sat the reporter, Roland Harrington, with his pad and pen. He began to write furiously. In the first row on the left was Sheriff Ferguson with a male deputy she had never met next to him.

L. T. Rice was standing in front of the judge's wooden bench with a sheaf of paper in both hands. Hilly smiled to herself. L. T. looked none the worse for wear dressed in a nicely pressed gray flannel suit. The white-haired judge, with a stern look, appeared to have been raising his gavel but had stopped in midair.

The uniformed deputy rose from his seat and slowly unsnapped his holster, but the sheriff leaned over and put his hand over the deputy's gun hand, shook his head, and motioned for him to sit down. Judge Winslow slowly lowered his wooden gavel and held one end pensively in each hand as he looked at the apparition that had just entered his courtroom. No one dared to breathe. The only sound in the courtroom was the four rotating ceiling fans.

The judge spoke first. "And, for God's sake, who are you?"

Before Hilly could reply, L. T. Rice proudly spoke for her as he turned back to the judge. "Judge, may I introduce my client, Hildegard Walker."

The judge said, "Can anyone else verify this…this…this woman's identity?"

The sheriff stood and calmly said, "Yes, Homer, I can verify that."

The judge looked up at the big clock over the double doors and then at his watch. "Counselor Rice, I have no choice but to grant your motion in the matter of Charles McHenry's estate." With that he banged his gavel down loudly on the bench in front of him. "Court adjourned!"

CHAPTER 39

Exit

The sleek Gulfstream G650 business jet sat in front of the general aviation terminal at the Detroit Metropolitan Wayne County Airport. Its airstair door just behind the cockpit was open, and there was a red carpet underneath. A nonstop flight plan to Zurich had been filed with air traffic control, and other required paperwork had been seen to. The jet was scheduled to depart into the clear fall evening in fifteen minutes.

The crew waited in the lounge area for their single passenger, although this particular G650 was configured to seat up to twelve passengers in total luxury. The flight to Zurich was planned at just over eight hours, so the crew this evening consisted of a captain and two first officers instead of one. The gray-haired captain sat in the crew lounge reading a book, one younger first officer sat next to him thumbing a game on his smart phone, while the second first officer, the lowest in seniority, was outside on the ramp with a flashlight making a final preflight check of the G650. The Gulfstream had been fueled. Tonight's flight would be 4,225 miles, well within the jet's 7,000 plus-mile-nonstop range.

Since there was only one passenger this evening, the charter company had assigned only one flight attendant. She was a raven-haired, sharp-tongued beauty in her early forties originally born in Lebanon. She had been with the charter company for some twenty years and could speak five languages fluently. Tonight's flight crew, all married men, were madly in love with her. She was a perfectionist and had seen that the cabin had been prepared to not only the charter company's high standards but to her own. She provided a level of service to her passengers unknown to most airline passengers. Woe to any company pilot, captains included, who crossed her. She let it be known that she owned everything from the cockpit door to the rear lavatory. She sat in the lounge across from the captain and the first officer reading a magazine with her legs crossed, nervously bouncing one foot.

A black Cadillac Escalade pulled up in the front of the terminal. The captain closed his book and placed it on the coffee table. Then he shrugged into this blue uniform coat with four stripes on each sleeve, adjusted his tie, placed the book under one arm, and went through the double glass doors onto the ramp, spinning one finger in the air telling the second first officer to climb aboard and start the auxiliary power unit. Usually the APU was running and providing the aircraft's heat or air-conditioning, but it was such a pleasant evening the captain had left it off until now.

The other first officer stowed his smart phone, and the flight attendant put down her magazine. They walked over to the glass double doors to the ramp and quite literally stood at attention, waiting for their passenger.

Two stern-looking men in dark suits and ties and telltale bulges under their left arms occupied the front seat of the Escalade. The driver exited the vehicle and went to the rear of the Cadillac SUV while the front passenger went to the right rear passenger door. Hilly waited until the man opened the door for her, then walked to the entrance to the terminal and waited patiently for him to close the Escalade's door and open the terminal door for her. She was learning.

Hilly walked purposefully into the waiting lounge and caught her breath for a moment at the sight of the sleek Gulfstream jet with the Swiss registration letters on the tail. The multimillion-dollar airplane with the red carpet under the door was waiting for no one but her.

She strode up to the dark-haired flight attendant while reaching into her Gucci black leather and canvas shoulder bag for her passport as if she did this all the time. She let out a huff of breath as if this was a large inconvenience.

Hilly thought she had cleaned up pretty nicely since that July morning in the Walker County courthouse two months ago. Her hair was longer now, and she had seen to it that it had been done perfectly, even covering those nasty streaks of gray, which she seemed to have more of when she finally had left Batavia, Kentucky. She had done her makeup herself at the Westin a few hours ago and hoped it would pass everyone's inspection. She wore an expensive, long-sleeved white silk blouse, which helped hide the bullet wound and the bandage she still wore. She wore the same gold necklace she had worn in the cave rescue those months ago paired again with her mother's gold art deco pin and simple diamond earrings. Her blouse was belted into gray woolen slacks. In the cool fall evening, she also decided to wear a light blue blazer. All very fashionable for a woman used to wearing sweat pants and T-shirts around the house.

The flight attendant reached out for the red Swiss passport with the white cross on the cover, and Hilly impatiently handed it to her, then looked at her Omega wrist watch. The flight attendant opened the passport quickly, thinking this US Transportation Security Administration requirement was certainly an impropriety for this class of passenger.. She flashed Hilly a million-dollar smile and handed Hilly back the passport, much to Hilly's relief.

Opening her purse to put the passport away, Hilly noticed the Escalade's driver carrying her Louis Vuitton leather luggage, two tan suitcases, across the ramp to the rear of the Gulfstream. The flight attendant followed her glance. "Don't worry, Ms. Wilz, we have complete access to your luggage from the cabin if you need anything." The flight attendant, who missed nothing, had also noticed Hilly glancing impatiently at her watch and added, "The flight is scheduled to depart on time, Ms. Wilz."

Hilly nodded and realized she hadn't spoken one word yet. Hildegard Wilz was the name on the Swiss passport. She had to get used to the new identity. Still learning.

The flight attendant and the first officer opened the double glass doors to the ramp for Hilly and stood on either side. The flight attendant flashed another dazzling smile, extended a hand toward the Gulfstream, and said officially in perfect English, "Welcome aboard, Ms. Wilz. What language do you prefer?"

Hilly smiled back. No one had ever asked her this question. "English will be fine." She instantly liked this woman.

Hilly slipped the Swiss passport back into her purse alongside her US passport, noticing her hand was shaking a bit. Also in her purse were her Swiss Army Knife, burner cell phone, and wallet. The wallet contained the new credit cards and $815 in cash and some change, her entire fortune at the moment if you discounted the Swiss *privatbankier* passbook next to it. All seemed in order, but before she zipped the purse shut she checked again to make sure the new lambskin pouch with the drawstring (the original one had simply fallen apart) was resting at the bottom. It was still there. She gave it a squeeze just to make sure. She knew the object inside might buy three of the jets she was about to board.

Her outfit was the real thing. She had purchased it and the three others in the suitcases in a shopping spree at a Saks Fifth Avenue in the northern Detroit suburbs, greatly depleting her savings. The leather Louis Vuitton suitcases, Gucci purse, diamond earrings, and the Omega watch were used and came from a big pawnshop outside Detroit, depleting her savings even more despite haggling with the owner.

She had been staying in a Westin Hotel at the airport for the past four days in a paid-for luxury suite until the air-freighted package had arrived at the hotel from Antwerp with the Swiss passport, Swiss driver's license, and the bank book the second day. Anton had included a note that assured her that all the documents were completely authentic and that encouraged her to check the balance in the bank account via a secure Internet connection to see if all was satisfactory. She had checked and had drawn a very big breath. He also told her in the handwritten note to act like a "rich bitch" and reminded her that the airplane was ten grand an hour.

Hilly walked on the red carpet and approached the Gulfstream's airstairs. The captain doffed his hat, shook her hand, welcomed her aboard his aircraft, and gestured for her to board. He smiled as he inhaled a pleasant whiff of Chanel as she passed by.

She climbed the steps, ducking under the opening a little and glanced into the cockpit, where one pilot was seated. The captain, the flight attendant, and the other first officer followed Hilly into the cabin. Hilly stopped a few feet down the aisle and tried not to gawk. She had ridden in a few small business jets over the years connected to investigations in the military and the Detroit PD. They had all been cramped and noisy with narrow aisles and low ceilings. Hilly took in the large cabin of the Gulfstream as the flight attendant came up behind her. On each side were three pairs of overly large seats facing each other upholstered in soft butterscotch leather. A glossy, highly polished wood folding table divided each pair of seats. On each table was secured a small crystal vase with a colorful flower arrangement. The cabin, with its polished wood accents, was bathed indirectly in soft light. A bright, adjustable LED reading light in the ceiling illuminated each seating area. Hilly noticed she could stand upright in the aisle with the ceiling some inches over her head. She inhaled before moving down the aisle. The cabin actually smelled good, a delightful scent of leather, light perfume, and fresh air.

The flight attendant came up behind Hilly and broke the spell. She extended a hand. "Sit anywhere you like, Ms. Wilz."

Hilly said thank you and chose the forward-facing seat in the middle pair of seats on the right. Before she sat down, she started to shrug off her blazer. The flight attendant was beside her in an instant to help her take it off, and then she carefully took the blazer forward, where she hung it in a closet, smoothing it out as she did so.

Hilly sank into the sumptuous leather seat and almost sighed. She carefully put her purse between her and the armrest. The flight attendant returned with a napkin and a champagne flute filled with a tawny, bubbly liquid. She proffered the flute to Hilly and said, "Ms. Wilz, my name is Layla and I will be at your service tonight. Would you like some champagne before we depart?" Hilly nodded, and the flight attendant first placed the cloth napkin on the table and then the crystal flute. Hilly picked up the glass of champagne and took a sip. Heavenly! "We also have a selection of beers, wines, soft drinks, and sparkling water." Hilly wondered to herself if they had some Royal Crown soda. "I will also be serving dinner an hour after takeoff or at your leisure." Hilly nodded and took another sip of the champagne, this time a little bigger.

Layla disappeared down the aisle, turning off the remaining reading lights and lowering the cove lighting. She passed Hilly and walked to the front of the cabin, still turning off lights, until Hilly sat in her own pool of light sipping her champagne.

The cockpit door was still open with its multitude of colorful lights and instruments. One of the pilots was closing the airstair door. He made some visual checks and then disappeared into the cockpit, closing the door behind him.

Layla appeared in the aisle with the champagne bottle and topped off Hilly's crystal flute. She stowed the bottle again in the forward galley and returned. "Sorry to bother you, Ms. Wilz, but by regulation I must give you a short safety brief." She explained the emergency exits, seat belt use, emergency oxygen use, and placement of the life vests. She also handed Hilly a remote to control the amenities at her seat then nodded sternly at Hilly's lap after she had explained the use of seat belts, and Hilly quickly set the champagne flute on the table and buckled up. Not even rich people do without seat belts she thought.

Layla went forward again and retrieved the champagne bottle. Hilly heard one engine in the rear start and then the other. Layla returned and topped off the flute once more. "Is there anything else I can get you to make you more comfortable, Ms. Wilz?"

Hilly took off the diamond earrings and placed them on the table. "No, Layla, you've been too good to me. And, please, call me, Hilly, short as you know, for Hildegard, the rest of the flight."

Hilly noticed the flight attendant make a slight frown at the familiarity. "Yes, ma'am, Hilly, from now on."

The flight attendant walked to the front of the cabin and spoke softly into a handset on the wall near the cockpit door. Then she lowered a jumpseat near the main cabin door and buckled herself into it, including shoulder straps. Layla smiled down the aisle, and Hilly now realized that the airplane had not been going to move until she, the lone passenger, was ready and comfortable.

The Gulfstream moved smoothly across the ramp toward the active runway. Hilly looked at her pawnshop Omega. It was precisely eight o'clock. A small line of airplanes was waiting for takeoff, but soon the Gulfstream was airborne and banking smoothly over the Detroit suburbs. Hilly took another sip of champagne, turned off her reading light, looked down at the city, and wondered if she would ever return. She felt like a combination of a character in a James Bond movie, a smuggler, and a person in some type of material witness program as she thought of the last six weeks.

CHAPTER 40

The Shit Storm

The shit storm started the instant Judge Winslow's gavel came down on his wooden bench and he pronounced Hilly as the rightful heir. She was suddenly in the eye of the storm.

The bailiff, whose name was Jimmy and who had been outside a fire exit stealing a smoke, came quietly into the courtroom only to find her standing in the aisle square in front of him swaying a little on her feet. He was surprised to see everyone in the courtroom on their feet, including the judge, and looking in his direction. Sheriff Ferguson and his deputy, Roy, were running up the aisle toward the woman standing five feet in front of him, followed slowly by that old coot of a lawyer, Rice. A state trooper then came through the door and almost knocked him down.

The sheriff reached the woman first and helped her into one of the nearby pew-like wooden courtroom seats. His deputy stood in the aisle nearby and spoke into the mike on his shoulder, calling for an ambulance, which, in fact, was barely over a hundred feet away, sitting in front of its bay being washed by the two volunteer firefighters on duty that day.

As the sheriff lowered Hilly onto the seat cushion, the bailiff and the state trooper stared wide-eyed when they saw that Hilly was armed to the teeth—especially the bailiff, whose job was to keep order in the courtroom. After she was seated, the sheriff noticed the wound on her forearm and the blood on the coveralls, but even so, held out his hand for both guns. Hilly obliged by unsnapping the holster, bringing out the Beretta, and handing it to him butt first. She told the sheriff it was empty, but he checked anyway by bringing the slide back. The Civil War–era Colt revolver was another matter. She pulled it gingerly from her waistband and handed the heavy, engraved pistol to the sheriff also butt first, explaining that she thought it was still loaded with at least four rounds. The sheriff gingerly took it and handed it with its dangerous 150-year-old black powder load and percussion caps to his deputy, Roy, who carefully held it with two fingers, barrel down. As it turned out later, no one present knew exactly how to disarm it.

The courtroom went silent at the sight of the two guns and everyone instinctively backed up a few feet into each other. L. T. Rice finally made it up the aisle to his client, looked at her, and put a finger over his lips. Then he demanded receipts from the sheriff, who was now desperate for a couple of evidence bags, for both guns.

The state trooper received a radio call about two more bodies and backed out the door. The two volunteer firemen had driven the soapy ambulance fifty feet to the courthouse and triple-parked near the state trooper's car. One of them shut off the Buick still idling by the curb on their way into the courthouse. They came into the courtroom pushing a gurney covered with a white sheet.

The judge, who had never seen anything like this in his thirty-year career, decided to sit down and yelled at his bailiff, "Jimmy, get this woman some water!" He would deal with Jimmy's absence later.

Hilly refused to ride the gurney and wasn't too happy about the ambulance ride either. Pride. But she agreed to ride in it if they left the lights and sirens off and let her walk out of the courthouse.

A crowd had gathered opposite the courthouse on the town square when they boarded. The two firefighters sat up front, she had refused any aid, and Roy the deputy sat in the back facing Hilly as they rode the five blocks to the small hospital near the high school. Hilly knew Roy was the sheriff's way to keep an eye on her. Roy had heard the stories about her by now, acted jumpy, and kept his hand on his holster the entire time. The shit storm wind was starting to pick up.

Sheriff Ferguson, after logging in the guns and placing them carefully in a safe in his office for the time being with Rice present, headed out to the rock pile near the bridge over the West Fork in his Crown Vic, where he had also learned there were two more bodies and some kind of old wagon in a hole.

At the hospital two doctors, one male and one female, and two nurses took Hilly into an examination room and tended to her wound which required twenty stitches. One of the nurses, holding a clipboard and pages of forms, asked Hilly personal and health-related questions. More importantly, yes, she had insurance. The doctors took her blood pressure, took her pulse, listened to her lungs, and took her temperature. Everything was a little elevated. Hilly almost fell asleep on the examination table. After they tended to her bullet wound—really a bullet-fragment wound—and told her they would by law have to report it to the sheriff's department, she laughed and told them she thought the sheriff already knew about it.

Finally, they took her to an empty hospital room with an adjacent bathroom and shower. Deputy Roy appeared again accompanied by a female orderly. He told her politely that she was under arrest, read her Miranda rights, and told her to empty her pockets. The first dark cloud of the shit storm had appeared on the horizon. When she asked what the charges were, he simply mumbled something about a criminal investigation and Sheriff Ferguson's orders.

After she emptied her pockets, including some loose change she didn't remember, and gave him her cell phone, the mini Maglite, her watch, and the webbed belt and holster, she asked the deputy seriously, "Am I going to jail, deputy?"

He replied, "No, ma'am, no cuffs or anything. Sheriff's orders. He just said to tell you not to leave town."

"Just like the old West." She quipped.

Roy couldn't help himself, hooked his thumbs over his gun belt, and simply replied, "Yep." He placed everything in a white kitchen garbage bag and left the room, to be replaced by the female doctor with two garbage bags—a large black one and a smaller white one—and a roll of tape.

The doctor said politely, "The deputy ordered me to be in the room to gather your clothing, sorry."

Hilly nodded and began to undress. When she was down to her bra and panties, the doctor held up her hand and said she had seen enough and gathered the pungent clothes and the ruined boots into the large black bag. She took the smaller bag and taped it expertly around Hilly's wounded forearm before pointing to the shower and telling her she would collect the underwear later. The doctor then left the room.

Hilly entered the bathroom and closed the door behind her. She noticed there was a neat pile of clothing resting on the closed toilet seat, on top of which stood a bar of soap and a tube of shampoo. The clothes were blue nurse's scrubs and underwear. A pair of white canvas shoes sat on the floor nearby. A clean white towel and washcloth were hanging on the rack in the shower.

She didn't emerge for twenty minutes, and when she did, she found Deputy Big waiting in the room. "Hey, y'all, I knew you was tough but not as tough as I'm hearin'."

Hilly asked seriously. "Are you here to drive me to the jail? Did the sheriff change his mind?"

"Don't be silly. No, actually, I'm here to drive you back to the Bluebird and tuck you in, sheriff's orders, Hilly." Then she handed Hilly three small medicine bottles. "Doc Kramer had to leave and said for me to give these to you." Big looked at the bottles. "He said one's an antibiotic for that arm, the other's some pain pills, and the third's some sleeping pills."

Hilly put the three plastic bottles in the pocket of the blue scrubs she was now wearing and followed Big out of the room, down the hall, through the small lobby, through the automatic doors, and out to the Tahoe waiting under the emergency portico. The afternoon heat hit her like a wall. Big climbed into the driver's seat. Hilly opened the front passenger door and hesitated. "What, no cuffs?"

"Yeah, no cuffs either, sheriff's orders. Though there's plenty that would like to see you in cuffs right now I hear. He's pissin' off everybody."

Hilly wearily climbed in, and Big put the Tahoe in gear and turned up the air. Big said, "I'd like to ask you all kinds of questions, but, you know, the Miranda thing and all, me bein' a sworn officer of the law."

Hilly just nodded.

Big stopped at the Bluebird's office, jumped out and retrieved a room key. Hilly could see Miss E. behind the counter craning her neck mightily trying to catch a glimpse of her guest as Big came back to the Tahoe. Big parked in front of Room 15 and handed Hilly the key along with her business card. "You're supposed to stay in your room for now; consider it motel arrest. If you want to go anywhere—*anywhere*—call that number." Big peered over her sunglasses at Hilly. "Don't go wandering off if you catch my drift, honey."

Hilly nodded and got out of the Tahoe. As she walked to the room, she glanced over her shoulder. The Tahoe hadn't moved.

The air conditioner was humming, and the room felt good after the heat and humidity. A stack of her clothes was resting on the end of the bed, all laundered and pressed by Miss E. On one of the bedside tables were two of Johnnie's chocolate doughnuts resting on napkins. Next to the doughnuts was a full ice bucket with two cans of Royal Crown Cola. Hilly went into the immaculate bathroom and set the medicine bottles on the sink under the mirror. She swallowed one of the antibiotic pills and a sleeping pill as she looked at her image. She thought she looked at least ten years older. She laid down on top the covers and stared at the ceiling. She slept for twelve hours.

The room was dark when she awoke. She walked softly to the front window over the desk and slowly pulled back the curtain. There was a white unmarked Crown Vic with a trunk antenna in front of her room parked next to a marked Kentucky state trooper cruiser. A cigarette flared briefly in the unmarked Crown Vic. They wouldn't let her leave for another five weeks.

Hilly slept a few more hours but was up by five. She brushed her teeth, took another antibiotic, and then spent twenty minutes getting her hair somewhat squared away. She slipped on a clean pair of jeans and a T-shirt. Her Nikes had been left with the professor and the Suburban, so she slipped on the canvas shoes she had worn back to the motel from the hospital. In the predawn light she saw both police cars still parked out in front of her room.

By six, she was starved and stepped out into the early-morning coolness, intent on walking to the office to retrieve a cup of coffee to go with the two doughnuts still on the bedside table. The two car doors opened simultaneously as she stepped outside. Hilly and the two cops, one obviously a fed in civilian clothes, stood there awkwardly until the young trooper in uniform cleared his throat and finally asked quietly, "Eh, Ms. Walker, where you headed, ma'am?"

"Just down to the office to get a cup of coffee, officer."

"OK," he said, as he gently shut his car door, "I'm afraid I'll have to escort you."

Hilly started down the walk between the rooms and the construction crew's service trucks. Lights were on in some rooms as workers prepared for another day at the dam site. "That's OK, officer."

When they returned to the room, the state trooper, clearly embarrassed, said in a low voice, "Sorry, ma'am; orders."

Hilly smiled and said, "I understand."

The state trooper walked to his car, turned, and watched as Hilly opened her door. "I almost forgot, ma'am. They want to see you in the sheriff's office at 0900. Someone will give you a lift." Hilly nodded and closed her door. Two blocks.

In the initial excitement in the courtroom the day before no one realized that Roland Harrington had taken some pictures with his smart phone. By eight o'clock, the story, "Pistol-Packin' Heiress" had appeared on the front page of the morning edition of the *Walker County Eagle*. An hour later, the story was picked up by the AP, then NBC, CBS, ABC, CNN, and Fox—and it was promptly buried. No one was interested.

Deputy Big came by Hilly's room in the Crown Vic at 8:45 and drove her the two short blocks up the alley to the town square. She escorted Hilly inside the sheriff's annex, down a hallway to a conference room where at least ten men including the sheriff—some in coats and ties—milled around, talking in clusters, eating doughnuts from Johnnie's, and drinking coffee. She spotted L. T. Rice and another man talking quietly in one corner.

The room went silent at Hilly's appearance. Rice and the other man approached her and asked if she had been read her Miranda rights and Hilly nodded. She had done many interrogations herself and recognized the setup. She became somewhat nervous being on the other side of the table, although she knew she had not done anything wrong nor, in her opinion, committed a crime. Deputy Big left, and Sheriff Ferguson pulled out a chair for Hilly. Hilly wished she had dressed better, but her good clothes had been ruined in the cave rescue.

The restless men in the room represented government agencies called in on the case in the last twenty-four hours: the FBI, the Drug Enforcement Administration, the Kentucky State Police, the US Forest Service, and even the Atlanta police department represented by a lone detective. All had been ordered to Batavia, had traveled overnight by various means, and were sleepless, unshaven, and wore rumpled suits and ties. Everyone thought they had an interest in the case about which more was being learned by the hour. These men were just the vanguard. The two motels in town were still booked full by the dam workers. The motels out by the interstate would do a booming business in coming weeks and some agents would just have to double up.

This was Sheriff Ferguson's case, and he introduced everyone to Hilly, Rice, and the other criminal lawyer who Rice had called down from Lexington because Rice himself was a potential witness. The other lawyer's name was Edgar Johnson, and he charged $300 an hour. He had left Lexington in his Lexus at five in the morning to be here. His were only the first billable legal hours that would start piling up in the coming weeks.

Sheriff Ferguson rubbed his chin and announced that so far the tally was seven dead men and he added, a mummy of some kind, and, don't forget, three dogs. At the mention of the dogs, all the men turned and stared at Hilly. The sheriff cleared his throat and said all the potential crime scenes had been secured.

Under the table Hilly was also counting with her fingers. She came up with "only" six bodies not including the mummy. She had shot four, maybe five people, and seen one thrown from the Opera Box. Maybe he was counting the mummy? She did not include the other assassin who had gone the other way in the cave. Missing? She remained silent as the sheriff counted off the bodies. Confusing.

The lawyer Johnson then asked for an hour to confer with his client whom he had just met. Despite some grumbling from everyone, the sheriff conceded, and the three retired to Rice's office above the Worm Café. They actually didn't return for two hours as Johnson heard the story firsthand.

Roland Harrington drove out to the bridge construction site to see about the discovery of a so-called mummy and the wagon and was surprised to see the area's rocky hillside guarded by two state troopers. Hilly's escape hole up above had been cordoned off by yellow crime tape, and there was a state detective on his knees peering down into something. So far no one had actually climbed down into the hole. The detective considered it too dangerous and was waiting for a search-and-rescue unit driving down from Frankfort, the state capital, and another cave rescue unit from Mammoth Cave National Park.. Harrington knew one of the troopers, and he was told off the record about some kind of cave up there. It was indeed a fact that there was a mummy, a wooden wagon, and a fresh body from what they could see. On his way back to his car Harrington spoke with some of the bridge construction workers, and they told him a story of a woman who had crawled out of the a hole yesterday morning. Harrington began to put two and two together. He wrote another story about the wagon and the mummy for the next day's edition of the *Eagle* and also put a wire story out. No other news agency appeared interested. As for the woman the construction workers had seen yesterday, Harrington thought for sure it had to have been Hilly Walker. He noted the fresh body in addition to the mummy on his notepad.

Friday afternoon Hilly, Rice, and Johnson met again with the government men in the sheriff's conference room, and, under the lawyer from Lexington's watchful eye, Hilly and Rice began to tell their stories.

The sheriff held his first of many news conferences later in the afternoon. The news broke that evening in Atlanta that Alex Kingman, the Atomic Furniture magnate and TV personality, had been found dead in the hills of central Kentucky in a marijuana plantation. All the Atlanta TV stations carried the story on the eleven o'clock news.

The three Korean businessmen left town and were never seen again.

The Kentucky search-and-rescue team arrived early on Saturday along with the National Park Service's Mammoth Cave rescue team. Most of the members of each team knew one another and had worked together before on rescues, but none had been involved in the type of rescue that was about to unfold over the next few days. They set up camp at the farmhouse and met with Professor Cunningham, whom they all knew and respected.

Members of the Kentucky State Historical Society were also called in to work with the cavers. They set about to carefully remove the mummy and the by-now ripe body of the Mexican assassin. It was later learned through fingerprints that his name was Roberto Sanchez and was wanted for murder in at least three countries. Even after the bodies were removed, it would take another week to carefully enlarge Hilly's escape hole with jackhammers and lift out the guarded wagon and strongboxes with a ninety-foot crane.

On Saturday afternoon, Hilly got to the point in her story where she told everyone that she had been a witness to the two Mexicans throwing the third man off the Opera Box. Eyebrows were raised and throats cleared. Notes were taken. Counting the ones she had shot in the lane and the cave, where was the third Mexican in her story? Yet another body somewhere? The cave entrance had been secured as a crime scene, and all bodies from the farm and the ridge, including the dogs, had been transferred by refrigerated truck to a morgue in Lexington because the Walker County coroner's facility was inadequate. The missing Mexican would possibly make nine total, counting the mummy and the body still below the Opera Box.. Everyone drew a breath with the news that there was the possibility of yet still another armed Mexican roaming around in Worm Cave, as they had all come to call it. Plans were started immediately to have the two cave rescue teams enter Worm Cave with armed men to bring out the body below the Opera Box. It was becoming a big, very unique operation. Roland Harrington continued to take notes and was beginning to smell a potential Pulitzer.

All the vehicles at the farmhouse, including Hilly's Honda, had been towed to the Walker County maintenance shop to be examined.

One of the Kentucky State Historical Society members that had arrived was found to be an antique firearms expert, and he finally unloaded the old Colt revolver. He confirmed it was a very special order Colt 1851 Navy revolver in excellent condition and then contacted Colt's Manufacturing Company in Hartford, Connecticut, with the serial number in order to maybe identify the mummy and a year of manufacture.

While extracting the Mexican's body in a bag over the wagon and out of the hole, two members of the Mammoth Cave rescue team took it upon themselves to explore the dusty passage a little farther and came back with a wild story of a huge cave beyond. Despite the excitement, nobody was able to return to explore the cave as a police guard was put on the hole over the wagon and strongboxes after the removal of the mummy and the Mexican. No one was allowed back into the opening. They were disappointed until they were briefed that evening by law enforcement officials and Professor Cunningham about the possible extraction of yet another body from a cave and another dangerous Mexican still in the cave as far as anyone knew. They would enter the cave by another opening the next day with armed guards and not be disappointed when they arrived at the Opera Box. The news of a vast, new, unknown cave, Worm Cave, circulated quickly in spelunker circles.

On Monday, a select few of the two cave rescue teams, Professor Cunningham, and four armed cops, two FBI agents and two state troopers, suited up in spelunking gear and entered Worm Cave at what was now called the farmhouse entrance. It took eight hours for the team to bring out Alvin's torn body and nearby broken Winchester. They found no sign of the other Mexican assassin, but everyone on the recovery team spoke of nothing else but the vast cave. None of the cavers had ever seen anything like it.

Roland Harrington interviewed some members of the team and wrote another story for the *Eagle* and put the story on the wire.

On Tuesday, the large US news agencies suddenly took notice of the stories coming from central Kentucky, and five national news agency satellite trucks and reporters headed for Batavia.

On Wednesday, lawyers and officials from the National Park Foundation and Department of the Interior began to arrive. Hilly and Camas Worm were keeping their promise of donating Worm Ridge and other lands to the government for a new national park. Rice, Hilly, and Johnson met with law enforcement in the morning in the sheriff's conference room, had lunch at the Worm, and then met with the park people in the afternoon. Camas Worm had his own lawyer now, a cousin from Somerset, Kentucky.

Hilly usually sat with Professor Cunningham at lunch and described the cave as best as she could while he drew maps. As it turned out while being pursued, she had explored the cave now more than any living person.

On the following Thursday, the wagon was finally removed from its tomb of 150 years. A large crowd attended the removal. Everyone commented on its perfect preservation in the dry, cool cave air. A locksmith picked the locks, and everyone held their breath as the strongboxes were opened one by one under the watchful eyes of the state police and the FBI. They were not disappointed. An inventory was begun. The estimate of their contents of gold and silver bars, coins, silver cutlery, gems, and jewelry quickly grew to the many millions. The age-old legend of buried treasure turned out to be true, after all. The state of Kentucky swooped in and claimed it all, saying that the find was in a public road right-of-way. News of the treasure spread around the nation on all the news outlets that day. The treasure was trucked to a Federal Reserve bank in Louisville by armored car.

Offers poured in for interviews from all the big TV news shows, including *60 Minutes*, *Dateline*, and *20/20*. Roland Harrington also put in a request for the *Walker County Eagle*. All offers were declined, even Harrington's, by Hilly, Rice, and Camas Worm.

During the second week, Hilly, always declaring self-defense, was taken to both scenes riding in the Tahoe with Deputy Big to reenact everything. Two of the law enforcement officials had her demonstrate, with their unloaded guns touching her forehead, just how she had disarmed Kingman. She took away their firearm each time and turned it on them quickly with no trouble as Deputy Big looked on and smiled. Hilly had gained respect with the law enforcement officials in the interviews as they considered her background and past record of service, she was one of them, but this brought that respect even higher.

Also during the second week, officials from the Internal Revenue Service and the Kentucky Department of Revenue arrived to enter into the discussion of the land donation to the National Park Service. Reporters from *National Geographic* and *Outside* magazine also rolled into town.

The morning meetings in the sheriff's conference room and afternoon meetings in Rice's law office had continued into the fourth week, when Hilly's Honda was returned to the Bluebird's parking lot in spotless condition and a full tank of gas courtesy of the Walker County maintenance shop, the head of which was remotely related to Ronny Henderson. Hilly drove it during the lunch break to Ben's Auto Repair while Deputy Big followed in the Crown Vic. A new starter was ordered, delivered by FedEx the next day, and installed in the Honda. The starter cost $293, but Ben refused to charge any labor for the installation as the Henderson boy was also a relative of his. Hilly thought the timing was right. Her monthly pension check, such as it was, had just been deposited in her checking account.

By the fifth week, the law enforcement officials were pretty well satisfied with Hilly's story and declared her innocence. A crime had been committed, but no one could be charged. They were all dead. Her Beretta 92FS and other possessions were returned to her, and she was told that she was free to go—but that maybe she could stick around a few more days in case there were any more questions. There would be some informal investigations by every agency later into the various role and influence of the Walker County Sheriff's Office, some members of the state legislature, Judge Winslow, Atomic Furniture Warehouse and its CEO, and even the Korean car company in the matter of Charles McHeny's estate.

By the end of the fifth week Hilly had been in Batavia, the tentative papers had been signed and sealed to lay the groundwork for the nation's newest national park. Some National Park Service people had balked at the name, but it was to be Worm Cave National Park into perpetuity, all 19,000 acres of it. Camas Worm, good to his promise, had donated all of his family's holdings on Worm Ridge, including some forested land north of the ridge. Hilly had donated all her inheritance north of route 153 directly to the National Park Service. The farmland south of the state route and the land out by Interstate 75 and the railroad the Korean car company had wanted was to be leased to the Worm family for twenty years at a dollar per year, and then it would revert to the National Park Service and the Department of the Interior to be eventually restored to its prehistoric prairie and forested state for all to enjoy. The state of Kentucky would also cede to the National Park Service its highway right-of-way surrounding the second entrance to Worm Cave. Most importantly, the IRS and the Kentucky Department of Revenue signed off on no tax liability for anyone in the deal.

Finally, a federal judge in Cincinnati issued an injunction stopping the Corps of Engineers from further work on the Sun River Dam project.

CHAPTER 41

Farewell

Hilly and L. T. Rice stood at the curb in front of the Worm Café. Rice, dressed in one of his best seersucker suits with the coat unbuttoned, worked a toothpick up and down. A cold front had passed through that morning with a few showers. The air was crisp and refreshing, fall-like, and the sun had already set behind the buildings on the west side of the square.

Hilly and Rice heard the Tahoe start in front of the sheriff's office as Deputy Big and Professor Cunningham backed out of the reserved parking spot to drop him off at the Fireside and for her to start her evening patrol. The deputy idled past them, blipped the siren, flashed the overheads, and gave them a backhanded wave as she drove down the square.

The meals at the Worm had, of course, been delicious. Rib-eye steaks and mashed potatoes followed by slices of apple pie topped with homemade vanilla ice cream. Good-byes had been said. Handshakes had turned into hugs.

Now it was Hilly's and Rice's turn. Lilly the Honda was parked nearby in the yellow zone in front of the post office, packed and ready for the road. Rice removed his toothpick and pointed to a bench across the street in the town square. "Why don't we go over and sit for a moment."

Hilly was anxious to leave before dark, maybe make Cincinnati that night, but she answered, "Sure, why not?" and took hold of the man's arm to help him off the curb.

They sat together on the bench with their back to the Worm and the large war memorial in the middle of the square to their right. Rice pretended to straighten out his pants leg for a moment, then faced his client. "Real nice what you did for the town and all with the new park, and I can practically retire when I sell those few acres you gave me on the west edge of town. But answer a question, please."

Hilly looked straight ahead and didn't say a word.

Rice pressed, "You found something in that cave, didn't you? I can't say what. I can't figure it any other way." His voice trailed off, "Yes, you found something...."

Hilly took his hand and leaned in close. He turned toward her. She nodded, kissed him on the cheek, and whispered, "You're a clever old SOB." Then she stood, fished Lilly's keys from her front jeans pocket, and walked over to the Honda. Rice twisted on the bench and watched her walk away, knowing he'd never see her again.

CHAPTER 42

Buried Treasure

Hilly accelerated west out of town on Route 153. The sun was just on the horizon, and she reached to pull down the sun visor. Soon she passed the mailbox and the long gravel drive to the farmhouse and barn. There were still some vehicles parked near the barn in the twilight under the trees. Security, no doubt. The story had run its course, and the news people and satellite trucks were off covering something else 24/7. The farm had not been part of her life growing up in Detroit, and she had only visited it twice when you got down to it. It had belonged to her just a couple of weeks. Both sides of the road now belonged to the US Department of the Interior. As she passed the place she looked over her shoulder, but there was no nostalgia. Nostalgia? Instead, she worried about future post-traumatic stress disorder that the shrink she was forced to meet with these past couple of weeks had talked about.

She drove a few more miles and then slowed. Just before the road began to drop into the West Fork's valley, Hilly made a U-turn and pulled off the pavement on the gravel shoulder. She was just past the speed limit sign. She rolled forward until Lilly's right front bumper almost touched the green, perforated metal pole supporting the Batavia Kiwanis and Lions Club's signs and threw the Honda into park and let the car idle.

Sure, she thought, Lilly had a new starter but you never know. She left the four-way flashers off so as to not attract any attention.

She reached under her seat and pulled out the garden spade. Brand new, it was painted a shiny dark green with a wood handle. She had bought it that afternoon at the True Value near the Ford dealer. The white price sticker, $5.99, was still on the handle. Although the dirt was soft, the spade would be much better for digging this time.

Looking ahead and in the rearview mirror for traffic and seeing none, Hilly climbed out of the Honda, leaving the door open and chiming in her haste. She walked around the front of the car, half slid down the gravel shoulder, and stopped between the first two rows of corn. The corn was much higher, over her head, than it was five weeks ago and ready for harvest. She sank to her knees in the soft soil just as the sun dipped below the horizon.

Digging with the spade, it didn't take long before she heard a satisfying metallic *thunk*. She put down the spade and widened the hole with both hands. Soon she uncovered the large, wide-mouthed Thermos jug, lifted it out, brushed off the remaining dirt, and clasped it to her chest. As she came to her feet between the rows of corn, the object inside tumbled to the other end.

———

As she frantically drove into town that day in the Buick, she had been searching for ideas when she had spied the Thermos, half full of coffee, with its red-and-green plaid sides and red cup for a screw cap on the passenger's seat of the Roadmaster. All the rows of corn along the highway had looked identical, and, remembering the winter fenceline scene from the movie Fargo, the metal pole and signs had made a convenient marker as she had slid the big Buick to stop on the gravel shoulder. In order to help dig in the soft earth she had found an old screwdriver on the Roadmaster's rear floor.

———

Hilly climbed up the shoulder, jumped into the Honda, laid the Thermos and the spade on the passenger's seat, and slammed her door. She switched on the headlights, put Lilly in gear, and made another U-turn across Route 153. She started down the hill, relieved that no traffic had passed her going either way while she made her dig.

At the bottom of the grade, she stopped at the T-intersection and then crossed the bridge over the West Fork, now westbound on Route 287. She noticed a cop car parked off the road just below the new cave entrance area. They were still guarding the area after all this time.

As she drove up the other side of the valley she watched her rearview mirror while nervously tapping the steering wheel with both thumbs, but nobody followed.

At the brightly lit interchange, Hilly turned north on I-75 and let out a sigh of relief. She drove the speed limit and made a Courtyard by Marriott just north of Cincinnati later that night. She fell asleep while clutching the Thermos tightly to her chest. Her Beretta lay closeby on the bedside table with nine in the clip and one in the chamber. She made her condo in Detroit the next afternoon.

CHAPTER 43

Touchdown

All the window shades had been lowered sometime during the night, and the interior of the Gulfstream was dark. The cabin was much quieter than other business jets with just the hiss of the slipstream over the fuselage and the distant hum of the two powerful Rolls-Royce engines at the rear of the airplane. Despite the dark and quiet, Hilly wore a complimentary eyeshade and comfortable earplugs provided earlier by the flight attendant who now stood in the aisle adjacent to Hilly, hesitating to wake her only passenger. The cabin had cooled, and Layla now wore a sweater over her uniform.

Although there was a divan in the rear of the cabin, the soft leather seats that faced each other slid forward to make a comfortable bed, and Hilly was sleeping on her left side with an arm over her head. With the remote device that controlled the amenities at her seat, she had lowered the temperature before falling asleep. Layla had covered her with a lambswool blanket at some point.

The flight attendant reached over and gently shook Hilly's shoulder. Hilly rolled over on her back but did not awaken. Layla gently shook her again—orders were orders—and Hilly raised her head. "Ms....er, Hilly, sorry to wake you, but we're just over the Irish Sea and soon the English

Channel, and the captain estimates we'll be landing in about ninety minutes."

Hilly pulled the eyeshade up onto her forehead and blinked, trying to remember where she was before it dawned on her. Did the flight attendant say the Irish Sea? Using both arms, she came up on her elbows, letting the soft blanket fall down onto her legs. She looked at her watch. She had been asleep four hours and had comfortably crossed the Atlantic Ocean. On past flights to and from Europe she had never had the luxury of sleep in a tight coach seat.

She stretched her arms over her head as the flight attendant waited. Then Hilly found the remote on the empty seat next to her, brought her seat up, and powered up the window shade. Bright morning sunlight poured into the cabin, and she squinted at the sudden change. Hilly looked at her watch again.

Layla answered Hilly's question before she had a chance to speak. "It's eight thirty-three local time in Zurich, ma'am. The captain says we will be landing at precisely ten oh one. It's a clear morning at the airport with light winds. The temperature is thirteen degrees Celsius."

Hilly yawned and stretched again. "Thank you, Layla." Then she remembered her purse and jerked upright. She felt its familiar bulge between the seat cushion and the armrest and relaxed. She pulled out the case containing her Ray-Ban aviators. Peering through the window, she saw it was a clear day. The ocean miles below was blue and covered with white breakers. There appeared to be land ahead, and she thought it must be southwest England, Land's End, if this was the Irish Sea.

Layla, waiting patiently in the aisle, said, "Why don't you freshen up a bit, and I'll start breakfast."

Hilly rubbed her eyes again, yawned, and replied, "Good idea." She used the remote again to power her seat fully upright, moved into the aisle, and tucked her purse under her arm. She was dressed in a complimentary full-length white cotton robe that she had been given when she had changed out of her clothes in the lav. She pulled it tightly around herself as she started down the aisle to the rear of the airplane. The flight attendant quickly folded Hilly's blanket and tidied up her seat area before going to the galley.

Hilly entered the lavatory and shut the door. The lights came on overhead and around the mirror. She noticed her clothes had been neatly hung on hangers to one side. She set her purse on the counter, faced the mirror, and blew out a breath. Despite just four hours of sleep and maybe a little too much champagne, she actually felt pretty good as she surveyed the damage in the mirror. Not good enough yet to whistle a tune but pretty good. She decided all she needed was a quick fix and, by the looks of it, Layla had laid out all the necessary tools on the adjacent counter. Hilly started by picking up the hairbrush.

Hours before, while they had flown over the wilds of Canada, the flight attendant had served a delicious roast beef dinner, almost Worm Café–like, sighing and profusely apologizing all the while for the lack of entrées as she didn't have time beforehand to contact Hilly and ask her preferences. The dinner was followed by a wee bit more champagne and coffee. Then Layla had brought out a chocolate éclair with a single burning candle. Hilly was asked to blow it out quickly because of the smoke alarms in the cabin. Yes, the flight attendant had known it was her birthday.

Hilly stopped brushing her hair for a moment and stared at the mirror. Yes, she thought, the big five-oh. Jesus.

After dessert Hilly had been treated to a first-run Woody Allen movie on a twenty-six-inch screen that seemed to magically appear as they neared the Atlantic Ocean. Hilly guessed the movie was probably pretty good—it looked like it took place in southern France, someplace she wanted to visit again—but she couldn't concentrate. She feared at any moment the sleek Gulfstream would suddenly bank to one side as the crew was ordered to take her back to Detroit, where the authorities would be waiting.

She put down the brush, turned on the tap, and splashed water over her face.

But, no, the jet didn't turn around, and now here we are at 40,000 feet starting to fly over the English Channel. Hilly took a white fluffy towel from a rack next to the mirror, dried her face, looked once again at herself in the mirror, and started to mentally go over the last hectic week.

———

Her pockets bulging with quarters, the initial call to Anton had been carefully made on a broken-down pay phone hanging precariously on the outside wall of a 7-Eleven miles from her condo. The conversation had been short. She followed his instructions, removed the battery, and then immediately crushed the cell phone that had saved her life in the cave before throwing it in a nearby trash can. That evening she had purchased a burner, an untraceable cell phone, from a Walmart. After giving him the number, she awaited further instructions from Antwerp.

Meanwhile, she had put a stop on her mail so it wouldn't pile up. The post office wouldn't show any concern for at least thirty days, maybe more.. Then she had withdrawn most of the money from her bank accounts but didn't close them. Her pension checks were automatically deposited electronically and she knew it might be years before the bank and the city were any wiser. All her bills were automatically withdrawn each month.

Hilly spent two days packing the pawnshop suitcases and cleaning the condo. Then she had simply left after setting the wall thermostat and turning off the refrigerator and leaving the doors open. She had lived there for twelve years, had acquired no equity in the place, and owed far more than it was worth thanks to all the shenanigans of the too-big-to-fail banks. In fact, one of those banks held her mortgage, so the joke was on them eventually. The American Dream, she thought as she threw the keys on the counter and walked out the door to her Honda.

She didn't have any close friends or family to miss. She had discovered that when you retire everyone says they will keep in touch but they don't. Her family was gone. A new life was definitely needed.

The furniture was left where it was. Getting rid of the Beretta was easy. She expertly field-stripped it into parts and threw half of the parts from a bridge over a tributary of the Detroit River and the other half from another bridge a mile downstream. Her old XP PC went over the railing next.

Lilly was another matter. She drove to a salvage yard in a rough neighborhood she knew about from her detective days, Vince's, a questionable junkyard and car-crushing operation. Vince was a grimy old character in dirty coveralls with an unlit cigar always clamped between his teeth. He looked Lilly over and said he would give her a hundred bucks for the car. When Hilly said she wanted to watch the car being crushed, he grinned, raised his eyebrows, and said in that case she would have to pay him to crush the car but he would let her pull the lever. Hilly agreed and hefted her two expensive suitcases from the trunk and her leather purse from the front seat. She dug five twenties from her wallet as Vince looked on. He apparently didn't recognize her from her police department days. Two of his men stripped the Honda of its battery, spare tire, and tires and wheels before a big forklift picked it up and set it in the crusher. The men had laughed at the old cassette tape deck in the dash.

Vince kept his promise and Hilly pulled the lever, and that was that. An inanimate object, Hilly thought, so why am I tearing up? She watched the car come out of the crusher now a foot high.

Vince led her to his greasy office and handed her an even greasier phonebook. She called a taxi, and one of Vince's men wiped his hands and helped her to the front gate with her suitcases, where she waited for a nervous thirty minutes for the cab, thinking all the while, if they only knew what was in her fancy purse. The cab driver loaded the bags into the trunk as she climbed in the back, then drove her to the airport Westin as instructed.

———

Hilly changed into her clothes, gave herself a final look in the mirror, pretty much passed inspection, and left the lav. The jet's cabin smelled of bacon and coffee. Layla served her a Worm Café–worthy breakfast as the Gulfstream descended over the middle of France. The touchdown was smooth as Hilly put on the diamond earrings.

There was another red carpet below the airstairs as Hilly alighted from the Gulfstream in the refreshing Swiss morning air. The captain and flight attendant waited on the tarmac on either side. They wished her well and said it had been a privilege to have flown her to the home country. Per Anton's instructions, Hilly had generously tipped them half her cash.

People held doors open for her again as she strode across the ramp into the general aviation terminal at the international airport, just as she had done in Detroit. She had taken the red passport from her purse and casually held it in her right hand as instructed. She saw through the next set of glass doors a silver stretched-wheelbase S-class Mercedes waiting at the curb. The trunk lid was up, and a man in a suit and tie and purple-tinted wraparound sunglasses was already loading her luggage. She noticed the license plate with the dark blue eurozone rectangle on the left. Below the gold circle of stars was a white letter B indicating Belgium. Another man also dressed in a suit and tie and wearing almost identical sunglasses was standing next to the open rear door of the Mercedes.

A young uniformed Swiss customs officer held one of the automatic glass doors open for her as she approached. He actually clicked his heels together and nodded as she passed. She had been assured by Anton that she would be "precleared" by customs. The Gulfstream G650's flight into Zurich had been blocked by Skyguide, the Swiss equivalent of the Federal Aviation Administration, so there was no public record of the flight. As Hilly walked to the Mercedes, she thought it was indeed a fact that the banks pulled the strings in this county.

Hilly entered the car, held her purse on her lap, placed her new passport into it next to the leather pouch, and took out her Ray-Bans. She stretched out her legs as the man in the suit gently shut the door. The other man finished loading the luggage; the automatic trunk lid closed smoothly with a barely audible click. The two men got in the car, and the driver started the engine. Hilly guessed both men were probably in their early forties; they definitely had that hard-core, shaved-head mercenary look. They were no doubt armed.

The man in the passenger seat turned around and put an arm over the seat back. He said to Hilly with a sudden bright smile, "Guten Morgen! Wie geht es lhnen?"

Hilly returned the smile and said, "Gut, danke."

Then the man said in broken English, "I vas told you, eh, like to be named Hilly, ja?"

She nodded, "Ja, Hilly bitte."

The Mercedes glided away from the terminal.

.

CHAPTER 44

The Diamantkwartier

The Mercedes entered the square-mile Diamantkwartier district near the grand Antwerpen-Centraal Railway Station. The drive had taken four and a half hours, and now it was midafternoon. There had been one quick stop at a rest area. Hilly was almost sure another Mercedes had followed them.

The driver cruised slowly along the busy main thoroughfare near the station which was lined with small retail jewelry shops on the periphery of the largest diamond center in the world. He turned right into a smaller side street and then left through lowered cylindrical barriers into a restricted street which was the heart of the Diamantkwartier. The driver soon turned into the entrance of an underground parking garage, powered down his window, and entered a code. The heavy door slowly began to rise as another Mercedes with two men pulled in sideways behind them blocking the entrance.

As they had left the autoroute and entered the city, Hilly began to recognize landmarks, and memories came flooding back of her time in Belgium as a NATO military investigator and later as a detective with the Detroit PD.

But she didn't recognize the parking garage. They were obviously going in a back door of some sort. She had been right though about the other Mercedes tailing them. It was now preventing any other vehicles from entering the garage behind them. Her Mercedes idled down a ramp into the garage as the door closed behind them. The car came to a halt midway down the garage where another man stood near an elevator door. The two men, who Hilly now knew as Rolf and Edgar, exited the Mercedes. Edgar, who had been the driver, opened the door for Hilly while Rolf scanned the garage. The three then approached the man by the elevator. Rolf and Edgar greeted the man by name and it was obvious as the third man unlocked the elevator that they all knew each other. In fact, the man opening the elevator with a key appeared to be a clone of the other two men. As the elevator door opened he smiled at Hilly, bowed slightly, and politely indicated she should board first. The three men followed.

The elevator took them to the sixth floor where they joined a main hall with granite floors and better lighting. Except for the men's greetings to each other nobody had spoken again as they approached a set of double doors at the end of the hall. The man who had met them at the parking garage elevator knocked discreetly on one of the doors. There was the distinct sound of a lock being thrown before both doors were pulled open enthusiastically by a small, almost totally bald man with a white goatee dressed in an elegant dark suit.

The three men stood aside as the man stepped forward with both arms out, smiled, and practically shouted, "Hildegard!"

Hilly smiled and met him just inside the wide doorway. As they hugged, she whispered in his ear in English, "Anton, it's been too many years." He kissed both her cheeks in the European fashion and then held her at arm's length. Anton was a diamond expert, and Hilly had worked with him when she was a NATO investigator in the army and later as a Detroit PD detective.

The Antwerp diamond trade was dominated by the Jewish community. Anton Epstein, a survivor of Auschwitz at the age of four, was the head of one of the largest diamond trading, cutting, and polishing companies in the world. His reputation as a *diamantaire* had no parallel. His influence in the diamond trade extended to all corners of the globe. He was on a first name basis with some of the most powerful men in the world, including bankers, CEOs, and heads of state. He employed thousands of people in the diamond trade in Antwerp alone. On the five floors below them at this moment were hundreds of his employees cutting and polishing diamonds. He had several other buildings in the Diamond Quarter and suburbs of Antwerp.

Anton Epstein stepped aside and, with a dramatic sweep of his hand, beckoned Hilly into the conference room. Hilly stepped forward still grasping her purse in front of her. The room was dimly lit and dominated by a long, rectangular stainless steel–and–glass table. It ran almost the length of the room. Framed portraits crowded the walls. The only light source was a bright, blue-white spotlight mounted over the far end of the table. The spotlight illuminated a small pedestal draped in black velvet. All the chairs had been pushed against the walls except one at the far end. In it sat a middle-aged man in an expensive suit with a gray-flecked beard and bushy gray eyebrows. On his right stood a Hasidic Jew in traditional garb. Behind them, two younger, tough-looking men stood against the wall with their hands folded in front of them. The man in the chair was Igor Cheryenko, a Russian oil billionaire and a personal friend of the Russian president.

Hilly stopped at her end of the long table and waited. The elevator man remained in the room with them as Anton locked the double doors, leaving Rolf and Edgar outside in the hallway. Anton joined her and pointed to the velvet-draped pedestal.

A bit dramatic, she thought, but she drew a breath and walked the length of the table with the Russian following her every move. She stopped opposite the pedestal, reached into her purse, and brought out the soft lambskin pouch. Slipping the purse over one shoulder, she slowly spread the drawstring and opened the pouch. She reached into it, hesitated, and looked at the Russian before she drew out the large diamond with one hand and gently placed it on the pedestal. Everyone in the room audibly drew in a breath. Even the expressionless security men against the wall raised their eyebrows. Cheryenko's eyes widened as did Epstein's who was leaning forward on his arms on the other end of the long table.

The stone was the legendary Pink Sunset diamond, and it reportedly had been last seen in New York over two hundred years ago. Its brilliance under the spotlight danced around the room and walls like a kaleidoscope as the pedestal started to turn slowly. At 101.4 carats, it was the largest pink diamond in the world. In the past it had been rated fancy, vivid pink, and was internally flawless. Its purity put it in the top 1 percent of all the diamonds in the world. It had been mined in India sometime in the middle 1700s and had weighed some 183 carats in rough form. The rough pink diamond eventually had been smuggled to Europe by ship, to Antwerp in particular. It had taken skilled diamond cutters over two years to perfect and carefully finish the round European cut.

The Russian snapped a finger, and the Hasidic Jew stepped forward carrying a small scale, a pair of white cotton gloves, and a loupe. He needed no tweezers for this diamond, and, after donning the gloves, his hand trembled at the honor as he picked the gem up between his thumb and forefinger, weighed it quickly, picked it up again, and then put the loupe to his eye.

Hilly stood nearby and smiled. She wondered if these men would like to know she had carried it around for a while in a red-and-green plaid Thermos bottle filled with coffee dregs.

The Hasidic Jew turned the diamond over and over in his hand and carefully inspected it before placing the diamond back on the pedestal. He turned and nodded at Cheryenko. The Russian stood so quickly he knocked his chair over. He whooped, reached out, snatched up the diamond in one hand, and turned it over and over under the light.

Hilly set down the leather pouch and walked to Anton at the other end of the table, who stood frowning at Cheryenko's antics. She said to him in a low voice, "I think you and I have some more unfinished business, ja?"

Anton smiled and said, "Ja, ja, follow me to mein office, Hildegard." He had always refused to call her Hilly for some reason.

The man from the elevator stood aside as Anton unlocked and opened the double conference room doors. Edgar and Rolf were still there on either side of the door and remained so as Hilly and Anton walked to the elevator. Hilly heard the conference room doors close and the lock turned.

Anton's lavish office was built into a front corner of the second floor. On the second floor, dozens of employees, most in traditional Hasidic garb but many not, were busy cutting and polishing diamonds. After riding the elevator down, Hilly and Anton stopped for a moment near his office door to watch. Hilly looked around the large, open floor literally humming with activity under bright shop lights. Amazing, she thought. All this for jewelry and tradition. Wedding and engagement rings, birthday and anniversary gifts, earrings such as the ones she wore at this moment, necklaces, and pins.

Anton let her watch the activity for a moment. "I vish you vould stay and be a guest at my home. My vife vould like to meet you. She is disappointed. Ve both vould very much like to hear the story of the cave." He swept his hand around the floor. "And I vould like to give you a rare tour, Hildegard." He held his office door open for her. "But I know you vant to 'hit de road' as you Americans say." He shook his head. "Vat is your hurry?"

The anteroom held three secretaries, all busy on the phone as they looked up and waved at their boss. A second door led to Anton's inner office. Three big windows with steel bars overlooked the busy cobblestone street below. Glass cases with sparkling diamond jewelry lined two walls. Anton walked behind his desk and opened a laptop computer. He motioned for Hilly to have a seat in an upholstered chair in front of his desk and only sat down himself after she was seated. Hilly sat silently as Anton frowned for several minutes as he worked the computer. Finally, satisfied, he turned the laptop around and smiled. "The transfer has been made and confirmed. I hope it is to your satisfaction, Hildegard."

Hilly could hear her heart pounding. The website was a small Swiss private bank in Zurich where an account had been opened. Only she knew the nine-digit account number. There was a window for those nine digits facing her and a black bar blinking on the left. She had memorized the numbers and now used the keyboard to type them. Then she clicked enter.

While Hilly had cleaned her condo, crushed Lilly, and waited four days in the Westin, a very secret and private auction in U.S. dollars had taken place for the diamond. At the end, two bidders were left: the Russian Cheryenko and another person Anton would only refer to as of Middle Eastern descent. The Russian had won the auction with a final bid of $118.5 million. Until a few days ago, the record price for any diamond had been a little over $80 million but, of course, this current record bid would never be made public. Anton and Hilly had settled on a deal, 60 percent to him and 40 percent to her; her share amounted to $47.4 million.

Hilly watched the screen briefly and then logged off. The account, her account, held 43,483,600 Swiss francs at the current exchange rate. She suddenly felt light-headed, took a few breaths, and turned the laptop around. Her pulse raced.

Anton asked, "Are you not feeling vell?"

Hilly fanned her face with one hand and replied, "Give me a moment, Anton." And thought, it had all come true.

Anton opened a desk drawer and stood. He reached across the large desk and placed some objects in front of her: two sets of keys and two manila envelopes, one small and one large. Then he sat, waited, and said, "Ven you are ready."

Hilly put a hand to her mouth and thought she might throw up right on his desk—the old adrenalin reaction—but the feeling passed and she quickly recovered. She relaxed a little, faced the diamond dealer, and nodded.

He pointed to the first set of two keys on a steel ring; both black fobs had four interlocking chrome rings. "I hope it is vat you vanted, Hildegard.

It vas not easy to find at the last minute." Hilly felt her pulse racing again and the bile rising.

He pointed to the second set of keys on a chrome ring with a plastic tag and a three-digit number. "This request vas somewhat easier. I also hope the apartment and parking garage is to your liking. It is in the section of Zurich neighborhood you requested. There is a year lease, and twelve month's rent has been fully paid, Hildegard." He then pointed to the large manila envelope. "In this von is your Swiss auto registration, green insurance card, and two additional credit cards on your account, all valid like the passport and driver's license. Ve had to pull many strings, as you Americans like to say. You drive a hard bargain, but worth it, eh?" He pointed to the smaller unsealed envelope and said, "You haf to open this von yourself, Hildegard."

Hilly picked up the envelope and opened the flap. She pulled out a sheaf of euro bills in small denominations and fanned them out with a puzzled look on her face. She was feeling better.

Anton continued, "A personal gift from me to get you on your vay, ten thousand euros. You are an honest woman." He extended his hand across the desk and they shook. Then he handed her a business card with a number penned on it. "My personal number. Call me anytime. I know many people. I just might have a job or two for a vomen like you in the future if you vant. Now I must return to my new Russian friend."

Hilly took the elevator to the ground floor with a security guard and walked through the company's small, glittering, retail diamond showroom with him. A female clerk behind the counter smiled at her. She smiled back as the security guard escorted her to the door and stopped. Alone, she was buzzed out of the building by the clerk behind the counter, first through an inner security door and then, after she stood between the inner and outer doors a moment, she was buzzed out of the outer door onto the street.

A dark blue Audi S4 quattro was waiting at the curb. Audi called the paint color Scuba Blue Metallic. The S4 was the more powerful version of its small A4 sedan. A police officer stood in the street directing traffic around the car while another uniformed security guard was loading the last of her Louis Vuitton luggage into the trunk. Hilly noticed the ZH Swiss license plates with a white cross within the small red shield adjacent to the numbers. Yet another security guard stood on the curb holding the driver's door open for her.

Hilly slipped into the black leather driver's seat. The guard closed the door and stepped back just as the other guard closed the trunk. He joined his coworker on the sidewalk.

Hilly laid her purse, the other set of keys, and the envelopes on the passenger seat, on which rested a Michelin European road atlas. The car surely had its own GPS system but she would have to learn it later. Anton always saw to the details.

She put one of the ignition keys in the slot on the steering column. The other dangled below. She wrapped both hands around the steering wheel and caressed it gently for a moment. The car smelled wonderful. Leather and new plastic.

The Audi started instantly and she let the engine warm up a bit. The gas tank showed full, Anton again. She thought to herself, over 300 horsepower, almost three times as much as Lilly. Gasoline in Europe was approaching eight dollars a gallon.

She reached into her purse and donned the Ray-Bans. As she pulled away, she saw the guards wave to her in the rearview mirror and the policeman give her a salute.

An hour later on the *autoroad* she stopped at a rest area and in the petrol station restroom exchanged the fancy clothes and heels for her worn Nikes, comfortable jeans, pocket T-shirt, and plain gray sweatshirt she had packed in Detroit but not before gagging a little for the final time in one of the sinks. She was still on a high. That adrenalin thing again. On the way back to the Audi she crushed her burner cell phone on the cement sidewalk and threw the remains in a refuse barrel. Then she placed the diamond earrings, leather Gucci purse, Omega, and other jewelry in

370

one of the suitcases in exchange for her Timex Indiglo Explorer with its new battery and her fanny pack, which now held her old Swiss Army knife, wallet, and sunglasses case. As she accelerated hard down the on ramp from the rest area, the road atlas was open on the passenger seat. Hilly merged with the traffic, flashed her high beans, moved quickly into the left lane, and accelerated again. She would definitely have to find a masculine name for this car. She turned the radio on and touch screened the seek feature. It settled on a station somewhere playing an old ABBA tune. She smiled. Her new life had begun.

EPILOGUE

People and Places

Sheriff Roscoe Ferguson was never implicated in any wrongdoing. The sheriff died of a massive heart attack the following October while campaigning for office. His opponent ran unopposed. Sheriff Ferguson was buried with honors in Arlington National Cemetery near his son. His wife succumbed to Alzheimer's disease a few months after his death and was buried alongside her husband. Their daughter died of a drug overdose a year later and was also buried in Arlington with the rest of her family at the government's discretion.

The following year Worm Cave became the nation's sixtieth national park by act of Congress and the president's signature. Two years later Worm Cave was designated a UNESCO World Heritage Site. Many years after becoming a national park, despite some controversy, three elevator shafts were dug into Worm Ridge for visitors, lighting was installed, and pathways were created. A modern visitor center and parking lot were built on the site where the old farmhouse and barn once stood. Paved roads with curbs, gutters, and streetlights were constructed from the visitor center up the ridge where the muddy track once existed to access the man made entrances. Worm Cave became accessible for all the world to see. The most popular tours are the Whirlpool, the Grand Canyon, Angel Falls, the Invisible River, and, of course, Concordia. There is also a special tour twice a week led by a park ranger for the adventurous to suit up in spelunker gear and enter the historic farmhouse entrance in order to stand on the Opera Box.

The injunction stopping the Sun River Dam was made permanent. The Corps of Engineers was ordered to reclaim both the dam and highway bridge sites. The reclamation would take two years. The Sun River and its tributaries were given National River designations and allowed to run free. The Sun River is still one of the few undammed rivers for its full length in the lower 48 states.

Trisha Worm received an anonymous full-ride nursing scholarship and graduated with honors as an RN from the University of Kentucky's College of Nursing in Lexington. She works at the Batavia Hospital but still pulls a couple of shifts a week at the Worm Café. She is still in the Army Reserves where she serves in a medical detachment. She quit smoking.

Judge Winslow's bailiff kept his job.

L. T. Rice eventually sold his acreage just west of town to two big-box stores and two motel chains and made a fortune. He practiced law into his nineties.

Upon high school graduation, Ronny Henderson and his cousin Jimmy Lee Bailey received anonymous full-ride scholarships to the University of Kentucky.

Emery Henderson never abused his family again but continued to drink. He would die four years later of cirrhosis of the liver.

Professor Cunningham retired from his university job and was hired by the Department of the Interior to oversee the exploration of Worm Cave. The main passageway was found to run under Worm Ridge from one end to the the other, a distance of ten miles. Twenty-two miles of cave have been mapped. The massive cave still has only two known natural entrances. No other natural entrances have ever been found to date. Worm Cave is believed to be the largest cave on Earth.

Roland Harrington did not win a Pulitzer Prize for his Worm Cave story. He now works for a Louisville newspaper.

Layla the flight attendant eventually became the director of operations of the Swiss charter company. The charter company has twelve Gulfstream G650s. They are efficiently dispatched world-wide.

Deputy Big receives an anonymous air freight FedEx package containing a large amount of cash every Christmas. Per her lawyer L. T. Rice's advice, she was told to keep quiet about the packages. She soon quit her deputy job to spend time with her children. Her husband still works at the Ford dealership in Batavia.

Camas and Leroy Worm still operate the Worm Café on the Batavia town square. Their family continues to make moonshine in the hills and hollows of Walker County. A person can still buy white lightning in glass jars off the loading dock at the rear of the Worm Café.

The Atomic Furniture Warehouse in Atlanta declared bankruptcy, closed all its stores, and parked all its trucks.

The other Mexican assassin's body was found two years later in a small passageway. Nearby was a broken flashlight and an empty cigarette lighter. There was no apparent third source of light. The Mexican had apparently died of a self-inflicted gunshot to the head.

Using the serial number of the 1851 Navy Colt, the mummified body was identified as that of Bryon Sanders. He is now buried in a cemetery in Louisville.

Billy the flagman, whose last name was Donovan, continued to work construction in the area. The following Christmas morning a new Ford F250 pickup truck, purchased anonymously, was delivered to his driveway by a Kingston Ford dealer salesperson. Per the anonymous buyer's instructions, there was a new stainless steel Thermos jug and a pair of Ray-Ban Aviator sunglasses placed on the front seat. Billy had smiled and understood. Later, he would become a supervisor on the construction of the Worm Cave visitor center. He was hired by the National Park Service a year after the visitor center was completed as a maintenance supervisor for the park, and he still works there. He has three children and continues to serve as a firefighter and paramedic for the Batavia Volunteer Fire Department.

A large portion of the treasure in the strongboxes was auctioned and brought the state of Kentucky's general fund approximately $8 million dollars. The wooden wagon, strongboxes, and some other Civil War era artifacts, including the fancy engraved 1851 Navy Colt revolver, were eventually put on display in an exhibit room in the Worm Cave visitor center for all to see and learn this story.

Hilly's condominium manager finally reported her missing. Two Detroit PD colleagues responded, found no evidence of foul play, and, although puzzled, finally concluded that it is not illegal to disappear and to not say goodbye. The case is still open.

The Pink Sunset diamond was spirited away to Russia and has not been seen since.

Hilly Walker continues to live and thrive in Europe under her new identity. She gave her Audi the name Fritz.

THE END

Made in the USA
Monee, IL
13 July 2023

39090918R10222